CW00376594

Silver in the Blood

by
Victoria Hyder

Victoria Hyder

One day, men will look back and say I gave
birth to the twentieth century.

~ Jack the Ripper

London,

1888

Friday 3rd August 1888.

The night sky was beautiful to behold. No heads bothered to turn up to look at the sweep of velvety black sky, speckled with small white stars. No heads, that is, except one young man who needed an extra breath of fresh air before heading into the hospitals theatre. The anticipation of breathing in the musk of harsh soap and ether was not something that roused his interest.

Dull orange lamplight bathed the flagstones and the porch that the other young apprentices were gathered upon. There was a cool note in the air that whispered off the Thames. It wasn't cold enough for the breath to mist, but it was enough for the men to take their overcoats –just in case. In the distance, the soft clicking of footsteps on the flagstones filled the otherwise still night. Glancing at his pocket watch, Thomas determined that it was already a quarter to eight. The lecture was due to start at 9 o'clock and they hadn't even gotten into the building yet.

"I suppose it's a good thing it hasn't gotten cold enough to snow yet," commented Rufus.

Thomas raised his eyebrows in agreement. Rufus was a tall, lanky man with a very thin neck. His hair was a mass of sleek copper strands swept across. His face was spattered with freckles that drew away from his –otherwise handsome –features.

"As long as we don't freeze in December, we'll be fine," Thomas said with a smile.

The truth was, despite it being the end of August, the sudden drop in temperature was a curious turn. Many elderly women lamented that it was to be the end of days, but Thomas found himself tuning them out more and more as the years passed. It was only a cool night, nothing untoward. They lived in London, the land where temperatures fluctuated throughout the year. His mother had even spoken of when she was a young girl, the Thames would freeze over, and they would have 'Frost Fairs' on the ice that could easily reach eleven inches in thickness.

A touch of nippy weather wasn't about to make their evenings unpleasant.

No; that was a job much better left to the crook currently prowling the streets of London. There had been horrid things in the newspaper. Thomas had read the articles, chills running down his spine whenever he remembered it. He caught himself speculating who could ever commit such horrid crimes, but it wasn't his place to go poking around. That was a job better left to the police.

In the courtyard, the clock struck 9 o'clock.

A key ground the gears in the lock and the large double doors swung open. A rush of warm air enveloped the student body as they shuffled forward onto the marble-tiled floor of the auditorium-like theatre. Shuffling around the circular levels, Thomas and Rufus found some seats on the lower ring of seats. As they shook off their overcoats and hats, their professor entered through the narrow door in a sweep of his long, black robes.

Taking his books out of his bag along with a quill and ink, Thomas had to take a moment to stare up at his professor, standing like a dark angel against the lectern. He was a tall man with slick, black hair that hung down to his chin, and a long nose. His skin was sallow but there was a hungry gleam in those dark eyes that made everyone's stomachs turn. He was a cold, calculating man, his voice deep and smooth as it resounded off the stone walls. His was a captivating presence that sank deep into the bones, and left his students enraptured with his teachings.

In short; he was a magnificent professor.

Fifteen minutes before the lecture ended -an introductory lecture to outline what they were supposed to learn over the coming months before Christmas–Professor Talbot turned to his array of dropsy-faced students and narrowed his eyes. So many insolent brats. It was a good thing half of them weren't paying attention, because then they wouldn't get another invite to the following lectures when the surgeries began. Most professors would relish in the extra money handed over at the end of every lecture, as a pre-emptive payment on the following week, however Talbot was not one of them. He'd rather teach half a class of interested pupils, rather than a full class almost completely filled with hopeless socialites.

Tightening his jaw even more, he stepped behind his podium and knocked the stand over. The crash resounded throughout the auditorium, the hundred or so students who had been slumped in their seats were suddenly on their feet and alert. Spinning around they searched for the source of the commotion. Upon finding that it had been Talbot, a great many cheeks flushed with embarrassment.

Thomas and Rufus shared a sly grin with one another.

"Now that I have your attention," Talbot intoned, his black glassy eyes passing over the pale faces staring up at him. "I'm sure you will all be interested to know what the curriculum will be consisting of, for those of you who can stomach it."

He gave a pointed look to a small cluster of young men

on the third row who had looked dangerously close to falling asleep.

"Now, for those of you who wish to excel your studies, I shall have it be known that for one week every month, there will be classes every night between 10 o'clock in the evening to 1 o'clock in the morning. For those of you who are interested, stay behind after this lecture and I shall inform you of what it entails."

Thomas caught himself before he was leaning against the brass pole that ran around the mahogany wall in front of him. Swallowing, he readjusted himself and straightened his shoulders. He'd almost dropped his notes. Rufus looked a little pale beside him and he couldn't help but suppress a chuckle. The auburn-haired man was not good with blood. He needed to do this series of lessons and hands-on study to actually get used to it, otherwise he'd have a hard time finding decent work in the field of medicine.

As Talbot continued to wrap up his lecture, Rufus leaned over and asked; "Are you going to wait behind to learn about the extracurricula lessons?"

Thomas shrugged. He couldn't deny that it filled him with a dizzying excitement to know what the man deemed worthy to extend lessons outside of time. "I think so. Even just to see what it entails."

Rufus nodded. "I don't think I could handle much more of that man, even if it were to guarantee me a job as soon as I graduated."

Thomas suppressed the urge to roll his eyes. Rufus managed when it came to academia, but he wasn't the brightest candle on the altar. At long last, the clock struck midnight and they were dismissed an hour early, since it was only an introductory lecture.

"Okay that's midnight. Get out," he enunciated his words, before turning his back on the students. He never left any room for questions, and at this late hour it didn't seem as though anyone had any.

Rufus stood up and, after gathering his books, he shot Thomas a strained look. "Are you sure you want to stay? You'll be walking home almost alone."

Thomas gave his friend a patient smile. "I'm sure I'll manage."

With a thin-lipped smile, the tall man nodded before he shuffled along the tight, circular row of benches towards the main doors. A soft breeze shuffled around the room as the rest of the class went out into the breathable air and made their way home. Thomas and ten other students were left.

When he turned back around, Talbot was pleasantly surprised that he had as many as eleven pupils staying behind for the extra lectures. He knew it wasn't going to be popular with half the current student body, and he'd probably only have three men turn up by the following week, but it was a risk he took every year. It was a risk that needed to be undertaken, because one day –despite his efforts –he wouldn't be there to carry these lessons through.

Stepping up to the lectern, he grasped the mahogany wood and smoothed his long, pale fingers over the varnished grain. "Now the rest of you have stayed behind this evening because you are either intrigued by the unknown subject matter yet to be disclosed, or you're thinking that this will mean you have to put less effort into your regular studying of the human body and its internals. On the latter, you are wrong; you will have to dedicate perhaps even more of your time to passing these extra lectures.

"You will all need to swear a declaration that whatever you witness within these four walls between the time the lectures start and end, will not be repeated to the outside world. This is of the upmost importance to the nation's security and the Queen herself is adamant for discretion."

Thomas furrowed his brown. Upmost security declared by Her Majesty? That didn't seem at all likely. Why would the Queen have any interest in the medical sciences? He shifted uncomfortably, the hard wood eating into the back of his thighs. His quill trembled in his hand as he prepared to take notes.

"Now a lot of you may have heard rumours about some of the subjects I like to teach?" Talbot drawled, his narrow, dark eyes surveying the room. A few young men squirmed in his peripheral vision, but he ignored them. He knew what people said about him, often when they thought he was nowhere near. "You may have been told not to bother wasting your time, that elements of the supernatural have no place in the world of science, medicine and our way of life. However, I am here to tell you that you are wrong."

A buzzing of hushed voices rippled through the room

Thomas felt the hairs on the back of his neck stand up on end.

"There are very few scientifically acclaimed accounts of strange and otherworldly diseases or dangers. Reports indicate that there are far more out there in the world that simply are ignored, given no treatment or a chance to recover and join society."

A hand raised near the middle of the fifth row of seats. Talbot narrowed his eyes but inclined his head. The voice that spoke was nasally and sounded rather pompous. "If there aren't any recorded cases then why are you bothering to tell us all of this?"

"One day, Mr. Renham, doctors will need to know of ways to cure such ailments. That is why the task has befallen whomever chooses to study these lectures, to create as many detailed notes and diagrams to be printed into a new volume for the medical sciences journals in Oxford."

Thomas swallowed thickly. To become published alone would be a huge achievement, the royalties wouldn't be amazing however it would certainly escalate his future career threefold if he was published in journals approved by the Queen herself. However, the was a strange feeling inside him, curling around like a snake, sending chills running up and down his limbs. His brain argued that it was merely the late hour and the unusually cool evening that awaited him outside the large oak doors. However ... what of the subject matter? Clearly it had not done Professor Talbot any harm, though Thomas did wonder if it had done the man any favours, being so involved in teachings of the occult.

Another hand rose.

"Professor, why exactly is there interest in the medical side of the occult?" the young man asked. Thomas felt some relief ebb into his chest. He was glad he didn't have to ask the question, no doubt, all of them were wondering.

"The reason, Mr. Fielding, is that there have been some strange and gruesome murders up and down the country. You may have noticed that even the police here in London are stretched pretty thin. It is my hopes that we shall have fresh corpses from any new murders.

"You young men are to help me research these bodies and determine if their cause of death was committed by a supernatural entity, and if not, why not? What else could it be? How do you know it is something else? Have you, yourself, discovered a new disease that will transform the medical world? We won't know. Not yet, at least. However, within the next fortnight I shall have more news regarding any autopsies."

Thomas bit his lip. His palms were clammy as he glanced back down at his notes. Was this really an enterprise he wanted to be involved in? He had a week to completely make his mind up and find the money for the tuition for the extra classes.

Talbot turned to eye them all with a flourish of his robes. "Alright men. If you wish to participate in these extra lectures, stay after your original lecture next Monday night. That is one week to make the decision. Dismissed!"

Stepping out into the dark street, Thomas drew in a deep breath. The crisp note in the air stung his lungs and the back of his throat, but it was a welcomed change from the oppressing atmosphere of the lecture room. Raking a hand through his hair, he looked up and down the street, the few young men who had stayed behind already ghosting along the pavement, their silver-headed staffs gleaming whenever they passed under a streetlamp. Thomas turned left and started making his way up the road, the rustling of leaves following him.

Walking home alone had never been an issue for him. He actually preferred when the streets were empty; it meant he could move with freedom and not have to worry about knocking into someone. He was grateful that he didn't have to walk for more than forty minutes to get to the hospital. It wasn't an issue now, however when the weather started to turn cold, he would need to find a short cut so that he didn't get ill.

Upon arriving at his lodgings, he slipped his key into the lock and went inside. Climbing the staircase, he didn't take his cloak off nor his hat until he was inside his room. His lodgings were small but homely. Living so far away from his parents was a disheartening truth to come home to every night, however Thomas had to keep thinking of how good this opportunity was. It wasn't many people who received a fully paid scholarship to study under the renowned Professor Stephen Talbot. Perhaps that was another reason spurring him towards the extra activities. He hoped it would aid him in becoming the Professors protegeé once the class had graduated. He liked to write to his parents every week to let them know how things were progressing for him. Normally, he wouldn't have written so often, however not only did his mother worry, but the postal service could take a while between London and Sheffield. He just wanted to make sure that if it did stop for whatever reason –perhaps a strike or bad weather –they'd have a flock of new letters to read.

Within half an hour, Thomas had a small iron kettle heating up over his fire and had managed to make up a dinner of cold meat cuts, warmed soup and half a loaf of bread from earlier that afternoon. It wasn't much –not like his mother's cooking –but it would suffice until morning.

Sat in his chair with nothing but the creaks and groans of the old house around him, Thomas finally let himself relax. He was disappointed that Rufus hadn't wanted to learn about the exciting new lectures. Perhaps it was the late hour of said lectures, but Thomas knew better. Rufus was squeamish. Why the auburn-haired man wanted to go into the profession at all still remained a mystery to Thomas, but he admired his friend's spirit.

Unfastening his buttons Thomas felt a cold weight settle in his chest as he pulled his chair closer to the low fire, his legs stretched out before him. It would be increasingly lonely if he were to study throughout the early hours of the morning and not have a companion alongside. He liked knowing his classmates. Sadly, the only ones who had stayed behind were not people Thomas tended to talk to.

Twisting the small ring on his right ring finger, Thomas sighed and glanced out of the window. The faintest hint of daylight was already bleaching the black from the sky. Vague shapes took on a sharper life.

'*I need to get some sleep*,' he thought as he banked the fire.

A yawn rubbed his throat raw as he sluggishly shucked off his clothes and dropped down into his narrow bed. It creaked under his weight. Sighing softly, Thomas resolved to watch daylight slowly waken the city.

He drifted off to sleep before the sun had fully risen.

Monday 6th August 1888.

Every part of Thomas' body felt over-sensitive to the room around him. His skin prickled at the grain of his seat. A touch of parchment on his skin made his mouth run dry. The dust made his eyes water and raw as he tried to focus on what the professor was saying to round off his current lecture, preparing to dismiss those that had no interest in the supernatural.

That meant that within five minutes, Rufus would be weaving his way through the circular rows of chairs towards the door. This was to be their first lecture and Thomas couldn't deny the knots he felt in his stomach. He hadn't gotten much sleep over the weekend, and he was trying to get his head around these middle-of-the-night lessons –and he'd only had an introductory class last week.

As the other students stood to leave the lecture hall –Rufus stopping to give Thomas a supportive grip on his shoulder before departing –Thomas shifted awkwardly as the coolness from the now empty spaces whispered against his skin.

The wad of money burned in his pocket.

The door banged closed at the top of the hall.

Talbot looked down the length of his hooked nose and studied the remaining seven men with his flat, black eyes. "I trust that each of you has the tuition fees I explained in our previous lesson."

It wasn't a question. Thomas always admired the bluntness of the older man's words. He didn't question people or their actions. He didn't even go in the other direction and make assumptions. He demanded what was expected of them and they, in turn, found no way to avoid complying.

A dull chorus of '*yes*' echoed around the room.

One by one, they each walked up to the podium and set their brown paper packets on the varnished wood before retreating to their seats. Talbot's face remained emotionless as he put the money out of sight and unravelled a blank canvas with a tug of his cane. Thomas jumped. Feeling a hot flush creep up his neck, he sincerely hoped that no one else had noticed. He tried to focus on the images the lantern slide was producing on the blank fabric.

He felt a cold bead of sweat dribble down the small of his back.

One by one, they each walked up to the podium and set their brown paper packets on the varnished wood before retreating to their seats. Talbot's face remained emotionless as he put the money out of sight and unravelled a blank canvas with a tug of his cane. Thomas jumped. Feeling a hot flush creep up his neck, he sincerely hoped that no one else had noticed. He tried to focus on the images the lantern slide was producing on the blank fabric.

On the blackboard there was an immaculately sketched diagram of the Vitruvian Man –only this one was different from the one Da Vinci had created. The one being shown from the projector was one that depicted the central figure as having hairy, muscular legs a tail and a wolf head with its feral expression and hair trailing down the human torso. It was – an unnerving sight. To think that such an inhuman atrocity could exist, it was enough to make the stomach twist. Thomas felt himself leaning on the edge of his seat. His note book threatened to spill out into the pulpit.

"For those of you who are unaware what this creature is," Talbot's voice rang out throughout the hall. "Please save your petulant wonderings until after!"

The lycanthropic man vanished, only to be replaced with another image. This time the canvas was showing the image of a full human skeleton, only this skeleton had been adapted in the most bizarre way; the feet were not simple, angular bones. No, these feet were drawn to resemble the enlarged structure of a bat.

Thomas squirmed.

It'd be incredibly uncomfortable to have feet like a bat, no matter how big or small they were. His eye wondered upwards to the rest of the structure looming over the human skeleton. They were wings. Thin, hollow and brittle they spread out from the original body in two large arcs on either side. Was this supposed to be an angelic being?

"I see I have caught your attention," Talbot's voice called out through the shadowed hall. "What do you call these two creatures I have shown you?"

Two hands shot into the air. Thomas merely pressed himself back into his seat, straining his ears against the sound of his hammering heart.

"You?"

"The first is a hellhound, sir! The second is possibly a mutation in the form of an angelic being!"

"Incorrect. You're wasting my time and yours if you don't think before you speak! You?"

"I think that –perhaps –the first image could be a depiction of lycanthropy s-sir."

"What's your name?"

"Neville, sir. Neville Locke."

"Well, Mr. Locke, it seems that you got something right. Goodness knows how, but we shan't demean miracles when they happen." The curl of his sneer sent a shiver through the room. "Now, who can name the second creature?"

Thomas was struggling to write and listen. In the dim light he was trying to mimic the diagram on the drop-screen before him, even going as far to annotate both of them as Talbot spoke.

"None of you?" Talbot spared them a disdainful look. "Not one of you men know even the common name for a creature such as this?" Silence met his question. It irked him. Straightening up even taller, he curled his long fingers around the podium. "That creature –children –is what is most commonly known as a 'vampire'!"

Hushed gasps came from various points in the darkness.

The temperature seemed to drop, and the wood seemed to harden under Thomas' legs. Was this man insane?

'Hear him out, Segdon!' he admonished himself. *'You've paid for the extra lessons, so you'd better pay attention!'*

"Now according to folklore these two creatures are very much polar opposites of one another. The skeletal structure differs drastically from one to the other."

"How would you know that, sir?" drawled a low voice from the back of the room. Thomas craned his neck but was unable to catch sight of the man who had spoken.

Talbot fixed the arrogant speaker with a dark glare. "Any imbecile who looks at the diagrams drawn, is evidence enough."

"And we're supposed to just take your word?"

"If you don't like it, Mr. Bradley, then by all means grace us with the sight of your back."

There was a tense silence before a faint huff came from the young man. Talbot did not take any prisoners when it came to the sharpness of his tongue. Flexing his shoulders, the black-haired man stood taller, like a Grim Reaper without a scythe. Flipping the black-board to a clean slate, he showed another diagram of a full-fledged vampire structure next to a werewolf structure. There were arrows and blank boxes pointing to various spots on each body that weren't akin to that of a regular human.

Thomas had to squint and lean forward in his chair to see the thin chalk lines clearly. He mentally cursed his short-sightedness. It wouldn't do to be a surgeon or any practitioner of medicine, if he couldn't see what he was working on.

'*Stop it!*' he snapped at himself as he focused on recreating the diagrams perfectly.

After they'd had about fifteen minutes to sketch, Talbot stood like a slim black pillar, his waxy features almost melting in the low light. The stench of beeswax and oppressive atmosphere felt like a weight pressing down over their heads. Brandishing his chalk like a wand, Talbot tapped one of the empty boxes –the one pointing to the vampire's mouth.

"Name it!" he called.

A hand shot up. "Fangs!"

"What is their main purpose?"

"To stun their victim as well as drain the blood from the jugular!"

Talbot was not the type of man to congratulate a right answer. His silence did it for him, as he wrote the word and abbreviated description in the box. Without a pause, he pointed to the next box indicating the fine, bat-like wings spreading out over the centre of the board.

"Name it!"

On and on it went for the better part of an hour until the majority of both sketched skeletons had been labelled. To Thomas, the werewolf was a far more interesting specimen; it had a unique bone structure since it didn't have separate appendages –it actually seemed to mutate from the human form to the other.

As he labelled the diagram in his book, Thomas couldn't help but regret his decision to study this supernatural nonsense. Of course it was interesting, but if it meant touching his book with his nose just to be able to see what he'd written –was it worth it?

"Now, gentlemen, over the next few weeks I will be sharing my lessons with some speakers, who are coming to London specifically to discuss their knowledge on the biological anomalies that are linked to lycanthropy and vampirism." His dark eyes silenced any murmuring in a heartbeat. "You'd do well to attend."

Thomas raised his head, his interest piqued.

Somewhere outside the bells chimed 1 o'clock in the morning.

Talbot seethed, his long, white fingers curling around the podium. "Very well. Class is over. Study the diagrams I have drawn for you. You'll need to memorise as much as possible."

As the class filed out of the classroom, a few lingered near the corner of the building, dragging on small white cigarettes. As Thomas slowly shuffled past them, not wanting to have a coughing fit because of the smoke, he heard their voices carry against the stone.

"That man is a raving lunatic!" one commented. "To think I paid good money to listen to this insanity!"

"Do you really think he is insane, Edward? Or are you just scared?"

A ripple of laughter lightening the mood.

"Why, there's nothing to be scared of!" the first speaker – Edward –stated. "The only thing I could be scared of is Talbot himself."

"How sure are we that this man isn't a vampiric daemon himself? He has all the traits about him."

"Don't say that you believe his drivel?" Edward barked.

"Of course not," said the second man. "All I know is that based on the texts he's had us read, he displays quite a number of those properties. Watch him next time if you don't believe me. He always wears black, he only teaches at night, we never see him in the daylight, and he has long, white fingers and hands, indicative of a lack of blood flow. Not to mention, he's rather imposing."

"'That could be applied to a lot of doctors," reasoned a third man.

Their voices drifted off as Thomas made his way out of the main courtyard and onto the cobbled streets. His heels clacked a little on the damp stones as he made his way to his rooms. The night air was heavy and damp. He pulled his cloak tighter around him, bowing his head to his chest. Was it possible that his teacher was a vampire? That really was the most amusing thing Thomas had heard recently. Talbot wasn't a vampire –he just couldn't be. Not to mention, Thomas was sure he had seen the sallow-faced man in daylight at least one time.

As soon as he was inside, he lit a fire and shrugged out of his damp clothes, changing into some fresh undergarments and wrapped himself in a dressing gown and a heavy blanket to ward off the chill as the fire grew. Now that he had much better light and was comfortable, Thomas drew out his notebook. His diagram was detailed enough however he couldn't help but looking at the lycanthropic skeleton. It really was abnormal in comparison to a classic human skeleton. But how? How was it possible for bones to mutate so quickly? For them to stretch and change shape –becoming canine in appearance. Even the facial muscles grew distorted and elongated once the creature was fully developed.

It all happened so fast! The idea of the physiological ramifications churned his gut.

"Am I missing something?" he wondered, as he ran a finger over the drawing.

A sudden idea came to him. Fumbling around he located a stub of pencil on the mantelpiece and drew more arrows from the page and listed questions that he was sure to ask in the following weeks lecture.

The following week, Thomas was eager to get to his lecture whereas the remaining seven young men seemed to be taking it as a chore. They had known of Talbot and his teachings. The workload and studying outside of lectures should not have surprised them. In fact, Thomas sat in the first row of seats for two reasons; one, so he was able to see the writing on the blackboard without squinting and two, so he could be easily heard when asking Talbot the questions he had prepared the week before.

It had already been an intense day for him. He'd made it on time to his previous lecture on new surgery techniques in regard to women giving birth, and had been a little squeamish upon seeing the large, detailed sheets Talbot had drawn up especially for them to study and memorise. Rufus had been especially pale during that lesson as, he told Thomas over the weekend, that he had started courting a young woman from North London. It was such a shock for the man to see the detailed drawings –he had to be excused for ten minutes. Thomas felt sympathy for his friend, he really did, however he was also seeing the poor man's training go up in smoke if he didn't quell his queasiness.

Now that the theatre was empty again, Thomas felt like he could relax a little more.

Talbot was doing a recap of their last lesson and asked if any of them had done extra studying, to which only three people raised their hands. Thomas included. Again, there was no approval, merely silence.

"Now, class, for this next session I am requiring you to study up on the chapters I have copied for you. They are medications and concoctions that have been reportedly proven to lessen the effects of those inflicted with lycanthropic tendencies." His voice was a low rumble that worked rhythmically with the darkness. "I want you all to study the exact production of each medication. Learn it by heart; sometimes you'll need to work from memory alone. Learning these tricks now will make life far easier later."

Thomas frowned, before taking the top sheet and passing them back.

It was a large sheaf of thin paper, the ink printed small alongside Talbot's inked drawings. He really was rather talented; at the very least the images were detailed enough so that it'd be easy to identify things, if he ever happened to come face-to-face with such an anomaly.

Thomas bit back a snort of derision.

Of course he'd see a werewolf! This was one hundred per cent true! He'd also buy a baby mermaid and raise it in a bowl on the windowsill!

"Now, class, gather your notebooks. We are to adjourn to the courtyard."

There was a stunned moment of silence before they broke out into a chorus of questions.

"You heard. Outside. Five minutes!"

There was no room for arguments. As a group, the shuffling of feet and gathering of leather-bound books filled the air as the doors were unlocked and pushed open. A rush of balmy air ruffled the loose papers lying on the empty seats.

The courtyard was black when they stepped outside. The lamps had been extinguished.

Thomas was stunned.

Did Talbot really have that much sway at the hospital?

In the courtyard, there were four brass telescopes positioned with a lantern resting by the legs. It was a curious sight, looking up at the night sky and –amidst the thin echo of chimney smoke –seeing brilliant white stars glimmering down at them. It was a calm, still night. The silence of the city was calming compared to the hustle and bustle that accompanied the daylight hours. The dampness had dried out from the previous week.

"Pair off, all of you. We're going to be mapping the lunar cycle of this month."

There was a murmur of intrigue as well as despair at having to stand in the evening air. As the other young men paired off, Thomas was suddenly aware that no one was migrating towards him.

'*Great*,' he inwardly sighed. '*Alone again.*'

Oh well, it wasn't an issue. He was no stranger to working alone. Setting himself up with the brass telescope, he looked into the scope lens and adjusted it so that the image of the sky was sharper. Attached to each telescope, Talbot had written them a series of coordinates to look-up and document.

Within the hour, whilst Thomas' fingers cramped around his pencil stub –he wasn't stupid enough to write in ink, not when he couldn't see anything –Talbot started patrolling along the line, his disapproving aura already making him sweat.

"On your own, Segdon?"

Thomas swallowed thickly. "Yes, sir."

"Are you having difficulties?"

"No, sir."

"Hand me your book."

It wasn't a request. Thomas lifted his notebook for Talbot to read. His own lamp swung from an iron hook. Talbot's face remained impassive as his dark eyes flitted over Thomas' handwriting. He was suddenly self-conscious about not writing in cursive.

"Don't forget to copy these out in ink as soon as you can," the tall man intoned, before passing the notebook back and continuing on his way towards the next in line.

It wasn't a compliment –but it was something.

For the remainder of the lesson, before the sky started to pale on the horizon, Thomas worked relentlessly to make his observations as precise as possible, before he packed away the telescope and carried it back into the theatre, following his classmates. Back at his seat, Thomas took great care in folding the papers into his notebook before tucking them away in his portfolio.

A group of the young men were talking and smoking outside yet again. Thomas kept his head bowed as he passed them. Thankfully, they seemed too weary to bother talking ill of Talbot or anything for that matter. From what Thomas heard along the pathway, their conversation hovered around what they were going to do for the remainder of that week. Thomas never had any such plans. At the very least he was going to be having an early lunch with Rufus come Wednesday.

The walk back to his rooms was calming; the promise of light made the damp grass glimmer. The streets were quiet, and the hush of rustling leaves made Thomas think of his calm life back home in Yorkshire. He definitely needed to get back to see his family at some point. For now, though, he needed to make them proud.

Thursday 16th August 1888.

Rufus raised his glass of ale and grinned as Thomas saluted with him. It had been a rough twenty-four hours since his last lecture with Talbot, and the cold and fatigue were only just ebbing out of his bones. He couldn't afford to have a fire going all night long. He'd had a good night sleep, though, and a large meal with his friend seemed like the perfect way to celebrate a solid rest.

"Are the lectures any good?" Rufus asked as their food was served to them.

"They're interesting," Thomas nodded, placing his napkin over his lap. It wouldn't do to stain his only good pair of trousers.

It was a nice place –not as high end as some of the noblemen were able to afford but it was definitely higher than his own personal preferences. It was classier than a local pub, but not as refined as a proper restaurant.

"He has a very detailed hand in regard to diagrams and reference images. Although he does seem to spring plans on us last minute. It's very ... unsettling."

"More unsettling than the way he handles cadavers?" Rufus blanched as he picked up his knife and fork.

"Well that remains to be seen," Thomas grinned. "We haven't done anything physically aggressive yet. Just mapping out the lunar cycle."

"Is that all?"

"And a lot of reading. That's why I've been trying to read as much as I can."

"Has he asked you to read any of these obscure books?"

"Of course!" Thomas tried to bite back his laughter. "I'm having to traipse to the library every day just in case another copy of '*Medieval Teachings of the Occult*' has come back in stock."

"That's a little obvious, isn't it?" Rufus asked, quirking an amused eyebrow.

"Yes and no. It's an obvious title, yet it seems to have gotten lost in translation."

"Where did it originate from?"

"England," Thomas deadpanned. "Which makes it even worse that I can't find a copy!"

"How is everyone else coping?"

"Apparently they've found copies. I'm not sure whether I believe them or not."

Rufus frowned but didn't have the secrets that Thomas needed. Sad, really. What else could he do? However, Rufus opted to change the subject. "So, do you remember I mentioned I was starting to court that young lady from North London?"

"Distinctly."

"Well I was wondering if you would like to have dinner with me and her at some point next week?"

Thomas tried to keep his composure. His smile was almost ear-splitting, however. "Good job, Rufus! I'm impressed! Has she already met with your parents?"

"Goodness, no! That's a torture I have reserved especially for tonight." He pulled a moody face, but the faint blush was enough of a clue. He really was enamoured with this lady.

"Your family will love her," Thomas stated with a confident smile. Rufus had a tendency to worry too much. "Besides, it's not about what your family thinks of her. It's more about what her family thinks of **you**."

"I know," Rufus intoned. "I have that nightmare awaiting me for this weekend."

"I'm sure it won't be that bad."

"They're from up North, Thomas!" Rufus hissed. It wasn't like it was a secret; every city in the world had a North and South. "How on earth am I to compete with that? I honestly think it's because I'm training as a doctor that her father's even letting me court her!"

Thomas kept his mouth shut. It wouldn't do to add to his friends worries when it came to his short-comings in the classroom. He supposed it could be an ode to Talbot's teaching style. Although, it did have to be said, that if one couldn't handle the way Talbot taught medicine, then perhaps one was not fit to become a doctor.

No. Rufus definitely didn't need to hear that.

It was almost a mercy when they finally paid their tab and made their way out into the bright sunshine. The heat was near suffocating, reminding Thomas of that one morning a week where he got to walk home whilst the rest of the city stirred in their beds. Still, he breathed in the scent of wildflowers, freshly baked bread, and the salty tang of the Thames as it sloshed lazily under the bridges. The sound of carriages rolling along, the clopping of horses' hooves and the sound of children laughing as they outran whomever's pocket they'd just picked –it was a strange symphony to readjust to. Thomas couldn't lie though; it was nice to be out and about in the city without feeling confined. Perhaps that's why Talbot taught at such odd hours?

Once they'd crossed over the Thames they went their separate ways; Rufus to go and spend time with his new lady-friend, and Thomas went off in the direction of the central city library. It wasn't how he wanted to spend his Wednesday afternoon, but he really needed that book. He wanted to prove that he was as smart as any of the other men in his class. That his scholarship wasn't just an easy-way ticket.

'*I'm just as good,*' he thought as he came face-to-face with the tall, double oak doors. '*I just need to find that book!*'

The library was cool compared to the heat that baked the streets outside. The still aroma of old paper, ink and dust was cloying and comforting. It truly wouldn't be a magnificent library without that smell. Feeling comfortable, he made his way up a few steps to the main desk.

The old man behind the desk looked up from his desk, barely moving anything except his eye muscles as he regarded Thomas with open resentment. "How may I help you today, sir?" he intoned.

"I was wondering if '*Medieval Teachings of the Occult*' has come back in stock?"

"Like I told you last week, sir, we don't stock that particular book."

"Could you at least tell me if you ever have?" Thomas asked, a bead of desperation swelling inside him.

"No, sir."

"Does you know of a store that might stock it?"

The old man narrowed his eyes. "No, sir. We only have a very small section dedicated to that particular subject. You're more than welcome to see if there are any other books that might be of use to you."

Thomas opened his mouth and closed it just as quickly. That was a helpful response compared to all the other times he'd questioned the man. Nodding politely, he edged his way around the weathered desk towards a small dark corner of the building. Sunlight never reached this particular bookcase –a perfect home for the books about the occult.

The air was musty, shafts of sunlight highlighting the dust mites that swarmed behind him.

Reaching out he trailed his fingers over the old, roughened leather books. Some of their spines almost crumbled under his touch. None of the titles jumped out at him, however, and as far as he knew, Talbot didn't have them on the pre-approved reading list.

"Not good ... Not good ... Not good ..." He didn't mean to mutter. It was hard not to in the austere silence. He must have annoyed someone in the neighbouring aisle, for a shadow fell from behind him, making it impossible to read the gilded letters.

"I take it you're not finding a particular book," drawled a low, sultry voice.

Thomas –despite sensing a presence behind him –jumped. Looking over his shoulder, he swallowed thickly as he came face-to-face with a tall blonde man with pure white skin and eyes as hard as steel.

"I'm sorry," he finally said keeping his voice low. "Was I disturbing you?"

"Yes and no."

Thomas frowned. "I'm sorry, sir –I'm not sure I understand."

"No; you weren't disturbing me, because I can accustom myself with everyone's personal tics, and yes; because I can tell that you're becoming quite vexed and I'm going to avail myself to help you. If you'll permit me?"

Thomas blinked. Stunned. "I'm sorry, sir, but I'm not sure you can."

The man smiled, his smooth pink lips merely a shade or two darker than his skin. "Allow me to be the judge of that."

Weaving his way completely into the aisle so that he was no longer blocking the light, the blonde man bent over to that his sharp eyes could scan the embossed titles. Thomas watched, too stunned to do anything other than breathe –and even that seemed to require manual focus.

"Do forgive me, young man," the stranger murmured, "but I'm not entirely sure what book I'm looking for."

"Oh!" Thomas felt his cheeks flush. "I'm sorry! It's ... um ...

'M*edieval Teachings of the Occult*'."

The stranger straightened up, his blonde hair shining in the shaft of sunlight. His face was sombre. "That's a rather dark book for someone of your age to be reading."

Thomas felt himself shrink down a little. Why did he feel so judged –like a naughty child caught stealing –when the man looked at him in that way? "It's –It's for my studies, sir. Required text from my professor."

"I feel as though you should redirect your studies, young man. Studying these subjects –well –it could very well warp your judgement."

Thomas smiled and shook his head. "Thank you, sir, but I must insist that I need this particular text."

A blonde eyebrow quirked. "Well, I must say your insistence is quite admirable."

"It's not here, is it?" Thomas murmured. He didn't need a reply. He knew that, even if the desk clerk wasn't good at his job, that the book wouldn't be here. Perhaps it was time he frequented another library?

"Unfortunately, no, it doesn't appear to be."

Suddenly aware that he had taken up a perfect stranger's time, Thomas backed up and dipped his head a little. "Forgive me, sir, I've taken up too much of your time."

The man smiled down at Thomas. "It's alright. I'm happy to try and help."

Thomas offered a smile. It was too natural.

He was about to turn away when the blonde man spoke up. "If it's any consolation, I have a couple of obscure books of my own on these sorts of subjects. I'd be happy to loan you a book or two, if you'd like."

Stopping dead, Thomas looked up with wide eyes. "S-sir ... you don't even know me."

"Perhaps we should change that." Straightening his light jacket, the man extended his hand towards Thomas. It was strange, almost poetic in the way the light cut through the gloom and painted the man's pale skin with the luminescence of the sun. Thomas shook the thought away. "My name is Philip Ridley."

Accepting the hand, he said, "It's a pleasure to meet you, sir. I'm Thomas. Thomas Segdon."

"Here's your tea, sir."

Thomas flushed awkwardly as the slim maid placed a silver tray on the wrought iron table. He felt as though he was in a dream, perched in a well-manicured terraced garden, shrouded from the city life that bustled on by in the streets below.

As Philip had led him through the London streets towards his home, Thomas had felt more out-of-place than ever. He felt too dirty, too scruffy too uncouth in comparison to the tall, blonde man who seemed to make even bricked pillars swoon in his presence. It didn't help that the man appeared rich enough to afford his own house-staff. Fiddling with his cuffs, Thomas was too aware that he hadn't bathed in a few days either. The faint whiff of ether still clung to his shirt.

If Philip noticed, he didn't hint at it.

As graceful as anything, Philip poured two cups of tea, milk with two sugars each. Thomas wasn't used to drinking tea in such a way. Sugar was a luxury in his home for a number of years, used mainly by his mother in regard to pastries and jams. It helped to earn them a little extra money when things got strained around Christmas.

'*Perhaps I should send mother a care package with my monthly allowance?*' Thomas mused as he watched Philip stir the tea with a silver spoon.

"So, Thomas, tell me about yourself?"

His glasses nearly fell of his nose, he was so startled.

"Um ... there's not really much to know, I'm afraid."

"Nonsense. How did you come to live in London?"

Swallowing thickly, he replied; "I was granted a full scholarship to study underneath Stephen Talbot in St. Bart's hospital. I'm –training to become a physician."

"So it's your first year?"

"Y-yes."

"My condolences," the blonde chuckled.

"I beg your pardon?"

"Stephen Talbot, I'm afraid, is my Uncle," Philip smirked. "I can sympathise with his erratic teaching methods."

Thomas sank back into his chair. This seemed –almost too much of a coincidence. "Did your uncle talk about me?" Thomas asked forlornly. "Is that why he sent you to help?"

To his chagrin, Philip laughed. "Honestly, running into you was not pre-planned. This is merely a coincidence. Try not to read too much into it."

"So am I to assume that you don't have a copy of the book I need?" Thomas challenged through gritted teeth. His hands tightened into fists in his lap.

Philip frowned. The expression looked wrong on his porcelain face. "I can understand your determination. However, I must disappoint you. No, I don't have that specific book. I have a fair few that you're more than welcome to browse."

"That's cheating," Thomas ground out.

"I beg your pardon?"

Looking up, Thomas narrowed his eyes at the older man. This was too perfect to happen to someone like him. It wasn't fair. He was trying so hard to be the best he could be. He wasn't going to take free hand-outs, not even from his own professor's extended family. Anger boiled in his skull. He just wanted to prove, on his own, that he was good enough. He didn't need to be baby-sat by the professor –or even his nephew!

He stood up abruptly. Philip blinked in surprise but otherwise didn't react. Thomas felt ridiculous –he had an opportunity better than most in that moment. With clenched fists and jaw, Thomas shook his head.

"I'm –I'm sorry, sir, to reject such niceties but I'm afraid I must decline your help." Taking a deep breath, he straightened up and looked Philip in the eye. "Thank you for your time. You've been most kind."

Philip regarded him. "Mr. Segdon, sit down."

"I have errands to run," Thomas lied. "I've taken up too much of your time. Have a pleasant evening."

Without a moment to lose, he turned on his heel and hurried on through the building, taking care to follow the route they'd used to ascend to the balcony.

Back out on the street, he gulped in the dirty, hot air and felt queasy. This was too foreign to him. What on earth was Talbot's game? Trying to force-feed him help from a third-party source? That was so harsh! Had he truly proven himself that incompetent during their last three lectures that his professor needed to ambush him with hands-outs?

His eyes burned a little. Cuffing his eyes, he ground his teeth together and started to walk in a direction. He wasn't entirely sure where he was going. He needed to cross over the Thames, that's all he could focus on. Making his way to one of the bridges was all he needed to keep in mind.

By the time he crossed over to his side of the water, the sun had sunk beneath the horizon, leaching the last dregs of pink, purple and orange from the sky.

Night had fallen by the time he stepped into his building.

The room was exactly as he'd left it. The window had been opened thanks to his landlord. Yet the fire –he hadn't left that burning. The hairs on the back of his neck stood up on end. His senses were on alert. Leaving the door ajar, he edged into the room. There was only one other door that led off from his small room –and that led into the washroom. Straining his ears, he tried to catch a sound of anyone else in the room.

Silence.

"Hello?" he called out, his heart leaping into his throat. Bending low, he grabbed a blunt chair leg from under his coffee table by the fireplace. His palms were sweating as he edged further into the room.

"Who's in here?"

The lock slid back. The sound dropped like a lead weight in his stomach.

The shock of blonde hair startled him. Philip regarded him with a vaguely impressed look. "Put that down, Mr. Segdon."

It was all too much. Thomas' arms quaked and faltered down to his sides. Philip looked so stark and clean, like a marble slab tossed in the slums. It just didn't fit! He was too clean, too neat, too perfect –so much so that he seemed to dwarf everything in the room.

"How did you get in here?" Thomas rasped out.

"I bribed your landlord. He seemed more than happy to take the money," Philip stated casually. "As a matter of fact, I'd consider moving. If your landlord is going to sell you out for a couple extra shillings –well, you wouldn't want him in charge of your rooms."

"How did you get here before me?"

"I asked my driver to bring me."

"Why?"

"I felt bad for making you feel inadequate and I wanted to apologise for my behaviour."

Thomas floundered for a moment. Philip hadn't exactly

done anything out of the ordinary for himself. It had simply irked Thomas, rubbed him up the wrong way because it had been thrown at him too quickly. He hadn't been able to process it. Dropping the chair leg back in its place under his armchair, he raked both hands through his hair and closed his eyes.

'*Breathe ... one ... two ... three ... breathe ...*'

"Would you like some tea?"

"I don't have –" he stopped as he opened his eyes. There, on his small table that he ate at, was a fine china set. Two teacups and a teapot. "You brought tea?"

"You seemed agitated. I wanted to apologise." He said it as though that was explanation enough. Thomas sat down in his other chair. It wasn't as fine as his armchair but in that moment he didn't think he'd be able to relax. He accepted a cup of tea. "I am sorry for making you feel suspicious of my uncle. To be perfectly honest, the only information I was able to get from him was your home address. It still took me some time to find out exactly where you lived."

"You didn't need to follow me."

"Perhaps not," Philip conceded, raising his cup. "I also didn't need to overwhelm you."

"Perhaps not."

The mimicry made the blonde man smile. Why did that make Thomas' stomach knot.

'*Nerves*,' his mind hissed. '*You're still jumpy from before*'.

"By way of apology," Philip continued as he set his cup and saucer on the table. "I am loaning you my books on the occult. I figured you'd have more use of them than I would for the rest of the year." He gave a lazy smirk to the astounded brunette man. "Although, I will ask that you return them as neatly as possible. Some of those are rare, unabridged first editions. Worth a good hundred or two."

"**What?**"

The teacup almost fell to the floor.

Philip looked at him. He wasn't perplexed. "They are rare books, Mr. Segdon."

"Forgive me, sir, but I can't accept this."

Philip sighed before reaching out and grasping Thomas' shoulder. "Listen to me, Mr. Segdon. There is something in you that is quite admirable. Harness that tenacity and use it to further yourself. It doesn't matter how you get the tools to perform the job, as long as you can perform it to the best of your abilities."

Thomas watched the older man and felt his muscles turn to stone. He bowed his head. "Okay –thank you for the generous gift."

"No thanks are necessary, Mr. Segdon. All you need to do is make sure that you try and excel at your studies."

Thomas frowned. "Why are you being so nice to me?"

"I have been away for a while. My father made a huge argument against me that I was a selfish, entitled brat. In a way, I have been trying to redeem myself."

"What does that have to do with me?"

Philip smirked. "I noticed you coming into the library over the last two weeks. Always asking or the same book and always getting the same answer." He straightened up and steeped his fingers in his lap. "I must confess, I felt a little pity for you. I was concerned that you were wasting your time. Time that could have been better spent elsewhere."

Thomas pressed his lips together in thought.

Philip watched his reaction and stiffened. He really was out of place in the small room. "I apologise," he finally said, drinking down the last of his tea. "I appear to have over-stepped my bounds once again. I need to work on that, it seems."

"It's not that!" Thomas gushed out as Philip stood from the armchair. "I'm –I'm just not used to good things happening in my life. It's hard to accept them."

"Never look a gift-horse in the mouth, Mr. Segdon," Philip said. "They bite."

Thomas looked down at his hands, feeling a little on edge about the entire day. "I'm not sure how to feel right now, but I will feel grateful come the morning."

Surprisingly, Philip let a slow smile cross over his mouth. "I believe I can accept that. However, it's rather late and I think we both need to be up at first light."

With a quirk of his eyebrow, he quickly packed away his tea-set, something Thomas was still amused by, before making his way towards the door.

Thomas hovered behind him, feeling awkward still. The entire day felt like a strange dream. At the door, he held onto the wooden frame as Philip looked in the entrance, blocking the murky yellow light from the hall.

"It was a pleasure seeing you again, Mr. Segdon." He held out his hand.

Thomas looked down at the hand and felt his own palm itch. "Um ... please, I'd really rather prefer it if you'd just call me 'Thomas'."

With a wide grin Philip grabbed his hand. "I think I can do that ... Thomas."

The growl made Thomas' stomach flip. Still, Philip gripped his hand an extra moment before disappearing down the steps and into the night.

Friday 17th August 1888.

Talbot had sent them all a letter instructing them to attend a lecture in the hospital on Friday evening. Thomas didn't mind too much; he'd merely been about to have drinks with Philip, but the blonde man hadn't argued when he'd popped around Thursday morning to decline the invitation. In fact, Philip had been more than happy to encourage Thomas to go to the impromptu lecture.

"You can't not go," Philip had said. "The man does not take absences lightly. He'll make your remaining lessons hell if you skip for no reason."

Raking his hair back out of his eyes, he adjusted his glasses and pushed his way into the theatre. The same smell of wood and beeswax cloyed at his senses as he shuffled around, making his way into the lower ring of benches. Everyone seemed to sit in the first two rows now; it wasn't productive to be 'taking a stand' by sitting too far out of the only source of light in the room. It made Thomas feel a little uncomfortable as he barely spoke to anyone else. It made for very lonely study sessions.

The late summer heat had seeped into the room throughout the course of the day, bleeding into the woodwork and exuding onto the small cloister of young men tugging uncomfortably at their collars. It was a dry awkward heat that ebbed out, making the process of thinking and paying attention to their professor a daunting challenge.

Thomas couldn't deny his curiosity when he saw a long table stretched out in place of the podium. Upon the surface were numerous specimens in glass jars backlit by about twenty candles. It cast a dull yellow glow over the first two rows of seats. The blackboard already adorned a large, detailed sketch of the human body –both inside and out. However, for once, Thomas' hands weren't itching to label diagrams all day.

Thanks to his other lectures with Talbot they had gotten onto handling real, human specimens. The smells made his stomach coil and his gag reflex threatened to flare up, but he managed to quash it down to focus on the task at hand.

"This evening we'll be correctly identifying specimens of the human body as well as matching specimens from acclaimed supernatural creatures."

There was a murmur among the students. Even Thomas felt his muscles tense. He could only see the top half of the jars from his vantage point. His palms started to sweat a little as Talbot swept from side-to-side on the slightly raised platform, the candlelight making his skin looked ever waxier.

'How do you know he's not a vampire?' hissed the voice at the back of his mind.

Thomas shook his head and tried to focus.

For this lecture they needed to partner up with someone. Thomas felt his stomach drop. This was going to be the lunar-mapping all over again. There was only so much work he'd be able to do on his own. As the rest of the class moved around to sit in three pairs, Thomas felt his skin grow hot as eyes landed on him, alone again.

Swallowing, he tried to ignore them.

The banging of the double doors made everyone jump. A shot of sticky air flooded the room dragging in the scent of baked cobblestones and dry grass. All heads had turned to look at the latecomer as he swept the doors shut as though they weighed nothing. Thomas frowned, almost rising out of his seat to get a better look. Apparently, being at the front of the classroom had disadvantages as well.

"Sorry I'm late, Professor," a sultry voice drawled. The tap, tap, tapping of polished shoes descending the stairs made Thomas flinch. A shock of platinum hair swam into view, and he thought he was going to faint.

It was Philip.

Talbot gave the younger man a haughty glare before straightening up over him. Thomas hadn't imagined anyone as tall as Philip, yet he was just on par with Talbot's hooked nose. "Don't bore us with excuses. Get an apron and gloves on and get to work."

'Wow', Thomas thought. 'He really doesn't go easy on his own family.'

Philip gave a sideways smirk, draping his cloak and walking cane into an empty seat before going to the back of the room where Stephen kept rubber gloves and aprons for manual tasks. When he stepped back into the light, Thomas was awestruck at how elegant the man managed to make chemical-soaked rubber look. It was impressive.

"Well what're you waiting for?" Talbot sneered at the seven young men. "Get the uniform on and stand at this table in two minutes."

"Sir, you haven't even told us what we're –"

"One minute, fifty-seven."

Thomas had never seen them move faster. As he moved over the raised platform, he walked past Philip as he was snapping the black rubber glove in place. The sound was so satisfying in the din of shuffling feet and stink of beeswax and formaldehyde. He slid his eyes over to Thomas and smirked. The brunette man had to focus intently on tying the apron around him and slipping his hands into a pair of gloves.

'Focus! You can't mess up now he's here!'

They split off into their pairs around the table. Talbot took centre stage, his own rubber gloves covering the sleeves of his tailored black tunic. He popped the glass lid off the nearest jar –that holding a human brain –filling the air with the toxic smell of flesh and chemicals. Thomas clamped his jaw tight. He was not going to vomit on the professor's specimens! They were hard to come by as it was.

"Today," Talbot's voice echoed despite the hostile level he always maintained. "We are going to be comparing human samples next to afflicted samples. Since the brain is the highest functioning organ in our body, you should acknowledge that it should be significantly different to an afflicted brain."

He was silent for a moment.

"Where are your notebooks?"

Without bothering to question him, seven young men hurried to retrieve their notebooks and begin doing as they had done in every other lecture; detailed diagrams and labels prepared for when the diagnostics were explained. As Thomas was sketching out the human brain, Philip chuckled quietly beside him. Was this amusing to him? Watching his uncle antagonise people?

By the end of the first hour Philip had a more prominent role in directing the class. This left Thomas alone with a very noticeable emptiness on the bench beside him. However, he reasoned it was a good thing. That last thing he needed was to be branded as a teacher's pet by the rest of the class. Philip was standing at the black board. He still had his rubber gloves on as he continued to label the two diagrams drawn. Talbot was standing off to the side, observing. Each time someone guessed an answer correctly, he made a small note in a pad tucked away in his sleeve.

He also made a note of all the incorrect answers.

Thomas found that he kept looking over when the book

came out. He focused on the board; Philip's sketches were quite remarkable –almost as good as Talbot's own. Had he taught his nephew, perhaps?

"Come on, men!" Philip snapped. He had no problem raising his voice to all kind of levels it appeared. "The Lupine brain is clearly different! Now I want you to tell me how!"

No one answered.

Philip glowered at them before turning to another blackboard and stabbing his cane at it. "Possible werewolf skull. What are the differences?"

Silence.

"Good God, men! How have you managed to trudge through your studies if you refuse to answer such simple questions?" he sneered. "First of all, the lupine brain is clearly accustomed to sitting in this oversized canine skull, however it is a fat hybrid of both a wolf brain and a human brain. The nervous system within appears to be similar, however a few of the nerves become inactive and new ones seem to emerge!" He drew a deep breath before continuing; "Now the werewolf skull is clearly reminiscent of a human one, however the jaw line elongates, and scarring is caused by the teeth!"

As a demonstration, he pushed five wooden fangs out of a replicated model on the side of the table. The wooden fangs slotted in when pushed, and retracted when he pulled. Could that really happen every month? Surely the pain when becoming human would make any man fear for his own life, let alone others!

Thomas hastened to scribble down everything he was saying. Not that he needed to; he'd already figured out the majority of what the blonde was prattling on about, but it was so intriguing to watch him lose his temper. Thomas hadn't the heart to stop him. Even his well-manicured hair fell out of place and into his eyes as he stabbed at the boards with his cane.

"Philip, control yourself. Otherwise we won't get onto the difference between human hearts and a vampire's heart."

Philip drew in a deep breath and squared his shoulders. Talbot having a calming effect on someone was almost as peculiar as the lectures themselves. Or perhaps it was the cloying chemical aroma in the air?

Somehow, describing and analysing the differences between a healthy human heart and that of a vampiric demon, was much simpler than comparing skulls and brains based on their size. Thomas could only imagine that the rest of his class simply didn't want to be yelled at or witness Talbot making notes throughout the rest of the lecture. Whatever it was, the other six seemed to be more attentive.

"So who wants to go first?" Philip asked, cocking a blonde eyebrow.

They were all crowded around the table. Two mechanisms had been set-up, each with a heart wired into it. Small tubes seemed to weave in and out of the valves. Faint smears of blood shone on the tables' surface. Philip was holding a syringe; in it was black writing ink. The experiment was to see the way the veins and heart worked when processing blood. Thomas itched to try but –couldn't. The needle gleamed in the candlelight.

"Human or vampire, who is going first?" There was a tight edge to Philip's voice now. There were a few faint whiskers on his jaw line. They seemed a lot darker than his natural hair colour.

"I'll go!"

Thomas barely remembered how it happened; one second he was pressing his stomach into the table, the next, Philips gloves hands slid over his own as he slipped the needle into the top of the valve. His hand tremored –proximity to the freshly cleaned blonde man and the chemicals was gut churning –and squeezed. Veins streaked across the organ before spurting out of the other valve. Easy and simple –a healthy human heart.

"Takes notes, gentlemen!" Philip stated, already armed with the second syringe. "Now, let's see what happens with the vampire specimen."

The whole class seemed to hold their breath. It was one thing to have an 'alleged' specimen, however to have an organ so fantastical was dizzying. Thomas tried to quell the tremor in his hand. His glasses seemed to slip a little down his nose as he slipped the needle into the valve. Ever-so-slowly, he pressed the plunger.

The veins were instantly black –no changes there. However, instead of spurting out the other valve, the ink seemed to soak into a solid ball in the centre of the muscle before disappearing. A stunned silence fell over their heads.

Thomas forced the lump in his throat back down. "What –just happened?"

"That, Thomas, is a very good question," Philip said. His tone implied that he would not be so forthcoming with an answer as he was his praise. Turning to the rest of the class, he stated; "What you saw was a stark contrast in how hearts are supposed to work. Unfortunately, it is as yet undetermined where or how the blood is used throughout the rest of the demon's body. This will be your homework!"

Thomas felt his head spin. Homework about hearts? Where was he supposed to find medical journals that detailed such anomalies?

The bell chimed when they were practically finished clearing away the hall. The table needed to be soaked and scrubbed, the aprons and gloves being tossed into a large canvas sack for thorough cleaning. It wouldn't do to contaminate the rest of their specimens –or indeed the other students –with the materials they were using. Not that it mattered to Philip or Talbot. The two men had given clear instructions before departing into a side room. Thomas couldn't stop himself from glancing over at the door. There weren't any raised voices, yet he knew that that didn't mean much in regard to Talbot.

He strained, trying not to look too suspicious. Not that the rest of the class paid him any mind. They rarely did.

He was the only one left in the hall by the time the door open and Philip marched out, his fists clenched and his jaw set. He looked rattled. Had Talbot admonished him? He stopped short when he spotted Thomas about to climb the steps to the door. "One moment, Mr. Segdon. I'll walk you out."

The weight of his presence beside him made Thomas feel a lot safer as he stepped out into the black night. They walked along mostly in silence, the tap, tap, tapping of Philip's shoes and cane on the cobbles filling the mild air between them.

"So how did you like the lecture?"

"I was surprised to see you there," Thomas admitted. "It was extremely satisfying though. I feel like we were soon to stagnate in our studies."

"Never underestimate my uncle," Philip stated archly. Softening his tone, he said; "Are you intrigued by the homework?"

"Intrigued and frustrated, yes."

"Why so?"

Thomas flushed, clutching his portfolio tighter under his arm. "The studies are difficult. I'll need to locate certain journals."

"Nonsense!" Philip waved him off with a smirk. "You don't need all that extra reading material. All you need is to think about what you saw tonight and make it articulate."

"What if I struggle? I don't want Talbot to look down on

me."

"If you like, I can give you some advice before next week's lecture?"

Thomas stopped in the street, looking up at the man with narrowed eyes. "Why are you trying to help me?"

"Truthfully?"

"Yes."

"Because I see potential in you. I want you to harness that and do great things with it!"

Thomas shook his head, "You don't even know me."

"Nor do you know me." He arched a blonde eyebrow, making Thomas squirm. His eyes were far too intense. "Trust me, Thomas. I promise you, I can help."

There was no denying that he was still hesitant. He couldn't help it. Perhaps it was from working hard all his life. He didn't like handouts, not even from friends. It's why he insisted on paying half the tab whenever he dined with Rufus, even if he couldn't really afford it. "Fine," he eventually said. "I shall accept advice. However, that's where I draw the line."

A slow smile spread over Philip's face. "Very well. I can agree to that."

As they began to walk, Thomas tilted his head up at the sky. It was like a vast black canvas, sparsely dotted with stars. "It's a half moon tonight," he observed. "We should have a full one in a couple of weeks."

Philip followed his gaze up to the sky. A chill whispered at the leaves.

"Indeed," was all he said as they drew closer to Whitechapel.

Monday 27th August 1888.

For the next couple of weeks, Thomas had to admit that he barely saw the inside of his rooms until the dead of night. There was a murmuring in the dark ends of the London alleyways. Talk of criminals cutting down people on their way home. It made him a little edgy when he made his way to and from his lectures, but other than that life seemed to carry on as usual. He did envy Rufus a little, getting to go home when the streets were still busy with the swarm of drunkards that lurked in every glowing doorway.

It was only once a week, he reasoned.

That Monday he awoke late in the afternoon when someone knocked loudly on his door. Grunting through his sleep haze, Thomas stumbled to the door. He still had five hours before his lecture at the mortuary with Talbot and the other hundred and fifty young men remaining, intent on becoming a doctor. Through bleary eyes, Thomas grappled with the door handle and finally got the door to swing inwards.

"Hello?" he croaked.

"You were asleep, weren't you?" drawled a cool voice.

It sent a shiver down Thomas' spine though not in the foreboding way it had the first time they'd met. Backing away from the light he rubbed the heel of his hand into his eyes. "I'm sorry –I didn't mean to be rude."

"Do you have lectures today?" Philip asked, ignoring the apology.

Finding his glasses and sliding them onto his nose, Thomas nodded. "Y-yes. At 9 o'clock."

"Perfect. That'll give us enough time."

"For what?" Thomas frowned.

"For dinner," Philip stated as though it were obvious. "I think you should be prepared for what's to come in your lecture tonight. I don't want you to be surprised."

Thomas felt his insides twist and turn. "What –what do you know?"

"Never mind that now. Put some clothes on and then we can have a decent meal before you need to be locked away in that dungeon."

"It's hardly a dungeon," Thomas chastised as he blindly groped for the clean clothes hanging in front of the stove.

Philip ignored him –thankfully –as he got dressed. He was torn between wearing something decent for wherever Philip was going to take him, and wearing something worn-out and old for whatever was to come in the lectures. In the wash-room, Thomas untangled his hair, scrubbed his hands and face and inspected his reflection in the small, cracked mirror before sighing. It was the best as he was going to get. Straightening up, he left the bathroom, steeling himself for the evening ahead.

Thomas was glad that'd he'd taken an extra few minutes to scrub himself free of soot and grime. He often wondered how Philip could stand being around him half the time. It was a wonder that the blonde man would stomach being in the same breathing space as him. Swallowing thickly, he pressed his back into the padded chair. This was definitely the place where cleanliness was born; even the glasses were real crystal! Not the fake, stained glass that wound up in everyone's kitchen –this was the real deal!

"You're fiddling again," Philip stated without looking up from the menu. Yes, there were menus in this place! No smudged chalk words on a black painted scrap of wood.

Thomas glanced down. He blushed. He was fiddling with

his shirtsleeves again. It was a habit he seemed to have when he was, as Philip put it, 'out of his element'.

"Sorry," he mumbled, stuffing his hands under his thighs. He glanced at the menu and felt the blood drain from his face.

'*Out of my element, indeed*,' he inwardly groaned.

"Have you decided what you want?" Philip asked.

"I ... um ..." Thomas blushed again. "Perhaps you should just order for me. I ... don't really have experience with this."

Philip looked momentarily surprised. His lips lifted into a smile, before signalling for a waiter. With food and a little more wine ordered –fresh, fruity wine that went straight to his head –Thomas relaxed a little as he eyed his surroundings yet again. It really was spectacular!

"How are things going in your lectures?" Philip asked.

"Rather well," Thomas admitted. "Talbot says that, if we're lucky, we might get more specimens to experiment with and see how they function." There was a muted silence before Thomas dropped his gaze to his plate. Suddenly, the room felt really warm. "Philip?"

"Mmm?"

"What purpose does it serve Talbot to study these things?"

Perhaps it was the wrong question, as a dark look crossed the blonde man's face. "Unfortunately, Thomas, my uncle is rather eccentric in his beliefs. If there is a mystery to be solved or a cure to be found, he will work on it until he's dead."

Thomas furrowed his brow. "Really? He doesn't seem the type."

Philip gave a small smile. "No, he doesn't, does he?"

That ended the conversation. Thomas tried not to think about it too much. What else could he do? He just needed to focus on his studies and hope that the theoretical work was up to Talbot's standards. He felt a little guilty, always talking about Talbot and his lectures with Philip, however he couldn't deny that -without those things -his life would be extremely monotonous.

"I was planning on going to see my family this week?" Thomas finally said.

Philip raised his eyebrows, a small smile crawling onto his mouth. "Have you not seen them since you came down here?"

Thomas shook his head. "No, unfortunately. I was only planning to go back at Christmas."

"Oh, so what made you change your mind?" the blonde asked.

"Just a feeling, I guess," Thomas shrugged. It was true. He hadn't known what had caused it, but over the last few days he'd felt this niggling at the back of his mind that he needed to see his family before the yule tide season. "Not to mention, my dad is the town Doctor. I'm sure he'd love to see what I've been studying."

"You mean the traditional lessons?" Philip quirked an eyebrow. "Not the extra-curricular lectures?"

"Oh no!" Thomas said. "My father wouldn't understand. He'd say that I was wasting my life away."

Philip chuckled. It was a low sound that made Thomas feel more at ease with himself and his company. "So how is it you're not teaching with Talbot?"

Philip shook his head. "I don't have the patience for it," he stated. "Besides, if I were teaching I wouldn't be able to see that look of concentration you get when you're trying to draw the diagrams."

"It's not concentration," Thomas huffed. "I can't see. I'm practically blind."

Philip rolled his eyes but didn't comment. They remained quiet for the next while, as they finished their meal and Philip made his way to pay. Thomas kept his eyes averted, not wanting to feel the twist of jealousy he felt whenever he saw someone with more dispensable money than he had. It was a stupid feeling.

Walking out into the sunshine, both men had to take a moment to catch their breath. The heat was like a heavy hand pressing down on their shoulders. Philip draped his cloak over his arm and proceeded to walk along the cobbled pavements, his cane clicking softly. Thomas watched the cane move, the silver head catching the sun. He couldn't deny that he didn't see the point of the cane. Philip didn't even have the suggestion of a limp. Was it a psychological thing? He wasn't sure, but he wasn't foolish enough to ask no matter how much it piqued his interest.

"So you won't be back until later this week?" Philip asked.

Thomas dabbed his brow with his handkerchief. "I'm leaving first thing in the morning and should be back Friday afternoon. It's not long but it was the cheapest ticket they had on offer."

"I don't mind lending you some money."

Thomas snorted and smiled. "Sorry, Philip, but I don't accept money from friends. I don't like charity in regard to my lifestyle. I saved up enough money and can afford a return ticket for a few days. That'll be enough time to spend some quality time with my family and relax. The city really is like a beehive."

Philip stiffened a little but nodded. "I suppose I can respect that. You want to be a self-made man and you're starting from the ground up. That's definitely admirable at least."

Peering up at the blonde man, Thomas was intrigued by the set of his jaw and the stiffness to his posture. "Are you anxious about me leaving London?" For some reason this thought made him smile.

Philip wrinkled his nose. "Not especially, no. I just worry that you'll grow homesick and want to stay there."

"I'm already homesick. Going home now is what's going to curb that."

Philip stopped and stared down at the brunette man. They were definitely a strange pair; an aristocratic blonde man with a cane and silk waistcoat and pocket watch staring down into the face of a young brunette man, with round glasses tucked around his ears, an old white shirt under a weathered waistcoat and slacks. Even the finer details –like their hair –were a stark contrast to the other.

"I just want you to be cautious, Thomas," Philip stated, all joviality leaving his voice. His tone –and expression – was severe. "There are murmurs going around that police are having difficulties with some type of killer. It could be nothing or it could be a one-off. Either way they are trying to determine the threat before alerting the papers." His arm shot out and gripped Thomas' upper arm. "I just want you to be safe."

A fluttering sensation ghosted through Thomas' chest. The sincerity and severity in those grey eyes was almost overwhelming. "I promise to be safe," he vowed, noting that Philip did not release his grip. "Not to mention, I'll only be gone a few days. If anything, you might be the one in danger."

Something flickered in those grey eyes that he couldn't perceive.

Thomas grinned. His arm felt naked and clammy when Philip's hand slipped back down to rest at his side. "Now, I need to pack my things and head on to my lecture. If you like, we could possibly have a drink afterwards?"

"At 11 o'clock?" Philip chuckled. "Maybe I will just see you off at the station in the morning."

Thomas felt his heart drop in his chest but ignored it. "Okay. I wouldn't want you to postpone any plans because of me."

"I'll see you tomorrow morning, Thomas."

How was it that the man knew just the perfect tone to say his name? It sent a shiver running through him. "Have a nice evening, Philip. Thank you for lunch."

"It was my pleasure."

They kept eye contact for a while longer, before Thomas gave a curt nod and made his way up the stone steps to the hospital building. At the double doors, he turned and blinked in surprise. Philip had vanished so quickly from the courtyard that he wasn't even sure he'd heard the crunch of the gravel. With a frown, he turned his back on the daylight and entered the soothing, cool gloom of the lecture hall.

A hand rested on his shoulder with a soothing squeeze. Thomas looked up into the gentle face of his mother as she set a bowl of soup down in front of him. It was piping hot, fresh from the stove, and smelled of 'home'. "I know it's the middle of summer, but this is a new recipe Mrs. Munnick gave me. When I heard you were coming home for a few days, I couldn't resist."

Thomas leaned his head on her knuckles and kissed her hands. There were slightly calloused from her being a seamstress, but she loved her work. Her hands portrayed that love and determination. It was one of the subtle glimpses of her beauty.

"Thanks Mama," he said, picking up a spoon and starting to eat. He didn't care that it scalded his tongue, it was delicious! "When do you think Papa will be home?"

"The sun set about an hour ago. I'd imagine he'll be back soon. Probably just finishing up with a last-minute patient."

Thomas shook his head in response. As he continued to eat, he was amazed at how relaxed the atmosphere felt. Even in their little cottage, the resonating aura from the town was humbling and cosy. In London, it felt as though even breathing was an expense that would line the tax-man's pockets. If they had been a good hundred or so miles south, there would be a tremor of anxiety in his mother's voice, panicking about what was holding his Papa up. Not here, though.

He was almost finished with his second bowl of soup by the time his Papa came in through the back door. He had no cloak or hat –the balmy air rushing in with him –and dumped his leather case on the floor.

"Thomas my boy!" he exclaimed as he crossed the kitchen and enveloped his son in a strong hug. Thomas gasped out with a grin as he awkwardly hugged his Papa back. James Segdon beamed down at his son as he ruffled his hair –a gesture that had grown with them through Thomas' infancy.

"Are you hungry, dear?"

"Absolutely not!" James stated shaking his head as he made his way over to the stove. Taking the bowl and ladle from his wife's hands, he pressed a tender kiss to her forehead. "You sit down and rest. I can serve myself."

Margaret smiled gently, before brushing her hair out of her bright eyes and making her way to sit across from Thomas. James served himself and his wife with a bowl of soup and some crusty bread. Thomas watched as his Papa touched her shoulder affectionately as he made his way to the head of the table, the firelight from the hearth illuminating their little family.

"So Thomas was do you plan on doing here for the next few days?" James asked.

"I've not thought about it too much," Thomas stated. "I just wanted to come home before the Christmas season. I might have a lot of studying to do then, too. I thought it'd be best to see you when I'm less frazzled."

"Is it really that difficult?" Margaret asked.

"Oh, I'm managing!" he said, feeling a hot flush creep up the back of his neck. "The professor is intense but pragmatic in his techniques. We've already gotten onto experimenting with real human organs."

"Already?" James raised an amused eyebrow. "You were almost too squeamish to touch a toad before you left to go down to London."

Margaret chuckled as her son grew flustered. "Honestly, Papa, I wasn't that bad!"

"Oh, yes you were!" James clapped his son on the shoulder. "We are proud of you, son. You have a great opportunity here. If you get busy, we understand. We just want to hear from you every once in a while, so that we know you're alive and doing well."

"So have you been making any friends down there?" Margaret asked, breaking a small chunk of bread off.

"I have a few, here and there," Thomas said in off-handed way. "I've recently befriended the Professor's nephew."

"That's a strange line to follow with," James observed.

"I know. It was purely by coincidence that we came to meet, but I have been fortunate in doing so. Everyone else has funds and ways to get some of the more delicate journals and textbooks I need for my personal study sessions. Thanks to my knowing Philip, I am able to gain just as much access to these materials as the richer students."

"Is that really fair that you would have struggled without this young man?" Margaret asked with a heavy frown.

"Perhaps not. The professor might have helped. I just never got to the point of needing to ask."

"Oh listen to him!" Margaret exclaimed, "He's getting a right little London accent!"

Thomas blushed as she pinched his cheek but didn't brush

her away. It was nice having someone taking care of him. It suddenly made all those long nights in his small lodgings feel even more claustrophobic and depressing. "Mama don't tease," he mumbled weakly through a grin as she cleared the table of the empty bowls.

Once everything was stacked by the basin, she turned towards them, drawing her light shawl across her shoulders. "I'm going to head up to bed. It's lovely having you back Thomas." She pressed a kiss to the top of his head and squeezed him gently.

He hugged her back, before watching her silhouette make its way up the spiral staircase. A shaft of moonlight peeped in through the narrow window and illuminated her trail. Turning back to his Papa, Thomas was surprised to see him carry over two goblets and a bottle of wine. Raising the goblets, they gave a silent toast and took a sip. The warmth of the wine and the fire mingled to make his mind completely relax.

"So, how're things really, down in London?" James asked.

"I've told you."

"I mean really, Thomas. Is something bothering you?"

"Honestly, Papa? I worry that I'm out of my depth," he shuddered. He hadn't wanted to admit it out loud. Wine really did loosen his tongue. Spinning the goblet in front of him, Thomas looked up and chewed his bottom lip.

"Everyone feels like that at one time or another," James stated. "Even I did when I was younger."

"Not anymore?"

"Sometimes I get it," the older man admitted. "If I've encountered something I've not much experience in. Or when I have a patient I simply cannot cure. Sometimes you just need to push through the indecision and make the only option sound like the best option."

Thomas hummed to himself and took another sip of wine. "I've ... been doing some extra lessons too."

"Oh? And what do those teach?"

"Promise you won't judge me?"

"I can promise to try," James teased.

"They're lessons based on the biological structures and functions of supposed supernatural beings."

Looking up, he winced at the expression on his Papa's face. He rarely ever wore it. It was a mixture of being stern and concerned all at once. "Are you saying you want to follow that lead of study?" James asked carefully.

Thomas shook his head. "To be perfectly honest, Papa, I don't know where the specimens come from –perhaps they are from another race of people –however I know that I am making headway. As long as I can improve my skills and techniques, I am certain that the Professor will be impressed."

"Do you need to impress him this much?" the older man frowned.

"If I am going to get a decent job in the city, then yes. His approval can make or break people."

"Well I can't discourage your determination."

Thomas jerked his head up. He frowned. Why was his Papa being so lenient? Most people he knew –even the more accepting ones –frowned upon what Talbot taught. It was only because he was a renowned Physician that the hospital board of directors allowed him to teach such things.

"Why –aren't you judging me?"

"Thomas, we all have to do things we don't like to get ahead. If anything, you might pick-up a more open-minded approach to some medical emergencies. That can only be a good thing."

Feeling his Papa's offhanded praised made the wine taste sour in his mouth. He didn't have the heart to tell his Papa that he was actually enjoying studying the extracurricular lectures after hours. He didn't go into any more detail though.

His Papa would tell his Mama and then she would worry about him.

Thomas didn't need them to worry.

Draining the last of his wine, Thomas pushed his chair back from the table and made his way over to the basin. It was a weathered old stone thing, naturally carved out of a large rock. It had a draining system to the outside which was useful, but other than that it was a strange thing. Hanging from the window frame were some painted glass beads. When the sun shone through, they'd catch the light and paint pretty patterns on the bare walls.

Almost every room in the cottage had them.

"I think I'm going to head up to bed," Thomas announced, turning away from the window.

"Alright son, you go and get some rest. You've had a hard day travelling."

Ducking his head, Thomas pressed a goodnight kiss to his Papa's unshaven jaw, before crossing the kitchen and mounting the spiral staircase.

Up in his bedroom at the top of the cottage, Thomas stripped down to his shirt-tails and slipped into the cool sheets. They probably hadn't been turned-down since he left for London. The whole room felt warm and uninhabited. It somehow made the place feel even more cosy and welcoming.

'*Perhaps I was more homesick than I thought*,' he mused as he laid on his back on the soft bed. With an arm curled under his head, he watched the blur of the clouds move across the chalky white moon.

It was beautiful.

It was hard to believe it was the same moon he saw whenever he walked home from the hospital in the early hours of the morning. This moon was softer, smoother and just more welcoming than that cold, hard disk that floated in the black sky. He wondered if —when he got back down to London —Talbot would make them create another Lunar map for the upcoming month. He wasn't opposed to the idea. He'd much rather do it while the weather was still warm.

Did he even wanted to go back?

Of course he did! He was anxious to know what they would get to study next as well as the outcomes of their experiments. However, as he let his head sink back down into the goose feather pillows, he knew that he was in no hurry. Not yet. He needed a few days to simply switch his mind off and be in a nurturing environment. Thomas couldn't deny that he missed his family. He was only human, after all.

'*What about Philip's family?*' asked a voice in the back of his head. '*He doesn't even mention his parents. Does he have siblings? The only person he speaks of is his uncle.*'

Thomas frowned. He hadn't really noticed it until that moment. Philip was always alone; whether it was at his home or when he spoke of his daily life —family was never present. How odd.

Turning onto his side, Thomas pulled the sheet over his shoulders and stared out of the moors just beyond the village lights. The hills were softly illuminated by the moon swelling in the sky.

'*It's almost full,*' he thought idly as he drifted off to sleep.

Friday 31st August 1888.

tepping off the train and onto the platform Thomas drew in a deep breath. It was still morning –probably only about eleven o'clock –but he hadn't wanted to run the risk of turning up late to Talbot's lecture with all his belongings in hand. Juggling his cases –one really an old leather case his mother had lovingly stocked food in for him –he managed to walk through the station without knocking into anyone.

Out on the main street he was greeted by the appearance of Philip's driver leaning out of a horse-drawn carriage. He had insisted that he hadn't needed an escort home, however the blonde man had been insistent. Now that he had extra luggage, Thomas had to admit that he was grateful for it. The man inclined his head as Thomas approached, before dutifully taking the two cases and strapping them to the roof. Thomas climbed up into the carriage and sighed as his back relaxed into the padded seat.

The ride to his lodgings was smooth as it could be on the cobblestones. It had rained the previous evening and the pavements were still sleek with drying puddles. He heard a slight commotion as they passed by Buck's Row. Frowning, he tried to see what had happened out of the window, but there was such a dense crowd that he could barely make out the rounded hat of a constable.

'*Oh well,*' he thought. '*Probably some drunkard getting into trouble.*'

Once he was home, he set the fire up. Whilst it bloomed

over the dried logs inside, he propped his cases on the small wooden table under the window and started to unpack the food. A lot of them were in air-tight clay containers. His mother swore by them and, to her credit, they did keep the food fresher for longer. He stocked them in the lower shelves of his cupboard that doubled as a pantry. At least he wouldn't be starving for the next couple of weeks.

By midday Thomas had boiled water for a shallow bath and scrubbed the train journey off his skin. As the warm daylight brightened his room, he lounged about in his armchair, pouring over his notebooks for Talbot's class. The few days away had cleared the cobwebs from his head and he could finally look on the workbooks with fresh eyes and insight. Perhaps they all needed a break. As he chewed on his thumbnail he was dimly aware that last night had been a full moon.

A tremor ran down his spine.

He hoped it had started to wane already even though it was unlikely. He didn't fancy walking all the way to the hospital on his own, especially with some sort of crime scene not too far away. Raking his damp hair out of his eyes, he picked up his stub of pencil and started making notes of the current lunar cycle along with added notes about some herbs his Papa had given him. There were a lot of ways that plant life effected the body –whether by ingestion or inhalation –it was fascinating to read up on.

Evening rolled around all too soon. Thomas didn't mind so much. He'd had a whole day of studying, eating, washing his clothes, and making sure that everything was back in its place. It was easier than coming home in the early hours of the morning and tripping over his cases. With his notebooks tucked under his arm, he set out through the dying light towards the hospital.

The chatter of the young men died instantly as they edged into the hall. Despite the cloying stench of the gas-lamps, there was another smell lingering in the air. Thomas recoiled at it, feeling himself shrink inwards as his eyes adjusted to the gloom. Talbot watched as they gingerly sat themselves down. On the platform behind him there was a sheet-covered table. There was no denying what lay underneath that table. Sure enough, when the Professor wordlessly ripped the sheet away, a gasp emitted throughout the room.

There, on the gurney, was a body.

Thomas felt a chill descend upon the room, despite the heat still pressing around the building from outside. What on earth had happened since he'd left? Talbot had said from day one that it'd be highly unlikely for them to use real-life specimens. Maybe the odd organ here and there, but an actual body? He was both curious and wished to remain ignorant all at the same time.

"As you can all see," Talbot started in his droll voice. "We have a corpse in the room."

Silence.

"As some of you have clearly heard of the attack in the early hours of this morning I can confirm that yes; this is the same woman who was murdered."

A wave of murmurs started up, but Thomas couldn't hear them. Murdered? Someone had been murdered not a stone's throw away from his front door? He felt ill. If he had been home last night would he have heard the screams? Would he have ignored it? Called out for her to shut up? Gone out to see if she was alright?

'Don't be a fool! There was nothing that could be done! You'd have mostly likely died too!'

65

He knew it was true. That didn't mean he had to like being so close to the danger zone, though.

"Before you ask any questions; they have already performed the autopsy. I have made copies for all of you to study before we begin this lesson. You'll have twenty minutes to read the notes. As of six o'clock this evening, this body was released into my care for the next forty-eight hours." He paused. "And yes, that does mean they'll be a lesson tomorrow night."

Only about two men sighed. The rest were far too intrigued by the prospect of a fresh corpse to work on, to care about another sleepless night.

Thomas was on the fence.

He took one of the reports and narrowed his eyes at it. His stomach knotted as he read what had been found on this corpse. The victim was known as Mary Ann 'Polly' Nichols –a known prostitute in the area. He felt physically sick at the listed wounds inflicted upon the poor woman. How had someone managed to do all of that in the witching hours of London town? Surely someone had been there to see? Hadn't anyone heard her pleas for help?

'*You can't be emotional in medicine,*' he heard his Papa's voice whisper in his ear. '*Everyone dies in the end, you just need to find the easiest way to help them live well. Getting emotional will only cloud your judgment and make it harder for you to progress.*'

Damn, his Papa had always known what to say.

"Time's up," Talbot stated coolly. "Aprons and gloves on and at the table in two minutes."

Despite being hesitant, most of the men strode over to the pegs and started to prepare themselves with the thick rubber gloves and apron. Thomas adjusted his glasses and drew in a deep breath before forcing his feet to walk to the table.

The woman was not that attractive. That was Thomas' first

thought as he looked down at her bloated facial features. The decomposition of the body had started almost a day prior, and the smell was enough to make anyone want to gag. Barely daring to breathe, Thomas observed –from his position by her left elbow –that this Mary Ann was definitely at the low end of the barrel if someone wanted a quick fuck in the dark. Her nose was long and jutted out from her face like a shark's fin, and her lips were thin. Her features were small, someone delicate –perhaps she had been attractive in her early years. However, she'd been greying at the temples by the time she'd been murdered.

Talbot lowered the secondary sheet from the body, exposing the sagging skin underneath. The breasts were limp and weighed off to the sides slightly. Her figure was rather plump as it broadened slightly to her hips. All her nails seemed chipped and off-colour.

"Since you can see the obvious wounds listed in the reports, I want all of you to look at the finer details. Tell me what you see."

Lips purses and reluctant heads drew closer.

"Feel free to move her if you so wish."

No one reached out for Mary Ann. No one wanted to be tainted by something so freshly touched by Death.

Thomas pushed his glasses up his nose and did a mental check from head to toe. There were the lacerations on her neck, the missing teeth, and the expanse of soft, doughy flesh that bloated in odd places. Then, at the abdomen, there were the deep slashes in her gut. It looked as though they went from right-to-left –towards the dominant hand.

'So, *the killer is left handed?*' he mused, as he continued to peer, trying not to knock his head against his classmate's.

What else was there?

"Do you want to turn her over?" he found himself asking. Everyone stiffened around him. Looking up, he saw the look of horror from six other young men. Poor Neville looked like he was about to faint.

"What are you talking about, Segdon?" Walpole hissed at him.

"Maybe something was missed? On her back?"

"Nothing gets missed in an autopsy, Segdon."

"Well then maybe something is written that isn't in the official report."

"And why might that be?"

"Well ..." he faltered for a moment. "If –If you found someone with occult symbols all over them –w-would you put that in the official report? The one that goes public in the papers?"

There was a moment of impressed silence. Of course there was something else! There had to be! They were studying supernatural biological anomalies –there was always something else, something hidden.

"So ...?"

"Alright men," Walpole addressed them. "On the count of three, roll her onto her side." Hands latched onto Mary Ann's limbs –even Neville grabbed a hold of her ankles. "On my count; one ... two ... turn!"

Her limbs flopped awkwardly down her front. Thomas and Edward stared, shocked at the state of the woman's back. Even with the surgeon's cack-handed excuse for stitches with the thick black wire, there was no denying the shape of the wound. This one had not been done by the knife that had eventually killed her. No; before Mary Ann Nichols was cut down in her prime –she'd first been brutally attacked by something. Something with a mouth as large as Thomas' forearm.

"What in God's name did that?" Edward hissed.

"I ... I don't know ..." Thomas felt his arms quake.

"What is it?" Walpole asked from the other side of the

heavy, ashen corpse.

"She was bitten!" Edward said, his voice breaking a little. "It looks as though she was mutilated by some sort of animal!"

"Lie her on her front!"

With some effort, they managed to get the corpse onto her front. Thomas was too horrified by the way her back looked to pay much heed to her flabby, drooping buttocks and pock-marked thighs. There were no other wounds on her back. She must have been attacked from the front by whoever had wielded the knife.

The bite wound itself was around twelve inches long –give or take. It had been done at a frenzied angle, ripping skin before finding a good spot to latch on to. Her spinal cord had been severed by the impact. That much was clear by the way the bones jutted out from under the loose flaps of skin. Layers of soft, yellow fat glistened wetly in the lamplight. The smell was rancid. It was enough to choke a horse. Thomas brushed a tear from his eye and stared at the wound. This one hadn't been touched by the surgeon's needles yet. That was a good sign. The flesh beneath the skin was all but destroyed. Bloodless veins hung like fine threads, dripping into the gaping hole. Thomas good see pinkish-grey organs resting like a slippery pile of snakes.

He felt the urge to vomit.

"How on earth was she still walking after this?" Walpole asked in disgust as he prodded at the loose skin.

"Perhaps it all happened within the same hour?" Neville suggested.

"If something that big was stalking around London don't you think someone would have seen it?" Walpole snapped, scowling.

Thomas watched the two of them bicker for a moment longer before leaning away from the corpse. Already, the air seemed more breathable. Blinking away the tears in his itchy eyes, he wiped his gloves down on a rag and went over to the chalkboard. He hastily drew a rough diagram of Mary Ann's corpse both from the front and the back. He used basic lines and arrows to show what wounds had been done and in what direction, as listed.

"Right so we've all come to the conclusion that the man who eventually killed her was left-handed, correct?"

A murmur of agreement.

"Right. So, in regard to the wound on the back –what can we see from this?"

"Whatever the creature was, it attacked instantly. There were no claw marks or anything. It was very precise," Walpole observed.

Thomas made a note. "How many of you know animals that are genuinely that controlled or precise in their attacks? One bite for one victim? No staying to make sure they're dead? No claw marks at all? Or other bites?"

"The teeth marks look to be that of a canine," Edward said. "However, an animal that big would have to be more of a wolf variety. Or a wild dog."

"We're almost in central London. Those dogs would be shot by the police if they were seen," Neville said.

Another murmur of agreement.

"So that only leaves one conclusion," Talbot's voice made them all jump. In truth, they'd forgotten he was even in the room. "This woman was attacked by both a werewolf and her human assailant."

"But ... in the same night?" Thomas asked with a frown. "That seems so ... unlikely."

A thin smirk played on Talbot's lips. "Exactly."

Walpole raised an eyebrow. "So you're telling us that either this woman just so happened to be targeted by both man and beast, or that the werewolf attacked a man and the woman just got in the way?"

"Think Mr. Walpole," Talbot intoned. "How many men do you know go walking around at that time of night wielding a weapon?"

"None?"

"Exactly."

The bell chimed one.

"Class dismissed," Talbot drawled. "Make sure you're all present for tomorrow night. It'll start at 9 o'clock so as not to disturb your schedules too much."

One by one, they slowly turned away from the drooping corpse to disperse of their rubber gloves and aprons. As he gathered his things and made way for the double doors, Thomas couldn't help but wonder what exactly he'd returned to in the streets of London town. Although as he made his way down the stone steps, he couldn't shake the feeling of being watched. The moon was still a swollen fat thumbprint in the sky and he was anxious to get into bed and draw his curtains closed against its raw light.

He also hoped that Mary Ann was not in attendance the following night.

Closing the door and locking it behind him, Thomas drew in a quaking breath of relief. However, he still did a check of all the dark corners, under his bed and the cupboards just to make sure that he was definitely alone. He was. Somehow that feeling made him even more anxious. The thought of being alone whilst something stalked the streets outside was sickening.

"You're being paranoid," he said out loud as he started to change for bed. He was only talking out loud to fill up the silence that seemed to swell and grow around him.

'*Like Mary Ann's belly,*' whispered his brain.

He promptly threw up at the base of his hearth.

Wiping his mouth he trembled as he doubled over on his knees, pressing his forehead onto the rough floorboards.

"Stop it," he hissed, tasting bile on his breath. "Stop making yourself ill. At least you didn't do it during the lesson."

That was a small blessing at least.

Wiping his face down Thomas drew in deep breaths and tried to calm his erratic heart. Rubbing his chest, he sat down on the thin bed, wincing as it creaked under his weight. It had been a long day. He'd been up since just after five the previous morning.

"You just need to get some rest," he murmured as he wriggled down under the blankets. He'd need to save for a thicker one come winter. With his glasses off the room dissolved into a colourless blur. Only the moonlight shone faintly behind his curtains, giving him a silvery box to stare at.

'Perhaps I'll go and see Philip tomorrow. I wish I'd gotten to see him today'.

He missed that the blonde man hadn't met him at the station, but he'd mentioned that he would most likely be busy. Thomas hadn't questioned him. There was no need. He would have just appreciated the company, to have someone to talk to about his few days away. Oh well, it would keep till the morning.

Soon enough, much to his relief, he drifted off to sleep.

In the distance, something howled.

Saturday 1st September 1888.

Thomas fiddled with his collar as he stared at the door. It was so immaculate and shiny, he felt like he was spending a fortune just being there. The silver knocker gleamed in the sunshine. Footsteps drew close from the other side. The door swung inwards, revealing Philip's butler.

"Ah, Mr. Segdon. Master Ridley is expecting you up in his chambers."

Thomas blinked, stunned.

Stepping through into the tiled hallway, he straightened his shoulders and nodded his thanks to the butler, before moving up the stairs. His shoes clicked on the floor as he came to Philip's bedroom door. Knocking, he waited in the hallway.

"*Come in!*"

Thomas entered the room, the sunlight catching him off-guard as he took in the size of the room. It seemed to stretch on forever, with gilt windows and thick, plush carpets and blankets. As he edged further inside, he caught sight of Philip sat in a tall chair, his blanketed legs stretched out on a footstool, with the newspaper in his hands.

"Good morning, Thomas," he smiled, setting the paper to one side.

Thomas took a seat in the vacant chair offered to him. "Good morning, Philip." In the sunlight he blanched at how pale the man looked; his skin was ashen, his eyes heavily circled and his hair lie flat and lifeless against his skull. "I'm sorry to say this but –you look awful."

"Your concern is touching," he said flatly. "Tea?"

"Please."

Despite Philip's pride, neither of them could ignore the way the teapot lid rattled as he struggled to hold it steady. As the brown liquid sloshed into the cup, Thomas' hands automatically caught hold of it. Unfortunately, Philip's clammy hands were caught between his own and the china pot.

Eyes bore into his own. They were a dull grey, flat like a cobblestone.

"Thank you," Philip murmured, relinquishing the teapot to his companion.

Thomas carefully poured two cups of tea –milk and two sugars for Philip –and handed a cup to the blonde. His hand seemed to tremble as he accepted the beverage, but Thomas didn't want to pry.

"So how was the lecture last night?" Philip asked, sipping at his tea. He sank deeper into his thick dressing gown. Thomas was getting hot and sweaty just looking at the layers enveloping the older man.

"It was ... intense," he exhaled.

He hadn't slept too well the previous night. Though he'd gotten to sleep earlier than usual after a lecture, he was plagued by the insight he'd gotten to '*Polly*'s' body –and that savage bite mark on her back. He shuddered, chasing the cold away with a gulp of hot tea.

"What did he have you do?"

"That's just it," Thomas hedged rubbing at the back of his neck. "I don't know if it's completely legal. It's definitely not public knowledge so ... um ... you can keep it a secret, can't you?"

Philip paused, his lip pressed to the rim of his teacup. Looking over at the bespectacled young man before him, he could practically smell the anxiety rolling off of him in waves. "Of course, Thomas. I hope you're not partaking in anything that would herald you as a pariah." He arched a fine eyebrow at his companion. "That'd be unfortunate."

"It –it would?"

"Of course. As a manner of speaking, I've gotten quite fond of you, Thomas. I'd hate for my uncle to jeopardise our friendship purely because of his eccentricities."

Thomas gave a twitch of a smile.

"So, what exactly is it that my uncle had you do?"

"Well –did you hear about the woman found murdered in Whitechapel?"

Philip narrowed his eyes. "Yes," he said slowly.

Thomas lowered his gaze and thumbed the rim of his cup. The China was smooth against his skin. "Well … Talbot somehow got permission for us to investigate her corpse. There were some … peculiarities."

"What sort of peculiarities?"

"Other than the sheer brutality of the murder …" He stopped again. The words just seemed to get lodged in his throat. "She … S-she had a huge section of her back missing – thanks to a grotesque animal attack."

Blonde eyebrows rose. "An animal? Ripping off a woman's entire back?"

Thomas nodded. "In one bite, yes."

The silence hung in the air like a fog, seeping into every fibre of fabric within the chamber. Philip's eyes were downcast as he tapped a rhythm on the arm of his chair. Thomas was on edge. Should he have not told his friend? Perhaps Philip already knew and was judging him? Perhaps he had no idea and was going to have an intense conversation with his uncle?

"What are your thoughts on the matter?" the blonde man eventually asked.

Thomas blinked and sat back in the chair. Philip was … intrigued? "Er … The class as a whole seemed to come to the conclusion that this was a larger than life beast. Something that can come and go and outrun most men."

"Why do you say that?"

"We're in the middle of London," the young brunette stated. "There's no way a hound of that size and stature could have snuck around the streets, even in the dead of night, and not been seen by anyone."

Philip nodded in agreement. "Fair point. So –from this – what can you tell me?"

"That ... the only person to see this beast, is dead."

"Anything else?"

"The woman was killed ... because she was attacked?"

"Well now you're assuming that this attacker actually knew of the wolf," Philip countered, "Perhaps he was just a monster who happened to get –what was the term? –sloppy seconds?"

Thomas pressed his lips together. "That's an awfully big coincidence, though, if we're entertaining that idea."

"Perhaps. However, the only other conclusion is that this poor woman was mauled by a –a -?"

"Werewolf."

Philip narrowed his eyes but inclined his head regardless. "Exactly. As much as I am close to my uncle, even I have to draw the line at some of his superstitious elements."

Thomas clenched and unclenched his fist. "I ... What if there's some truth to any of this?"

Philip let out a soft sigh. "I thought you wanted to be a doctor, Thomas."

"I do! Of course I do!"

"Then why are you giving this so much thought?" Philip asked, curiously.

Thomas turned to stare out of the window. It was a bright day with a light breeze. The colours were so vibrant under the sunlight. Everything within the room suddenly seemed to dull in comparison. Philip was right; why was he wasting his precious time worrying about some form of mythical beast? For all he knew, Talbot had created that ghastly bite just as a way to ignite their imaginations? Thinking about it now, Thomas had to admit that it sounded too convenient. They were studying supernatural beings and all of a sudden, one turns up on their doorstep? Ready for dissection? Their professor just barely managed to secure the rights to the body? That all seemed too neatly cut.

Shaking his head, he felt the back of his neck heat up. "I ... I suppose you could be right."

"I'm sorry Thomas," Philip frowned. "I didn't mean to offend you. I've known my uncle for years. I know what he's like. These night time lectures won't amount to anything useful in your future career as a physician."

"You seem to have a rather hostile view towards your uncle despite readily teaching one of his lectures," Thomas observed rather coldly. He hadn't meant to change his attitude so quickly, but he had paid a handsome sum of money to study with Talbot and –nephew or not –he didn't like it when anyone insulted his professor and, by extension, himself.

"My views on my uncle have nothing to do with this," Philip chided. "I just don't want to see a dear friend lead down the wrong path to a dead end."

"How're you so sure it will?"

Philip shook his head, rubbed his temples and sighed. "Let's not talk about this anymore. I'm getting a migraine."

"Do you want me to get your butler?"

"No, no," Philip waved him back down into the armchair. "I'll be fine I just –don't wish to discuss my uncle anymore."

Thomas wanted to argue that Philip was the one who had been curious, however seeing how the blonde man's head lulled heavily into his hand and the purple hue of his fingernails, he felt a surge of panic bolt through him. "Try not to move," he said. "You're not well, Philip. Let me get a bath ready for you?" Philip have a sigh but eventually nodded.

"Good. Oh –er –what's your butler's name?"

"Mr. Jenson."

"Thanks." Thomas hurried over to the door and stepped out into the long hallway. "MR. JENSON? MR. JENSON?"

It took a few moments, although it felt like a lifetime to Thomas, before the clicking of shoes on the polished wood floors could be heard. The middle-aged butler appeared, his cheeks pink with the heat. "Yes, Mr. Segdon?"

"Mr. Ridley requires a hot bath and a well-lit fire. He's coming down with a fever."

"I shall arrange a bath right away, sir. I'll notify his uncle at once!"

"Oh, there's no need for that!" Thomas gushed, feeling awkward. The butler frowned at him. "I'm studying medicine with his uncle. It is most likely just the heat; his body is out of sync with the heat, so we need to get him warm again." Still the butler frowned, clearly not entirely convinced. "Please?" Thomas urged. "I assure you, I know what I'm doing."

"Very well," Jenson conceded. "However, if any ill befalls the young master, the consequences shall fall upon your head, is that understood?"

"Yes, of course."

Steam rolled over the brim of the large copper bath. It was hot inside and out, as the maids had placed it on the hearthrug before the large fireplace. Fire crackled in the grate. They had closed the curtains upon Philip's insistence. The sunlight seemed to hurt his eyes. Thomas couldn't help but feel a prickling in his skin as he'd rolled up the sleeves of his undershirt.

Philip was lying in the bathtub, floating as though he were suspended in the hot water. The faint film of bubbles and soap made the water look like frothy milk. It worried Thomas; Philip was already extremely pale, however now that his skin was against something so white, he just looked ashen. As though all the colour and freshness had been leeched from his skin.

His skin was still clammy to the touch and his lips and tongue were pale.

Thomas tried not to let his technical mind interfere with making his friend well again. He took his time rubbing soap and oils into Philip's skin, letting him soak in the scented water, before scrubbing him down with a sponge. His eyes stared straight ahead, unseeing, like two grey glass windows.

It got to the point that Thomas just assumed the man slept with his eyes open.

"Thomas?"

He flinched, stopping in his motion of washing soap suds off Philip's arm. "Y-yes?"

"Tell me about your home."

"My home?" Thomas frowned. "What're you talking about? You've seen where I live."

Philip rocked his head back and forth. No. That's not what he wanted. Thomas frowned as the firelight cast soft shadows over his companion's haggard features. His blonde hair hung in damp tendrils over his skull and his cheeks looked gaunt. His Adams apple almost burst out of his throat, he looked so thin. "N-no ..." Philip rasped. "Where you come from ... your parents?"

Thomas breathed a laugh. "You don't want to hear about any of that."

"Please?" he rasped.

"Oh ... Okay." Thomas cleared his throat. "Well my parents were childhood sweethearts. They began courting as soon as they were able. My Mama was a maid, and my papa was training to be a doctor."

"Mmm ..."

"My Papa looks like I do. They say I have my Mama's eyes though."

"... Lovely eyes."

Thomas felt his cheeks flare. He kept on scrubbing. "We live in a small cottage with well down the bottom of the garden. Mama grows herbs and vegetables and takes care of some of the elderly. She doesn't make a lot of money, but she always makes sure people are fed well.

"Papa is different; he's eccentric –that's what mama says. He likes finding new cures and easier ways to perform surgeries. They're not as big as the accidents you get in the city. More just sprains and breaks, but every once in a while, someone needs an amputation of something growing off them in the wrong place –He likes his work."

"That's good." Philip's head drooped around to rest against Thomas' propped up elbow. He seemed to hesitate for a moment before pressing his cool cheek harder against the younger man's skin.

"I think that's enough smelling salts for you," Thomas murmured, standing up and heading over to the fire. Swiping a towel up from the copper grate places in front of it, he went back to the tub and beckoned for Philip to sit up. "Come on, let's get you dried off and into bed."

Thankfully, Philip didn't protest as he let Thomas dry him off and leave him standing in front of the fire whilst he fetched some nightclothes. Once dressed, Thomas bundled his friend up in an armchair pulled over by the fire and fed him soup before leading the blonde man over to the large mahogany bed when his eyelids began to droop.

"Goodnight Philip," Thomas murmured into the dimly lit room as he closed the chamber door behind him and left.

The London streets were bright with lamplight, moonlight and the sickly glow that poured onto the pavements from the open doors of the taverns. The aroma of cheap beer and roast meat hung, like dripping clouds in the air, as Thomas bowed his head and ghosted long the streets through Whitechapel. Nothing seemed to lurk in the shadows –nothing other than the usual ruffians, homeless tramps or drunk prostitutes.

The air was warm, yet whenever he passed by the cramped houses or under a bridge, he felt a tremor run down his spine. It was as though all those glowing eyes in the gloom were turning in his direction and watching him. He knew he was being ridiculous. There was no denying it. After his conversation with Philip, all he needed to do was keep moving quickly and get home.

'Maybe Philip was right about all this?' he thought, as he loosened his collar a little more. 'All of Talbot's lessons are making me paranoid.'

The further he walked, the quieter the city seemed to grow. Even the lapping of the Thames was left far behind him. The gentle murmurs of generic nightlife faded away to a whisper and then –silence.

It had always unnerved him, how in the early morning hours right after his lectures that the entire city seemed to die. The silence was overwhelming. Drawing in deep breaths, Thomas found himself straining his ears for any click of shoes on pavement, or the growl of a beggar's gut. Even the rustling of his own trousers was enough to make the hairs on his arms stand up on end.

"Nearly home," he murmured.

The clouds drifted lazily in the breeze, letting more silvery light dribble down onto the pavements. Chimney smoke seemed to cease at night, letting some of the stars peak down.

"A few more streets ... then I'll be fine."

The moonlight poured down like a heatless sun, melting the skin off his bones, manipulating his flesh and burrowing through the very marrow of his bones.

Every pore seemed to stretch, as though thin worms were wriggling out into the cool, evening air. Each tendril exploded into thick, dark hair that covered every inch –even the fingertips.

Bones cracked –like lightning –through the silence.

Flesh and muscle stretched and reformed to mould over the skeletal figure. Every inch of the flesh burned, seared and pulsed as new tissue created a cobweb over the veins.

So many new scents; rotting meat, salt water and piss.

Something else –something alive!

Fresh, hot, blood –rushing, pumping, bubbling in veins that scurried quickly over warm cobblestones.

Thick, heavy feet scrambling over the pavements. Clacking of claws, panting of breath, thick heavy coat shimmering in the dim light. Lamplight flashing on the fangs, in the eyes, and fur rippling with anticipation.

It was hot rage –burning, unpredictable –like fire!

A mad frenzy making the brain fizz and froth and bubble down the back of the throat.

There!

In the shadow thrown by a narrow building. There was the flesh –the mound of hot blood fuelled by fear! He could smell it! Taste it on the air! Trailing down from the rooftops, using the night as a cloak, shying away whenever eyes gleamed through the gloom.

Quivering hunger and feverish desire mingled in the air as a pair of bespectacled eyes narrowed in the darkness.

Laboured breathing –sweat –cinnamon stink rolling through the still air. Oh, how his mouth watered!

Towering tall through into the pale light. A deep, guttural growl

–new jaw unhinging, dripping.

The man let out a yell!

So loud to the new ears! Why was it so loud? Growling louder drowned out the terror piercing through his brain but not enough. No, it wasn't enough!

A blur of black and silver. A cut through the night. Burning – hot, red blood running into the gutter. His? No, of course not.

Manic laughter filling his ears – "BEGONE FANGED DAEMON!" –what was this sorcery? Backing up past brickwork –nails scraping on brick and growls failing to drown out the Warlocks words.

Daemon? Daemon? Daemon? NO!

Running –so much running! Heart drumming painfully, muscles screaming, brain burning! Safety –HELP! Running –never stopping –hardly breathing –NO!

THERE! HOME? NO?!

Panic! So much panic! Blood –pain –agony –retracting!

Sunrise …

Monday 10th September 1888.

Another emergency lecture had been called.

It was almost no surprise when they found Talbot waiting in the hospital theatre with a covered body on a mortuary slab. The stink of formaldehyde hung heavily in the air. It was cloying to the lungs and burned steadily through the senses. That evening they didn't even bother sitting down with their notebooks. They merely set their belongings aside and made their way to the apron booth.

It had already been a long day. After the previous week, Thomas was still getting used to going out after dark. It was nerve-wracking whenever the sun sank below the horizon. Darkness was his enemy now, but there was nothing he could do to hide from it. His allowance didn't amount to much and he was already down to his last candle stub. He'd had to go to the hospital for two days to get his wounds treated. Talbot had come in to see him, even treated the wound and had stated that it would most definitely scar.

Great.

He still had to wear bandages –the wound was going to take a while before the tissue full healed over the grisly rip. It made his gut quake whenever he had to change his dressing. Having to look at where his flesh was literally torn in half –it was vile! He had asked Talbot how his nephew was, considering the condition he'd left the man just two days prior. Talbot had given him an unreadable look and stated that Philip would need a few extra days rest, and that his illness was not serious.

That was a minor relief; at least he wasn't worrying whilst he was cooped up.

Now that he was out of the hospital, he was anxious to try and get back into his normal routine. It didn't help him too much that he got inhumanly anxious whenever night fell. Most evenings he would walk most of the way home. However, it was that last part –that final leg of the journey – that was the hardest part.

His friends had been good to him though; Rufus took a little extra time out of his way to make sure Thomas got as close to his lodgings as possible. It was difficult, however, on the Witching Hour lectures. At the very least, in the last week since the first brutal murder, Thomas had managed to have more time to himself, to gather his thoughts and even pay more attention to his own friends' needs. More specifically, meeting the new woman in Rufus's life.

Her name was Daphne Rothschild; she was petite, book-smart and had a father very high-up on the medical board. If anything, it seemed to add more pressure to Rufus for being squeamish around blood. Although –Thomas thought –the last few lectures he hadn't shied away as he'd used to do. Perhaps she was an encouraging influence on him? She was a determined one, that much could be said for her. She was pretty too; she seemed like she had the entire package. Thomas was genuinely pleased for his friend. If their courtship progressed as well as they'd imagined it would, then there were sure to be some wedding bells by the end of the year.

Unfortunately, it also drew attention to how lonely he was. He didn't have anyone to spend his evenings with. He only had Philip –and the man was often busy. They met up on his timetable. Not that Thomas had a timetable –but it would have been nice to have some control.

None of it had really helped his mental state as another body was found near his lodgings.

Every time he walked by Whitechapel, the shredded skin

on his arm seemed to itch.

Glancing over at the covered woman, Thomas felt cold dread drip down his spine. What was going on? Why were there so many women being attacked? Why was it only women? Thomas seemed to be the only one who'd managed to escape the beast —but why? Was it simply attracted to the female sex? He really tried not to think about that night. He'd had a policeman visit him in the hospital and had to go down to the station to make an official statement. They'd asked him all sorts of questions that he couldn't really answer.

What attacked you that night?
Why were you walking around so late?
Who was the man who helped save you?
Had you been drinking or inhaling opium?

Well —that one had been an obvious '*no*' but that still didn't make the events of that night any clearer. His glasses had been knocked off when he'd been thrown down onto the pavement. He didn't know what exactly had attacked him —but he'd heard it. That growl —it felt so savage and bloodthirsty. It made bile rush up his throat whenever he thought of it.

As for the man who'd helped save him? He honestly had no idea. He had a low, smooth voice —entirely in control of himself, even in peril. He'd worn gloves and a cloak. His hat had been low, but Thomas had caught sight of a thin, black moustache and thin lips.

That was all he'd been able to offer the police. He felt useless, but had been allowed to leave soon after.

It didn't help that, once back in the lecture hall, everyone else treated him with a little more caution and concern. Thomas didn't like being invalidated, but his arm still quaked whenever he tried to use it for something practical. Talbot had assured the class that he'd sustained no other injuries. In other words, he hadn't been bitten.

Annie Chapman's corpse was almost identical to Mary Ann's; the same right-to-left slashes across the throat and abdomen, her features beaten and swollen from gas bloating inside her corpse. Her teeth were very fine in comparison to most prostitutes, and –as with Mary Ann –she bore no other wounds.

Until they turned her over.

The bite mark was as savage as the first. Although there was something else stuck in one of her shoulder blades.

"What the heck is that?" Walpole asked as he held a lamp close to the gaping wound. The smell of wet, old meat turned their stomachs, but they continued to stare into the corpse regardless.

Thomas peered closer too, not that he was able to contribute much to the inspection. Whatever was stuck through the bone, was thick, shiny with blood and fat, and about as long as his ring finger. He watched as Walpole used a pair of pliers to wriggle the thing out and hold it up in the light for everyone to see. Thomas paled. "Is –is that a tooth?" he grimaced.

"Correct, Mr. Segdon," Talbot intoned. "Here, gentlemen, we have a genuine werewolf tooth. Look at how long it is and imagine about thirty of those ripping your skin from your bones."

Thomas suppressed the urge to vomit.

"As for the corpse," Talbot continued. "What can you tell me about this one?"

"The wound isn't fresh," Neville squeaked. One would think he was still going through puberty. "It's been open and festering for a few days –maybe even a week."

"So when can we assume the wound was inflicted?"

"Possibly around the same time as the first corpse," Walpole said.

"So ... she somehow managed to survive a week before

getting killed by this psychopath?" Thomas asked. "How is that even possible?"

"Well by the looks of things, despite a vast amount of blood loss, none of her major organs were damaged, unlike the first. Once bound, I'm sure she could have struggled along for a time."

"So ..." Thomas frowned. "This was ... another 'mercy' killing?"

"That's absurd!" Walpole sneered, although he didn't quite believe his own words.

Thomas cast a look around at his other classmates. They were all wondering the same thing. He felt his skin itch under the bandage. Thankfully, Edward spoke up.

"Sir?"

"What?"

"I ... uh ... We were wondering what is the purpose of looking at these corpses?"

"To educate you."

"I think what he means," Neville stuttered. "Was ... well ... why are we the only ones studying them? Shouldn't we tell the police of our findings?"

Thomas bristled at this and wanted nothing more than to disappear at the back of the theatre. He'd had enough of police for the time being. They'd started to double the curfew patrols around Whitechapel but he highly doubted that anything would come of them.

"You are here to study and understand that these beasts are unable to be killed by any normal means. Otherwise, that 'psychopath' as you called him, would have killed the animal already." Talbot narrowed his eyes at the seven of them. "I hope you paid attention to that, at least."

"What exactly are we meant to have missed?" Walpole seethed.

"That this vigilante clearly has no idea what he's doing. At least, not fully, for he has not managed to kill the creature."

"He might have maimed it?" Neville suggested.

"Only if his blade was made of silver," Talbot stated, bored.

Thomas wondered if he'd ever become desensitised like that.

"Now, silver is a werewolf's enemy, much like garlic is to the vampire," his voice droned out throughout the cavernous theatre room. "So, if you only cut a werewolf with a silver blade, what do you think happens when the creature turns back to his human form?"

"He'd be maimed as a human, wouldn't he?" Edward asked.

"Depending on the depth of the cut in its werewolf form, it'd either be a cut or a very dark bruise. It'd mostly be in the regions of the body that are covered by clothes. Anything on the face would –no doubt –be bandaged or concealed from the public eye."

Something about that last comment stuck in Thomas' mind just as the bell chimed in the courtyard.

The lesson was over.

Gathering all his notebooks and satchel, Thomas wrapped himself up in his cloak one-handed, and made his way up the stairs. They seemed to go on forever. His head was swimming as he neared the entrance, the feeling of fresh air making him shudder and shy away from the wide, dark open spaces beyond. He'd just gotten out of the courtyard when a hand came down on his shoulder.

He let out a yell as he whipped around.

"It's okay, you don't need to make so much noise," Philip admonished, as he gripped Thomas' good shoulder.

Thomas jerked out of the older man's grip, wincing as his injured arm strained against his body. His heart was a panicked blur in his ears and it turned his stomach. He leaned back against the gate, urging his breathing to get under control. His head was a mess as he ran a hand through his hair and drew in deep breaths. "Philip what are you doing here?" he rasped out, the balmy air calming to the back of his throat.

The tall man furrowed his brow. "Surely you've heard?" he said. "Of course, you have. You've probably had the body in that hospital."

Thomas glowered up at the man, but he turned his head the other way. "Yes. Another woman was attacked."

"No doubt my uncle believes it to be linked to the last one?"

"Yes. So do the local police."

Philip snorted in derision under his breath. "I meant in regard to what killed her."

"A werewolf?"

"You don't agree with him?" Philip asked, frowning.

Thomas felt his shoulders sag. "I ... I don't really know. After what happened last week, I just –I really just want to go to sleep and never wake up."

A dark shadow passed over Philip's face. "Don't talk like that," he hissed. "You have no idea what it means to talk like that."

Thomas continued to glare but didn't say anything. He simply pushed himself off of the gates and made his feet move over the pavements towards Whitechapel. Philip straightened his shoulders and made his way after Thomas at a slower than usual pace. His cane clicked against the stonework underfoot. They walked side-by-side in silence for a while, as clouds rolled over the sky overhead. The darkness felt oppressive, cold, and foreboding as they made their way through the narrow streets. Thomas found that he wanted to move closer towards his companion, feel the heat from his body, to feel secure. The bone in his arm ached as he bowed his head, teeth clenched. He needed a hot fire, some tea, and his bed. He didn't want to be in London anymore. He didn't want to be *alone* anymore.

He wasn't safe!

Nowhere was safe!

It wasn't just the prostitutes –it was anyone and everyone who stalked through the street at the witching hour of the night.

"So where have you been?" he found himself asking. All he wanted to do was drown out the aching silence that burning through his ears and resided within his skull.

"I've just been a little ill," Philip stated. "I appreciate you taking care of me as you did. My ailment didn't ease up until a few days ago and so that's why I've not been able to see you for most of the last week."

Thomas gave an exasperated sigh. "I took care of you because you're my friend, Philip."

"I'm sorry I wasn't able to offer the same to you last week," Philip said, coming to a halt on the corner of Hanbury street. The entire corner was roped off since early Saturday morning. Thomas was sure he could see the shadow of where Annie Chapman's corpse had been, her vagina-less body sprawled out for the world to see.

He turned his head away, not wanting to see it.

"It's fine," Thomas murmured. "I lived."

Philip cupped the brunette man's face in his hands and tilted it upwards. "You're traumatised."

Thomas wanted to jerk his head out of the hot, pale hands. At the same time, if felt comforting to have human contact that wasn't invasive, like those doctor's hands. "I'll manage, Philip," he replied tightly. He averted his eyes, wanted to scurry back to his lodgings as quickly as possible.

"That's not an answer, Thomas."

"What do you want me to say?"

Silence.

"Let's get you home."

They continued to walk in silence. Around the next bend, Thomas caught sight of his lodgings. "You didn't need to walk me home," he said, somewhat awkwardly as they stood in the shadow of the building.

"I'm not having you walk around in the dead of night, right next to the crime scene, alone."

Thomas shuddered, desperately needing to change his dressings. "Well ... thank you." He fumbled awkwardly with trying to open his door and balancing his satchel of notebooks. The strain on his arm was painful. A notebook slipped out of his arm and slapped down on the alleyway floor. "Shit!" he cursed.

Philip bent down and picked the book up. It seemed wrong for someone so immaculately dressed to stoop down in the dirt of the city. Thomas hastily accepted the book back. "Let me help you to your room," Philip offered, extending his hand as for the satchel. Thomas opened his mouth to protest but was promptly silence by a finger on his lips. "Don't argue with me, Segdon. Just turn around and get upstairs. It's too late to argue on your landlord's doorstep."

Thomas clamped his mouth shut before turning around and making his way up the stairs. Philip followed.

The stairs creaked underfoot. The woodwork seemed rougher underhand, as did the stink of the mould and piss that seemed to exude from most of the other rooms. In the top floor there was the distant sound of dirty, drunken slurs and moans as a bed creaked under the weight of two fat sweating bodies. It made Thomas feel hot and self-conscious. Philip was a large, imposing shadow in the darkness. His very presence swelled within the corridor, as Thomas groped for the key to his room.

The key turned in the lock.

The door swung open.

Within twenty minutes a fire was burning in the grate, and both of their cloaks were hung on the rickety stand behind the door. The curtains were closed against the waning moon and Philip was seated in the sagging armchair whilst Thomas was perched awkwardly on the small wooden stool. He wasn't sure how it had happened, but Philip was tending to the wounds he'd sustained on his arm from the week prior.

"You don't need to –AH! –do this," Thomas hissed through his teeth as Philip cleaned the wound with hot, salt water. "That stings!"

"Stinging is good," Philip murmured quietly. Thomas watched as the blonde man worked meticulously, his arm cradled in the finely clothed lap. It felt wrong and comfortable all at the same time. "It means it's healing well."

Thomas didn't have the heart to argue.

"I know you don't want to talk about it now," Philip hedged, still not making eye contact. "However, I think it'd be good for you to talk to someone about what happened that night."

Thomas shook his head. All his muscles were suddenly tense again. He could feel knots tightening in his back at the very thought. "I don't think I need to. It was a bad experience, but I survived it. I just need to take things one day at a time."

"London is becoming a danger zone," he insisted. "I ... I worry that every time I open the newspaper I'm going to see your name printed up on the front page –as another victim."

Thomas felt a pang in his heart. "Philip, this killer only seems to be going after women."

"For now."

"So, for now, can't we just assume that I'm not in any danger?"

Philip let out a growling sigh, before looking up at the young man. Thomas flinched back at the intensity of that glare; there were so many dark, tormented moments in those eyes that they rooted him to the spot. He felt the air escape his lungs as he watched Philip's pale pink lips move around words that hung silently in the air between them.

"I'm sorry –what did you say?"

Grey eyes narrowed.

"I said that no; we can't take risks in regard to your safety. One day I am going to read your name in the obituaries and I'd rather not have that day come any time within the next few years."

Long, pale fingers gripped Thomas' arm. He let out a strangled cry as the neat nails dug into the open wound. Beads of blood bloomed to the surface, staining Philip's fingertips as he leered over him, his breathing harsh. "Like it or not, you have people who care about your well-being. Stop being so selfish and let me help you."

"I have!" Thomas whimpered. He couldn't move out of the grip. It was like an iron weight had clamped down on his arm. "You've helped me already, Philip, what more can I let you do?"

"I just want you to accept my help when I offer it." The words appeared calm and even reasonable, however the grip on his arm was still hard and strong. "I loathe the idea of you walking around in the darkness."

Thomas squirmed, the raw flesh burning on his arm. "Why do you even care so much?" he snapped.

"Because I care about *you!*"

Thomas didn't have a chance to breathe before his head was yanked forward and a savage pair of lips ensnared his in a violently hungry kiss. He tried to push away at first, but Philip seemed to possess a strength that his lithe frame belied. He was helpless as he was imprisoned within those arms on that stool, the firelight and the kiss burning him both inside and out. Tears of pain clouded his eyes as he let Philip attack his mouth. It wasn't unpleasant –just brutal!

He gingerly responded just to see if it would make Philip stop ... but it didn't.

It just made Thomas want more.

Tuesday 11th September 1888.

Thomas jerked awake, breathing heavily.

He cast blurry eyes around his room and winced at how hard his heart pounded against his ribs. Sunlight poured in through his window –hadn't he closed the curtains last night? Grinding the heel of his hand against his eyes, he drew his knees up and tried to shrink down into the mattress, shying away from the brightness. Even sighing seemed to make his brain fizz inside his skull. What time was it?

His pocket watch read 11:12 o'clock.

How and why had he slept so late?

His throat felt sore, and his arm felt like a dead weight as he cradled it in his lap. A faint memory lingered on the periphery of his mind, but he didn't have the energy to entertain it. Not now. It had been a long week and all he needed to do was take it easy. Maybe spend the day in a library, soaking up the works of doctors before him and having to work in forced silence – it'd be more peaceful than his lodgings at least.

His lips still seemed to tingle at a memory he wasn't sure was real. The pain in his arm, however, was.

He took his time getting himself washed and dressed for the day, taking extra care to soak and wrap his arm in fresh bandages. Perhaps he should write to his Papa and see if he had any herbal remedies that might help?

The streets were easier to navigate in the daylight. They helped to reset his thinking and spend the next ten or so hours convincing himself that he was being an idiot before the sun eventually set. He kept his head down and his arms pressed at his sides. His feet seemed to weigh too much as he walked up the steps and disappeared between the doors of the library. Hunched over a small wooden desk in the corner, Thomas reread the letter he'd penned to his Papa.

Papa,

I'm sorry to write to you so suddenly but I need your advice. I was attacked last week by some form of beast that's been lurking around London. I'm fine, except for a rather aggressive claw mark on my arm. It measures approximately 7 inches long down my forearm. The tear is around 1 inch wide. It appears deeper than on first inspection. I was wondering if there were any remedies, you'd know of to counteract the itching of the wound? It doesn't seem to be healing too well.

Your son,
Thomas.

P.S. Tell mama not to worry. I truly am alright. The beast may have been lycanthropic –if that makes any difference.

It was a crudely worded letter, short and abrupt unlike his usual style. However, he knew his Papa. He responded well to short, matter-of-fact requests. Hopefully any replies would arrive within the week. Setting the letter aside, he pulled a small leather-bound book in front of him. It listed various healing uses of certain wild plants. He tried making notes. He was determined to find a way to treat werewolf wounds –but how? Surely this would excel him as a top-level student?

He stayed in the library until the bell chimed 6 o'clock. There was no way around it; he would have to drag himself back home with very little accomplishment. Even his notes wouldn't help him too much in finding a cure or a wild plant that would lessen the effects of a werewolf's bite. Perhaps it would calm down when a new moon appeared in the sky?

He didn't know. The very idea made his wound itch.

Hugging his arms around his waist, he bowed his head to the pavement and made his way home. He just wanted to clear his mind and focus on what else he could offer to his own personal dilemma. He had another check-up with the local doctor in the next couple of days. He hoped the swollen red skin would ease up a little; nothing was more disconcerting than a doctor having to look away from an injury. He was just about to cross the street when a loud yell ripped through the fog in his mind and the wind was knocked out of him. Without knowing how, he'd ended up on the pavement, his palms grazed and a pain in his side. There was a ringing in his ears and his lower back felt like it had been set on fire.

What the hell had just happened?

A hand touched his elbow, attempting to drag him to his feet.

"Is he alright?"

"He just stepped off the road!"

"That poor boy!"

Thomas tried to sort through the yells as a familiar scent hit his nose. Peering up through his –thankfully still intact –glasses, he caught sight of a familiar sharp face and bright blonde hair. "There's nothing to see here, ladies and gentlemen!" Philip called out, his voice a sharp stab through Thomas' dull senses. "He's just taken a nasty turn!"

Nasty turn? Had he? What was going on? Before he could get himself together Philip had a firm grip of his arm and was guiding him away from the road. The pavement rushed by under his feet as he let the taller man take him along towards a familiar street. Thomas was dimly aware of being let into

Philip's front door, up the polished staircase and into the bedchamber. None of it truly registered until some time later when the aroma of hot tea and lemon hovered under his nose.

"Here drink this."

Thomas blinked himself to reality with a jolt. "Er ... thank you ... What am I -?"

"Shh, we can talk later. For now, you need to drink."

Thomas took a sip and shivered. They sat in silence the dimness of dusk settling into the room. The fireplace and lights were already on. There was a dull thrumming in his forehead and the tea did little to chase it away.

"What happened?" he asked again. He didn't know how much time had passed but the sky was now completely dark outside.

"You were so distracted," Philip stated. "You walked out into the middle of the road without looking where you were going. You were almost run over."

Thomas let the words sink in. He was almost knocked over? Why hadn't he heard the yells or the horns? Why hadn't he heard the horse's hooves? He let out a sigh and drank some more of the tea. It was sweet, hot, and sugary. Not his preferred drink but it was chasing his headache away.

"Why were you there?" he rasped.

"I was walking along to run some errands and was just in time to rescue you."

Thomas furrowed his brow. "Where ... um ... Where's my satchel?"

"Your satchel?" Philip frowned.

"My bag it has notes and journals and research in it." His eyes went wide. "Oh God! Don't tell me I've lost it! Professor Talbot will kill me!"

"Oh what? This thing?" Philip held up a rough leather bag. It looked as though it had seen better days and the way Philip was touching it, you'd think the leather was poisoned with something that could cause the skin to blister.

"YES!" Thomas saw black stars dot his vision. He gratefully accepted the bag into his lap and stroked the worn hide. "Thank you ..." he breathed. "I don't know what I'd do if I lost this."

"It's just a bag, Thomas."

"I guess ..." The tone of the younger man's voice belied the fact that there was more history to that bag than picking it up at a market stall. "Nothing got lost out of it, did it?"

"Not as far as I'm aware," Philip said, taking a sip from his own teacup.

"That's good at least."

"So what were you doing up that side of the river when you didn't have a lecture this evening?" Philip asked.

"I was doing some extra studying," Thomas shrugged. He set his satchel down the side of his armchair and drew in a deep, pained sigh. Another sip of tea seemed to curb the pain. The itch in his arm was receding a little too –maybe he was imagining it, he couldn't be sure. "This tea is really good," he hummed, sinking lower into the chair.

A slow smile curled Philip's lips. "I'm glad you like it. It's a home-blend. I can get some made for you, if you like?"

Thomas nodded that he'd like that. His eyelids were drooping. Everything felt so cosy around him in that moment. The air was warm and soothing, the tea was calming like a salve on every internal scar both physical and mental –soon he was asleep.

Sunlight burning –hot smells! World waking up –daylight! Colours! Brightness! Everything hurt the eyes.

Smells grew stronger –pungent, putrid, vile! Clogging the throat and the nose and the brain!

Hairs retracting –bones breaking –shrinking –cold ice in the veins, heart hammering loudly, deafening, dying! Where was God? Where was safe?

Reborn –new light, new smells, new skin. Alleyways strewn with blood and shit, smearing the bare feet. Rancid! Flesh raw and prickly, feeling every dust mote and pebble.

Staggering ... brain adjusting ... remember to breathe ...

Remember to think ...

Remember to speak ...

Keep to the shadows. Running, scrambling, sniffing the air? Empty! Nothing to smell but you!

Home? Home? Where is home?

Home ...

Thomas peered up at his reflection. His skin was sallow, he hadn't shaved in a while and couldn't afford a new razor just yet. His hair was a greasy, black mess and his eyes were bloodshot. He hadn't slept too well the last few nights.

Whenever he did manage to sleep it was usually fitful. That only made him feel more tired when he made use of his days. He was sleeping later and heavier and his brain was often a sluggish mess in the daylight hours in between. He'd felt completely rude and as though he were in another world when he'd attended a luncheon with Rufus and Daphne on Wednesday. He'd gotten a reply from his Papa the day before with a small paper packet filled with deep indigo coloured plants. The bold letters that had been printed on the packet read:

'DO NOT HANDLE WITHOUT GLOVES!'

Said plants were now in a clay pot on his mantelpiece. The letter from his Papa had been somewhat encouraging but not terribly insightful.

'Thomas,

First of all, I shall not tell your mama about what you told me. As long as you are safe and well that's all that matters. I am here if you wish to discuss it more.

These plants are commonly known around these parts as 'Devils Helmet' –clearly you can see why. They are known to be extremely poisonous, so be sure not to touch them unless you are wearing gloves. They can be mixed into a paste or a salve with some other ingredients (recipes included on the back) or a small part of them can be dried out, crushed and mixed to become a home brew of tea. They can be quite poisonous still if drunk excessively and are also highly addictive.

Try to take care of yourself, okay?

All my love and concern,
Papa'

Thomas had instantly been wary of the plant currently drying itself out on his mantle. He had no desire to start drugging himself to such an extent. He'd just carry on using the laudanum doses his doctor prescribed him.

Not that they were doing much to cure his wounds.

He touched his new dressings gingerly, his mouth tasting bitter at the memory of having his wound sterilised and dried out before new bandages had been wrapped on. A tremor ran down his spine. He rubbed a rough hand down his face and looked at the window in his reflection. The sun was hovering on the horizon, slowly sinking within the last hour before dusk officially fell. His lecture was due to start within that hour. He still needed to bathe himself and try to look presentable enough before showing up at the hospital.

'*I wonder what horror will be waiting for me today.*'

Thinking about those prostitutes made his throat constrict. Maybe he just wasn't up for being a doctor. Perhaps he'd need to just help his Papa back home, instead of broadening his horizons down in London. Clearing his throat, he turned to heat some water on over the fire for him to wash in.

Standing in just his undergarments, he shuddered as a chill pimpled his skin. He scrubbed his face, hands and under his arms, before running the bar of cold soap over his legs. His body steamed in the tepid room. Scooping up handfuls of water, he sluiced the soapy scum off his arms, back and genitals before air drying in front of the low fire.

Once he was finally dressed, Thomas sighed.

He just needed to get to the hospital. Once he was there, he'd get into the rhythm of things. A chill crept down his spine; something was waiting for them all in that theatre he could just *feel* it.

The sound of the door closing behind them echoed around the cavernous room. The air smelled stale and like it hadn't been cleaned since their last lecture. Of course it had been –something else was causing that rancid smell. Perhaps it was the huge object covered in a muslin sheet that Talbot had erected in the centre of his platform. 'I knew it!' Thomas inwardly sneered as he sank down onto his usual bench near the front. There was light shuffling around him as the other six young men settled down around him and leaned forward, expectantly watching the sheet covered object.

Talbot was not there yet.

Strange.

After five minutes of waiting around with no indication as to where their current lesson was going to go, Walpole leaned forward on his bench and eyed the object. "So how many guesses there's another prostitute under that sheet?"

Silence followed his question.

"It looks too big to be another whore," Edward said, frowning up at the platform. "Perhaps it's a man this time?"

Walpole smirked. "I dare one of you to take the sheet off."

"WHAT?" Neville gasped. "Are you mad?"

The other man shrugged.

Thomas watched as Neville shook his head, the blood draining from his face. Edward scoffed but didn't object.

The silence made Thomas ache in his bones.

"At least six of you have some respect for the way I try to teach restraint and patience among you lot!" Talbot's voice echoed out. It rebounded off the walls like the crack of a whip and made them all spin round. The grim-faced Professor stood up from where he'd been sitting in the middle of the back row and began to descend the stairs to the floor of the theatre.

He swooped past them like a spectre, his black robes billowing.

"Now that I've piqued the interest of you all," he stated bluntly, his dark eyes cutting at Walpole a fraction longer than the rest of them. "We can begin the lesson."

He tugged the sheet off the object.

Thomas' heart exploded in his ears.

There on the table –under the bright lamps and reeking of chemicals –was the body of a wolf.

At least –it looked like a wolf.

The body was covered in coarse, matted grey hair that looked as though it was thick with mud and other bits of filth. Thomas wrinkled his nose yet craned his neck to try and get a better vantage point. Yet the head appeared strange. In fact, the skull looked a lot smaller than the rest of the body.

The skin around the skull was sickly, greyish and looked as though any hair growing there was thin and greasy. Around the hairline there appeared to be bright blue and purple veins pressed up against the skin. The rest of the face seemed to be a collision of two mammals merged together.

His stomach squirmed.

It was so unbearably unnatural but at the same time it was hard to look away from something so grotesque. The patches of hair were spaced out in irregular patches, giving the creature the appearance of being mauled by –something bigger.

"Sir?" Edward raised a hand, even though that wasn't standard practice in their lectures. "What exactly is *that*?"

"*That*, Edward, is the first smart question anyone's asked for a while." A few of the others around Thomas bristled at that comment. Thomas often thought that the man was callous to his students in order to keep them grounded. Medicine was an ever-evolving practice; they were always discovering new medicines, new procedures and new treatments.

"For all of you also wondering the same thing, this creature before you, is something I managed to pick up down South in the Sevenoaks region."

Talbot had captured it? Somehow it felt foreign to think of Talbot doing anything more energetic than gliding from point A to point B.

"That, gentlemen, is what we have been studying for the last several weeks. It is either the exact one –or related to the one –that has been slaughtering those prostitutes during the Witching Hour for the last month."

Thomas felt his throat run dry. His wound was starting to itch, the thin fibres burrowing their way into his open pores like ticks. He ground his back teeth together as he watched Talbot curled his long, gloved hand into the thin, greasy black strands of hair on the creature's skull and lifted it off the table. Getting a full view of the things face head-on was a shock that churned the stomach. Thomas almost choked on the stomach acid that raced up his throat.

"This, gentlemen, is what we in the teachings of the occult call '*Lupinotuum Pectinem*' –more commonly known as a werewolf."

Friday 14th September 1888.

Thomas took his time disinfecting himself and pulling on the rubber apron and gloves. Every sound, every breath seemed to put him even more on edge. He felt as though he were hypersensitive to the world around him. The hairs all over his body were perpetually on end as he raked a gloved hand through his hair, adjusted his glasses and took a deep breath before turning to face the corpse shackled to the operating table.

He wondered why the creature had been chained up, but Talbot insisted that it was necessary on the off chance that their tampering with the corpse caused any strange or possibly dangerous outcomes. Thomas remained unconvinced as he drew in a deep breath and joined his fellow classmates at a safe distance around the operating table.

Talbot didn't make any move to speak.

They watched him in silence until Neville piped up.

"Sir –how exactly were you able to capture this –thing?" he hedged, his voice a higher than it ought to be.

"Magic," Talbot drawled.

"No, really sir?"

Talbot narrowed his eyes but didn't repeat himself. "I simply tracked the animal and attacked when it was in a weakened state. For example, at the first break of sunlight."

Thomas itched at his arm.

It had been two weeks since the last full moon –yet this body was still fresh. How was that possible? Was the myth that werewolves only changed at the full moon just that? A lie? He chewed on his lip. He didn't have the heart to ask the question.

"You may be wondering how this corpse is still fresh considering we're midway into the moon cycle?"

Silence.

"As it happens, I had this creature in my possession for the last two weeks. I have been testing a draught that is meant to make these daemons docile. Suffice to say, this beast died before I was able to perfect the dosage."

"Was this the creature that attacked those prostitutes?" Neville asked.

"No. This one was not the creature that stalks our streets. Although knowing that there is more than one within a twenty-mile radius is unsettling to say the least."

Thomas swallowed, trying not to look at any one place too long. His arm was really starting to burn through the bandages. He bit the inside of his cheek and flexed his fingers through the rubber gloves. A tremor ran down his spine. Talbot's words blurred into white noise. The lights seemed to grow dimmer and his retinas burned in his skull.

Something clapped him on the shoulder.

He jumped, his head jerking up. His eyes burned, everything felt sharp and painful and his skin felt electrified. He could feel sweat beading over his clammy skin.

"*Are you okay Thomas?*"

Swallowing, his mouth dry, Thomas nodded. He could feel Talbot's eyes burning through his skin, but he ignored it. Pursing his lips, he forced his hunched shoulders straighter, every bone rigid and grinding under his skin. He'd missed something but there was no time to explain as a scalpel flashed in the lamplight.

Talbot was wielding the weapon.

As the older man hacked away at the corpse –the sound of the bone saw working its way through a leg, skull plates and shoulder blades filling the room –the group of young men watched on in horrified rapture. Never before had they –or anyone else –seen what they were currently witnessing. The stink of blood filled the air as one-by-one they took turns in emptying the buckets down the drain in the corner of the room. Neville threw up when the brain was removed. As previously stated it was much larger than the human brain suspended in formaldehyde. Walpole handled it as he dried excess goo from the organ and slowly eased it into the large glass jar.

Thomas was relieved he wasn't the only one sickened by what they were doing.

Everything about this thing was larger in comparison to its human counterpart; as one side of the mammal's head was midway into becoming human –it was easy to compare to a fresh sample. The manual work was the easy part. It was when studying the empty chasm of bone and muscle and thin layers of oozing fat that was disquieting.

Neville was given the task of dissolving any left-over flesh from the skull before setting it out to dry for further examination. Thomas had never seen a human man looking greener than Neville did in those moments. Edward was given the task of bagging up the entrails and disposing of them in the furnace down the corridor. The smell was so rotten it churned their stomachs. The air cleared a little once the bag was dragged away.

"What happened to the man who –*became* this?" Walpole asked, wrinkling his nose in disgust as he swept a heap of mottled grey fur aside.

"He died."

"I can see that! I mean ... Is there a missing person's report? Is there a family to notify of his death?"

"That's already been taken care of."

"How?" Edward asked.

"I sent an official statement from the police station down

Sevenoaks, showed them the body and they have written to the family with a death certificate signed by myself," the professor explained coolly, his features expressionless as he flexed his gloved fingers around a bone saw. "Whatever is left in the furnace we shall send to the family for the creature's funeral."

"But sir," Thomas piped up licking his dry lips. "Who was the man?"

"He was of no concern to us," Talbot said.

"But you do know who he was? Even ... like this?"

"Of course, Mr. Segdon." Talbot lowered the saw onto the table and folded his arms across his chest. His expression darkened a fraction, his eyes glinting like still, black pools in the night. "There is always a way to extract that sort of information from someone –even in a lycanthropic state. This man told me himself before he died, who he was and where he was from. From that alone, I was able to locate his family."

"But sir -?"

"Do not pity this creature, Segdon. He is dead. Knowing who he was will not bring him back nor humanise what was left of him."

Thomas felt his jaw click shut.

A few pairs of eyes watched him as Talbot eased off his gloves and went to change out of the apron and resume his usual position beside the podium and the large blackboard. Thomas swallowed any other questions that had danced on his tongue, and instead went about scrubbing the blood, fat and pus stains from the metal examination table. They all sluiced cold water over their scrubbing hands, wincing at the temperature through their thick gloves, and continued until all the tainted water flowed away.

Before Talbot dismissed them by the toll of the bell in the courtyard, he set them to their task of lying out the bleached werewolf skeleton on the table. It was like fitting all the pieces to a large, white puzzle. Now that all the flesh, oozing wounds and fur had been stripped away it was fascinating to see the deformed shape of the half-turned skull, the way the bone fused awkwardly and misshaped itself. The way the bones fit neatly, and at the same time irregularly, to create such an unholy beast.

Still, having it spread out before them in such a black-and-white way was phenomenal!

Once the skeleton was laid out, the bones still emanating a faint chemical smell, Talbot directed them to sketch out the skeleton in their notebooks and to annotate said diagram and identify any non-human bones they found. Thomas was surprised as it seemed like the tamest personal study assignments they'd ever been assigned.

The bell tolled 1 o'clock in the courtyard.

"That'll be all for tonight," Talbot intoned. "Clean up and get out."

Considering how tired they all looked and felt, the young men were more than happy to hand in their rubber aprons and gloves and take their time to get ready to leave. The evening's events had taken a toll on Thomas' mind as he slowly packed his satchel away and slung it over his shoulder.

As they made their way up to the door, Talbot's voice made them all stop in their tracks.

"We will be having a lecture at ten, Monday evening. I want you all there with your current work completed and up to date. After that, there will be no lectures for two weeks until the start of next month. If I need your presence prior to then, I shall notify you."

"But sir that's short notice," Edward said.

The pale, sallow face looked up at them, thin lips pressed into a line. "Yes."

"Well ... What if some of us have plans?"

"Cancel them."

"But sir —"

"I said dismissed. Or did you fail to pay attention?"

The two men stared at one another for a while. Thomas felt a tingle run down his spine. The weight of Talbot's gaze always left anyone staring back at him feeling —sick and weakened. It was peculiar. It was almost as though he had a power over people that no one else was able to understand.

Stepping out into the cool evening air, Thomas drew in a deep breath of chimney smoke and Thames water. He stood at the top of the hospital steps for a while, taking in the sight of London stretched out before him, like the burning embers of a dying fire. The first bead of light would shatter said darkness in a few hours. The silence would be broken, too, with birds chirping and the shop vendors opening up for the day.

For now there was just stillness.

It had become one of the things that Thomas had started to indulge in, since his night lectures had started. Drawing in a deep breath, quieting the buzzing anxieties in his mind, Thomas made his way down the steps and out of the courtyard. Raking a hand through his tousled hair, he made his way East towards his lodgings, whereas everyone else seemed to veer off in a westward direction. As he walked through the streets, his breathing filled his ears and the sound of his shoes clicked softly on the cobblestone road. A few people still milled about here and there so he wasn't completely alone. However, the further he moved through the narrow streets, the quieter it became.

He was about half-way to his lodgings when he caught sound of another pair of heels clicking nearby. It tickled at his senses but he focused on the pavement as he wove his way down a side alley into a neighbouring street.

The heels followed him.

His heart spiked a little as he tried keeping close to the houses, not wanting to be caught unawares from the side.

'*You're being paranoid,*' he told himself. '*A lot of people live this way and the pubs are only just closing. Get a grip.*'

His breathing grew harsher.

The wound on his arm prickled and burned.

The mysterious person continued to follow.

'*Please, just get me to my door!*' he silently prayed to his feet –God –anyone who would listen. '*I'm nearly there, just let me get inside!*'

Blood bubbled in his ears, drowning out the sounds of his feet and the other Witching Hour noises. Only his heartbeat and the prickling white noise fizzing in his bones filled his ears.

What if it was the murderer? What would he do then? Could he outrun him? Fight him off? What if his disembowelled body ended up on the front page of the papers? In Talbot's next class?

He started to sweat.

A hand landed on his shoulder and he was sure he screamed before blacking out.

Warm darkness.

That was the first thing that Thomas thought of when his mind drifted back into consciousness.

Where was he?

"I can see your eyelids moving," murmured a low voice. "Wake up."

Despite the heaviness of his muscles, Thomas obeyed his –saviour? Captor? –and opened his eyes. Everything was still blurry, but he was just about able to make out the pale outline of his sparse furniture in his lodgings. That was a good sign. Right? Blinking through bleary eyelids, he squinted in the direction of the shadow that loomed in the armchair parked in the middle of the room. His throat was dry, and his joints were still from sleeping awkwardly.

Patting himself down he winced; he was naked under the thin bedsheets.

"Where am I?" he asked uselessly.

"Your place."

"Why?"

"I brought you here."

Thomas narrowed his eyes. "Why did you bring me here?"

A pause. "Where else would I bring you?"

Rubbing the heel of his hands against his eyes, Thomas drew in slow calming breaths and tried to organize his thoughts.

I'm in my own house.

I'm not in much pain.

I seem to know this person.

They were following me.

His eyes snapped open. Peering up through the greasy strings of his fringe, he squinted at the other man. "You were following me," he stated.

"Of course I did," the shadowed figure shrugged. "How else am I meant to know you're okay?"

"Goddamnit Philip!" Thomas sneered, banging a fist into the wall. "We've talked about this!"

If the blonde man was perturbed by the plaster that chipped away from where Thomas had struck the wall, he didn't show it. He merely kept his face expressionless, before folding his hands in his lap. "If you'll recall," he said. "I let you talk. I decided not to listen to your concerns."

"So what? Your concerns outweigh my own?" Thomas

sneered.

"No. You are, however, far too unconcerned for your own well-being. Someone needs to look out for you, and I daresay your landlord wouldn't think twice about burning your belongings and renting the room out again."

He had a point. Thomas hated that, but it was true.

"What were you even doing around here at that time of night?"

Philip let out a weary sigh. "I was waiting for the lecture to finish of course. I ran a little late and had to walk a fair bit before catching up with you."

"I was nearly home! Why did you need to give me a fright?"

"That was an accident and I apologise for it."

"Philip please," Thomas cupped his face in his hands, restraining the urge to yell out. "I'm having a very bad week. The nightmares aren't going away, my wound isn't healing the way it should and I think I'm getting a bit on edge walking around in the dark all the time. So can you please do me a favour and *LEAVE ME ALONE?*"

"After what you've just told me? I hardly think so."

"Philip –please ..."

"Thomas, enough. Until the danger has passed I want to be able to look after you. You know my door is always open if you don't feel safe."

"You live further from the hospital than I do!" Thomas protested heatedly.

"Yes, but in a well-lit part of the city as opposed to those back streets you weave through."

Thomas tightened his fingers into fists. "You're being ridiculous!"

"And you're being an incessant pain!"

"Fine! Then leave!"

Narrowing his eyes, Philip stood up. Thomas flinched away as he crossed to the bed and towered over him, looking so frail in his undergarments. His skin was losing its lustrous sun-kissed look and his ribs were starting to poke out a little too much. "You're neglecting yourself," he intoned.

"I've been ill! I was attacked, in case you'd forgotten."

"Why do you think I'm here?"

"No offense, Philip, but I really don't think you could fend off a werewolf!"

'*Especially if I'm one too,*' echoed in his mind. He shook the thought away. There was no need for that.

"Come and stay with me tonight."

The offer caught Thomas off-guard. He spluttered uselessly, his body flushing a bright pink as he self-consciously drew the sheets up around his chest. "W-why?"

"So I can help take care of you. You're not well, like you said. You need some supervision."

"I'm not a child!"

"Then stop acting like one and get dressed," Philip demanded.

Twenty minutes later Thomas found himself clumsily keeping pace with the blonde man as they frogmarched through the London streets. Thomas had a hat pulled low over his eyes. The summer sun was burning his retinas. Surely it hadn't been that bright last month? His clothes felt itchy on his skin. Philip had given him time to wash and redress his wound, but the angry red and purple welts didn't seem to be healing at all.

Once at Philip's place, a bath was ordered. Thomas didn't hear what was being said at the door, his muscles tense at bathing so early on such a lovely day. Not to mention, he still had his notes to go over. He couldn't dawdle on those –

"Thomas?"

Blinking, the green-eyed man frowned. "Sorry –what?"

"I asked if you were alright," Philip said. "You've not

touched your tea."

Thomas glanced down and nearly jumped out of his seat. Not only was he resting in a plush velvet armchair but at some point he'd even been handed a cup of tea –when had this happened? Why couldn't he remember? His skull started to throb, and he groaned. Shifting the teacup onto the table, he dropped his head into his hands and hunched over.

"My head –why does it hurt so much?"

A hand rested on his shoulder and squeezed. "Come here Thomas. Let me help."

Weakly, Thomas shook his head but didn't protest when the man took him by the wrists and helped him to stand. He let his head bob weakly, watching through half-closed eyelids as pale hands unfastened the buttons of his waistcoat, shirt and loosened his slacks. He only shuddered a little as his legs were bared to the air.

He was guided by his wrists over to the bathtub. The heat from the water sent shockwaves rippling through him.

He was about to lean back and settle in the tub he was greeted with the view of Philip, pure white and naked, dark gold hairs trimmed neatly between his legs and under his arms. He swallowed drily at the man lowered himself down into the frothy water. His stomach tightened as the water rose around his shoulders. The aromas tickled at his senses but all he could focus on in that moment was that Philip was leaning closer to him. The world blurred as Philip lifted the spectacles from his face.

His breathing came out in ragged gasps.

There was nothing but the soft rays of sunlight shining in through the window and making Philip look ethereal. Thomas had to focus on anything else just to keep himself from having a problem. Unfortunately, Philip took it upon himself to take a bar of soap in his hands, rub vigorously until his fingers were dripping with lather, and took Thomas' arm and started to wash him. It was a peculiar feeling, having someone else's hands all over you. The way Philip's fingers ran over every inch of skin, up under his armpit, over the curves of his collarbones, and down the ridges of his ribcage. It sent shivers running through him.

"What are you doing?" Thomas murmured as Philip reached his lathered fingers under the frothy water to massage Thomas' thighs. Tipping his head back, the brunette let out a low, guttural moan. "That feels nice."

"If you like, once you're clean, I can help you relax properly."

Thomas let out a shuddering breath, his erection straining heavily just inches from Philip's fingertips. "If ... If you think it would help."

Philip smirked a little. "I definitely think it would help you."

Thomas shuddered, his breaths coming in shallow gasps. He let his eyelids close and focused solely on the sensation of Philip's long, firm fingers running down his calves, over his ankles and pressing firmly in the dimples in his thighs. It made a sulphuric heat pool in his stomach. Stars flashed behind his eyelids and he was tense all over, biting on his bottom lip. Philip's hands moved further up his thighs and wrapped roughly around his –

"Philip no! I'm –!"

He came hot and heavy in the frothy water, before sagging back in the bathtub. "Oh my God!" he cried out, covering his face with his wet hands. He sank lower into the tub in a vain attempt to drown himself. "I'm so –I didn't mean –Oh God Philip don't look at me! I'm disgusting!"

There was a pause. "Why would I think you're disgusting?"

"I just –I did that –while being touched by you –by a man!"

"Did you enjoy it?" Philip asked, his voice a low rumble.

Thomas looked down, Philip's wet, gold hair obscuring his view of his clear grey eyes. A tremor ran through his stomach.

Licking his lips, he felt blood rush through him. "Y-yes ... I did ..."

"Good."

Thomas barely had a moment to think before Philip was on top of him. He whimpered as Philip held his head in place, slipping his tongue down his throat, his hips slipping easily between Thomas' knees. Thomas felt his insides flip as he felt Philip –hard and urgent –rubbing against him. The pressure between his legs made his hips jerk slowly but firmly against the press of Philip's body.

He craned his neck back over the edge of the tub, his fingers reaching up to rake through Philip's hair, as the older man ravaged his neck. Every time those sharp teeth grazed a sensitive spot over and over –Thomas vibrated with arousal as they rutted together. He wanted more –he didn't know what more even was –but he was in a frenzy that couldn't be controlled!

"Philip I –"

"What do you need Thomas?" Philip growled in his ear. "Tell me what you need from me!"

"I –I –I don't know!" he groaned out, spreading his legs even wider, letting Philip slot closer against him.

"Get up," Philip growled, pulling away.

Thomas whined at the loss of contact, craning his head up to pant heavily. "Wh-why did you stop?"

Philip clutched the sides of the tub, his teeth barred, "Turn around."

Thomas frowned. "W-Why?"

"Do it."

On trembling hands and knees, Thomas managed to turn in the tub and braced his body over the back end. The cool air made his skin prickle with goose pimples. The hairs on the back of his arms and neck stood up on end. Worrying his bottom lip, he frowned into the shadows of the room beyond him. '*What am I doing?*' his brain screamed as his eyes fell onto the mutilated arm. Philip had unwrapped it for his bath. '*What are you thinking letting this happen?!*'

Everything went blank as he felt Philip's hands on his hips. They squeezed him roughly, wet thighs pressing against his buttocks. He let out a hitched gasp as a hand wove around his chest, up around his throat and tipped his chin back. Teeth on his neck made him tremble, his hips bucking backward, feeling the thick erection, wet and ready against his cleft.

Thomas felt pain and fire tear through the blank mess of his mind.

"Wha-What're you -?"

"Relax," came Philip's guttural voice.

"But I –"

"Relax."

Thomas closed his eyes and tried to relax as he felt Philip's long, smooth finger slowly tease him. Suddenly he felt hot, tight and sweaty and didn't know how to react, how to relax, how to *breathe* with Philip pressed up against his back, slowly easing in and out of his body. It was a sensation he'd never imagined feeling –it wasn't entirely unpleasant either.

However the thought of having Philip completely inside him –he choked.

"Shh, it'll be okay," Philip purred. His free hand worked on the tense muscles in Thomas' back. "Trust me."

'*Do I trust him?*' Thomas thought, leaving his body.

From his space on the ceiling, he watched as his body indulged in the sensations Philip was giving him. Arching back into the blonde, displaying himself ready and willing his face contorted in pain and pleasure as Philip readied himself and pressed into his body.

Body and soul clashed together and Thomas let out a long yowl of painful pleasure.

He didn't last long. Being stretched like a thin sheet of

rubber tight around Philip was both exhilarating, frightening and unlike any other pleasure he'd experienced on earth. Everything was brimming and burning inside him. He wanted to weep with pleasure whenever Philip hit that one perfect spot inside him.

"Oh Philip!" he cried out. "Yes! Please, don't stop!"

Philip did as he was asked. He gripped Thomas' shoulders, his thumb stroking his neck whilst thrusting his hips faster, harder, deeper until pleasure lanced through him like electricity. His mind spiralled as he shot his load as he plunged into Thomas up to his hilt. He felt all his muscles strain and tense as he threw his head back and cried out.

Thomas collapsed over the rim of the tub as Philip finally stopped spasming behind him, the grip on his neck finally loosening. Philip was still between his thighs, bracing himself over Thomas, his hands gripping the side of the bath. Thomas couldn't do anything. He focused purely on breathing in … and out.

Philip quickly rinsed himself in the tepid bathwater before climbing out on quaking legs. Thomas didn't pay attention to anything but soon felt a warm towel drape over his shoulders. He trembled, his body finally realising just how cool the room was.

"Thanks," he breathed as Philip took the time to get him up, out of the tub and dried off in front of the fire.

As the room was cleared, Thomas remained in a borrowed robe, perched in an armchair pulled up to the fire. Despite the bath and how thoroughly he'd been cleansed, the burning in his rear made him feel –dirty. Soiled.

Tainted.

The thought made bile burn in his throat. He clenched his muscles tightly as he watched the tall, blonde man stride from place to place as though nothing had happened, as though this was a normal occurrence –as though Thomas wasn't his first.

More bile rose in his throat.

"Why did you do that?" he breathed into the dying light.

Philip stopped his hunt through his many drawers for some night shirts for them both to wear, and turned slowly to frown at his companion. "Excuse me?"

"Why did you –do that –to me?" He couldn't look up. Couldn't see the pity, the callousness in those grey eyes. It could cut him too deeply.

Philip stiffened and straightened up. Suddenly, the room became a chasm between them. "I thought it was what we both wanted," he admitted.

"I never said I wanted … to be … to do …" his voice broke. He pressed his lips together and huddled up tighter in the armchair.

"Thomas *what* are you so afraid of?" Philip asked, coming into the warm glow of the fire.

Thomas clenched his eyes shut. *'I'm scared that I'm a demonic beast! I'm terrified I'll wake up one day and have your mangled corpse in my bed! Your blood staining my teeth and nails like a macabre painting!'*

"Thomas? Talk to me."

"How many others?" he finally rasped.

"I'm sorry?"

"How many other men have you –done that to?"

Philip licked his lips, his own stomach turning in knots. "Do you plan on reporting me to the authorities?"

Thomas' head jerked up. "No! Of course not I just –I *need* to know."

"Fine," Philip sighed, raking a hand through his damp hair. "If you must know –I've only ever had experiences with two other gentlemen. The first was my father's old butler at our manor. It was only a few kisses and some light touches. I was fourteen at the time. When father found out, he shot the man dead before he could get off the front porch." He paused, licking his lips and thinking about how he'd watched from a parlour window as Lionel had tried to flee and been toppled forward onto the green, a spray of red blood painting the white roses. His stomach churned inside him, the weight of Thomas' eyes on his face.

"The second man was about eight years ago, when I'd just turned twenty-three. I met him in a nightclub. I had thought everything was happy and enjoyable until father sent me a clipping, stating that he had married in the week he told me he was going abroad." He let out a cold laugh. "He tried to continue the affair but –I'm not that sort of person."

"But you will happily –b-be with men?" Thomas cursed his trembling lips.

"No." Philip shook his head. "I'd happily be with *you*. If you would so wish, that is. If not –there's no reason this has to change anything."

"Is that why you live alone?" Thomas asked, pulling the robe tighter around him.

"It helps," Philip acknowledged. "Though originally it wasn't my choice. This was father's way of –keeping me at bay."

"I see."

Philip watched the younger man for a while. His heart ached in his chest and he couldn't put his finger on the emotion he felt. Longing? Trepidation? He wasn't sure. "There's a nightshirt on the bed for you," he murmured. "Have a nice rest."

Thomas started. "W-where will you sleep?"

"I have another room I can stay in," Philip said. "It's fine. You need your space. That, at least, I can give you." He stood up and made to leave.

"Philip wait!"

"Honestly Thomas," Philip reached out and placed a soft hand on the younger man's shoulder. "One night won't hurt you. Okay? You're safe here."

Thomas looked up at the blonde man and felt his insides spin uncomfortably. He both wanted time to reflect and also to have Philip by his side. The conflicting emotions made him feel uneasy. "Okay ..." he murmured, watching as the blonde man gathered another nightshirt in his arms and made for the door, his silver embroidered robe billowing slightly around his ankles. "Goodnight."

Philip turned at the door, his eyes sullen and downcast. "Goodnight Thomas."

Marble —stone —wood —cool, balmy air —sticking to the teeth, to the eyes, to the fur to the blood! Cloying and suffocating, spiralling inside, electrodes attaching to every notch on the spine, burrowing deep into the brain like a tick. Radiating poison through the soul and turning it black!

Anger —rage —bloodlust —hunger!

Scraping paws under the skin, begging for release.

OUT! OUT! OUT!

Smell the blood —smell the soap —feel the flesh run down the throat!

COMING FOR YOU!

Bright eyes, soft skin, so fine, so pristine, so perfectly human! Sleeping unaware. The perfect trap. Slither the moonbeams down the throat, twist the soul and the bones and the brain and release!

Rip you apart, bite your heart —scream, scream, SCREAM!

Friday 21st September 1888.

Thomas didn't know how it happened, but it was about four days before he realised he'd not been to his lodgings for a while. His landlord would most likely rent his room out again soon if he didn't show his face, so he had to deal with the gruelling task of telling Philip that he was going to work from home for the day.

That day, however, turned into a worthless nightmare.

He stared out of the window for over an hour before jerking back to reality and realising that there was a large spot of ink spreading across his notebook page from where he'd been tapping the end of his quill on his book. He'd cursed and had to rip about three pages out of his journal and toss it into the cold fireplace.

He'd sat at his table, hands pressed under his chin as he stared out through the shaft of sunlight that fell across him. Eventually, his mind had snapped, he'd tossed his things into his satchel and hurried down into the street and along the road to Philip's side of the bridge.

The blonde man had let him back into his home and had given Thomas his space when he'd asked for a room with a desk so that he could work. There was something he couldn't explain, as he'd been left alone in Philip's study, about the feeling he'd felt as soon as he'd stepped over that threshold. It had felt calming –which had surprised him. He hadn't realised how on edge and jittery he'd felt until he'd stopped and breathed with firm, marble floors under his feet.

Thomas hadn't been able to get to work straight away. Instead, the dark-haired man had taken great pleasure in rifling through Philip's papers, books and the drawers that dotted the dark panelled room. He knew he was invading the blonde's privacy but there was –something –something he couldn't put his finger on. Something that tickled his nose, fermented at the back of his mind, and coiled like a salamander on the flaming rock within his gut.

Finally, he found it.

In the top desk drawer, right at the back, beyond a pile of neat papers, loose quills and a small coins purse –there was a small burlap pouch tied with a drawstring that felt somewhat crunchy as his fingers poked and prodded.

'*What is that?*' he thought as he dropped it onto the desk. His fingers tingled a little from where he'd touched the pouch. The smell was ... familiar. Where had he smelled it before?

Drawing in a deep breath, he stepped away from the desk and ran a hand through his hair. Turning his eyes around the room he stretched his arms up over his head. "Oh, what am I doing here? What the hell am I doing here?"

'*Do some work!*' his brain snapped irritably.

Rolling his eyes he pinched his nose. He knew he had to work. He knew he had to impress Talbot in order to continue the course in the New Year. There was nothing in his brain, though. Everything was utterly blank.

The clock chimed for midday.

He'd been useless and listless all morning –how was that even possible?

Out of the corner of his eye the small burlap pouch sat harmlessly on the desktop, bathed in the sunlight filtering in through the ornate windows. It felt as though the smell was getting stronger, like the sun was helping the aroma to permeate the room and his senses. Feeling a twisting in his stomach, he snatched the bag off the top, opened one of the small casement windows and tossed the sack outside into the courtyard garden below.

When Philip returned at dusk, he was greeted by a room that no longer resembled his study. It looked as though an extravagant ritual had taken place; the floorboards and blackboards he'd kept in storage, now adorned tons of notes, diagrams and symbols copied out from various dusty tomes. As the light faded away outside the latticed windows, Philip's eyes fell upon the hunched over figure of a topless Thomas seated in the centre of said symbols.

A tremor ran down his spine as he closed the door.

"Thomas?" he hedged, tightening his grip on his cane. "What have you been doing in here?"

"I have found a variation of alleged cures for the werewolf malady through these textbooks!" he panted, turning his frazzled appearance toward the blonde. "I'm sorry –I needed to map it all out to understand it better."

Philip frowned down at the state of his floor. It wouldn't be cheap to get it varnished again. "The boards weren't enough?"

He didn't expect an answer to his question –and he didn't get one.

"Thomas, you need to get some rest."

"I'm fine."

Pursing his lips, Philip tried again. "Thomas, please? Join me for dinner? You need a break."

Thomas let out a rough laugh. "If I stop now, I'll lose my train of thought!"

"Didn't you take notes?" he asked, browsing over the papers littering his desk. There were so many balls of scrunched up paper that it made his brain hurt just looking at them. "How can you even concentrate when the place looks so messy?"

"I'll write it down later!" Thomas waved him off. "I'm missing something –but I can't work out what!"

Philip tried to start clearing up the notes, but the shuffling noise of paper caught the younger man's attention. "NO!" he yelled out, hurrying over and snatching the notes from the blonde's hands and spreading them messily out over the desk once again. "Leave them as they were! You'll muddle them!"

"They're already muddled!" Philip snapped.

They glared at each other for a moment before Philip relented and backed away from the desk. Instead, he went over to the symbols on the floor completely perplexed. He hadn't even realised he had chalk in his possession –but there it was, as clear as day marring his floor.

"Thomas –what is all this?" he asked, dreading the answer in his bones. He tugged at his collar, feeling the airlessness in the room. "Why are you doing this?"

"It's for my thesis," Thomas murmured over his shoulder.

"Thesis for what?"

"Talbot's class."

Philip furrowed his brows even further. "And what exactly is your thesis about?"

"That werewolf bites inject an extra chromosome into the body and it becomes triggered by the Lunar cycle."

"Right ..."

"And every four weeks the body tries to repel said chromosome but it doesn't work, instead attacking the hosting body."

"So you're thinking that the werewolf toxin –is like a parasitic entity?"

Thomas turned wide, surprised eyes towards the blonde. "I ... y-yes."

Taking off his overcoat, Philip tugged up his trousers and crouched down, his fingers gingerly tracing through the chalk symbols on his floor. "I'm assuming you're not trying to isolate any herbal remedies that may be able to control, or extract said parasite?"

Thomas gave a breathless little smile. "I am ... how do you know?"

"I've been studying under Talbot for years. I'd be a junior lecturer at that hospital by now if it weren't for my own maladies."

Thomas looked over at his companion. "Is that why you don't get along with Talbot?"

"We get along the way we always have. He ... helped me when my father threw me out."

"What did he do for you?" Thomas asked.

Philip didn't answer right away. "He helped me to –get control of my urges. Tried to make medicines that would control my illnesses and the –side-effects."

"Did they work?"

Philip shrugged. "It's an on-going process."

Thomas nodded and dropped his focus back to the desk, littered with all his notes and workbooks. "I'm sorry about the mess! I'll clear it up!"

"I think you need to have a rest, Thomas. Go and rest then join me for dinner. The mess can wait until later."

"But ... Philip I can't take a break!"

"Take a little one. Then I'll help you with your research okay?"

"But –that's dishonest!"

Philip let out a bark of laughter. "Do you really think Talbot acquired those bodies completely legally?"

Thomas blinked as though he'd been struck. "I –well –no, I suppose not. I –I hadn't really thought about it."

"Maybe next time you should think about it."

Thomas pursed his lips and gathered his things from Philip's desk, taking great care not to jeopardize the order they were stacked in. Philip watched the younger man for a moment or two, before heading for the door. "I'll have dinner prepared for 7 o'clock. Try and be presentable by then. I'll let you sort yourself out."

Thomas watched as the door closed and left him alone – surrounded by symbols and dried herbs.

Later that evening as the two young men were eating in the dining room, Thomas was all too aware of how loud everything seemed. He rubbed at his ears and tried to pay attention to what Philip was talking about in regard to the attacks around London. Hardly any of the words sank into his mind, however, as he'd been consecutively out of 'harm's way' for at least two weeks. On top of all of this, his current workload for Talbot's class was bordering on an overwhelming magnitude. As he slowly ate his way through his food –a struggle for him as his stomach seemed to shrink away from the very idea of digesting –he watched the blonde man through the light of the setting sun filtering in through the latticed windows.

"... *Thomas?*"

"Y-Yes?" He blinked back to the moment.

"Did you hear a word of what I said?" Philip asked, his voice tight.

"I ... No, I'm sorry. I don't think I did."

"I said, that if you like, I have a small apothecary contact over in Camden Town. I have an appointment with him in two nights' time to pick up an order for Talbot. If you'd like, you're more than welcome to join me. Perhaps we'll be able to find a few herbs that might be able to aid your studies."

"Oh! Gosh –Philip, no, that's far too kind of you!"

"Nothing kind about it. I want to help where I can. If I can, I will."

Thomas chewed on his bottom lip but decided not to say

anything.

After another half hour of stiff-jawed chewing, Thomas was relieved of the arduous task when his plate was taken away. He had to politely decline dessert as his eyes had slowly gotten heavier due to the good, fruity wine and the ache radiating from his jaw. Maybe he didn't have the strength to study anymore tonight? Rubbing at his eyes he leaned back in the dining room chair and let out a soft sigh.

"I'm sorry Philip. I think I may need to sleep."

Philip's eyebrows rose up a notch. Setting his own glass of wine down –his silver signet ring gleaming from his finger – he looked over at Thomas and pressed the back of his hand to the man's forehead. "You're a tad warm," he remarked.

"A fever?"

"Perhaps." Philip set his napkin aside and took Thomas' hand, guiding him out towards the main hallway. "Let's just get you upstairs and have a quiet night."

Thomas willingly obeyed.

Within the hour he was propped up in thick, over-stuffed pillows, curtains drawn against the night sky and lamplight of the streets below. The fire crackled merrily in the grate at the foot of the four-poster bed. Thomas shuddered every now and then despite the summertime heat. Philip made sure to appear every half an hour until 11 o'clock that evening, bringing Thomas some sweet, fragrant teas and cool rags for his forehead to break his fever.

Thomas didn't mind –at that point, Philip was a most welcome break in his black, hazy, heated headache.

Whenever Philip dabbed at his forehead or held a cup of tea to his parched lips, he felt warmth wash through him. It was serene and calming. There was something sweet in the tea, something that soothed his senses. He wasn't entirely sure what was in it –he needed to remember to ask first thing in the morning. The final time that he was visited during the

night, he was pleased when he sank down into sleep —letting
the flowery, perfumed tea coax him into dreams.

A bell above the door tinkled as they walked in.

It was a calm, warm night and only the taverns up and
down London were open and accepting punters. Prostitutes
and drunk men crowded in alleyways and cackled, however
none of these low-life sounds came close to the bubble that
Thomas found himself in when he was around Philip Ridley.
As they stepped into the low-lit apothecary, they were greeted
by Philip's client, a tall man with weathered skin and wiry,
electrified white hair sticking up in all directions. He waved
them inside.

"Don't just stand in the doorway, lads, I need to keep the
average room temperature at thirty-five, you know."

Philip gave Thomas an encouraging smile before closing the
door behind them.

Thomas advanced into the unfamiliar shop, his eyes lighting
up at the hundreds of thousands of glass jars and bottles that
lined the shelves. From the floor to the ceiling, green, brown
and clear glass gleamed in the glow from the candles in their
sconces mounted on the walls. The air was heady with a rich,
flowery scent that made Thomas sway a little from side-to-
side. It was dizzying as he craned his neck up to view the
stained glass domed window at the top of the spiral staircase.

It was beautiful.

Philip chuckled. "So you like it, then?" he asked, his hand
creeping up to rest in the small of Thomas' back. He startled
but didn't pull away.

"It's wonderful!" Thomas beamed.

Philip shared a glance with the shop-owner, who inclined

his head to the back office. Philip nodded before murmuring into Thomas' ear. "I'll be right back. Mr. O'Callaghan needs to sign over some papers before giving me the order. Try not to touch anything."

"Can I read the labels?"

"They'll be plenty of time for that," Philip grinned. There was something in his smoky grey eyes that made Thomas' insides quiver.

Philip closed the office door behind him and adjusted his eyes to the lower light within. "Do you have all the specimens for my Uncle?" he intoned in a bored manner.

"Yes," O'Callaghan grunted. "Although I must have you know, Master Ridley, I gave up on this sort of work years ago! Your family needs to get some new contacts!"

"What can I say? Stephen likes you."

O'Callaghan scoffed. "A fat lot of good that's done me."

"Money is Money."

O'Callaghan ran a hand through his wiry hair as he gingerly selected bottles from a shelf behind the desk. "So what is your Uncle doing at the hospital these days to warrant such ingredients?"

"He's not told me that," Philip answered honestly. "I pop-in to aid from time-to-time but that's all."

"Pity. You had potential."

Philip swallowed thickly but didn't respond. He leaned back against the desk, cane trapped between his clasped hands. "I hope you don't mind that I brought my companion to your store at this late hour. He works with my uncle and doesn't have the same resources as his classmates."

"Of course not," O'Callaghan shrugged, setting down some vials on the desk. "I am surprised, however, that you're feeling remotely charitable."

Philip bristled, narrowing his eyes. "I am charitable. I just choose to not make a song and dance about everything I do."

O'Callaghan raised an amused eyebrow as he finished taking bottles off the shelves behind the desk. Setting everything down, he picked up a heavy-duty leather case and started aligning the bottles in the built-in racks within. The sound of glass on metal and wood twinkled in the silent office as he worked. Every ingredient had been ticked off of Talbot's list.

"So," O'Callaghan broke the silence. "What's the real reason you're keen to help that young man out there?"

Philip arched his eyebrows at the shop owner. "Why does it concern you?"

"Well if you're being honest in wanting to help him, I don't mind giving him some work here. I could use someone to help me take inventory every two weeks."

"You don't seem like you need the help."

"Fine!" O'Callaghan waved his hand, "I don't need the help, I would like the help. I'm not as young as I used to be. There is nothing wrong with having some extra pocket money to aid your friend in his studies, am I right?"

"I ... I suppose not. I would need to ask him first, of course."

"Very well. I can also provide him with discounted herbs if he requires it."

"Now I need to wonder why you really want to help," Philip asked, straightening his posture even more. His palms were beginning to grow clammy in the airtight office. He felt his jaw starting to ache and his insides prickled.

"Truthfully?" the old man sighed. "Business is slow. I have no one to give deliveries and as such, I'm losing a lot of prestigious customers. I feel that your young friend could aid me in that regard. The errands would only be a one day a week job and inventory every two weeks. I'd pay and give discounts. If –after a few months –my sales have not improved, then I can let him go."

Philip swallowed. "I'll let you know what he says."

"Good. Now shall we join your friend?"

Philip inclined his head, leaning on his cane as he made his way out of the office.

O'Callaghan didn't follow Philip. He claimed he needed to go into his residence at the very back of the shop, leaving the two young men alone. Thomas was crouched down, his glasses pushed up high on his nose as he read the labels of various brown tinted bottles on a low shelf by the spiral staircase. Upon noticing Philip, he turned his head and smiled.

"Hi –is everything okay with your order?"

"Yes, fine, thank you."

Thomas frowned at the clipped tone. "I've not complicated things by being here, have I?"

Philip peered up questioningly before shaking his head. "Oh no! Nothing like that, don't worry." Moving closer, Philip rested a hand on the younger man's shoulder. "So have you seen anything you think might help with your studies?" O'Callaghan's offer danced on the tip of his tongue, but he couldn't bring himself to voice it –not just yet.

"It's hard to tell," Thomas flushed a little. "There are so many herbs here and –well –I need to smell some of them to know."

"Well I'm sure we can sniff a few."

"Won't Mr. O'Callaghan mind?"

"Oh, we're only having a sniff," Philip chuckled. "As long as we don't spill anything."

"Okay," Thomas turned his eyes on the rows upon rows of bottles and vials. "Um ... how about ... this one?"

He plucked one from the shelf. The label read 'WORMWOOD'.

Thomas popped the stopper and took a deep breath –and coughed. "Oh gosh, no!" he choked, replacing the stopper and wiping a tear from his eye. "No, no, no –dreadful stuff!"

Philip chuckled. "Try another one."

"Okay…" Thomas bit his lip, eyes scanning the shelves in front of him. "What about this one? 'WILLOWEED.'"

"Give it a go."

Thomas popped the cork and held the bottle up to his nose. The aroma was sickeningly sweet and seemed to reach up his nose to tickle his brain. It felt … uncomfortable. "Oh Gosh – No! That one … makes me feel weird!"

"Okay not that one either," Philip smirked, replacing the corked bottle back on the shelf. "How about third time lucky?"

"Are you sure?"

"Might as well. Since we're here."

Thomas felt like a kid. His eyes roamed over all the glass bottles until they landed on one in the far corner of the bottom shelf. The glass was smoked black with a small purple ribbon tied limply around the neck.

"What's that one?" Thomas murmured as he plucked the bottle from the shelf. The label was a little worn, but he was able to read the calligraphy when he held it up to the light.

"What have you got there?" Philip asked, his voice low and husky in Thomas' ear.

It made his stomach flip.

"I … I uh … don't really know."

He popped the cork and –time stopped.

This was IT! THIS was what he'd been searching for!

Drawing in long, deep breaths of the flowery aroma, he felt fear, pain and aches disappear into a distant memory. He was all too aware of Philip's hot hands burning through his clothes on his back, the feel of his hip pressed against Thomas' thigh –the way his breath rushed over the nape of his neck.

"P-Philip?"

"Yes Thomas?"

There it was again. That low, growling voice. It made his

insides stutter and flare like a fire being brought back to life. Turning around to face the blonde man, his breath hitched. He felt as though his heart and lungs couldn't function anymore. A tremor ran down his spine. "I ... Philip I ..."

"Tell me." Philip hooked his finger under Thomas' chin, leaning closer so that he could smell the aftershave balm tainting the brunette's skin.

"I ... Can I ...?"

"Tell me, Thomas. What do you need?"

Thomas swallowed thickly before reacting. He grabbed a handful of Philip's silk waistcoat and tugged their bodies closer. His senses were mad for the blonde man in front of him; everything was overwhelmed by 'Philip'. He could smell him, hear him, feel him, and now he just needed to –

Philip was momentarily surprised when Thomas kissed him. It was hot, urgent, and completely without fear. He wrapped an arm around the young man's back, trapping him in the kiss. His free hand threaded through the tight waves of black hair, clutching at it, his mouth greedily accepting the hungry kisses Thomas lavished upon him.

"Mmm! Thomas, Thomas, Thomas! Stop!" he urged, his own mouth refusing to acknowledge the danger of being caught as he continued to nip at Thomas' red lips. "Later!" he growled out, forcing himself to step back. "Wait a little longer. Let's pay and go *home*."

Thomas panted, his pupils dilated with lust as he looked up at Philip without seeing him. Eventually, he drew in a deep breath and nodded.

Straightening himself up, Philip took the small black bottle from Thomas' hand and called O'Callaghan out from the back office so that he could pay. Once everything was all paid and packaged up into the briefcase, Philip dragged his companion out of the shop and marched him through the blackened streets of London towards his abode.

Thomas didn't complain.

As soon as the front door was slammed shut and the case of bottles tossed beside the coat rack, he found himself pinned up against the rough wood with Philip clawing at his clothes, mouth and teeth biting, kissing and licking as much of the exposed skin as he could reach. It wasn't enough, though.

"Philip!" Thomas gushed out, red-faced and breathing heavily. He trapped the blonde's face between his hands, staring deeply into those dark, lust-filled eyes. "Philip ... take me."

"Take you where?"

"I don't give a fuck where, Philip, I just need you to take me. Now!"

Neither was sure which of them had grunted first. All Thomas was aware of was the heat, the strength and the ferocity with which they wrestled each other up the stairs to the master bedchamber. Clothes were ripped, buttons skittered across the wooden floorboards and the rest was lost in a filthy, hot, dark mess of sweaty skin, blood, sex, and the most painfully blissful release either man had ever had.

Wednesday 26th September 1888.

Thomas woke up to bliss for the fifth day in a row. He'd never known how liquidised the human body could feel in the throes of passion. Sleep was nothing but a welcome darkness that snuck in when his body was utterly and completely exhausted beyond respite. This particular day had been a slow build-up, burning away sleep at the furthest corners of his mind, sensations ebbing into each muscle as he finally cracked an eyelid open. Upon squinting down at the rumpled bedclothes, his stomach jolted as he watched the red, swollen lips swallow him whole —and the guttural moan filling the bedchamber.

Between his raised knees, Philip's mouth worked miracles before the full weight of his body crushed down on top of Thomas, knocking the air from his lungs before his grunts and moans were silenced by greedy kisses.

To Thomas, it was heaven.

He was desperate to have more of the older man, even having the strong, pale naked muscles pressed roughly against him, gyrating against his hips, slicking a wet trail against the brunette's stomach. To be able to touch the man like in such a way was ... incredibly arousing! He couldn't understand it!

How had they done this for nearly five days straight?

Thomas was in awe as Philip peppered his body with enough bite marks to resemble a plague. Every time those teeth grazed his skin, Thomas found himself arching quickly into the touch —almost like he'd been struck by lightning. Raking his hands through Philip's blonde hair, he rubbed himself feverishly against the other man, already aching for more and —at the same time —wanting to drag their activities out for as long as possible before they were called down for breakfast.

"You're finally awake?" Philip smirked, taking Thomas' hands out of his hair, and pinning them up on either side of his head. Thomas grunted as the blonde man sat up and hooked his hips over his own. "So, we have some time before breakfast is ready –what would you have me do to you?"

"Ohh I don't know!" Thomas blushed, his eyes never properly focusing on the man looming over him. "I just – Gosh! I'm still new to this!"

Philip smirked wickedly, delighting in how innocent the younger man was. Oh, but he had a wonderful body to play with –a little thin perhaps –but he was agile and that was more than enough to keep him interested.

"There's no need to be shy with me," he crooned, "I've been inside you, after all."

His cheeks flared bright pink, making Philip chuckle.

"So? What do you want from me?"

"P-Philip ..."

"All you have to do is tell me."

"I ... I don't know!"

"I think you do," Philip purred, running the tip of his tongue around Thomas' nipple. Muscles tensed underneath him as his breath hitched. "So, you're either going to tell me –or I'm not going to let you out of this bed until you beg me to."

Thomas laughed nervously, shielding his face with his hands. "You're so cruel, Philip!"

"Cruel?" The blonde man crawled up until he was bracing himself over Thomas' head, the brunette's legs bent awkwardly between their bodies. "I'd never be cruel to you," he purred, raking his long, pale fingers down the length of Thomas' throat. "I just like having some fun with you."

"Your idea of fun is very rough and twice as dirty."

"Were you complaining last night?" he smirked, nipping at Thomas' earlobe with his teeth.

"THAT'S NOT THE POINT!"

Laughter rang out through the room as Philip continued to nibble and tease at the sensitive tanned man stretched out beneath him. Burying his nose in the crook of Thomas' neck he inhaled the scent that had soaked into their skin from their bath the previous evening. It made his insides cramp with pleasure. He'd managed to scrounge enough of the herbs into the hot bath and as soon as they were both in the water all form of animalistic cravings inside them were let loose. Thomas didn't understand how the herbs were able to do such a thing, but he wasn't about to complain –not yet at least.

After their amorous activities, they dressed and went down to breakfast. Thomas was able to eat a larger helping of food this time round, whereas Philip seemed to still be humming from their torrid bedroom antics. He only took some herbal tea and some oatcake –not very filling but he insisted that he'd be fine.

"Are you sure you want to work the entire morning with just that little bit of cake inside you?" Thomas asked, frowning as Philip stood and made to leave.

The man arched a perfect eyebrow before leaning down, close enough for his blonde hair to tickle Thomas' cheek.

"I'd rather be inside you," he growled. "Alas, I must bid you *adieu*. I have errands to run, and you have more studying to do. You have the entire case of vials to sort through still. They'll be going to Talbot's office tomorrow night, so make sure you use your time well."

Thomas bit back a smile. "Yes, *sir*."

"Good boy." He secured his cane between his hands, turned

on his heel and strode from the room. "Make sure you write up your notes coherently! I want to make sure they're legible before you showcase your findings!"

Thomas shook his head a little. The tea was indeed almost too sweet for his senses, but he powered through three more cups –it was addictive –before finally tossing down his napkin and making his way up to the study to take another look at the herbs from Mr. O'Callaghan.

In the light of day, with every bottle set out across Philip's desk –the task suddenly seemed rather daunting. There were over thirty bottles! Surely some of them he could dismiss without sniffing them? His Papa worked with numerous herbs as it was, there was no need to smell the ones he was already familiar with. Unfortunately, even weeding out the bottles he knew the contents of, he was still left with eighteen to go through.

Grabbing his notebook and a quill, he drew in a deep breath and started going through the bottles. The first one had a label that read 'KNOTGRASS'. He popped the cork and sniffed at the spindly plant inside and noted –nothing. He had no adverse reaction to this weed. With a frown, he placed the bottle to one side, scribbled a quick note in his book and reached for the second bottle in line.

'*This is going to be boring,*' he thought to himself, already eyeing the other bottles and vials with disdain. '*Oh well, it'll be over within the hour*'.

That thought, however, did little to console him.

The next bottle read 'NUX MYRISTICA'. Grimacing, he popped the cork and –sneezed!

"NUTMEG?" he choked, as he shoved the bottle away. "Who the hell uses nutmeg in medicine?" It was a foolish question, for his own Papa would often give small sachets of the powdered root to be used by his patients. He made another note –literally translating the Latin label to its

English meaning.

"Useless people not identifying their own stock," he grumbled as he waded through the rest of the bottles.

Within the hour, as he'd predicted, he came down to the small black bottle once again. Judging from its contents there was only a small amount of this herb left so there was no need for him to crush any or rub anything on his gums –some of which had left a bitter aftertaste that no amount of tea or water had been able to get rid of. Not like this last one. No, this was the one that was strangely calming. It was like a soft, sickly sweet perfume that soaked deep into the nervous system.

The label was quite faded. It began with an 'A' –but he needed to carry it over into the sunlight to be able to read the worn letters.

"A ... ACON ... I ... ITE. Aconite!" His face split into a triumphant grin. "Aconite! Great! Now ... Oh, dear."

He bit his bottom lip and frowned. Aconite was a plant that had slowly but surely been restricted to growing in Northern England and Scotland. It was particularly hard to come by. Thomas couldn't use this for his studies! What would happen if Talbot needed some urgently? He'd probably ship Thomas up to Scotland itself to harvest as much of the plant as possible. A shudder racked through his body.

"I don't really want to do that," he sighed. Casting a look at the blackened glass, he dropped himself into the armchair. It creaked under his weight.

The heady aroma teased at the periphery of his senses. He tried to ignore it but –it kept creeping in! He knew he'd smelled that aroma somewhere before. Almost constantly in fact. Where –had that been?

A knock came at the door.

"Come in!" he called.

"Pardon the intrusion, sir, but would you like a cup of tea?" the middle-aged maid asked.

"I ... yes that would be lovely thank you."

Waddling over to the table beside his chair, the maid quickly poured a cup of tea, milk and no sugar, before bowing out and shutting the door quietly behind her. The silence was almost over-whelming as life continued on the streets outside the window. Birds chirped as a soft breeze blew through the trees. He was missing something vital; he knew that. The aroma still clung to his skin. Reaching up, he took a sip of the tea. It was sweet –hitting the back of his throat –but the effect was instant. He felt calm wash through him like honey.

Taking another sip he felt almost dreamy.

And then another ... and another ...

'*Something in the tea*,' his brain hummed, like a faraway echo. '*There's something in the tea!*'

Sitting bolt upright, he stared at the teacup in his hands. It wasn't even warm. He'd been in such a daze for a long time, enough for the tea to grow cold in his hands. His bad arm started to quake a little as he licked his dried lips. "What ... the hell ...?"

Was he being ... poisoned?

His throat tightened. What was going on here? Setting the cup to one side, Thomas stroked his hair out of his eyes. His skin was started to grow sweaty.

'*Don't panic!*'

"It's okay. I'm okay. I'm not dying yet ... okay, stay calm, stay calm, stay calm!" He launched himself out of the chair and started to pace the hearth. What the hell was going on? Had Philip been poisoning his tea? Why? Why would such a pragmatic man do such a thing?

Not knowing was killing him.

'*Find out what's in the tea!*' his brain screamed through the panicking, white noise. '*Go down into the kitchens and find out what's in it!'*

The kitchens were cool and empty. Luckily for him, Philip liked to keep his place overly organised. Within ten minutes Thomas found the cupboard that had all the tea, coffee and other herbs that could possibly be needed in one's diet. He pried open the ceramic jar labelled 'TEA' but as soon as he held one up to his nose –he frowned. They smelled like regular tea leaves. Biting his lip, he frowned and rummaged through the rest of the cupboard. He could smell a faint hint of that aroma –drawing him nearer. It was definitely coming from the same place. Eventually he pulled out a small wooden box. It didn't have a label.

Strange.

Popping the lid off, Thomas was hit with a pungent wave of the odour. It wasn't unpleasant just ... too much of a good thing. It looked familiar. Pouring some into his palm Thomas turned from the kitchen and returned to the study. On the desk, under the lamplight, both the herb used for his tea and the one from the black bottle were ... exactly the same.

His insides cramped. He threw up the contents of his stomach into the empty grate.

Cuffing the back of his mouth on his shirt sleeve, Thomas let out a low breath and decided that there was only one thing he could do before Philip got back that evening. He needed to go and get some answers from Talbot. He wasn't even completely sure he could trust the sour professor but ... he knew Philip better than anyone.

He was the only one who would know the answers.

Talbot was writing up some notes in his office in the

lower level of the hospital. He preferred the silence that often unnerved the other faculty members and the entire student body. The only people who braved it down there were the men who worked in the boiler room, and that was usually just to toss unclaimed bodies into the furnace. When a knock came from the windowless door, he merely drew his eyes slowly from the document he was working on.

Sighing, he popped his quill back into the inkwell and droned, "Come in."

The door creaked open and admitted the last person he expected on a Wednesday night. Straightening back in his chair, he quirked a dark eyebrow. "Mister Segdon, what can I do for you?"

The young bespectacled boy braved a few steps into the room, closed the door behind him, and stood to attention. "I ... I need your help identifying a substance and its general properties."

Talbot suppressed the urge to roll his eyes. With a stiff hand, he beckoned for the item in question. A small paper packet was placed on his desk. With lips pursed into a tight line, he tipped the contents out onto his ledger, and, after a brief moment of poking and sniffing, he leaned back in his chair and cast an unamused look at his student.

"*This* is what you're disturbing me for?" he drawled.

Thomas nodded. "Aconite, yes sir."

"Why is it so important for you to know the properties of this herb, Mister Segdon?"

Thomas pressed his lips together. His bad arm trembled a little as he gripped the vacant chair for support. He didn't bother to seat himself. "I ... Feel that this plant could help me in my studies and for my thesis I just need to know as much as possible about what it is and can potentially do for patients."

"Well that would depend."

"On what?"

"On what your patients are suffering with."

"Considering our topic of study is lycanthropy, professor that seems a fairly invalid question."

"Perhaps," Talbot nodded. "However, we have also studied other creatures, such as daemons and vampires, have we not?"

"Neither of those holds any interest for me, sir," Thomas admitted, his eyes downcast. He didn't like to admit his own morbid curiosity for the macabre creature. Whenever his arm itched it reminded him of that traumatic night and how, if he was ever in need of a cure by the next full moon, he'd have it on hand.

Talbot didn't respond right away. He narrowed his dark eyes and leaned even further back in his chair until his shoulders were pressed up against the rough wood. "I may have a book that could help you with his particular direction of study."

He stood up from his chair, towering over everything in the room like a grim figure. He drifted over to his bookshelf and withdrew a small book. It had thick yellowed pages and looked stained and worse for wear. Thomas dreaded to think how faded the ink within would be. As Talbot brought the book back over to the desk the younger man noted that it was bound in dark purple leather, rusted studs in the corners with faded gilt writing embossed on the cover.

"That's a rather old book, sir," Thomas managed to croak. "Are you sure I'll be able to find what I need in there?"

"Quite sure," Talbot drawled. He pushed the book over towards Thomas with one long, bony finger. "In here are the names of herbs and plants –some long since extinct or hard to find –along with their names, meanings, and various ways to use them. I think it will benefit you to experiment with them."

"You mean like ... making my own medicines?"

"Medicines, draughts, poultices or balms, yes."

"How will I know if any of them work?"

"You have a wound don't you?" Talbot bit out. "Why not test some on that and see if it works?"

"On my arm?" Thomas paled. "But I ... No! I can't! What if it gets worse?"

"Worse than not healing at all?"

"I ... I um ..."

"You cannot become a Doctor of Medicine if you fail before you even try," Talbot stated in his '*classroom voice*' –a voice so loud and commanding that it drowned everything else out. He sat himself back down at his desk and bent his head over his neglected documents.

Thomas took that as his cue to leave.

Straightening down his waistcoat and shirtsleeves, he gingerly reached out and took the textbook in hand. It was heavier than it looked and the pages inside were indeed thick, yellow and had all manner of stains on the edges. His heart did a strange little twist as he ran his thumb over the faded gilt words. Was this the book he'd been searching for in the library all that time ago? Tucking the book under his arm, he made his way across the room and after some awkward jiggling, managed to get the stiff door free. As he was leaving, Talbot's voice caught him before he'd completely disappeared.

"Mister Segdon where exactly did you come across this much Aconite? You do realise it doesn't grow in the London area."

"Y-Yes sir, I'm aware of that."

"Then where did you get it?"

"Well ... there was some in the order you placed at O'Callaghan's but he only had a small bottle left."

"And the rest?"

"I ... well ... I don't really know that it's my place to say, sir."

"Mister Segdon, if you haven't noticed by now my methods of teaching and acquiring a fair number of our test subjects haven't exactly been orthodox methods, so spare me your melancholy dramatics and answer the question!"

"Well sir ... I found some at Mr. Ridley's residence."

"You found it?" the professor drawled, the disbelief etched into those cold, hard eyes.

"Y-yes sir. In the kitchen."

"Why on earth would it be there?" he sneered.

Thomas shrugged, hugging the book to his chest, and backing up through the door. His heart was hammering, and he could feel himself sweating. Even the pores on his bad arm seemed to gape open, exuding sweat and grime from within his body. His gut twisted.

"I ... I couldn't say sir," his voice cracked under the pressure of breathing. His vision blurred a little, and black spots started to pop before his eyes. "I ... I think ... b-being used in ... the tea ..."

"The tea?"

"I'm sorry sir but I really must go!" he gushed out, trying desperately not to vomit in his professor's office. He'd already ruined one fireplace he didn't need to start spewing his guts up on everyone's hearth.

Turning his back on the surprised look on Talbot's face, Thomas sprinted as fast as his unstable legs would permit. It wasn't that he was worried about implicating Philip, he was sure the blonde man had answers for the findings –he just really needed some breathable air!

Once in the courtyard, having caught his breath and cooled his burning muscles, cold sweat slicking the back of his neck, Thomas swiped his black fringe out of his eyes and pulled the book out from under his arm. It was almost stuck to him. Leaning back against the cool stone of the building, he opened the front cover and leafed through a few pages before coming to a paragraph that piqued his interest.

'There are over two hundred and fifty types of Aconitum, the three main ones being Wolfsbane, monkswood and aconite that now only grow in wild places. Aconitum species are a small trumpet-shaped plant that is highly toxic to both humans and animals, though recently they have been successfully used in medicines for pain relief, heart sedatives, and to induce swelling.

The flowers of the plant have healing properties and can be used for medicinal purposes, however it is the leaves of the plant that are highly toxic and should be avoided, unless for the purpose of poisoning. The roots of the plant can also be used as an ingredient of medicines, though none have been successful to date.'

"The leaves are poison?" Thomas choked, his hand darting to his trouser pocket. In there he felt something dried and crisp. Under the lamplight, he saw the remnants of what he'd given to Talbot. The herbs from Philip's tea box were almost too dry to make out the colour –but they weren't sharp or pointed like the leaves in the book.

No –there were only the flowers.

Eyes darting back to the book, Thomas reread the paragraph and felt his stuttering heart calm down a little. Only the leaves were poison. Relief washed through his body. Wiping his hand down on his trousers, he closed the book, tucked it under his arm and started to make his way to the open street. His relief didn't last long though. As he walked through the austere streets, cold sweat clinging to his limbs like a second, irritating skin, another thought entered his mind that echoed louder than his own footsteps.

'The aconite was in the tea.'

Though the rational part of his mind concluded that it may have simply been for pain relief, something that clearly both young men were in dire need of, the softer, darker thoughts wouldn't let that be the clear-cut answer.

'*The aconite was in the tea.*'

Why did Thomas feel the addiction to drink so much? Was it truly to purge himself of the pain inflicted upon him by that Hell beast?

'*The aconite was in the tea.*'

Perhaps there was another reason. Thomas stopped short under a large oak tree, wiping the sweat from his upper lip. His throat was dry, his heart beating uncomfortably. What if there was another reason? A darker reason? A reason that was too painful to even think about let alone say out loud? It wasn't as though Philip had told him what he was drinking after all. Clearly, he was only drinking it so as not to arouse suspicion.

'*The aconite was in the tea.*'

Or to use its other name ...

"W-wolfsbane..." Thomas let the word tumble from his mouth in a broken whisper.

Panic, dread, pain and reality started to wrack his body, the ground unhinged from under his feet as he collapsed back against the tree, the Thames turning into a glittering snake, twisting and writhing through his blurred vision as he dropped.

"He ... H-he thinks I'm the wolf ..."

Cupping his throbbing head in his hands, he let the tears come thick and fast, letting them burn trails down his numb cheeks.

"H-he thinks I-I'm the w-wolf?!"

Throughout the quiet, dark streets of London a cry was heard that would rip the soul to pieces. It wasn't, however, the cries they'd dreaded to hear of a savage beast claiming another victim. No; this time it was the cry of a young boy in desperate need of his Papa.

Sunday 30th September 1888.

Thomas was surprised that he received a letter that morning, instructing him to be at the hospital for another lesson. Considering Talbot had travelled up to Scotland the morning after Thomas had gotten information about the plants he'd found; the summons was peculiar. Who was going to be teaching the class with Talbot out of London? Did another unscheduled class mean that something else had happened? Thomas hadn't been sure if he was even going to bother attending; most of his notes hadn't been written up neatly in his presentation journal –the finalised findings that he'd present to Talbot at the end of the course.

He surprised himself as he walked through the large wooden doors of the theatre. He pressed his lips together, breathed deeply and made his way down the aisle towards his usual bench at the front. On the raised platform there were two gurneys with two bodies hidden under starched sheets.

He felt his insides lurch.

"What ... on earth is going on?" Thomas murmured as he sank down into the hard seat, ignoring the shuffling of the other young men finding their spots. Upon seeing the two covered bodies, their hushed tones magnified throughout the cavernous room.

"Who's taking this class?" Neville asked.

"I have no idea," Edward replied, helplessly.

Thomas felt his wound starting to itch under his bandages. He'd been hiding out at his old place for the last few days since his discovery. He'd had to coop himself up and hadn't been able to go out and get new dressings or ointments for his wound. It seemed to be getting worse with the more stress he put himself under. There was nothing he could do about it. The last time he'd gone outside, he'd almost bumped into Philip. He'd had to run and hide in a nearby shop and weave his way through the crowd so as not to be spotted. It had been hard but eventually he'd made it back home.

He hadn't spoken to the blonde man since the morning of his discovery.

A part of him felt bad for the silence he'd instilled upon their strange, budding infatuation. However, the other part of him was glad. He deserved to be isolated. Whatever was going on was sure to reveal itself within the next few days – until then he needed to focus on the two bodies lying before him on the operating tables.

The door to the hallway banged open.

Despite being right at the front and able to hear the footsteps approaching, Thomas still startled worse than Neville. His body was stewing in his own grime, sweat and odour. It was repugnant –but thankfully no one else had seemed to comment on it within earshot.

Through the doorway waddled a large, round man with horn-rimmed glasses perched on his bulbous nose and his thin greying hair clinging to his scalp like a cloud. "Good evening gentlemen. As Professor Talbot is out on assignment for the next week or so, I shall be leading you in this case."

"I'm sorry, sir, but who are you?" Neville asked.

"I am Dr. Stanhope and I'll be leading you through this autopsy tonight."

"What's happened?" Bennett asked.

"Another two bodies have turned up with similar wounds as the other prostitutes from the last two months."

"Why do we need to dissect them?" Edward asked. "Isn't it obvious we won't find anything new in these two corpses? Why must we desecrate them in this fashion?"

"I do not question Professor Talbot's motives, I simply do as he's instructed me," Stanhope stated, holding his hands up in surrender. "I'm merely here as an official witness to these proceedings."

Casting a look around at his classmates, Thomas scratched at his wounded arm before standing up and making his way towards the back of the operating platform. The other six men followed suit, as they dressed in the rubber aprons and gloves. The bodies were in a much more grotesque state than the previous victims –at the very least the one labelled '*LONG LIZ*' was much the same as the others.

It was the second victim that was in a horrifying state.

The two small, airless breasts lay flat and wrinkling on her chest, sagging slightly on either side. There was a greenish discoloration across her abdomen and the rough-handed stitching running up her body was like wires pulling old, weathered hides together in a rumpled line. Thomas blanched as he looked up at the woman's face; there was a deep cut across her face running right down in an angle over the jaw on the right side of her cheek. The cut went through the bone and divided all the structures of her cheek, except the membrane of the mouth. The tip of her nose was hanging on by a few thin strands of flesh, another cut having severed straight through and split the top lip. The skin on her cheeks flapped like grey leather wings.

Neville had to run to the sink and throw up at the large, thick slab of greying skin that moved too easily from a deep gash running from the inner left thigh, up to her labia. Thomas didn't blame him –he felt quite sick too.

"Well?" Stanhope's voice broke through their horrified trance. "Get to work. Unpick those stitches and take a look inside."

"Is it me or is he far too excited for this?" Bennett murmured darkly.

"Maybe a little," Thomas murmured.

"Who wants to do the honours?" Bennett goaded, scalpel aloft in his hand.

"Why don't *you* do it?" Edward hissed.

The dark man shrugged his shoulders before poking the sharp blade through a loose hole in the sewn-up skin –and gently working it through the rough stitches. Pus oozed from the wound, the foul smell pervading the air, causing them all to choke. Powering through the nausea swelling inside him, Thomas aided Bennett in cutting the last of the stitches and peeling away the grimy folds of skin. They smacked down on either side of the corpse, the milky white of her eyes staring up through her bloodied eyelids –or what was left of them.

With quaking hands, Edward removed the detached ribcage and stomach, placing them to one side. If anything, moving the internal organs seems to make the smell gush out of the corpse like a noxious gas.

"What –do you see?" Neville asked from his spot by the sink. He looked a sickly green colour his arm wrapped limply around his stomach. A sheen of sweat glossed his brow.

Narrowing his eyes, Thomas returned his attention to the innards of the corpse. "It ... appears as though some of the colon is missing."

"How much?"

"About ... one ... maybe two feet."

Bennett clenched his jaw tightly before pointing a gloved hand lower. "Look there. The left kidney is gone. These cuts were done with a clean precise knife but whoever did it had a lot of time on his hands. Otherwise, he wouldn't have bothered in cutting her eyelids."

"Why would a wolf need a kidney?" Edward asked.

"Perhaps it wasn't the wolf. Perhaps this is from that killer that's in the papers. The one who's getting all the credit for these crimes."

Thomas shrugged. "All the wolf did was bite them. This man is in fact killing them."

"They're mercy killings!" Bennett protested.

"Okay. They're still dead."

Bennett scoffed but didn't object. It was sound logic after-all. They had been working on all the corpses relating to this case –there was no denying any of it. He went back to work examining the lower abdominals for further oddities.

"This is so strange," he finally murmured. "Nothing else seems to be greatly injured. The cut on her throat was the obvious cause of death; she was probably bleeding out whilst he cut out her kidney."

"But who would need a kidney? For what purpose?" Neville asked weakly.

"Well when one of us meets this esteemed killer, we'll ask him, shall we?" Bennett sneered.

Neville clamped his mouth shut and remained silent.

"Don't go on at him," Thomas said. "The only reason any of us seem safe right now it because this killer seems to target women –namely women of ill-repute or ones who frequently drink."

"That's not all, it would seem," Bennett muttered.

"What do you mean?"

"This man seems to have some medical knowledge."

"How can you be sure?"

"Whoever targeted this woman knew as sure as you or I, where to locate a human kidney," the dark man stated. With the scalpel he prodded weakly at the dried-out innards where the knife wounds had torn through the flesh. "See here and here? These are clean wounds. No random hacking or callousness like you'd see from a butchering."

"So ... this may be the work of a begrudged medical student?"

"Possibly," Bennett muttered. "Or a medical professional."

A hush fell throughout the hall.

"What are you insinuating young man?" Stanhope's voice cried out, sounding eerily loud in the silent hall. "Are you implying that an esteemed member of the board of doctors has committed these atrocious crimes?"

"Well sir it does stand to reason –"

"I won't hear another word of this!" the rotund man snapped, smacking his book on the wooden podium. "No member of this board is capable of such horrors! We take a sacred oath to heal and protect members of society! We do not kill them for no reason!"

"Sir, if someone feels they are aiding society –"

"NOT ANOTHER WORD, WALPOLE!" Stanhope sneered. "One more accusation out of your mouth and you'll be dismissed from these lectures!"

The threat hung in the stale air.

"With all due respect, sir, we have an obligation to report any findings to the police in order to aid their investigation," the dark man stated in a chillingly calm manner.

"Well, if that's the case, Walpole, you'll have a lot of time after tonight since you'll no longer be welcome to participate in these studies."

"You don't have the authority to do that!"

"Professor Talbot put me in charge, so I think you'll find that I do."

"I make my payments to Professor Stephen Talbot," Bennett stated, advancing on the red-faced round man with thinning blonde hair. "So, for the time being I shan't attend these lectures. However, as soon as Talbot is standing back behind that podium, you mark my words I shall be back."

Stanhope scoffed and shook his head, "I'd like to see you try."

Bennett narrowed his eyes, threw down his rubber gloves and apron inside the corpses gaping gut, before storming up to his seat. Retrieving his belongings, he made his way to the main doors and slammed them loudly on the way out. The rest of the six men –Thomas included –stared after him in shock. Had that really just happened? Bennett knew too much and was one of the ones who had the more logical theories on the matter. He could expose all of what they knew to the public. He could expose everything that the hospital –and Talbot – were doing. Most of it wasn't even legal to begin with.

Casting glances around at the other five, Thomas sucked in a shallow breath and gently prodded at the mangled woman before him. There was a silent agreement around the table; they needed to sew the body back up and leave as soon as possible before anyone else was dismissed.

The clock struck 1 o'clock in the courtyard.

The remaining six young men hunched their shoulders against the cool breeze. No one said anything as they hurried along through the gates and went their separate ways home. Thomas was dreading returning to his cold lodgings. The dodgy little brass bolt on the bedroom door would hardly suffice against this killer. The maniac was clearly upping his game and Thomas felt sick with fear as he made his way along the streets towards his building.

Most houses were silent, the windows blacked out as the night wore on. All was quiet in the surrounding streets. Thomas' footsteps were magnified in his own ears as he cradled his injured arm to his chest. The smell of the formaldehyde and the pus that had leaked out onto their gloves seemed to have stained through the rubber and onto his hands. He knew he was being paranoid, but he could still smell it. It made his gag reflex lurch up, tightening his throat.

"Just get home, lock the door and you'll be fine," he murmured to himself.

Thankfully, he managed to make his way up to his own room without any incident, panic attacks or suspicious footsteps following him through the backstreets. His key echoed as it turned in the lock before he pushed his weight against the door. It creaked loudly as it swung inwards. As he'd predicted, like every other night, the room was quiet, empty and had a chill festering in the darkness.

"You're finally home then?"

Thomas let out a cry of panic as a match hissed to life. He scrambled with the door, his hands unable to work the door handle. Two strong arms wrapped around his waist and rocked him gently from side-to-side as he struggled.

"It's okay, Thomas," the familiar voice crooned. "It's just me, calm down. Breathe –in ... and out ... in ... and out ..."

Tears of fear dripped out of his eyes as he pressed his forehead so hard against the door, he was sure he'd go through it. He hunched over, his chest tight as he gasped desperately for air. Slowly, sensation ebbed back into his body. He was suddenly aware of his chipped nails digging into the wood. His stomach uncramped and he mentally thanked God for not letting him piss himself.

"Thomas?"

"Fuck you!" he snapped, weakly shoving the man off him and whipping around to sneer at him. "What the hell is wrong with you? You can't just break into my room and not expect me to panic!"

"I didn't mean to startle you –"

"I'm not done!" Thomas yelled. He advanced a few steps. "What do you think you're achieving here? I have to deal with corpses and the constant fear of nearly bumping into a murderer –you can't expect me to welcome you with open arms! You're lucky I don't carry a knife for my own protection!"

Philip waited patiently in the middle of the room; his hands clasped behind his back as he waited for the younger man's temper to abate before saying anything else. Thomas paced back and forth for a while, his heart hammering in his ears as he raked sweaty hair out of his eyes. He could literally smell his own fear staining his skin. It was a good thing it wasn't another full moon yet, otherwise he'd have been easy prey for the were-beast. After about ten minutes –and a thorough examination of his rooms –he was satisfied that there was no immediate threat on his life. He took his time and retrieved his satchel from where he'd flung it across the room in a panic. Thankfully, nothing had been broken or stained.

Setting his belongings aside, Thomas turned with a strained expression to the blonde man standing before him. "So? Why are you here?"

"It's been about three days since I last saw you. I wanted an explanation for your sudden departure –and I'd like to know why you made such a mess in my kitchen on the way out."

"Your ... oh," Thomas paled at the memory.

"Yes. 'Oh'," Philip repeated. "So, would you care to explain to me why you left so suddenly? And why you ransacked my cupboards?"

Thomas clenched his jaw tightly but didn't respond.

"I mean, honestly Thomas, if you were hungry all you needed to do was ask."

Through his damp glasses, Thomas glared as the blonde man seated himself in the threadbare armchair beside the hearth. The air between them was quiet as Philip took some time to add kindling to the fire and struck a few matches, letting some old newspapers catch alight. Soon, warmth spread throughout the room, leeching the cold from their bones. Thomas watched as the '*JACK THE RIPPER*' headlines turned to ash before him.

"I didn't want to be around you. I still don't."

"Why not?" Philip asked, leaning back in his chair and quirking a blonde eyebrow. "What have I done to offend you?"

A quip was on the tip of Thomas' tongue about all the sodomy they'd gotten up to over the last week. How he'd let Philip abuse and arouse his body was something that God would spit on them for. However, he swallowed his retort and shifted his weight from foot-to-foot. Philip watched him expectantly. "I ... I found out what you were putting in the tea, Philip."

"The aconite?"

Thomas blanched but nodded. "Y-yes."

"And you panicked over this because ...?"

"I did some research," Thomas stated, seating himself on the edge of his bed. It was flimsy and sagged awkwardly under his weight, but he didn't move. Any other place to sit was within close proximity to Philip –close enough to smell the soap that clung to his skin –and that was something he couldn't handle right at that moment. "I know what that herb is used for. I know it's used in rituals for ... f-for ..."

Philip narrowed his eyes. "For ...?"

"For ... w-werewolves."

Philip let out a bark of laughter. "Oh, dear Lord! That's the best thing I think I've heard all year!" He continued to laugh, actually having to dab at his eyes with a handkerchief. "Oh, my word. Oh! Thomas –oh my I can't breathe!"

The younger man watched Philip laugh in his armchair, his body flushing with embarrassment. It rolled off him in waves and seemed to stink worse than the corpse he'd been elbow-deep in. He waited for the laughter to subside before he tried to talk.

"I don't need your mockery, Philip," he bit out. "I've read plenty of books and they all say the same things; this herb is used in the ritualistic curing or attempted curing of people suffering from a lycanthropic disposition."

"Oh," Philip smirked through the firelight. "It's rather arousing when you talk like that."

"It arouses you when I talk like Talbot?" Thomas pulled a face.

"I meant in an authoritative way, but no matter. You've killed my spirits." He cocked his eyebrow again. "What else did you read about this herb?"

"T-that it can be used for helping with fevers, headaches, and stomach ailments."

"Did it ever occur to you that *that* was what it was for?" Philip coaxed.

"Well of course I did!" Thomas snapped. "However, considering all this treachery going on, and the fact that I was *attacked* –can you honestly blame me for jumping to that conclusion? That you wanted to cure me?"

"So what if that was the case?" Philip asked. "Don't you want someone looking out for you and trying to help find a cure for you?"

"But I'm not –that's not –Philip, that's not what's going on here!"

"Thomas the only thing going on here is that you made a drastic conclusion -a very deluded one at that –which I can only put down to the stress of these late night classes, your lack of sleep and our activities over the last week –and you've worked yourself up into such a horrid frenzy!"

Thomas felt his jaw drop.

With a sigh, Philip stood up and made his way over to the bed and settled down in a crouch in front of the younger man. He gripped Thomas by the shoulders and looked him square in the eye. Thomas leaned back with narrowed eyes, the firelight behind the blonde man throwing the pair of them in heavy shadows. "Thomas, I need you to listen to me very carefully, okay?"

Thomas nodded.

"You are not a werewolf. Say it."

"I am not a werewolf."

"I was only scratched by a werewolf. I was not bitten."

Thomas rolled his eyes and repeated the words.

"Philip was not trying to poison me."

Thomas glared but managed to trip over the words.

"Philip only uses the herbs for pragmatic medicinal purposes, like headaches and to calm his heart."

Thomas didn't know why but he felt a swell of affection flood through his chest. Philip had told him that he'd had many health issues and that Talbot had helped provide the medical treatment throughout the years. Perhaps Philip was right? Maybe all the sleepless nights had warped his perception of medicine and their proper uses, as well as the grimms tales been proported by the papers. At the very least, Professor Talbot would be gone for the next two weeks. That should provide a reprieve for him and give him a chance for some much-needed rest.

Swallowing past the lump in his throat, Thomas felt himself sag awkwardly in Philip's grip. "Can you forgive me Philip?" he asked, his eyes tearing up behind his glasses. He suddenly felt his eyeballs grow raw and scratchy in their sockets. "I never meant to accuse you of such things."

Philip gave his shoulders a squeeze. "I suppose I can forgive you. On one condition."

"Oh? What's that?"

"Let me take you back to my home. I promise we don't have to do anything your uncomfortable with. I just ... I want to help you get some proper sleep."

"Wasn't the tea supposed to do that?" Thomas quipped.

"It did, for a time. However natural sleep will aid you better, I think."

"How do you plan on accomplishing that?"

"Come back with me and I'll show you."

Despite the stress his heart and mind had been under over the last couple of days Thomas had to admit that the thought of sinking into a lavish bed –clean and freshened up –with Philip there to watch over him until he fell asleep, was an enticing proposition. Gathering up his satchel and journals, Thomas decided to leave.

Following Philip down the narrow, dark staircases Thomas was led out towards the cobbled streets. He kept close to the taller man, listening to his cane click-click-click against the stone before a large black carriage came into view at the end of the road two streets away. How had he never noticed it those other nights? Stepping up into the carriage, he felt his stomach lurch as Philip shut the door and the wheels creaked as the coach moved. They crossed through the streets and over the bridges towards the familiar, nicer streets where Philip resided.

Within the hour Thomas had, as predicted, gotten a quick wash in a stone basin filled with hot, soapy water, a freshly laundered nightshirt and been tucked into the four-poster bed that he was tempted to think of as 'his'. That was dangerous territory and he needed to remind himself not to wander down that road. It was hard not to, though, as Philip settled down on the edge of the bed, dressed in a nightshirt and a velvet robe.

"How're you feeling?" he asked. He pressed the back of his hand against Thomas' forehead and hummed softly.

"Much better. I'm feeling quite t-tired ..." he trailed off as a yawn cut him off.

Philip pressed a finger to his lips. "Shh, we can talk more tomorrow. You need to rest as much as possible over the next few days."

Thomas wanted to protest, but Philip's finger pressed firmer against his mouth.

"I said '*no talking*'," Philip smirked. He gently lifted Thomas' glasses from the end of his nose and set them on the nightstand. "Get some rest, Thomas. You've had an awfully long night."

Just as he was about to stand up and leave, Thomas reached out and snatched at his wrist. "Wait!"

Philip waited, both eyebrows raised.

"Can you ... stay and talk to me a little while?"

"Are you sure that won't keep you awake longer?"

"I ... I just like listening to your voice," Thomas admitted. "I think it'll help me sleep."

"So I bore you?"

"*No!*".

"Calm down," Philip said. The mattress dipped as he slid up onto the bed and gently threw a thick cover over his legs. The faint chill in the air was easily magnified in the large, stone house. "I'll stay as long as you need."

Thomas listened to Philip talk about nothing in particular; the news of the day, his favourite things to do in summertime when he'd been younger and any plans for the end of the year, nearer Christmas time. None of it was important and yet Thomas let every word soak into his brain. Philip's voice washed over him more calming than any cup of tea he'd ever drunk. He wasn't sure when it happened, but he was sure he felt Philip's long, thin fingers threading through his mass of black hair. It was soothing and relaxed him into a state of comfort he'd never known. All of it was the perfect combination to eased Thomas into sleep.

When he finally felt the younger man's breathing relax and grow laboured, Philip let out a soft breath. The faint aroma of aconite-tea still perfumed the air. Thomas was relaxed around him now and that was the important thing. There was no need for him to worry about what the herbs were needed for any longer. Philip had said his piece and as far as he was concerned, the matter was closed. He didn't leave Thomas' bedchamber that night. Instead, he got comfortable on the goose feather pillows, eased the younger man into a more nestled position against his chest and continued to stroke his black hair.

Through the gap in the curtains, the rooftops were bathed in the silvery glow of the moon through the thin sheaf of clouds drifting in the breeze. He lay that way for a while watching as the sky lightened outside towards the first break of dawn.

Thomas slept soundly on his chest.

That was all that mattered in that moment. Thomas' health was his top concern.

There'd be a full moon in another two days –they'd have more mania to deal with then.

Tuesday 2nd October 1888.

*I*t was in the early hours of the morning that restlessness roused Thomas from his sleep.

Cracking an eyelid open, it took a little while before his brain remembered the events of the previous evening. His fuzzy vision made out the engraved pillars of the four-poster bed holding up an elaborately embroidered velvet canopy. In any light, the curtains took his breath away. The mattress underneath him was plush and cushioned his aching joints perfectly. Had he really slept through the last twenty-four hours?

'I guess I needed it after seeing that body.'

Thomas shifted on his side and found that the expanse of mattress behind him was cool to the touch. His heart sank low in his chest. It made sense that Philip would retire to his bedchamber as promised. Thomas couldn't help but feel somewhat disappointed though. He wouldn't have minded waking up to a warm embrace.

'Maybe if you want someone to hold you, you should go and ask for it.'

Thomas had never been one to ask for such things. If something good happened then he'd be glad for it, and if something bad happened, he'd simply take it in stride. He'd never really been one to go out and manipulate his own destiny for personal gains.

Restlessness settled into his bones, and he let out a weary sigh. He needed to stretch his legs out a little before attempting to sleep again. It had been the same, even when he'd lived up North in the family's cottage. He'd go out in the early hours before dawn and wonder around the fields out back. As long as the cottage was in sight –he'd leave a candle in his bedroom window as a beacon –he'd feel safe.

Swinging his legs over the edge of the bed, Thomas had to shift himself forward a few inches until his feet touched the cold, wooden floorboards. Chilling tremors racked up his legs but he clenched his teeth, blindly touching around for the slippers Philip loaned him. Once on, he slowly shuffled towards the door and eased the latch up.

The door creaked a little as he opened it.

The dark hallway beyond was still as expected.

Thomas found that he was grateful for the slippers, not only because they kept his feet from freezing on the wooden floors, but also because they made his footsteps virtually soundless as he slipped out of his bedchamber. The hairs on the back of his neck stood up on end as he made his way towards the main landing –and suppressed a gasp. Up above his head there was a huge, latticed window. He'd never paid it much heed before but now as he looked out at the Heavens stretched high above him, his heart lurched. The stars winked down at him, as though they knew something he did not. The moon was swollen –on the very precipice of being full.

'*One more day.*'

He itched at his bandaged arm. He truly couldn't believe that it hadn't started healing yet. With a frown he had to force his attention from the moon and made his way along the corridor towards Philip's bedchamber. As he left the brilliant moonlight behind him, Thomas felt that he could breathe a little easier. The sooner the police caught up with that madman calling himself '*the Ripper*' the sooner they'd all sleep a little better.

Once at Philip's door, Thomas hesitated before knocking. There was no answer or stirrings beyond. He tried again.

There was still no answer.

'*Well it is nearly dawn.*'

Thomas knocked again, louder.

When there was still no reply, he decided that he had two choices; he could go into the room and disturb Philip that way, or he could run back to his own bed like a coward with his tail between his legs, and hope that he never embarrassed himself like that again. He was rooted to the spot for a moment, his legs trembling with fear and the cold seeping into his skin. He always ran away from anything remotely exciting. He took a huge risk coming down to study in London in the first place. Despite his injuries and the horror he'd seen –he knew he'd never trade any of those experiences for a calm, quiet life like his Papa.

Drawing in a determined breath, he raised the latch and went in.

The curtains were open, letting in the bright moonlight. It shone into the room, bathing everything in its ethereal glow. The fireplace stood white and proud, the soot-stained cavern within making it appear like a large mouth. The latticed windows created a dark pattern on the floorboards and rug. It fell upon the four-poster bed and exposed the empty mattress and cold blankets therein. Thomas was both confused and worried at the bed. Where was Philip? What on earth would wake the man up at such an hour?

'*Perhaps he couldn't sleep, just like you?*' he pondered.

Turning his back on the room Thomas went in search of his companion. Where could he look first? The kitchen? The study? Pursing his lips, he decided to go through the room's floor-by-floor, his hand trailing on the wall for a guide, leaving the moonlit landing behind.

The study was empty as was the dining hall and the kitchen. All of the rooms served no purpose other than making Thomas' panic creep into his mind and slowly spiral out of control. Bracing himself back against the kitchen counter, he chewed on his thumbnail. That's when his eyes caught sight of the eerier glow coming from under –a wall? Standing up, Thomas crossed the room and went over to the panel of wall that seemed as air tight as the rest.

He knocked against the wood. It was hollow.

With a frown, Thomas felt along the panel with his fingernails and finally felt a chill brush against his fingertips. There was a door there he was sure of it. Finally, his palm pressed against a smaller panel in the woodwork and the whole section of wall seemed to slide inwards. His heart in his throat, he pushed his weight against the hidden door and felt it sag to the side. Beyond, a stone spiral staircase was exposed. It would have been pitch black inside if it hadn't been for the eerie golden glow rising from somewhere below.

'*Do I really need to go down there?*' he asked himself.

'*Do you want to find Philip?*'

Biting the inside of his cheek, he stepped through the doorway and slowly descended the spiral staircase. It was tight, the stonework damp with the cold. It seemed to suck the air right out of his lungs. Why would Philip need to sneak down here during the Witching Hour? The slippers muffled his footsteps as the light grew brighter.

The staircase ended in a narrow archway. Before him there was a two foot long stone hallway which opened out to a beautifully bricked circular room. It was huge –probably as large as the dining hall up above. It looked as though it had numerous alcoves spaced around the edges expanding the general size with five other, small rooms. Almost every shelf and hollow in the walls was filled with candles of varying sizes and heights. All were lit and dribbling cream wax down the stonework.

Thomas was in awe as he took in the bookshelves, the trunks, the vials and strings of herbs and bulbs of garlic hanging from the ceiling. This room looked like something Talbot would desire in his own home. In the centre of the room there was a large copper bathtub that Thomas himself had bathed in. Candles had been arranged in a circle around the base. Feeling conscious that this place was meant to be hidden for a reason, Thomas was about to back away and retreat up the staircase when a hand shot out of the bath.

He screamed.

The pale white arm was covered in a thick, opalescent goo that seemed to slide over the skin. The nails of the hand were sharp, a dull purple colour and very long. His vision blurred in fear. Every part of his body seemed paralysed as he watched the body pull itself upright. The jaw seemed stronger and more muscular than he was used to on any human –and the way it opened exposing fangs ... it was all too much!

Thomas was dimly aware of the flagstones impacting with his skull as he passed out.

Lurching upright, Thomas panted for air, sweat staining his skin. Everything was sweet and sickly and made his head spin as he groped over the pillows for a goblet of water. What was going on? Where was he? How did he get back up to bed?

"Hey, calm down it's okay."

"NO!" he cried out, fighting weakly against the two strong arms that wrestled him down. "Get off me! Demon! Demon!"

A hand clamped down around his mouth.

"Keep your voice down!" Philip hissed in his ear. "People are trying to sleep!"

Thomas struggled against it, but Philip was far stronger than he was. Eventually he had to subside, lowering himself into the mattress, his muscles as stiff as stone as his eyes surveyed the room around him. Everything seemed normal, just as he'd left it earlier. Panting heavily against Philip's hand, Thomas squinted around the room. The curtains were closed now so it was profoundly difficult to make anything out through the gloom. Snatching Philip's hand off his mouth, Thomas struggled upright.

"How did you get me back up here?" Thomas hissed.

"What?" Philip slurred. His voice was low and sluggish, as though he'd just been asleep. He hadn't though –how could he? The moon appeared high in the sky. Not much time had passed since Thomas had found the room under the kitchen.

"How did you get me up here?" he repeated.

With a heavy sigh, Philip forced himself away from the plush pillows and leaned up. He cracked an eye open to look at the dishevelled brunette man beside him. "What in God's name are you prattling on about?"

"I saw you," Thomas intoned. "Downstairs. In that secret room under the kitchen."

Philip was silent for a moment. "Thomas, neither of us has left this room. You fell asleep on my chest. I don't think I –" a yawn fractured his thoughts. "-I don't think I'd been asleep long. You woke me up."

"But ... But I saw –"

"Thomas you were having a nightmare. That's why you woke up."

"Don't lie to me!" he snapped. He pressed his forehead to his knees and clamped his hands over his ears. "I know what I saw, Philip! I know you were performing a ritual!"

Philip groaned and grabbed Thomas' wrists and jerked them away. Hooking a finger under Thomas' jaw he turned the younger man to face him. "Thomas, it's late. I'm tired. You haven't been sleeping properly for weeks and you're having nightmares from your trauma. You need to rest."

Thomas shook his head as he mulled everything over in his

head. He'd been in that kitchen several times. He'd never seen any lights or moving panels before —so why would it suddenly appear now? His mind scrambled to try and cling to the nightmare —but the more rational part of his mind refused.

"I'm not tired anymore," he mumbled.

He was bone-tired to the point that even moving his facial muscles was causing him distress. He felt the warm weight of Philip's arm snake its way around his chest and draw his body back against the firm chest. A shiver ran down his spine as Thomas realised just how cold he was. He let himself be cradled back against the man's chest and let out a shaky sigh. It was so unfair for it to feel this warm and safe in the arms of a man who could probably rip his throat out with his fangs if he so wanted.

Philip's long, cool fingers threaded through his hair, soothing the aches away that had built up over the last few weeks. He let the blonde man knead and massage the stiff muscles up and down his back, neck, and shoulders. Even though Philip was tired, his efforts eventually relaxed Thomas to lie down properly, his eyelids heavy. By the time his hysteria had subsided, he dared to think that he was comfortable having Philip pressed firmly against his back. Sleep numbed his mind and his senses and soon the gloom grew heavier until sleep enveloped him.

The following morning Thomas awoke to bright morning sunshine with the curtains thrown open and a heavy fog clouding his mind and making him groggy. He rubbed at his eyes and grabbed his glasses before checking that everything was, in fact, as normal as he'd expected it to be. It was. Despite everything, Thomas let out a sigh of relief, feeling lightheaded as he scrambled out of bed and made short work of washing, shaving, and getting dressed for the day.

He was only in his shirt, trousers and suspenders by the time he skidded to a halt in the dining room doorway with his velveteen slippers.

Philip looked up from the newspaper as Thomas slid awkwardly into the chair adjacent to him. "You seem in a better mood," he remarked, as he lowered the paper and took a sip from his teacup.

Thomas helped himself to a cup. "I wouldn't say a better mood, but I definitely feel as though I've slept."

"I'd say I'm glad to hear that, if you hadn't woken me up at three in the morning with your nightmare."

Thomas had the decency to look sheepish. "I'm sorry about that. It just —seemed so real."

Philip reached out and gave the younger man's arm a reassuring squeeze. "Don't think on it. We all have nightmares. Even I didn't sleep well when I first moved to London."

"Really?"

"Of course not. How could I? Everything is so noisy all the time. Luckily, Stephen kept me company when he wasn't at the hospital."

"Were you and Talbot close?" Thomas asked, trying to keep his voice light as he ladled some porridge into his bowl.

"We were," Philip nodded. "However, we —drifted apart as I got older. My studies kept me busy, and his schedule kept him away from the house all hours of the night. Eventually, he signed the house over to me and got himself a room nearer the hospital."

Ah, so that was why it was a two-bedroomed house.

"Have you heard from him since he went away?"

Philip shook his head. "No. He's not the sentimental type. If there is some ground-breaking discovery or news, he'll either deliver it in person or I'll be reading a eulogy non-too-soon."

Thomas' head snapped up. "Maybe you two should make more time for one another?"

Philip snorted into his tea. "I don't see that coming to fruition I'm afraid."

"You don't know unless you try."

Narrowing his eyes, Philip hummed thoughtfully. "I think I'll continue to deprive you of sleep."

"Why is that?"

"You're sickeningly optimistic when you've had more than five hours."

Thomas tried to bite back a smile as they continued to eat breakfast. Once finished, Philip ordered the plates to be taken away. Thomas smiled gratefully up at the maid.

"So, what are your plans for the day?" Thomas asked.

"I need to head up into town and have a word with some other suppliers. Stephen asked me to check in on his stores since apparently the order I got for him last week wasn't sufficient enough." Casting a look over at his companion Philip asked, "How about you? What do you plan on doing?"

"I was going to head into town and meet up with Rufus and Daphne for dinner later tonight."

"I'll probably be heading back around the same time, would you like me to meet you?"

Thomas shook his head, "I couldn't ask you to go out of your way for me. I shouldn't be back late."

"Well if you need anything let me know before I leave." Philip gave his shoulder one last squeeze before standing up and making his way up to his bedchamber to ready himself for his departure.

When Philip left, they exchanged a brief handshake. As intimate as their night-time activities were, they didn't need to go alerting just how close they were to the house-staff. Thomas watched from the staircase window as Philip strode confidently down the street to where his carriage was waiting for him. Raking a hand through his hair, Thomas returned to his bedchamber and took all his journals into the study so he could sit down and focus on writing up his notes in a new leather-bound journal to present his findings for Talbot. He'd include the erratic, rough-draft as well, but he was sure that having a clean version for the doctors observing his work – should he ever be lucky to get that sort of privilege.

'You really do like to live in a fantasy world, don't you?' his brain admonished as he leaned back in the stiff-backed chair and stared through the open window.

As he rolled over the events of the previous evening in his mind, a sickening feeling clawed its way to the forefront of his mind. There was something about that nightmare that felt all too real. He couldn't put his finger on it but –something about it wouldn't leave him alone. Tossing down his quill he stood up from the desk and made up his mind. Enough was enough, he needed answers whether he liked what he found, or not.

Taking the stairs two at a time he made his way to the kitchen.

Keeping his ears strained for any approaching footsteps, Thomas made his way over to the wall panel. There was a long, narrow table in front of it holding bowls of fruit, a sack of potatoes and half a loaf of bread wrapped in a dishcloth. Had that been there before? Pushing the thought aside, Thomas picked up one end of the table and eased it around at an angle, so he could access the wall. He pressed against the wall half hoping that the panel would sink in and expose the hidden passageway.

Nothing happened.

He ran his fingernails along the grooves but didn't find any releases. Frowning, he found the panel he was sure he'd pressed on before. Still nothing. He pressed as hard as possible, but the wall didn't budge. Even knocking on the wall provided nothing. It didn't sound hollow anymore.

Maybe it had been a dream?

Sinking into a chair, Thomas frowned at the panel hoping beyond anything that a light would suddenly start glowing from beneath it.

"I guess I was wrong after-all," he sighed.

He ran his hands through his hair before dragging himself to his feet and replacing the table back against the wall and the utensils and food on top of it. Casting one last look over his shoulder, Thomas resigned himself to working on his findings for the remainder of the day, only taking a break to have some of the chowder the maid made him.

That night Thomas was the first one to arrive at the restaurant. He'd taken some extra time with his appearance that evening; he'd paid to have his hair cut and a professional shave at the barber's shop. He'd used some sort of wax that Philip seemed to favour in his hair to keep it neat and from falling into his eyes. He'd even managed to persuade the housekeeper to let him borrow one of Philip's older, small suits so that he didn't look too out-of-place in the refined restaurant. He couldn't deny he still felt out of his depth. He was surprised that Rufus had booked such a place for dinner, but there was nothing that could be done. Daphne was a fine young woman, and she deserved the best.

Movement by the entrance drew his attention up from his wine glass. Rufus and Daphne were just handing their coats to the young steward, before making their way over to the table. Thomas smiled at the perfect picture they made; Rufus looked well-groomed compared to how he used to look when they'd studied together, even his red hair seemed to glow with a coppery brilliance.

In comparison, Daphne was an angel; her soft caramel

coloured hair was curled into shiny ringlets that spiralled down her back and over her shoulders, her warm brown eyes gleamed and her bright blue dress seemed to leech all the colour out of her surroundings.

She was radiant.

"I'm surprised to see you here first," Rufus remarked good-naturedly as he drew out Daphne's chair for her to settle into.

"You and me both," Thomas replied. "I had nothing else to do today so I made sure to prepare myself."

"It's good to see you again, Thomas," Daphne smiled brightly as she shared a look with Rufus. "It feels like ages since we were able to get together like this."

A waiter came over and took their order before bringing over a bottle of wine.

Once everyone had been poured a glass, Rufus turned his attention to his friend. "So, tell me Thomas, how have Talbot's lectures been since all these grizzly murders have occurred?"

"Rufus!" Daphne hissed, her eyes scanning the occupants of the nearby tables.

"It's okay, darling, all of London and beyond knows of this man. I just want to know how Thomas' been fairing when he has to go home in the early hours of the morning alone."

"It's actually been okay," Thomas placated. "My friend, Philip, does a lot of business in the evenings so when he's able, he accompanies me home."

"Doesn't Philip fear for his own safety?" Daphne asked with a frown.

"He has a carriage that he has stationed near my place, so that when I'm home safely, all he has to do is walk down the road and get driven home."

He opted to leave out the part where he had been residing with Philip for the better part of a week.

"Oh! That's clever of him," Daphne beamed. "Really, it is a wonder those classes are even held during such terrible times."

"Well, Talbot is out of town now," Rufus stated. "So all his classes are postponed until he returns."

Thomas opened his mouth to state that Dr. Stanhope had in fact taken over the night classes, but seeing how his friends deemed him '*safe and sound*' for the foreseeable fortnight, he didn't have the heart to shatter their illusion.

Their food arrived and they commenced eating.

By the time their dessert had arrived they were all rosy-cheeked and feeling rather merry. Pouring himself another glass of wine, Thomas pointed his glass at the happy couple. "So, when should I expect a glossy invitation to your nuptials?"

Daphne flushed. Rufus went red too, however he also seemed to swell with pride. "Actually, we were thinking of sometime in the New Year."

"Really?" Thomas felt as though his face were too animated. "When, exactly? I don't want to be tired from these lectures and not able to attend."

"We were thinking of sometime in February," Daphne said.

"I shall definitely make sure I have plenty of time off to prepare myself."

"Oh, you have to give a speech as well!" Rufus chimed.

"Oh, yes! Thomas you must!"

"A speech?" he frowned. "Why?"

"You're going to be my best man of course!" the redhead stated.

Thomas felt his jaw drop. "What? Rufus I'm honoured! Are you sure you think I'm the best person for the job?"

"Of course you are!"

"Thomas, we both want you to be involved," Daphne assured him, resting her small hand over his own.

Thomas squeezed hers in return and clapped Rufus on the shoulder with his free hand. "I'm sincerely honoured to be your best man and hope that it will be the happiest day of your lives."

To say that Thomas was lighter than air when he left the restaurant later that night, was an understatement. He bade Daphne and Rufus a pleasant evening at the bridge, braced himself against the brisk breeze that rippled across the Thames' surface, and tried to focus his mind and vision on the route back to Philip's home. He almost wished he'd taken one of Philip's canes in order to twirl it around with a jaunty little jig to his step. Alas, there was no such '*jig*' as the lamplight around him was swallowed up when he stepped into a street of narrower buildings. The wine had left him feeling light-headed as he raked a hand through his hair, noting how feverish he felt.

At least there'd be a warm bedchamber awaiting him at Philip's.

As he wove his way through the narrow backstreets and houses, he couldn't help but feel apprehension seep into his bones as he missed a step and felt himself step into a momentary nothingness. It caused his heart and stomach to lurch. He had to brace himself against a lamppost on order to regain his breathing. Rubbing a hand on the back of his neck, he counted to ten over and over in his head whilst drawing in air.

"Okay, you're nearly there. Just a few more streets and you'll be safe."

His advice felt hollow to his own ears. Straightening up from the lamppost he adjusted his dinner jacket before making his way along the street. The houses loomed over his head. They seemed to sag inwards under the pressure of the grime that coated them. He couldn't judge the people living in there, though. Up until a month ago he'd been one of them.

'*I really want to get home to Philip*,' he found himself thinking as the sound of the Thames faded into the distance. '*I need to feel his arms around me.'*

He would never be able to pinpoint the moment when he'd started feeling envious of Rufus and Daphne's relationship. It had happened at some point during the meal; he watched how they interacted with one another –how Daphne would place her hand on Rufus's forearm or brush a strand of hair behind his ears, or the way he would kiss the knuckles of her hand affectionately –it all reminded him of the things he would never be able to have. He hadn't even known he'd wanted any of those things until tonight.

Maybe they could have that if Philip gave his house staff the night off?

Just as he was mulling over that particular possibility, something crashed into his side.

He cried out as he collided with the pavement. The effect of the wine made the sky and street spin out of control. He rolled onto the side and threw up in the gutter. He tried to brace himself up on his forearms, but a rough hand grabbed the back of his neck and shoulder.

"Stay down, Thomas! Keep still and don't make any sudden noises!"

Thomas froze as the pressure disappeared from his shoulder. He tried to keep still all too aware of how clumsy even breathing felt in that moment. A guttural roar resounded through the black street, sending horror racing down his spine and spiking through the alcoholic haze in his brain.

Who had spoken to him?

How did he know his name?

He didn't recognise the voice –he barely knew anyone in London.

Rolling onto his back he winced when he realised everything was blurred. He'd lost his glasses. There was the scuffing of feet, yells, and the sound of something being struck over and over again. Another howl pierced the white noise buzzing in his ears. It resounded throughout every house and surfed across the Thames. It was like the beast wanted its voice heard all the way to the moon itself!

Thomas was frozen to the pavement.

He could just about make out the shapes of a tall man in a black cloak with a cane –or was it a sword? –striking at the tall, greyish brown beast that lunged, leered, and snapped its foaming jaws at the newcomer. Was this ... the murderer? The maniac? Thomas wasn't sure whom he should fear most!

As slowly as possible, he groped his way blindly across the pavement, sliding himself into a dark alley. His breathing sounded like gunfire in his own ears. Edging out, he ran his hands behind him against the wall as a guide. Panic and sweat fermented through his borrowed suit and the taste of fresh vomit clung to this teeth and tongue.

What a waste of a meal.

The acidic taste of blood and wine pooled around his teeth. His foot caught on a loose cobble, and it skittered off out of his bubble of blurred vision. The snarling beast seemed to stop for a moment. Thomas' heart stopped. Without thinking, he turned on his heel and ran, completely ignoring the yells that followed him down the street.

"THOMAS NO! YOU CAN'T OUTRUN IT!"

The thing that would forever scar him was how close he could feel the beast behind him, almost as though its wet breath steamed against the back of his neck. And the howl – he'd never forget how his blood curdled at the sound.

That was what his nightmares were made of.

Wednesday 3rd October 1888.

Philip banged the doors against the wall, barely pausing for breath before tearing up the second staircase on his left. Taking them two at a time, he hurried to the second floor, sweat soaking the underarms of his shirt. Hurrying through the ghastly yellow light, he felt his senses spinning as he finally made it to the third-floor ward. Panting heavily, he counted the black painted numbers on the doors before he found the one he needed.

The glass rattled as he threw the door open.

"Sir! Our patients are rest–"

"You!" he sneered, grabbing the white-robed doctor by the lapels. "Where the damn hell is Thomas Segdon?"

"Sir, I'm afraid we cannot divulge a patient's information –"

"Did I stutter?" Philip snapped, shaking the wiry man. "Now tell me where Thomas Segdon is!"

Before the sputtering man could utter another syllable, a short, rotund man with horn-rimmed glasses waddled into the doorway. "Are you asking after Mr. Segdon?"

Releasing the doctor, Philip whirled around. "Where. Is. He?" he spat.

The portly man inclined his head, "Follow me, sir. He's just down the hall."

Philip stormed after the man in question. As they marched along the grotty looking floor, the older man spoke to Philip; "Are you a relative of Mr. Segdon?"

"He is my friend," Philip bit out.

"Then where are his family?"

"He doesn't have any."

It was a bald-faced lie but Philip couldn't run the risk of

being denied visitation rights on the minor technicality that he wasn't related by blood. As Talbot was out-of-town, the responsibility of Thomas' health fell upon his shoulders. Not that he wanted it any other way. He felt beyond accountable for the younger man's current condition –whatever that may be. They came to a stop outside a door.

The man turned to peer over his glasses at Philip. "I must warn you, sir, that his condition hasn't improved much from when he came to us this morning."

"What condition?"

"It appears he was attacked sometime last night, and an older gentleman brought him in."

Philip's head snapped up. "An older man? What did this man look like?"

"I wouldn't know, sir, I wasn't on duty at the time. It should be in the police report."

"The police were called?"

"Of course, sir. Your friend was attacked. It needed reporting."

Philip nodded. Their conversation was starting to circulate. "So, what is his current state?" he asked, managing to keep his voice level. "Is he awake? Can I go in and see him?"

"I'll need you to sign some –"

"I don't believe you understood what I said," Philip cut in, seething. His hands were clenched tightly around the head of his cane. "I'm going in to see my friend. After, I am going to the police. If you waste *any* more of my time, there's going to be another casualty."

The man swallowed, his fat throat bobbing awkwardly. "Sir –"

Philip ignored him. He simply turned on his heels and marched through the door onto the ward.

As soon as he caught sight of Thomas, his heart stopped

in his chest. He looked so pale, as white as the sheets he was lying on, his glasses were missing. He looked simply absurd without them. Thomas belonged with glasses. It was like a fish and water.

Draping his cloak over his arm he strode towards the brunette's bedside and sank down into the waiting chair. Up close the extent of the damage was worse –much worse. He sucked a breath in through his teeth and cupped his face in his hands. He didn't know how long he stayed in that position, hunched over in the seat with the sounds of the hospital milling around behind him.

Thomas remained motionless on the bed. The right side of his face was wrapped in gauze and his exposed eye was shining dark purple under the harsh lights. His wounded arm was bandaged even thicker and resting in a sling out of the way, so doctors and nurses had access to his body. He seemed to be breathing well enough on his own, but then Philip had no idea of the extent of the damage that had been done. Philip didn't even know what had actually happened to his companion.

'*You need to speak to the police as soon as possible. This nonsense has gone on far enough!*'

Gripping his hands in his lap, he drew in deep breaths. He needed to keep his temper under control. Seeing Thomas practically lifeless was making him irritable and feverishly angry. There was no real way he could protect Thomas, not from the outside world. Maybe being in the hospital, recovering, was the best place for him. It was incredibly difficult simply sitting down and letting the world carry-on as though everything was normal beyond those walls.

Swallowing thickly, he leaned back in the chair and watched with dull eyes as nurses bustled in and out of the ward. Pressing his lips together, he checked the charts at the end of Thomas' bed, but it didn't tell him too much, other than his wounds were mostly superficial.

Clipping the chart back on the bedrail, he flexed his aching shoulder muscles and straightened up. There was no use waiting around. The sooner he got down to the police station, the better.

On his way out of the ward, he stopped by the desk at the end of the hallway. The ward matron raised her eyebrows at him as he cleared his throat.

"Can I help you?" she asked.

"I want you to make sure that Mr. Segdon receives the top quality of care until I return."

"I'm sorry, sir, but the hospital is full of patients. I cannot prioritise one over hundreds of others."

Glaring, Philip dipped his hand into his pocket. Unfolding a one-pound note, he slapped it on the counter.

"See to it," he demanded, before turning on his heel and striding from the hospital.

Down at the police station Philip couldn't help but feel a smidgen of pity at the men who willingly came into the narrow, dank building every day for around fifty years. They seemed to want to be branded as heroes yet at the same time, it wasn't the nicest place to stare at when the streets were quiet. Being a patrol officer didn't seem appealing on any level to the blonde.

He was sat in a stiff, battered chair waiting for the officer who had attended Thomas' case to come and speak with him. Although as far as anyone seemed concerned, the incident had been reported and no one else had been at the scene, so who on earth could they arrest for the assault? Thomas was in hospital now and was recovering from the vicious attack so, as far as they seemed concerned, their job was done.

All that was left was filing the paperwork.

Philip did his best to reign in his impatience, but it was

becoming increasingly difficult. He found himself tapping his feet, his cane and constantly checking his pocket watch.

"Mr. Ridley?"

His head snapped up. A wiry man with a pencil thin moustache and too much wax in his receding hair beckoned him from a doorway just behind the main desk. Standing up from the stiff chair, Philip followed the man into the tight, airless room. The walls were the colour of the underside of a bridge, and it turned his stomach to even imagine what was behind the tall filing cabinets. Settling down in the chair, Philip eyed the man as he shuffled behind the tight desk and sat down, the chair creaking with his weight.

"So ... Mr. Ridley, is it?" he frowned.

Philip glared at him.

"What is it I can do for you today?"

"I need to know what happened to Mr. Thomas Segdon last night," Philip stated. "I believe an incident was reported sometime in the early hours of this morning."

"Ah, yes. Young mister Segdon. Yes, we got the incident report come in at around midnight last night."

"I need to know what happened, exactly."

"I'm afraid we cannot release that information, sir," the officer said.

"Why not?" Philip bit out. "And if you dare breathe a word about how 'you're not a relative' I will be sure to file another report about an officer being brutally attacked in his office by an unknown assailant."

The officer tensed and straightened in the chair, "Sir, are you threatening an officer of the law?"

Philip stretched his mouth into an ugly, thin smile. "What gave it away?"

They glared at one another over the desk.

"I think I need to go and get my supervisor," the greasy-haired man said. He stood up from his desk and edged his way around the room towards the door. It banged shut behind him, leaving Philip along in the suffocating little hole of an office.

After only a few minutes of silent stillness, the door opened once again and someone with a vague air of authority came in and replaced the greasy-haired weasel. He was a broad man with muttonchops and a thick greying moustache on his lip. His brown suit looked almost vibrant compared to the dingy walls.

"So, I take it that you're the '*arrogant blonde prat with no regards for the law*'?" the man asked, with a wry smile.

"That would be me, yes," Philip replied.

"Philip, we've talked about this. You can't harass the green ones."

"I'm well aware, Reuben, but I have more pressing matters on my mind at the moment."

"Ah. Regarding ye little friend?"

"Yes. He was attacked last night and still hasn't woken up from his ordeal. He's under heavy medication and seeing as he had no relatives in London, I am his sole carer. Any information that can help him needs to come to me immediately."

"Philip, even if I wanted to let you have that sort of control over him, you know I can't. We need to locate any relatives he might have."

"He's an only child from a small family that live up North."

Reuben scribbled a note down in the file. "I'm sorry, Philip."

He actually did appear sorry, which was worse than anything else Philip had heard today. Running a hand down his smooth chin, Philip bit his bottom lip and looked down at the file under Officer Harper's large, meat-cleaver hands. "Can I at least have a copy of the file?"

"Philip –"

"You need to send a copy to the hospital anyway. Just let me be the one to deliver it."

Reuben hesitated.

Philip lowered his voice and leaned closer over the desk. "You know I'm going to find out one way or another, Reuben, so just let save us both a lot of trouble and let me be the one to deliver it. The more information that they have, the better chance they have of making sure he lives."

Harper's beady eyes gleaned in the dim light. "It was that serious?"

"It still is. His life is hanging by a thread Reuben. I want him to have the best fighting chance he can get." He paused for a beat. "Please?"

The tall, broad man remained still for a moment, deliberating on what such an action would have on his career. He was already a superintendent. He was at a comfortable middle-ground and –if the current murders were solved –he could be up for a promotion. Then again, if anything came back to bite him in the arse it would no doubt be this. Lacing his fingers together, he leaned his elbows on the desk and stared directly at the man across from him.

"If I let you have a copy of this report, for your own records, you are to burn it as soon as you have memorised the information."

Philip nodded, his heart beating heavily in his ears.

"On top of that, I should expect a high-praising letter to my superiors about my aiding you along with a form of Christmas bonus."

Philip smirked, keeping his voice low. "Would twenty pounds be enough?"

Harper's eyes nearly bulked out of his head. It was so off-putting hearing rich people shrug at the idea of such money. He could still see people deliberate as to whether or not to buy a pennydreadful. Trying to remain calm, he shrugged, throwing hefty shadows against the drab walls.

"Whatever amount you deem acceptable, Mr. Ridley, that is entirely upon your head." Opening the file, he took out a sheet of paper and slid it across the desk. "Guard this with your life and burn it as soon as you're able."

"What about the copy you need to send to the hospital?" Philip frowned.

"I'll make another one."

"Won't that arouse suspicion?"

"I'll just say that the incident was traumatising, and the paperwork got filed incorrectly. It's still fairly fresh, so it shouldn't be strange to anyone."

Philip took the papers and folded it into his cloak pocket. "I appreciate this, Reuben."

"Don't forget, Philip. You owe me."

Standing up, the blonde man inclined his head. "I'm sure you'll collect it."

"Maybe I should yell you out of the office?" Harper raised his eyebrows in amusement.

"Fine. I know you'll want to gloat that you have some dregs of authority left," Philip smirked.

Harper smirked as he leaned back in his chair. He indicated for Philip to leave. As soon as the door was open, his deep voice boomed forth from his throat.

"DON'T EVER TRY AND THREATEN ME, RIDLEY! OR THE NEXT TIME I SEE YOU IT'LL BE IN THE MORGUE!"

Philip gave a subtle wink before turning on his heel and making a dramatic exit with lots of door-slamming and snarled insults over his shoulder.

Back at his own home, he was sat in his study by the window with a steaming cup of tea and a teapot sat in front of him, the police report splayed out on the desk before his eyes. It wasn't even much of a report, not compared to the ones he'd seen. He'd seen newspaper articles with more detail and depth to it. It was barely even a page worth of information, and he was making sure to read through it over and over just to make sure that the words sank into his brain.

'**DATE: WEDNESDAY 3RD OCTOBER 1888**

TIME OF INCIDENT: 00:37

NAME OF VICTIM: MR. THOMAS SEGDON

AGE OF VICTIM: 17 YEARS OLD

SCENE OF THE INCIDENT:

The young man was claimed to have been found splayed out on the end of the road leading towards Whitechapel road. The victim appeared to have several abrasions to his legs and back, an already wounded left arm and his glasses [found later about inspection] had fallen and were smashed beyond repair. He looked to have a lot of blood and bruising around his face, a cut running over his left eye.

The incident was reported by an older gentleman [approximately thirty-eight years old] with black hair, moustache and a walking cane. He identified himself simply as Mr. Black [name most likely a pseudonym. To be confirmed at later date]. Mr. Black gave a brief statement off the attack and fled the scene before emergency services were able to attend.
Mr. Segdon was hurried to St. Bartholomew's hospital and was attended by physician, Dr. Anderson.'

That was all it said. Even the name 'MR. BLACK' was an obvious dead-end. Something about the entire thing made Philip's insides turn. Last night was a full moon and the wounds appeared consistent with that of the werewolf that seemed to be lurking in the shadow of every house.

Resting his head in his hand, he couldn't help but feel utterly lost in that moment. This would have been the perfect opportunity to go to his uncle for advice and get a better insight into these events. He tried to shy away from that mythological side of affairs ever since Stephen had gotten a promotion and been able to teach lectures in the dead of night. That had all started five years prior, and somehow it had all intertwined to this point.

He took a sip of tea and instantly regretted it when his stomach cramped.

That was happening far too often lately. Maybe he needed to travel up North and drag Stephen back down in order to give him a medical diagnosis. Smoothing down his dishevelled blonde hair, Philip read through the brief report one last time, before taking a box of matches out of his desk drawer, striking a match and holding it under the corner of the creamy paper. It caught alight easily, spreading quick and hungry until he had to drop it into a crumbled heap in his teacup.

Smoke plumed up into the air. It scratched at his throat and made his sudden thirst for more aconite tea. '*No,*' he thought. '*I need to go back and see Thomas.*'

His body was fighting against the urges though. His bones were aching as though he'd run a hundred miles in his sleep, his brain was fuzzing at the edges, and he felt as though his teeth were floating and his nails were ready to wriggle loose and fall out. His chest felt cramped as though there were two extra lungs inside, crushing the life out of his primary organs. It was an indescribably horrible feeling but there was no form of medication he could take that had any effect on it.

It was an ailment from his childhood that refused to disappear. Stephen helped manage the aches and pains with the tea and sometimes balms when blemishes appeared with no memorable cause, however even those were losing their effect. The recent events happening in London weren't helping matters either. His worry for Thomas was even worse, growing every moment he didn't see those bright eyes. He knew he was being overbearing; he dreaded the thought of someone so perfectly endearing slip through his fingers.

'Go to him!'

That settled matters.

He didn't bother making preparations for dinner as he fastened his cloak around his throat, snatched up his cane and made his way out of the house to where his coach awaited. Barking his orders to the driver, he was suddenly rolling on his way towards the hospital. The ride took no longer than twenty minutes, the cobblestones making his stomach lurch. As he stepped out, he took in several deep breaths of the cool, damp air before marching his way across the street and in through the tall, double oak doors.

Thankfully, no one gave him any hassle this time when he asked for Thomas Segdon's room. There was only one problem –Thomas wasn't in the same room when he got up to the third floor. Seething, Philip stormed out of the ward and, upon seeing the fat doctor from earlier that morning, he charged towards him and snatched the front of his robes.

"WHERE IS HE?"

"M-Mr. M-Ridley I –"

"TELL ME WHERE HE IS!"

"Sir! Release him!" another doctor snapped, grabbing at Philip's arm.

It took another two doctors to pry his hands from the

rotund man –whose name he later learned was Stanhope. The second doctor who'd manhandled him, roughly took Philip to one side, and demanded to know what was going on and if he continued to behave in such an unruly way again, they'd have to physically remove him from the building.

Philip glared down at the doctor. "Tell me where Thomas Segdon has been moved."

The doctor straightened up as though someone had dropped snow down his collar. "He was given money by a benefactor. He has been upgraded to a private ward up on the fifth floor."

"What?" Philip hissed, rage pricking like ants in his veins. He wasn't allowed to put any money towards Thomas' life or well-being, yet a stranger was doing so, to what end? Showing Philip up? To make him appear uncaring and unfeeling towards the young man he'd kill to protect?

He froze at the thought, but only for a moment.

Yes, he'd kill for the boy.

"You said the fifth floor, yes?" he repeated, his breath harsh and stinging in his throat.

"Yes."

"Take me to him."

"Sir –"

"You either take me to him, or I'll see you never practice medicine again, do I make myself clear?"

The doctor pursed his lips but, thankfully, didn't argue anymore. Instead, he grasped his clipboard to his chest and motioned for Philip to follow him. Two flights of stairs later and the older man departed, leaving Philip outside the door of a room with grim, grey light bathing the room within. Drawing in a deep breath, Philip pushed the door open and went in.

Thomas' condition hadn't improved much from that morning. The dressings of his wounds seemed fresher, and he appeared to have more charts and medication to be given at various intervals throughout the day. He didn't have that before. Apparently good health was something that money *could* buy.

Feeling envious, Philip settled into the plush chair at the head of the bed and read through the charts and lists strapped to Thomas' clipboard. On the very last page there was the information sheet about Thomas being liable for such a space, the amount it would cost weekly –a surprisingly affordable amount, even if one was on a tighter budget – and the official signature of the Head of Medicine and the benefactor themselves. Philip felt blood drain out of his head when he saw the signature and read the printed name underneath.

Mr. X. Holland

The script was neat and swift. If it was an alias, it was well-versed and practised. Philip sat there for hours afterwards, fingers pressed to his lip in thought, mulling over the evidence mounting up. Mr. Holland had reported the incident, maybe had even borne witness to it. He clearly returned in order to give Thomas as much comfort as possible. That meant he would most likely return a third time.

Philip prepared himself for a long wait.

Saturday 6th October 1888.

It took three whole days before there was any improvement to Philip's state of mind. Three whole days of being at the hospital as long as physically possible at Thomas' bedside, just waiting for the day this Mr. Holland appeared. At around midday on the third day, Philip was just reading that morning's paper when the door to the private ward creaked open. Expecting it to be a nurse or a doctor, Philip looked up with a bored expression, and froze.

"You?" he exhaled, standing up and coming to stand between Thomas and the tall man.

"Good afternoon, Philip. I must say I expected you to leave at some point."

"I did," Philip bit out. "I go home for a few hours every day."

"I see. Not during the evenings?"

"No," he narrowed his eyes. "Why?"

"No reason," Holland shrugged and tucked his tinted glasses into the pocket of his overcoat. "Merely a question."

Philip straightened up, crossing his arms. "Why are you here?"

"I came to see young Mr. Segdon here and to examine his condition."

"Why should his health concern you?"

Holland narrowed his eyes. "I think you'll find *that* is none of *your* concern, Mr. Ridley."

Philip sneered. "As long as he is alive, it *is* my concern. Now get out of here before I have you removed."

"You're not in a position to make threats," Holland smirked. "I'm the one paying for this private room, need I remind you."

"Your money is useless here. Stop paying if you like, I can

easily afford this ward without your charity!"

Holland blinked slowly. "What's with this anger, Philip? Surely you have no objections to family helping you in dire times?"

Philip bristled at the word. Any family he'd had had turned their back on him after they'd buried the butler. From that moment on his father made a point of trying not to hire men. However, with an estate as big as theirs, men were needed to do the intensive labour. So, it was decided that Philip would be shipped off South, to live in London. In a way, he was lucky that Stephen wasn't disgusted with him the way his own parents were.

Maybe it was because they weren't blood related therefore Talbot had nothing to lose by associating with Philip and any rumour that may have followed him like a hissing shadow. The thought was of little comfort as Stephen was still out of town.

Clenching his fists tightly under his arms, Philip steadied his emotions as best he could. He felt weak, flustered, and sweaty but he needed to be strong for Thomas. The kid needed someone to protect him. They stared at one another for a while, the tension sparking like lightning between them. Philip held his gaze, unyielding. Eventually, Xander turned away.

"Very well. I'll take my leave." He turned towards the door. It creaked open. Turning his head slightly he let his eyes scan Philip up and down. "I'd be careful if I were you, Philip."

"Why?"

"I have a friend with similar –*ailments* –as you. Tell me; has it been particularly hard for you over the last few days?"

"I've just found out my friend was attacked and left to die in a sewer!" Philip spat. "Of *course*, it's been hard for me!"

"I see," was all he said as he replaced his tinted glasses on his nose. He patted his top hat firmly into place and strode out of the ward.

Philip remained standing. Despite getting rid of the man, he didn't feel as though he'd won that argument. He clenched and loosened his fists. He ground his back teeth together – why were they sensitive? –and turned his attention back to Thomas. God, he looked so small lying in that bed. Philip felt his stomach squirm as he sank back down into the chair and rubbed a hand down his face. They couldn't carry on like this. Thomas needed to go somewhere safe. London was far from safe. Despite Philip's best efforts the kid had still been in harm's way whenever he set foot outside after dark.

It was as though he attracted the attention of dark and ominous beings.

'*You need to send him home, back to where he came from,*' his brain hissed in his ear. He tilted his head to the side,stricken. He didn't want Thomas to go anywhere. It'd make him paranoid and manic. '*You need to let him go back to his safe, boring life in the country. He'll have a better chance at growing old that way.*'

What was the point of growing old if they didn't enjoy the life they lived?

His heart felt like a ball of lead in his chest, crushing everything else beneath it as it sank lower and lower, suffocating him. Biting the inside of his cheek, he walked over to the wash basin in the corner. There was a small, square mirror above it that caught the light. Philip cast a brief glance at himself and almost jumped.

He looked *ghastly.*

His hair was lank, and his skin was a grubby reddish colour. His eyes were flooded with red veins and his lips were pale and dry. He rinsed his face with water and scrubbed his skin raw. It wasn't a pleasant experience, but he couldn't walk around during the day looking as he did. He dabbed his face down on the dry flannel that had been left on the edge of the sink. The rinse-down hadn't done much to alter his appearance. His shoulders sagged in defeat.

"I can't let you stay here," he murmured to himself as he stroked Thomas' uninjured hands. It was limp and cool to the touch. He gave it a tight squeeze and hesitated before kissing the knuckles. "I'll take care of it, okay?" he murmured quietly. "I'll be back soon."

With one last look over his shoulder, Philip left the ward.

Thomas awoke to an empty hospital room and the sound of someone bustling around his bedside. His vision was blurry and seemed narrower than usual. His arms felt too heavy to move and his mouth was papery and raw. Every part of him was desperate for moisture. He parted his lips and tried to call out for help, for water, for anything –but the only thing that came out was a quiet, hiss of breath. He tried shifting his body about, but everything felt heavy and wrong. Even his brain was screaming from the inferno inside his skull.

He didn't know how long he was in that state of hazy limbo before someone noticed he was awake.

Two nurses and a doctor swooped into the room and without moments of blurry white movement, Thomas felt his body being forced up into a sitting position. His joints and bones seemed to creak with the effort. It made his head spin. He needed to vomit –but the acidic taste would blister this throat.

"*...Okay now lie him back down ...*"

Thomas felt the pressure on his back weaken and his body eased back against the pillows. He tried to move his mouth, but he wasn't entirely sure if the nerves in his jaw were responding properly. He soon felt like the room was empty, vacuous around him. It made him feel uncomfortable. He wasn't even sure if he was hungry. Everything seemed to start spinning a little if he tried to focus on it for too long. Whenever he tried to clear his mind, images of that night set his brain on fire.

Eventually his eyes drifted ...

Time no longer made any sense in his mind.

There were so many fragments of time, both bathed in daylight and suffocated under nightfall. It depressed him to think that he'd been there for hours or days or –Heaven forbid! –months without realising. It made him feel sick and burning. His clothing clung to him and he was sure that his bedding hadn't been changed in ... however long it'd been since he'd last woken up.

Suffice to say he only had one thought; to see Philip.

Since he wasn't there to visit him, Thomas could only assume that he hadn't really been awake for that long. Philip would have come and visited him at some point surely. He itched to see the familiar flash of blonde hair and clear grey eyes. He needed that familiarity to anchor him down. He needed the brush of skin against his own, the feeling of someone looking at him as opposed to through him.

He was suddenly aware of how the corpses must have felt.

The fifth time he woke up he managed to get someone's attention. They began bringing him meals –just soup and a small piece of bread that made his jaw ache when he chewed – along with water to drink. Something more routine made him better able to track the days. It only helped a little though, because if he didn't respond to them, they'd simply leave and take the food away with them.

On the seventh time he woke up he was able to remain awake for a few hours, as boring as they were. Philip still hadn't come to visit, and with the regular food and water he was gradually getting the use of his voice back. The nurses had given him sympathetic looks and smiled when he'd asked after Philip. None had heard from him, but his name was now on their registry for the room payments, so Thomas could stay for as long as he needed to recover.

Thomas didn't know how to feel about that.

The twelfth time he woke up Thomas was able to glean some more information. His chest still ached tightly that Philip still hadn't bothered to show up and see if he was okay. It made bitterness and resentment grow inside his chest. Although all the empty hours sat up in bed gave him a lot of time to think over the work he'd done. It was all very well and good explaining what he observed but to go the extra mile and find a cure –if that was even possible. He was sure he'd been so close to something before he'd gone out with Rufus and Daphne.

That's when another seed grew in his chest.

Why had neither of them come to visit him? Did no one know he was in the hospital? Had they kept his attack out of the paper? He needed to remember to ask the nurses when they came back with his evening meal.

The only thing he could think about in the meantime was various ways to try and use aconite in some remedies that might help with the complications that came with turning into a werewolf. He mulled over the possibilities, trying to remember as much as he could from his journals.

'*The transformation of a wolf occurs at the full moon of each month. The wolf ruptures organs and shatters bones and break the skin. Perhaps a cure that makes the skin strong enough to withstand breakage.*'

A seal perhaps? Silver infused bandages? Or would it be something to do with ointment? Or a balm?

'*An ointment would sink through to the skin and perhaps even into the bones. It would need to be incredibly long-lasting and sustainable.'*

Would that be enough? Generally, most medication needed to be injected into muscles and absorbed through the stomach. Perhaps he needed something digestible as well? He gnawed on his chapped lips and wondered what other things could combine to make a possible cure.

What if it didn't work?

There was always that risk. That it wouldn't work. However, if they couldn't cure the wolf ... would it be possible at the very least, to sedate it? Perhaps if he could invent some form of sedating drug that would make the wolf less dangerous –at least that would be a start toward finding a cure. That was surely helpful to the world.

Imagine; a tame werewolf.

It made him feel flushed with excitement. If only he wasn't stuck in the hospital, then maybe he could get some work done.

Two weeks.

That was how long he had been in the hospital. He felt sick to his stomach when he was finally told that, if he was fighting fit and had somewhere to go, he could rejoin the outside world. The only frustration was that it took another two days after being told said good news, that he needed to be fitted for some new glasses as his old ones had been crushed.

He begrudgingly got the new glasses and had to resign himself to wearing an eyepatch underneath it for another week.

On the day of his discharge Thomas was relieved to see a shock of sleek red hair peeking out over the crowd. As soon as Rufus caught sight of him, his freckled face split open into a large grin. Crossing the tiled room, he offered Thomas a cane to help with his walking.

"How are you feeling?" he asked as he held the door open. Together they walked down the stone steps of St. Bartholomew's.

Thomas eyed the tall man warily. "I'm feeling okay. A little dizzy now and again."

"That'll pass in time."

They walked in silence until they got down to the pavement.

"Why did neither you nor Daphne visit me?" Thomas asked. The anger he felt bubbling in his chest was sickening. Being alone in that hospital had made one thing very clear to him over the last two weeks; he was completely alone in this world. He had to fight his own battles.

"Daphne doesn't like hospitals and I've been taking my doctoral exams early. I'm sorry I couldn't make time to see you. I did write you; didn't you get them?"

"Evidently not," Thomas ground out.

"I truly am sorry. I came today to see you and was told you were being discharged. I waited around for you."

Thomas supposed that was something.

"Would you like to go for something to eat?" Rufus asked as they walked through the dim October sunshine. "I don't doubt that you've had enough of hospital food."

Over lunch they talked about all the things that had happened to Rufus and Daphne over the last fortnight. Wanting to become a fully licensed doctor before they were married, both of their parents had contributed Rufus to getting extra tuition and studying. It had been intense and had taken a lot of hours –sometimes even going on until midnight which had left the man ragged for his own classes.

Thomas secretly thought that it was somewhat justified.

Rufus was going to be taking his final exams that Friday afternoon. He was tense and stressing about it, but he was also excited. At this point, he almost didn't care what field he was tossed into, as long as he was a certified doctor, he would have some esteem in the new social circles he'd be entering, via Daphne's family. Thomas listened as attentively as possible, his mind often wondering to his own dilemmas. He needed all his notes to start properly formulating a plan. He needed to experiment with various ingredients and make a series of antidotes and balms —and noting their recipes —so he'd be able to eventually test them. Although testing would require an actual ... werewolf.

The notion put him off his —rather small —main course.

They discussed the upcoming wedding over dessert. Somehow, sweet cakes and tea were much more appealing to Thomas in that moment. It seemed to melt like caramel over his nerves. When asked about what he had been up to before being attacked and hospitalised, Thomas' mind drew a blank. A lot of his memory was still distorted between what was insomnia-induced hallucinations and what was real. Eventually he settled on a small truth.

"I think I may have met someone," he said.

"Oh?" Rufus paused, his fork hovering just in front of his face. "Anyone I know?"

Thomas had to catch himself before he said Philip's name. "No, no you don't know them. It's relatively new so I don't want to spoil things by declaring it to anyone just yet."

The redhead nodded sagely. "I understand. I was nervous when I started courting Daphne because —well! You've seen her! She's so far out of my league I'm still having to pinch myself in the mornings to make sure I'm not dreaming."

Thomas knew that feeling all too well, too. He often couldn't believe everything had happened in the dark of night, until Philip's hand lingered a little too long on his back, or his leg. A tremor ran down his spine.

He needed to see Philip.

Thankfully, Rufus had another study session to get to. Once

he had paid, Rufus helped Thomas up and they exited into the street. Thomas watched, leaning heavily on his borrowed cane, as the redhead man climbed up into a coach and was wheeled away into on-coming traffic. Left in the afternoon sunlight, Thomas drew in several shallow breaths, his body rejecting the food that he'd just eaten. He clamped his jaw shut in order to keep it down. Eventually, he managed to make his way in the direction of Philip's house.

Once there, Thomas hobbled out onto the pavement, the cane almost buckling under his weight. He'd needed to come here anyway, considering his belongings were still there. How had it been two weeks, when everything else still looked the same? His stomach churned uncomfortably inside him. The house loomed before him; tall, white and majestic –exactly what Thomas thought of Philip when he was kneeling over him, glowing in the moonlight. Shaking his head clear, Thomas stumbled awkwardly up the pale grey steps and knocked on the door. He felt as though a hundred eyes were peering through curtains and burning the back of his neck.

There was no answer.

He knocked again, louder and longer. It *was* a large house, after-all.

Eventually, Mr. Jenson the manservant answered the door. He regarded Thomas with his same nonchalant expression. "Hello, Mr. Jenson, I don't know if you remember me?"

"Mr. Segdon, of course I do," the old man stated. "Was there something you needed? Your room has been left as it was. Master Philip was insistent on that."

"Thank you, that's very kind of you. And helpful." Adjusting his position against the cane, he continued; "I was actually looking for Philip. I have a few matters I need to discuss with him."

Jenson frowned heavily. It was the first real expression

Thomas had seen him make. "I'm sorry, Mr. Segdon. Master Philip isn't here."

"W-What do you mean he isn't here?" he asked, his voice a strained whisper as he tried to fight against the heated flush creeping through his body.

"I was sure he'd have told you. Master Philip has left London."

"Did he say for how long?" Thomas asked desperately. "It's –it's important –I need to see him!"

"I truly am sorry, Mr. Segdon. Master Philip has gone out of London – indefinitely."

Thomas felt his leg buckle and the cane skid out from underneath him. The cold concrete step hit his hip hard. He barely even grunted in pain, the numbness spreading through him like a poison. He didn't even react when Jenson's hazy voice called for assistance from the housemaid, nor did he react when he felt hands grabbing at him. He stared into the void as the daylight was closed out by the thick front door.

Indefinitely. Philip was gone indefinitely. The word made him feel sick, cold and numb. All he could hear was that word ringing in his head. He wanted to hide away from everything.

Philip was gone.

Indefinitely.

Friday 26th October 1888.

Thomas was grateful to Jenson and the housemaid, Henrietta, who let him stay at Philip's house. He didn't know what he would've done otherwise. It had been a long week and the effects of his attack and drugs still hadn't faded from his mind. They gave him persistent nightmares and it woke him up, choking on his own phlegm and sweat. Thankfully, the house-servants didn't seem to mind. They insisted they were happy to help.

Once that concern was dampened down, Thomas found it easier to work.

He spent as many daylight hours as he could, his head bent low over his journals and scraps of papers and making detailed notes and diagrams for various sedatives for lycanthropy. He also wanted to create some salves or balms that would work on injuries given by a werewolf. Like his arm. The thoughts of experimenting various medicinal ointments on his own scar filled him with a slow-burning dread. There'd be no real antidote if something burned, irritated, or ate away at his muscles.

'*Maybe I need some mice to test on*,' he thought idly as he drank another cup of aconite tea. It really was addictive.

Running a hand through his hair, he decided to stretch his aching legs and go down to the main hall. He needed to see if anymore of his parcels had arrived. He couldn't very well start mixing concoctions without the proper equipment set up. Thankfully, everything was mail-ordered and due to arrive by the following Monday.

He had cleared the furniture in the study off to one side, so he had more room for his experiments and then departed the house to get the other equipment and test subjects he needed. As soon as some of the experiments proved effective, he could take a risk on himself.

Later that evening, hunched over his desk with his shoulders threatening to break and his neck aching, Thomas had his new glasses pressed high on his nose and was mixing a bubbling concoction over a small, controlled flame. It had a sickly, pungent aroma and he was almost sure it was melting his ladle. The smells were making his head spin. He was trying not to put too much of his hope into the first batch, but he couldn't help himself. Of all the things happening right now, he needed something to go right.

By midnight he had at least ten different substances brewing on a low heat. His back was as stiff as his walking-cane and sweat soaked his shirt and made it stick to his skin. Wiping his forehead on his shirtsleeves, he couldn't help but feel as though he had achieved something. Underneath each little black cauldron, he wrote down which variation it was along with the recipe he'd used. He knew he was being anal about everything, but he needed everything to be just right. The last thing he needed was to be ridiculed for forgetting a simple ingredient or how many times he'd stirred it.

Before the break of dawn he'd fallen asleep on the desk. He was roused from sleep by a hand on his shoulder and the sweet smell of aconite tea hit his senses like a bucket of cold water.

"Mr. Segdon?" the housemaid gently shook him, the fog in his brain making it difficult to react properly. He grunted, rubbing at his eyes and shuddering as the early morning sunlight fell over him.

"What time is it?" he slurred.

"It's half past eight, sir," she stated, setting the small breakfast plate and teapot in front of him. "You also have a visitor."

Thomas frowned heavily. "A visitor? Did they say who they were?"

"I'm sorry sir," she shook her head. "He was adamant he needed to see you. I showed him into the front parlour."

"Very well."

He took a sip of tea. It rubbed away some of the chill from his insides, perking his senses up a little. He needed his wits about him to deal with the type of man that Philip dealt with. With a weary sigh he stood up, drained the last of his tea and made his way downstairs to the front parlour.

Pushing the door open he stopped short when he saw a man standing tall and proud in a top hat, a cane hanging limply over his wrist. He was stood before the tall dark bookcase, his eyes scanning the gold embossed lettering from behind his tinted glasses. His hair hung around his shoulders in dark brown curls that were somewhat tamed by the short top hat on his head.

Thomas cleared his throat.

The man turned to him and then a slow smile stretched his lips. "Ah, good afternoon young man."

"Hello sir," Thomas inclined his head. "I'm afraid if you're here to see Mr. Ridley, he isn't in town at the moment."

The man chuckled, a deep throaty sound. "Actually, Mr. Segdon, it was you I'd come to see."

"I'm sorry? I think you might have the wrong person. I don't know you."

"You're Thomas Segdon?"

"Yes, sir."

"Then it is you I'm here to see."

"What is it you wanted to see me about?"

"According to an old acquaintance of mine, you are currently in the process of developing a drug to be used in regards to people afflicted with ... lycanthropic tendencies."

Biting on his lip, he pressed the door closed behind him and swallowed hard. "Sir I don't know what you're -"

The man held up a hand. "Let's not waste time with nonsense, Mr. Segdon."

Thomas clamped his mouth shut.

"We both know what you've been purchasing lately and the type of experiments you are conducting."

Thomas felt as though the room was spinning around him. He braced himself back against the door for support.

"I am not here to report you to the police or the board of directors at the hospital," the man stated, idly flicking an invisible speck of dust from his overcoat sleeve. Straightening up, he fixed Thomas with a firm stare. "This is more of a beneficiary visit."

"In ... er ... what way?" Thomas asked, his brain feeling dizzy. He needed to sit down but didn't want to appear weak in front of this man. This man who shouldn't have the knowledge he currently possessed of Thomas and his private workings.

"I am here to loan you any of the funds you require in order to find a cure."

Thomas blinked, taken aback. "Why would you have any interest in my work? It's just ideas! I have no idea if any of these concoctions are going to *work!*"

"That matters not. You're trying and that's what matters to me. If you require any special monetary funding, just send word for me and I shall contribute to your projects."

All words seem to evaporate on Thomas' tongue.

The man smirked. "I'll let you process my offer, Mr. Segdon, but know that it will not be around for long. As for your current experiments," he stated, flexing his long fingers into a pair of sleek black gloves. "For each one I wish to purchase a small sample of each."

"I –but they're –they're not really for sale!" Thomas hedged.

"I'll pay you a pound per vial."

Thomas was at a loss for words. Eventually he said the only thing he could think of. "They're still cooling, sir. They're not ready for bottling yet."

The man chuckled low in his throat. It was deep and rumbling, akin to the growling of a dog. "I shall come back this evening then, Mr. Segdon. Remember, a vial of each? I shall bring the money with me. Have a think of my other offer as well, and we can discuss a written contract if that makes you feel more at ease."

He was about to take his leave when Thomas finally snapped to his senses and called out after him. "Excuse me, sir! I –I'm not sure I can sell these creations without knowing what you plan on doing with them."

Stopping at the door, the man turned to face the young brunette, so close that Thomas caught a sickly-sweet scent radiating from the man's collar. Was that -? Could it be -? Aconite? His head spun. The man opened his mouth and murmured, "Let's just say I have a –close friend –with similar afflictions to your own."

Thomas felt a tremor run down his spine.

There were *others*?

Before he could ask any more questions, the tall man tipped his hat and departed from the room. Thomas was left stunned and speechless. He took deep calming breaths and tried to process the information. There were more people who had been attacked by werewolves and hadn't been murdered? Even stranger still, this man –whom Thomas just realised he hadn't asked his name! –seemed to be harbouring one of said victims from the law and the public eye. Why had they not spoken out? At each one of the crime scenes and newspaper articles not once were any witnesses mentioned.

His head was reeling.

There was another five days until the next full moon. He suddenly felt his chest grow tight, as though he were suddenly racing against the clock.

'Don't be silly! You have plenty of time there's no need to panic! You already have several test recipes cooling down at this very moment!'

That thought gave him a small bead of hope –but then the thought of getting more money for a small vial of each poultice and balm, along with some extra spending money for equipment and maybe even some rarer herbs from O'Callaghan's apothecary. That thought alone made his stomach bubble with promise.

Thomas knew the real reason he was hesitating –he missed Philip. The blonde man would know what to do in that sort of situation. If anything, Philip would have been the one to pay for everything and anything Thomas' heart desired! After all, he'd paid for the majority of the private ward at St. Bartholomew's! Philip would have known what he should do about this mysterious man.

With nothing else to do, Thomas went upstairs to finish off his cold breakfast and bottle his current potion experiments.

As night fell so did Thomas' stimulation. He'd done everything on his current to-do list, including getting a dozen mice from the local bread factory. They ran rampant in there and he'd spent a good hour or so setting a non-lethal trap to capture them in. Now that the mice were caught, the potions brewed, and the small vials bottled and labeled for the mysterious bureaucrat, Thomas was left with only two options; one was to simple call it a night, have some tea and go to bed. The other was to start testing the draughts he'd brewed on his mice.

'Maybe you should wait. Maybe this mystery man should be the

one to test it on his friend. Then you can replicate the results.'

It wasn't the worst idea in the world, but Thomas also knew he'd end up being the one held responsible. Besides, if this man's 'friend' was afflicted by werewolf wounds, then perhaps he too was as mild-mannered as Thomas. He didn't deserve to suffer.

Just as he was pondering on the decision, a booming knock resounded from the front doors. Within moments, the housekeeper was scuttling into the room, her drawn features looking a little puffy.

"There's a gentleman at the front door, sir," she stifled a yawn against the back of her hand. "Shall I let him in?"

Thomas nodded, "yes, please do. I shall be down in a moment."

"Yes sir," she bowed her head, about to close the door.

"Joan?" Thomas called out.

"Yes, sir?"

"Once you've shown him in you can go to bed. I can handle everything else." He offered her a smile.

"That's very kind of you sir." She seemed like she truly meant it as she left the room and closed the door gently behind her.

Upon entering the front parlour, Thomas was struck by a sudden sense of déjà vu. Everything was happening as it had before, the only different being that the sky outside the window was now black, only punctured by the faint light from the streetlamps. He closed the door as quietly as he could behind himself, before turning to address the man.

"So you kept your word?"

"Of course, Mr. Segdon," the man gave a knowing smile. "I am a man of my word. A rare thing these days."

"Indeed."

Cocking a black eyebrow, the man turned to address

Thomas. "I shall come right to the point, Mr. Segdon, I'm desperate."

"D-Desperate?"

"Yes. My friend is ailing, and I need to test-run your drugs."

"Sir, they haven't been tested to any degree. I don't know if they're safe for human ingestion!"

"That's not a matter of concern," the man stated bluntly. "My companion has ailed in this manner for many decades. He is exhausted. You are the first person to have some idea of what could lead to a cure."

Thomas rubbed the back of his neck, not really knowing what to say. To have to suffer from werewolf wounds for such an extended period of time would no doubt drive anyone to such a desperate turning point in their lives. Thomas felt his stomach grow tight as he wrestled with his conscience.

What if he handed over the vials and over the next few days a death was reported? Listing him as the creator of said unknown drug? It would finish his entire career before it had even started.

No, it was too risky.

Adopting a posture he'd seen Philip use a hundred times, he decided that he was going to do the professional thing and put his patient first. That was his duty as a future doctor.

"I'm afraid before I can do anything else, sir, I'm going to have to insist on seeing my would-be patient."

The man tightened his square jaw. "My companion is unable to leave the house in his current state."

"Then I must insist that you take me to him at once."

"Mr. Segdon, you are not in the –"

"Need I remind you, sir, that I am training to be a doctor?" Thomas ground out. "You have come to buy something off me that has not been tested and might very well poison your friend! Now, before either of us takes any risks in this matter, I am telling you now; take me to him!"

They glared at each other through the glow of a few candles.

Thomas held his ground, every muscle in his body ready to strike out if the man tried to do anything to him. He wasn't good at confrontation, but this man was insisting that Thomas risk his livelihood and put his head on the chopping block for some man who –despite the similarities in their situations –was a complete stranger.

Finally, the man sighed.

"Fine," he intoned darkly. "My carriage is parked outside. We can take it and go and see my companion. Then will you sell me the vials?"

Thomas regarded him with a reserved expression. "I'll consider it."

The carriage-ride was tense. The air between them hummed with suppressed anger and the creaking of the carriage wheels on the damp cobblestones. Nothing stirred beyond the lace curtain as the horses' hooves briskly drove them through the narrow streets. The almost-full moon hung low and fat in the sky. As they moved away from Philip's house, Thomas was flooded with dread. Had he just made a grave mistake in getting into this stranger's carriage? What was going to be on the other end of this trip? What if he'd just signed his own death certificate and not let anyone else know where he'd be going? What if his name ended up on the front page along with an article about his brutal murder?

What if Philip returned just to realise that Thomas had done a million stupid things in his absence?

A tremor ran down his spine.

After about an hour or so, the carriage finally slowed to a halt. The man next to him barely shifted as his door was opened and he stepped out, the carriage jostling at the loss of weight within it. Thomas followed suit, wanting this evening over with as soon as possible.

Why had he even agreed to this?

They'd stopped on the outskirts of London. The houses dotted around were all detached and spaced a lot more distantly compared to the London streets he'd gotten used to. The house itself was a very tall, narrow, dark building that looked as though it had seen better days. The brick work was loose in some places and there was a fair few bald spots on the roof where tiles had gone missing over the years. It was dilapidated and rather upsetting to look at. All the windows stared down at them like black, soulless eyes. Thomas stared up at the house, his mind reeling. Without hesitation, the older man stepped through the iron gate and made his way up the path toward the front door.

Thomas had to jog to catch up to him.

"What're we doing here?" he hissed through his teeth, the bite in the air making his body ache.

"You wanted to come and meet my friend," the older man stated bluntly, drawing a key out from his cloak and slipping it into the lock.

It groaned. The door swung inwards.

The hallway beyond was dark. Striking a match, the man lit a lantern on a side table and held it aloft. "This way," he instructed, leading Thomas down the narrow, somewhat dusty hallway towards the opposite end of the house.

'This is it!' Thomas thought. 'This is where my body will be found in ten years' time.'

Yet there was something about the whole ordeal that didn't ring completely untrue. There was something being kept from him he was sure about that. It was the reason he'd secreted a small blade in his jacket pocket. It clinked against the small vials he had with him. Stepping down the hallway, Thomas had to strain his eyes for anything that moved in the darkened corners. Doorways gaped like black mouths waiting to swallow him up on either side. The only source of light was the lantern held over the other man's head. Outside the wind howled and made the entire house bend beneath it.

In the back room, which served as a kitchen, the older man was waiting for him, his hand poised on the handle of a weathered door. It looked as old and battered as the rest of the house. Thomas felt claustrophobia set in as the dark walls seemed to edge closer and closer, the air growing stale with each breath.

He needed to get out.

"He's just down here," the man stated.

"Down there?" Thomas repeated, indicating the door. "Down in the basement? Your friend is ill, and he lives here, in the *basement*?"

"Yes."

Thomas wanted to scream, to shake the man, to run and set fire to the house and anything that might be awaiting him in the basement. A sudden image flashed; the image of a circular stone room, a large tub with milky, frothy bathwater and a long, pale hand stretching out of it ...

He gasped, his body coated in sweat.

"Are you alright?"

Thomas shook his head. "I'm not going down there."

"I understand your apprehension, but we really are against the clock here."

Thomas glared up at the man. His face was hard to read by candlelight. If Thomas had known him better, he'd wager that the man was –afraid? Afraid of what? His pending actions? The murder he was about to partake in? Or was it simply that he really *did* care for his friend? Something plucked at Thomas' heart.

"Okay," he finally exhaled slowly, his chest tight. Every muscle and nerve frantic with fear. "Take me to him."

Together, they descended the staircase. It was narrow and tight, the paintwork peeling off in large, greasy flakes. Thomas grimaced through the darkness and brushed his hand clean against his cloak. About halfway down, something grunted. Thomas froze. There was the grating sound of metal against stone. It set his teeth on edge.

As they drew nearer, the grunting grew louder. Mice scurried off into corners. Something shuffled and brushed awkwardly against the stone floor and Thomas felt the bottom drop out of his stomach. The man continued, holding the lantern high. Light fell –at last –into the furthest corner of the room where a broken bedframe held up a stuffed mattress. A mutilated nest of blankets, furs, and rugs had been strung together to cover the trembling, sweating body of –a man?

Blinking, Thomas rubbed at his eyes to make sure he wasn't seeing things.

It was. It was just a man. A very ill man, no doubt, but there was absolutely nothing inhuman about him.

The grunting turned into groans as the lantern was set on the ground beside the head of the bed. Watching warily, Thomas observed the older man kneel down on the gritty, cracked floor and reach out an ungloved hand toward the man in the sheets. As tender as one would be with a child, he brushed the sweaty strands of hair aside.

That's when Thomas saw it; the eyes!

They were empty! There was nothing in them –no colour, no pupils, no whites, nothing! They were just glossy and black, as though someone had poured tar inside a skull and left it to set. He felt bile burn up the back of his throat as he looked in the rest of the features; raw scars across the face, sallow skin, cracked, parched lips and puncture wounds where teeth had set in –sharp teeth!

The air around him was suddenly hot and acrid.

He felt the hairs on the back of his neck stand up on

end as he watched the man interact with this –daemon. Every fibre of his being was screaming at him to run but he was paralysed. He didn't have anywhere to run to. He had begrudgingly left the safety of Philip's townhouse and now he was on the outskirts of the city, in an unknown location and no one knew where he was!

He panicked as the reality sunk into his bones.

Fear burned like acid in his stomach as he looked over at the creature again. It was clearly sleep-deprived, it's movements erratic and disjointed. Its head lulled from side-to-side, jaw slack and eyelids drooping but never closing for more than a second or two. It was so much worse than he'd feared. This man had not suffered wounds from being *attacked* by a werewolf.

He was one.

Saturday 27th October 1888.

Thomas nearly screamed when he backed up against the wall.

In that filthy nest of blankets and rugs the creature writhed closer to the glow of the flame, his limp hands pawing in the hair towards the man in the top hat. He still wore it and only in that moment did Thomas realise how bizarre it was. Especially since the older man was crouched down in a very pristine outfit and crooning to the creature!

"Shh, shh, it's okay. I know it's painful," he hummed gently, threading his ungloved fingers through the rather matted, sweaty hair clinging to the daemon's skull.

Thomas clamped his eyes shut. His ears were unable to block out the sound of the guttural moaning from the animal's throat. It was almost like a deep whimper of pain. He needed to get out, to leave. It wasn't healthy for anyone if he remained in that basement.

The grating of metal on stone made him sick.

"I –I'm sorry!" he finally found his voice. It came out broken and scared, but he didn't care. "I can't –I can't help him!"

The man turned his gaze to him, the glow of the single candle wavering as the daemon's laboured breathing gushed against it. "You've not even looked at him, yet."

"I can see well enough!" Thomas retorted. "You lied to me! He wasn't attacked!"

"If we're going into semantics, Mr. Segdon, then yes, he was attacked. Only his case is much more severe than yours."

"It's a full moon in a DAY! Do you really think chains are – are enough to –?"

He trailed off as his foot brushed against something. He

looked down and was just able to make out something long and white on the stone floor. Was that –was that a human limb bone? He felt somewhat numbed to it.

"These chains are all I'm able to do to keep him here."

Thomas turned his nose up. "They don't work, do they?"

The man swallowed but didn't reply. "Can you just look at him, Segdon? Please?"

Everything inside Thomas was screaming '*NO!*'

Clamping his jaw tightly, he moved a little closer until he could smell the blood, the decay, and the stench of soiled sheets. "You keep him like an animal?"

"He's too weak to move much. I want to do more for him, but I am limited in my power and resources."

"It doesn't seem that way to me," Thomas bit out. He was shot a glare for his efforts.

"I did some reading a few months back," the man continued. "The Greeks and Romans used to believe that a state of severe exhaustion could cure men of his malady. Unfortunately, over said few months nothing seems to have changed anything. I thought if I could exhaust him enough after one of his excursions –it would help."

"Did you –try anything else?" Thomas hedged.

"A number of things."

"Such as?"

"Why do you care?"

"In order to help, I need to know what he's been subjected to."

"Well –there was some nonsense about calling out his Christian name as soon as he'd changed or in the midst of the night. It didn't work and honestly, I'm amazed anyone ever believed it could be that simple."

The thing grunted and lurched.

The thick collar around his neck dragged him back.

Thomas backed away, out of reaching distance. "Sir, please,

you cannot keep him here! He's a danger to us! How have you not been bitten yet?"

The man's shoulders sagged. "I've had a number of close calls, but I have been able to keep myself safe."

"Sir I don't think I can –"

"Xander."

Thomas blinked. "I –what?"

"My name is Xander. Xander Holland."

Thomas' mouth worked soundlessly for a moment before shaking himself back to the moment. "Okay, Xander, I don't think anything I do is going to be much good for him. He –he can't go on like this. He's barely even a man anymore. You need to let him go."

"HE'S MORE THAN A MAN THAT YOU COULD EVER KNOW!" Xander hollered, slamming his fists into the wall.

Something splintered and cracked but it was too dark to see what. Dust and chips of plaster drifted down from the ceiling. The creature strained against his restraints, mouth hanging open as it groaned and salivated down his front. Thomas cast it a terrified look. He didn't want to be there anymore.

"I'm sorry but I don't think there's anything else I can do. Maybe if you brought him down to the hospital when Stephen returns he might –?"

"No!" Xander barked out. The creature jerked again at the loud noise. "He can't know of this."

Thomas furrowed his brow and tried to process the information. "You –You know Stephen?"

Hunching his shoulders, Xander gave a stiff nod. "Yes. I know him."

"Personally or ...?"

"We were in school together if you must know."

"School?"

Xander sighed heavily, a growl through his barred teeth. "We were in medical school together."

"*You* were training to be a Doctor?"

"Yes. I got all the way up to my final exams before getting expelled."

"So –you're technically trained as a doctor?" Thomas asked.

There was a pause. "Yes. I am."

The wounds were precise, locating the organs within and making accurate incisions and lacerations across the body.

Thomas stared at the man as he crouched down and continued to smooth down the matted brown hair of the daemon wriggling awkwardly in the nest. He tried to make sense of the information he was being given. Was there a connection to all of this? It was possible that the Ripper was trained to be a doctor. Very few men actually passed the final exams. Even Rufus must have struggled. God, it seemed like a completely other life away.

Standing a little straighter, Thomas tried to contain his nerves as he addressed the man before him. "Sir, I'm afraid he's too far gone. Nothing can be done for him in this state."

"Do not condemn this man for what he is!"

"I'm not!" Thomas snapped back, his raised voice having a strange effect on the creature. Its ears pricked as though listening for his next move, its nostrils flared, and it stilled in the dim light. It was unnerving to watch those tar-black eyes swivel around to face him.

Lowering his voice, Thomas tried to keep his muscles from quaking. "Look at him, sir. He is barely even human at this point. He wasn't able to complete his ... his ... *transformation.*"

The word sounded awful and alien on his tongue.

"He's as human as you or I!"

"I'm –I'm so sorry, Xander, but ... I don't know anyone with eyes like that. Or ears or hands or elongated feet with claws." Tentatively, he reached out and put a consoling hand on the older man's shoulder. "You need to let him go."

"I promised him I'd do all I could," Xander murmured, his

lips barely moving as he squeezed the long, clawed fingers of the beast. It was such a tender embrace that Thomas found himself recoiling just a little. "Can't you at least look at him? Properly? A secondary opinion, if you will?"

"A secondary opinion would be from Talbot, and I haven't the faintest idea where he's gone."

"I see."

Thomas pursed his lips. Turning his back on the scene, he stopped in his tracks. There, under the staircase, was a horrible old bathtub. It was rusted and discoloured from disuse –but perhaps it would serve its purpose. Biting on his lower lip, he raked a hand through his hair and fought the vision that flashed at the back of his mind.

A stone circular vault under the townhouse ... garlic and herbs hanging from every corner of the ceiling ... a large tub with milky liquid within ... the pungent scent of wolfsbane in the air ...

"Is there a well around here?" he found himself asking before he banished the idea.

"Around the back of the house. Why?"

"I –I might have an idea –but it's dangerous. We'll need to act fast."

Xander, clearly perked up by any remedy good or bad, rose from the floor. "What do you need?"

"We'll need a lot of water to heat up and to bring that old tub upstairs."

Xander cast a filthy look at the offending object but didn't voice his concerns. Instead, he inclined his head and turned towards the staircase. "I'll see to it."

Without another word he disappeared.

As the door clicked shut, Thomas' momentary relief was extinguished by the panting and ragged breathing of the beast in the corner. Its wet breath panted against the candle, casting long, shadows dancing around the room. He felt fear and adrenaline spike through his heart. Curiosity got the better of him, he couldn't deny, as he carefully crossed the room, slowly. The black eyes followed him, unblinking, as he crouched down a little farther than Xander had been. He had no desire to cradle the beast's paw in his hands. However, he did push his glasses up his nose and inspect the creature in the light of the quivering flame.

Its skin was like mottled tissue paper, pulled tight over a disfigured skeleton. It was like the one they'd cracked open and studied in one of his earlier lectures; the jawline was too long for any normal mans but too square and strong to be anything other than a wolf. The eyes were wide, almost as large as his own fist, and completely black. The teeth were short but sharp and yellowed with poor hygiene and blood. The forehead was far too large and streaked with dirt and sweat, adding a strange swollen appearance to the animal. The ears, too, were far too large and pointed for a human skull, even one as currently misshapen as this beast's.

The odour of old meat on his breath was enough to make Thomas heave.

He stood up on stiff legs and backed away. His lungs protested, and his injured arm itched and burned under his bandages. He pressed down on the wound, relishing the sting, before eyeing the shuffling creature before him. He had another idea, one he hadn't tested or made any sort of brew for, one he wasn't sure would even work. He'd looked it up in an old German text –or rather the other components that had failed –and was positive he'd isolated the key ingredient that could help in such a dire matter.

The vials weighed down in his breast pocket.

It would be worth a try at least.

"*THOMAS*?" a voice called from above. "*THE WATER IS BOILING! WHAT ELSE DO YOU NEED?*"

Casting a wary glance at the beast in its nest –that was currently sat on its side like a dog listening to its master's voice –he replied, "I NEED YOU TO HELP ME CARRY THE TUB UP!"

The swollen moon hung in its almost-full state just over the horizon. It glowed a deep, luscious yellow colour and peaked in and out between clouds. Behind the house, Xander and Thomas had set up the bathtub in a patch of barren dirt. Xander stood back, watching with interest as Thomas tried to recreate the candles in the patterns he'd seen in his dream. It was difficult reliving such a moment when the thought alone made him queasy.

Still, he pressed on.

Once the patterns were made, they filled the tub with hot water. Thomas mixed in as much garlic and aconite as he could find in the house –a surprising amount considering the rarity of the herb –and let it stew in the water. By the light of over a hundred candles, he nodded his head for Xander to go and bring the beast up. As soon as he disappeared inside the house, Thomas pulled out one of the small vials in his breast pocket. It wasn't one of his experiments –this was something else entirely. Something that cost a fair bit to acquire.

Silver flakes.

He only put a pinch into the bathwater. It frothed a little, the bubbles burning a pale violet colour in the moonlight. His stomach knotted. There was no way to know if this would work. He'd read up about the properties of metal in an archaic little journal, easily overlooked.

Grunting broke the natural silence.

Whipping around, Thomas watched as the creature –easily

seven or eight feet tall –lope awkwardly on its misshapen legs, it's grotesquely long arms draped over Xander's shoulders. He suppressed a grimace, backing away to the other side of the bathtub. Without a word, Xander gingerly coaxed the creature into the water.

As soon as its elongated foot sank below the murky surface, it lurched. It tried to wrestle away but it appeared to be weak in its current state. Xander, despite his crooning and gentle words, had no issue in manhandling the beast into the tub. He yelped and groaned as water sloshed over the sides, soaking his clothes. Grinding his teeth he slung heavy chains over the top.

Thomas grabbed them and pinned them down.

Submerged, the creature foamed at the mouth, its jaw snapping around the chains, teeth on metal grating through the air. Grinding his teeth, he grabbed a vial from his pocket and caught Xander's gaze as he struggled, his arms in the tub keeping the creature under. Only its snapping jaw could be seen.

"Try and steady its mouth!" Thomas ordered. "I need him to drink this!"

"Will it work?" Xander barked.

"I don't know!"

There was a pregnant pause in which Thomas almost expected the older man to change his mind. He was surprised again when he saw Xander dig his thumbs between the snapping jaws –Thomas took note that he wore thick gloves –and pried the disfigured mouth apart, exposing the mouth and back of the throat. As quickly as he could, Thomas clumsily tipped the vial over the jaws. He tried to make sure all of the liquid went down but it was difficult to tell with the amount of bathwater splashing around.

A cold wind gushed around them.

Candles flickered in the breeze but didn't go out.

The beast stopped struggling for a moment. It choked the liquid down and stilled. Thomas held his breath, not wanting to trust anything for a moment. Just like that, the silent night was ripped apart around them by the howling. It tore through the darkness and echoed out into the distance. It was the most heart-breaking sound that Thomas had ever heard. It vibrated through his bones, threatening to make them shatter.

The thrashing suddenly started again.

"What's happening?" Thomas asked, feeling guilt surge through him like hot oil. He was meant to be the one with the knowledge, yet he was completely clueless. Everything they witnessed henceforth would be ground-breaking for all of them.

Xander wasn't listening to him, however.

He was too focused on the werewolf.

Snarling and agitated the wolf tried to attack Xander's arms and hands but the man was protected and, though he struggled too, was more agile. Against the howling of the choking beast, Thomas was able to make out the voice of the older man.

"Richard Lexton listen to me! I am your friend! You are not this animal! You are Richard Lexton! My friend, come back!"

With a forceful shove, Xander pushed the beast underwater.

"Richard Lexton you are human! You are just as human as I!"

Another shove. More splashes and guttural gurgles.

"RICHARD LEXTON!" his voice called out through the other noise drowning it out as the wolf disappeared to the bottom of the bath. Xander's head nearly rested on the rim. He was shaking. "... Come back to me."

Another gust of wind tore at their clothes. Thomas hadn't realised he'd been holding his breath until the thrashing stopped. Everything stilled. The water bubbled and rippled, calming itself like a creamy lilac pool. He was suddenly all too aware of his heart hammering against his tight rib-cage. His brain caught up with the reality of the situation and he started to sweat profusely despite the cold. Swallowing, he stood upright and peered into the bathtub.

Nothing stirred.

Xander's arm was hanging limply in the water, his head bowed forward, and his shoulders hunched. Thomas cleared his throat, the sound echoing loudly in his ears. He didn't know what he wanted to ask. He didn't even understand what was going on, in that moment.

The silence screamed around them.

Every breath was a thunderclap.

A tremor ran down Thomas' spine. Tears pricked in his eyes. Had he done it? Had he killed a man? An innocent? His stomach churned inside him. He sank down on the ground, wincing as gravel bit through his trousers and pressed into his buttocks. Raking hands through his greasy hair he felt as though he was going to vomit through his own guilt. What had he done? Just as he was preparing a speech in his head for Xander and how this was clearly the best thing for that creature, something broke the smooth surface of the bath water.

A white hand shot out.

It was as white as a bone, the nails long and grey. Both men fell back, away from the tub as the fingers latched around the rim of the tub. The liquid had congealed, growing thick like a skin across the top. It stretched like an amniotic sac as the body of a man slowly rose out in a hunched position. The lilac slime broke away, sliding off the skin as the creature tossed its head back, gasping desperately for air. Thomas stared, horrified, as the now human mouth stretched and gaped, its emaciated body quaking as the substance oozed off and into the tub.

Before Thomas could comprehend what had happened,

Xander shot forward towards the tub, his arms instantly wrapping around the skeletal man, holding his head upright to breathe properly.

"Richard?" he breathed, his voice breaking with hysteria. "Is –is it really you?"

The other man was too weak to reply. His head lulled against Xander's chest, staining his brocade waistcoat.

He remained paralysed as he watched Xander use his shirtsleeves to scrub the sticky matter off of Richard's face. He scrubbed his eyes clear and tugged it out of his hair. With great difficulty, Richard was lifted out of the tub, his bony limbs knocking against the metal sides, making Thomas wince at the sound. He flopped into the dirt, reminding Thomas of when he'd watched the village cows giving birth, before Xander draped his jacket over the scrawny shoulders. A hacking cough grated through the air.

"Thomas go and get a fire started! Now!"

Thomas obliged, feeling like a scared child being shooed away from an adult conversation with the promise of puzzles and sweets. The escape was a relief; he felt unbearably useless, guilty and responsible in equal measure. It made him feel sick.

In the dark house, he forced his cold, stiff fingers to arrange a fire in the grate. Five burned-out matches later and the tinder finally caught light. It took a while for the fire to get going but once it did, Thomas busied himself with tidying up the front parlour, clapping dust out of the cushions and forcing all the furniture closer to the hearth, wincing as it squeaked against the worn, splintered floorboards.

He crouched on his haunches for a while, watching as the flames leapt and swallowed the branches whole, crackling and spitting out warmth that he'd missed. His mind was numb; slowly trying to absorb what had just happened without understanding a single moment.

Richard banged into the room, startling Thomas to his feet, his body hanging from Xander's neck. He was naked except for Xander's overcoat that hung off him. Together, they managed to get Richard over to the sofa. A small dust cloud puffed out as he dropped onto it, nearly rolling off onto the floor. Xander kept him grounded on the sofa and repositioned the coat over Richard's private areas. Thomas found himself flushing and turning his gaze away.

'*Look at what you did!*' his brain admonished. '*You brought a man back from a demonic state! You did well!*'

Thomas found that he couldn't take pride in the moment. He still wasn't sure what had happened or able to understand. Peering over the rim of his glasses he watched as Xander smoothed the damp hair back and pulling a thin, grubby blanket over the lower portion of his companion's body.

"Thank you, Thomas. You've done me a great service."

"It was a risk," Thomas found himself saying, the words bitter, his mouth moving of its own accord. "For all we know, I could have just as easily have poisoned him."

Xander pursed his lips in understanding. "Regardless, whatever you did seems to have worked."

Thomas sighed wearily, not wanting to argue the matter anymore. Richard appeared to be his 'normal self' as he drew in deep, laboured breaths against the flat, sofa cushions. Even in the firelight he looked like a complete wreck of a man; his hair was thinning –even slicked back with the potion – his skin stretched tight over his skeleton and his eyes were sunken. Dark bruises were around his eyes and his ribs poked out. Even through the overcoat the bulbs of his spinal cord could be faintly seen.

They sat in silence. Thomas slumped back against the armchair, the weight of the entire situation pressing down on the back of his skull and shoulders. It felt as though his cranium was about to shatter and explode. He cradled his face in his hands and pressed against the burn of sleep-deprivation. Out of the corner of his eyes, he watched as Xander loomed over Richard's deflated body. It was such a tender image, the way he carded his fingers through the slippery hair, down the hidden neck and over the covered arms. He squeezed the man's limp hands as he struggled to breathe against the cloying dust.

"Will he ... be okay?" Thomas asked lamely.

"He just needs rest," Xander stated in a quiet, matter-of-fact tone.

Thomas draped his arms across his knees and watched as Xander doted on the unconscious man sprawled before them. He tucked him up to make sure he was kept warm before the sun rose through the slat blinds. He offered a drink at some point, but Thomas didn't remember. He wasn't even sure if he'd even responded.

It was all such a blank.

He just kept staring at Richard. He looked like such a normal, humble man. A quiet schoolteacher perhaps? A mild-mannered merchant? He looked like everything the beast had not; he looked calm, gentle, and conservative in his ways. The only real indication that he'd been through such a traumatising ordeal at all, were the lacerations marring his complexion. Some were deep and raw, bruising heavily around the edges in a myriad of colours from dark pink to yellow and green. Others were pale lines that glowed silver in the firelight.

As the sky paled through the blinds, he felt his raw eyes grow tired and his eyelids droop. His head tipped backwards. Noises faded to white noise in the far distance. He didn't care anymore. For the moment, the imminent danger had passed and that was all that mattered. He'd figure out the ins and outs of it later, after some sleep. He tucked his legs underneath his own, his cold skin making his insides churn.

'*I'll warm up soon ...*' he thought as he burrowed down into his coat, trying to get comfortable.

With the conflicting sounds of Richard's laboured breathing, the soft, crackling of the fire and Xander's erratic pacing in the hallway, Thomas drifted into a troubled, dreamless sleep.

Sunday 28th October 1888.

Thomas sat bolt upright in a panic. He was dripping with sweat and panting. He checked his head, neck, body, and legs before gradually willing his heart to calm.

Peering around himself in the feeble shafts of sunlight pouring in through the slat blinds, he frowned. It took his brain a few moments to completely understand where he was, however as soon as it did, he sprang from the chair. Fear played a concerto down his spine as he spun in circles, trying to organise his thoughts. His eyes fell upon the sofa; it was empty. Not even a crumpled blanket was left in its place.

His breathing grew erratic.

'What the hell is going on? Where is everyone?'

Tearing through the rest of the house, floorboards creaked and splintered heavily under his weight as he checked the dusty rooms upstairs. All were empty, the furniture draped in dustcovers. All rooms were the same. There was one final room at the end of the hallway; it didn't have any dustsheets in it, but it still made for a sombre bedchamber. The colours were muted, and it looked like a hasty set-up at best. As though neither of the two mysterious men had been living in the run-down house for long.

Gripping the doorway in his hands, he didn't know how to feel about being left stranded in a run-down house outside of London. At least there was no immediate danger. The house was silent around him. Only the quiet sounds of countryside twittered outside the windows. There was nothing to worry about. Nothing at all. So –why didn't he feel as though he was safe?

'*Get out of here!*'

He whipped around, eyes scanning the dimly lit hallways,

rooms, and back kitchen. Everything was quiet and still. There were jumbled prints in the dust but other than that, nothing else had been disturbed. Pressing his lips together Thomas managed to locate his cloak slung carefully over the edge of a beaten chair in the small kitchen. Quickly shrugging into it, the worst of the cold ebbing away, Thomas was about to leave when he noticed a note on the tabletop. Peering closer he saw his name scrawled on the front.

'*Thomas,*

I'm sorry to have left you but Richard needed to be taken somewhere more secure. He panicked about being exposed so I drugged him and took him to another location. He'll be fine.
In the meantime I have left you some money for a train back into London. Take the rest of it and brew as much of that formula as possible. If I am able to help in anyway, I'll find you.

God be with you.
Xander'

Thomas frowned at the last sentence. Xander hadn't seemed like a particularly religious man, however after the nightmare of the previous evening, Thomas had to admit that God had to be real. There was nothing more terrifying than believing he resided on a planet with devilish beasts without a God somewhere out there, watching over his immortal soul.

Tucking the money into his pocket, Thomas spun on his heel and marched himself out the front door.

In the pale daylight, grey clouds blocking most of the sunlight from his vision, Thomas stared up at the house once he was a safe enough distance away from it. Just being outside and on the road in front of it had him breathing a little easier, a little calmer. It was such a rundown old house that it was a wonder the strong gale-force wind hadn't forced the roof to cave in on itself. It looked like a horrid black smudge on the bleak terrain, all the shrubbery around the house had overgrown on itself and dried up completely, leaving nothing but brown ivy vines threading over one side of the house –and in some cases through a few of the windows –as well as old trees that had long since stopped bearing fruit.

Fingering the money is his pocket, he reluctantly turned his back on the dilapidated house and decided to turn right at the road and walk up. Hopefully at the top of the hill he'd be able to see which direction a town was and, from there, get a train into London. It was probably a long walk back and he'd have more chance of asking for a lift from a passer-by, but something told him that carriages didn't frequent this particular road.

With a sigh, he began making tracks.

By midday Thomas had managed to make his way back to London. He took a small detour before returning to Philip's townhouse, stopping in at O'Callaghan's apothecary to pick up some more of the ingredients he needed to create more of his formula as instructed. Not that he was doing so for money or Xander or anything of the like. He needed to do it for himself, above all else. Thankfully, the old man had exactly what he needed in stock, including the silver flakes. He hadn't been sure what had worked, but he was determined to replenish his reserves just in case.

The last thing he needed was to run out of silver for whatever reason.

Back in the relative comfort of the townhouse, Thomas

tried to organise his scattered thoughts. Some tea helped to drive the chill from his aching limbs. Once calmed and perched at the large mahogany desk with his recipes spread out before him, he retrieved the empty vial to see which one he had tipped in. On the cork, he had inked a number '3'. Flipping through his journal he came to the pages he'd written down each recipe and the actions taken to brew each one.

Good.

He had a starting point.

Now, the potion had worked, but its effectiveness could have been put down to a number of factors working in their favour. It wasn't guaranteed that it was a cure or if it had merely forced the Richard's body into its original state since he'd been closer to human at the time.

'*Had it even been a cure? How do I know it would work again? Being in a half-fledged state looked to be soul-destroying. As though something feasted on the physical body while the mind continued to burn with the unholy daemon within.*'

His skin crawled at the thought.

As he cast his eyes around the room, he felt his shoulders sag. The entire house was far too big for him to be comfortable with. It had been different with Philip. Somehow, he'd driven the emptiness out of all those vacant spaces or made them immaterial to the present moment. Now, all Thomas could feel were those large vacuous rooms panelled in wood, like a hundred coffins awaiting him behind every door.

"Philip," he breathed out slowly, "Where did you go? Why did you leave without telling me?"

What was so important that he hadn't been able to stick around and help Thomas when he was on the brink of a breakthrough? He rubbed a hand over his mouth and sighed, trying to keep his mind focused on the task at hand. He had to brew the potion just so, otherwise it would be rendered useless. He couldn't afford to tip the brew down the drain.

He worked long into the night.

He forced himself to keep going until he could barely concentrate, and the potion needed to sit for twelve hours before he added the last of the ingredients. Pulling the door of the study to, Thomas finally retreated to his bedchamber, his eyes red and raw from being awake for too long. It was a wonder he'd been able to focus at all, considering he'd barely slept last night.

As he made his way down the corridor and across the landing he stopped short at the top of the stairs. Through the large ornate window, a thick shaft of silver moonlight bled into the hall, bathing everything in is corporeal glow. He stared up at it, the light magnified by his new glasses. It was like the moon was calling out to him, soothing the madness that buzzed within his skull.

His fingers twitched, as though aching to reach out for something.

The wound on his arm started to throb.

Grinding his back teeth, he forced his eyes away from the moon and finally felt like he was able to breathe again. Keeping his head bent low, he made his way down the dark corridor until he came to his bedchamber and went inside. Shutting the thick velvet curtains against the brilliant moon, Thomas undressed with frantic hands. The hairs on the back of his neck stood up on end as he lit a candle in his undergarments. Perching himself on the edge of the bed, he braced himself against his knees and took a few deep, calming breaths. It still caught him off-guard every so often, as he took note of the décor and the opulence of the house.

Philip had expensive taste or at least, Talbot did.

The entire house oozed of the finer things, money, and

decadence to such a degree that Thomas felt uncomfortable looking at it for too long. Or maybe that was his paranoia stemming from the moonbeams pressing up against the curtains, like phantoms desperate to slide into the room as he slept.

'*Stop it! You don't need to work yourself up! There's nothing to be afraid of.*'

Changing into a nightshirt, he climbed in between the cool sheets and settled back on the pillows, ignoring the nerves that flickered in his stomach. It had been a long time since he and Philip had shared the bed, but it was a fond memory. Just looking at the expanse of empty bedding on his left side made him crave the blonde's touch even more.

All too soon, the events of the day caught up to him and he passed out.

The following morning Thomas managed to wake up on his own. It seemed like a rarity these days. Usually, Joan, Henrietta or Jensen would knock on his door and inform him that breakfast was being served. It made him nervous whenever any of them did it.

Maybe they'd finally gotten the message.

Taking his time, he washed, shaved, and made sure his wavy black hair was as neat as possible before getting dressed and making his way down to the dining room. He was relieved when he saw a piping hot plate waiting for him. He ate quickly, his mind already itching to continue with brewing the medicine and get it bottled before lunchtime. Joan appeared just as he was heading towards the kitchen with a tray of his things. She blushed and apologised that she hadn't been there, over and over, until Thomas assured her that it was fine.

She took the tray from him and scuttled off, her cheeks

glowing red as she descended the few steps down into the kitchen.

On his way back upstairs, Thomas halted when he caught site of the letter waiting on a side table. Frowning he looked down at the envelope with his name scrawled on the front in elegant script. Was this from Xander? His heart sank. He hadn't given the man much thought since returning to the townhouse and he felt guilty. Turning the envelope over, he tore it open and unfolded the thick parchment inside. It wasn't from Xander; that was both a relief and a concern.

It was from Talbot.

'*Mr. Segdon,*

Please attend a lecture at St. Bartholomew's hospital at 10 o'clock on eve of 28th October. Be punctual.

Talbot'

It was blunt, barely even worth the effort of parchment and envelope, but it was a request he wouldn't be able to ignore. It had been over two weeks since Talbot had postponed their lectures and now, he was calling an emergency one for that evening? Thomas felt his chest grow tight. This was perfect timing, surely? He'd found some sort of way for a werebeast to be rendered relatively harmless. All he needed to do was take Talbot to one side after the lecture, show him his findings and proceed from there!

'*How will you tell him the draught is effective if you can't tell him about Richard?*'

"I can just say that I used it on myself and the wound started to heal."

'*But you haven't used it on yourself and your wound is the same.*'

Thomas frowned, dimly aware that he was talking to

himself.

Tucking the note into his pocket he made his way upstairs to continue working. At the very least, he needed to have some vials filled and stoppered properly before even considering telling Talbot of his current findings.

As the day wore on Thomas found himself glancing at the ornate clock on the mantelpiece. It was hard to ignore its ticking and the grandfather clock down the hall didn't help matters as it announced every hour. He ate lunch with Joan, insisting that he didn't care if she ate with him. She'd looked at a loss for words but had gingerly sat herself across from him, her mannerisms tight and precise for the first ten minutes before she finally relaxed. It had been a nice change of pace at any rate, and she genuinely seemed interested in the work Thomas was slaving over, even if she didn't understand some of the more complex terminology.

Thomas was glad; he felt as though they'd connected on a deeper level.

Once all the potions had been poured into vials, flasks, and anything else he could get his hands on that were made of glass, he stoppered them all, labelled them and then found that he had nothing more to do for the time being. It felt oddly dissatisfying to have accomplished a rare feat and not have anyone to acknowledge it other than himself. It left him feeling hollow. Would Philip have been proud of him, or would he have admired in a distant way? Would he have been able to help Thomas with testing everything on mice? Thomas had fed them five drops each of the potion and none had perished. They'd just become really sleepy and slow in their movements.

It was something, but Thomas didn't think it would be enough for Talbot's approval. All it would do was prove that the medicine wasn't poisonous. That was hardly ground-breaking. It didn't mean that it did what Thomas claimed it could –not without dragging Richard and Xander into the matter.

Before he knew it, it was eight o'clock at night.

He ate a quick, cold dinner, made sure he packed his research materials and journals into his satchel before hurrying out of the house. He took Philip's carriage through the narrow streets to the hospital and pressed a silver coin into the driver's hand and told him to have a drink on him, the lecture would most likely take a while. Thomas just hoped he remained sober enough by the time he was let out.

The lecture hall hadn't changed at all. It was still dull, gloomy, and stinking of beeswax and formaldehyde. His eyebrows rose in surprise when he saw that Bennett had returned to the lecture with a grim sort of determination in his dark eyes.

On the raised platform in the centre of the theatre, there was a large cage covered with a grubby cloth. Something clinked within but before anyone would start murmuring among themselves, Talbot swept into the room like a giant bat, his robes billowing in a non-existent breeze. He came to rest against the podium, looked perhaps a little thinner in the face but otherwise unchanged by his time away.

"At least you all made it on time," he drawled after a few moments of tense silence as his black eyes loomed on each of their faces. "I trust your studies have been productive."

No one replied.

Something clanged in the cage following by deep, heavy panting. That provoked some murmurs and worried glances at the covered thing. Talbot appeared unaffected.

"Now, I'm sure you're all wondering what I've brought back

with me from my travels."

Thomas swallowed thickly, his skin prickling with piping hot fear. He'd heard similar sorts of noises before, very recently in fact, and the dread that pooled in his stomach only made matters worse. Talbot paced before them, his black robes sweeping against the marble floor.

"I was able to discover information about the werewolf culture and various alleged cures that would make your minds *sing* with the impossibility of it all. However," he paused to lace his fingers together. "None of that is important, for I was able to procure something far more valuable."

With a swift tug, the cloth fell away.

A collective gasp shattered the silence as they looked upon the foul creature within. Thomas felt physically sick at what he saw.

Crouched low in the cage, resting on its haunches and the obscenely long forearms was another half-fledged werewolf. It had somehow gotten stuck midway through a transformation. It was grotesque; of course, Thomas had seen something akin to this creature the previous evening –had it really only been then? –and was not as stricken at the rest of his classmates. It was still a ghastly sight. Its skull looked as though it had been pressed sideways against two slabs of metal, its jaw looked askew as one side was a human jaw, the other side was a wolf jaw, and it melded in the middle. The hair was pressed thinly and flat in streaks against its veiny skin, and its black eyes flickered around the room without comprehension. Saliva dribbled from the too-big tongue lulling out of the mouth.

It was a grotesque parody of a human face.

Neville had vomited on the bench in front of him. No one blamed him –they were too transfixed by the beast before them to care. Thomas was frozen in his seat, cold sweat staining his feverish muscles. His mind was running at a million miles a minute as he tried to remember how to breathe. Talbot had done something almost impossible. He'd managed to capture a werebeast. The only viable explanation was that he'd managed to poison or hinder the creature; there were lacerations and oozing wounds scattered across the pale, greasy skin like pock marks.

The creature loped from one side of its cage to the other, barely even moving in half-circles as it panted and pawed at the steel base with its long nails. The sound set Thomas' teeth on edge.

It turned and stuck its half-formed muzzle through the bars.

His breath hitched.

He'd known there was something disturbingly familiar about the creature, only made more evident now as it had turned its more human side of its face toward him. He could recognise the ghost of the cheekbones, the dip in the earlobe and the distinct colour of the eyes as the blackness dripped like black tears out of the socket. Shock started to wrack through his body, jerking his muscles and making his jaw tremble with the pressure to fight against the emotions warring within him. Turning his attention to Talbot, he found that the man was staring down at him with narrowed, unblinking eyes. There was no doubt in his mind that he knew what he'd done. Perhaps not at the time of wounding and mutilating the beast, but it all became clear as the moons effects dwindled.

All the while the beast had been starved of both sunlight and moonlight, making the transformation back to his human state painfully slow and torturous. Proven by the black tears slowly dripping down the gaunt cheek. Thomas wondered how anyone could do such a thing to another human being. How could someone make another human being live through a brutally slow reformation of their very skeleton? Thomas looked up at the man and stared hard into his blank, black eyes.

'*How could you?*' he raged silently.

He looked back at the cage just as the beast raised its muzzle as high as it could and let out a long, mournful how.

'*No, not the beast,*' his mind pierced through the rage. '*Philip.*'

Not the beast.

Philip.

Philip.

Sunday 28th October 1888.

~Part 2~

It was Philip.

The beast was Philip.

That was the only thing running through Thomas' mind once he'd connected the dots. His body was exuding sweat and his mind was a mess. He curled his hands into fists, nails digging sharp crescents into his palms. The small bite of pain wasn't enough for him to tear his eyes from the salivating creature before his eyes. Around him the faint hush of his classmates murmuring started up and –for once –Talbot didn't silence them. He wanted to watch them squirm.

The creature –*No, Philip!* –shifted in the cage, its long claws snaking through the bars. One eye was still tar-black and the other was a murky grey colour, a black streak running down the cheek.

'*Philip, what's happened to you? Why didn't you tell me?*'

He felt emotions warring away inside him, but none more than the surge of protectiveness he felt as the hunched over beast, slobbering down its front with soft whines echoing out of its gaping mouth.

"Sir, what do you expect us to do with this creature?" Neville asked.

"We're going to study it," the Professor stated. "We're going to study it and see if any of the old rituals worked."

Thomas' stomach clenched. He'd read those old books, inhaled the dust and ignorance that bled into the ink. None of those rituals had had any distinct results, other than a mutilated corpse that needed to be burned. Talbot couldn't do that, could he? Not to his own nephew? Surely there were limits to the man's thirst for success among all else?

"Is that what we're doing tonight?" Bennett drawled, his interest piqued.

"No," Talbot swept his gaze over them. "I just want you to observe. Take notes, make observations, and let it aid your studies."

It was more than that. Thomas could tell by the way Talbot had dangled something so strange and hideous in front of their eyes. This was a test; he was testing their limits as well as their loyalty. He was most likely trying to trap Thomas into revealing everything and anything he knew.

He was tempted.

It was blatantly a trap for information –but he couldn't risk anyone else in the room recognising Philip. Not in this state! It would ruin him forever! Chewing the inside of his cheek, Thomas tried to tune everything else out as Talbot droned on in the usual slow, congealing rhythm. Maybe if he stayed behind after class and spoke to Talbot privately in his office? It was the only way he'd be able to buy Philip some more time, for what he didn't know, but he just couldn't risk having Philip exposed naked and covered in his own faeces.

Sweat tricked down the back of his neck.

He couldn't subject Philip to such a fate as described in those books. Not after everything the man had done for him, taking him in, and offering to help fund his research and experiments. There needed to be another way. Thomas felt himself slip into a daze completely stunned by what was going on around him. He was both pumped with adrenaline, wanting to dive across the wooden benches, rip the cage open and let Philip run out into the open streets, and at the same time he was rooted to the spot, stiff with fear at what might happen if he were found out.

The bell chimed in the courtyard.

Slowly and nervously, all six of the other men gathered their belongings and made for the door. All eyes kept darting back over their shoulders to look at the beast panting in the cage. No one wanted to turn their backs on it for long.

As soon as the doors closed, Talbot turned to Thomas. "Don't you have somewhere to be, Mr. Segdon?"

Thomas squared his shoulders. "I was actually hoping to speak with you, sir. I have some queries regarding my personal study, and I was hoping to gain some insights from you."

He needed to keep himself calm. There was no telling who lurked in the hospital grounds at such a late hour. Any mere mention of Philip's name could easily be printed in the papers by morning.

"Very well, Mr. Segdon, let us reconvene in my office."

Clutching his satchel tightly under his arm, Thomas moved across the theatre floor, feeling the sweat grow cold and irritable on his skin. He passed so close to the cage he could smell the rot of flesh, feaces, and blood. Bile shot up his throat. He choked it back down. He kept his eyes focused on the tiled floor, fearing that if he looked up into those mismatched eyes, all his bottled-up energy would emerge in a violent, feral rage. He bowed his head and kept going.

The tight, dank office hadn't changed since the last time Thomas had set foot in there. It was still yellowing and damp, like a lot of the long-forgotten books in the local library, but there were a larger number of journals and papers littering the desktop in an orderly fashion. Not like the mess Thomas had created throughout Philip's study before he'd –left.

Shutting the door behind himself, Thomas turned to address Talbot. The man stood in the middle of the room, arms crossed against his chest, looking down his long nose at his student. As soon as the door clicked shut, Thomas exploded.

"He's your nephew!" he spat, every vein pressing up to his skin. The room blurred out, leaving only Talbot as the focus point for his hatred. "How can you do that to your own flesh and blood? He's your *nephew*!"

"I'm aware of that."

"*Are you?* Then tell me why he's chained up in that cage!"

"I don't see how you'd have missed it," Talbot curled his upper lip in distaste. "He's currently not in possession of his mental faculties. He'd tear your spine out through your mouth given the chance."

Thomas flinched but wasn't deterred. "You don't know that! He's in a half-formed state! He's not dangerous like before!"

"Perhaps not compared to his full lycanthropic state, no. However, he is still stronger than any mortal man alive today. It's too dangerous."

"I'm sorry, sir, but I can't let you perform those rituals on him!" Thomas snapped, positioning himself in front of the door. "It will kill him! There are so many other avenues to explore!"

"Why do you think I was gone so long?" Talbot groused. "I tried them all."

"You can't have otherwise something would have worked!"

"Segdon, I understand you have a profound sense of respect and empathy for my nephew; however, I am afraid his ultimate needs have to be acquired and met through me. He's my responsibility now and how I decide to proceed is my decision alone."

"Please sir," he whispered. "I may have something else we could try."

Talbot stopped mid-step and turned his narrowed gaze upon Thomas.

Breathless, Thomas tried to focus on the pattern of the tiles underfoot.

"What do you mean by that?" Talbot asked slowly.

"While you were away," Thomas' voice tremored a little as he dug his nails into his satchel. The leather was pockmarked with half-crescents, a true sign of his inner turmoil. "I created a series of medicinal draughts that have healing properties for those afflicted by lycanthropy."

Talbot cocked a black eyebrow. "And how were you able to test their effects without a werewolf?"

"I ... I came across one last week." It was a small lie, twisting the timeline, but Thomas feared for Richard's exposure only a little less than Philip's.

"How ... convenient for you."

"It was a coincidence, sir. However, I was able to test one of my experiments. It seemed to have worked, although I can't be sure how long-lasting the effects were."

"Why not?"

"I fell asleep. By the time I woke up, everyone had scarpered."

"I see."

"Please, sir? We can at least give it a try? It can't do any more harm than keeping him locked up like a savage animal."

"It's for his own good," Talbot stated. "That cage has silver embedded in it. If he tried to break out, he'll be burned."

"Is that what silver does to them?" Thomas murmured, momentarily awestruck and sickened. He'd doused Richard in silver; had the poor man felt as though he were being burned alive in that bathtub?

Stephen didn't comment. Instead, he sighed wearily. "I suppose at the very least, there is no real harm in giving one of your concoctions a trial-run. He's been kept awake for some fifty-eight hours already. Another trivial attempt to render him weakened in his current form."

Thomas pursed his lips. Despite how primitive the torture

had been, there was no denying that not getting a set number of hours sleep a night severely impaired one's mental faculties and basic motor functions. There was some minor logic to it but at the same time it wouldn't be nearly enough to render a were-beast harmless. How they were going to keep Philip restrained during the process was another mystery entirely. Richard had been severely weakened by the time Xander had dragged Thomas to that old house. He wasn't convinced that Philip was at the same level of exhaustion.

"How are we going to restrain him?" he finally asked.

"We'll need a number of people to help. The mixture of scents will confuse him, only then can he be restrained."

"Will we need the shackles?"

"Yes."

Thomas let his chin drop into his hand. The idea of shackling Philip up was terrifying –he'd never imagined such a horrible idea! It set him on edge and made his skin hot and cloying over his skeleton. He raked a hand through his hair. This was all too much.

"Does this mean that you'll have to involve the other men?" Thomas finally asked.

"Yes. We'll need as many men as we can get."

"What will you need me to bring?"

"A vial of the antidote as soon as you're able. I want you to explain to me exactly what you did last time and make sure that we replicate it as much as possible. If we can achieve the same results, then we may just bring Philip back from the brink."

Thomas pressed his lips together.

He needed to hold onto hope.

"I'll bring as much as I can. We can go over some of the more intricate details then."

Talbot inclined his head before dismissing him.

Later that night as he laid in bed staring up at the brocade canopy, Thomas listened to the sounds of the night around him. He was exhausted and needed some time to rest before the following evening, but he wasn't able to sleep. His mind kept turning to Philip and how things would have been if he'd stayed at the townhouse. Would he have disappeared into another room when the full moon came? Would Thomas have been able to restrain him and keep himself safe? Or would Philip have ripped his throat out before disposing of the house servants?

'By midnight tomorrow you could have the old Philip back. You need to focus on that instead of all the negatives. You need to try and remain positive!'

That was easier said than done. He couldn't help but think about Xander and Richard and their daily lives. How did one incorporate a werewolf into their life? What precautions needed to be taken to ensure everyone's safety? Would he have to chain Philip up in the basement? Would he needed to bind the beasts muzzle to stop it from biting him? If so, how would one do such a thing without help?

It was all so confusing.

More than anything he missed the blonde man's company, his dry humour, the way he carried himself with grace even in the privacy of his own home. Thomas felt his insides twist painfully. He needed to make sure that, no matter what happened tomorrow night, Philip would live throughout the ordeal.

Throughout the entire day, Thomas was jittery with nerves. His mind was entirely preoccupied with the repercussions of what could go wrong that night. All he wanted to do was to rush ahead to the following morning to see if everything worked out or not. The not-knowing and anticipation was crippling. He was barely able to touch his breakfast and stressed over every detail in his journal. He didn't want Talbot to criticise his work above all things right now.

'*You're doing this for Philip!*'

Gently placing the stoppered bottled into the stiff doctor's bag he'd bought from O'Callaghan. The man had insisted, saying that he'd gotten a new one for his deliveries. Nevertheless, Thomas had paid him decently for the weathered case. It had been a Godsend since he had to pack as many vials as possible to take with him to the hospital that night. His hands trembled as he placed the last one in, and snapped the case closed. Stealing a glance at the clock, he felt himself tense up as he saw that it was just gone 7 o'clock.

It was time.

Taking a carriage to the hospital, the vials twinkling softly in the case in his lap, Thomas felt his heart beating heavily beneath his ribs. What if everything went wrong? He didn't want to be responsible for Philip's death. Every fear escalated itself in his mind until he was dripping in a cold sweat, his hands damp as he clutched the handle of the leather case and marched up the stone steps to the hospital. He was sure he held his breath the entire time until he knocked on Talbot's office door.

"*Enter.*"

Thomas twisted the doorknob and walked into the office. Nothing had changed from the previous evening. Thomas tightened his hold on the bag handle. Placing the case on the desktop, he looked at Talbot as the older man looked from the few sheets of parchment he was reading.

"Did you bring the formulas?"

"I brought my journals as well. Hopefully you find them

detailed enough to understand the thought process behind them."

Talbot held out as his hand. Thomas dug his neatly written journals out of the bag and carefully handed them over. It felt as though he were handing over a piece of his soul. Talbot didn't invite him to sit down; he merely flipped the first journal open and began to read. After a few minutes of standing awkwardly in front of the desk, Thomas sat down across from his professor, placing the case gently under his chair. He watched the older man flipping through the book, each page turned was another nerve plucked.

After about twenty minutes he swallowed thickly. "So – what do you think?"

"This is an interesting take on the information we have."

"Do you think it's worth a try?"

"Considering you don't fully understand which part of the formula worked or why, I'm inclined to say it's not worth the risk." Thomas felt his stomach drop. "However, despite his current state, Philip is still my nephew. I'm responsible for him. I don't want to see him die. At least, not like that."

"So –you're going to let me try it this way?"

Talbot inclined his head, handing the journals back. "I don't see what we have to lose."

"So when the others come –what do we tell them? We can't tell them that it's Philip. He'd be ruined!"

Talbot dismissed his concern with a wave of his hand. "That's easily taken care of. If we do manage to transform him back to his human state, he'll be so ragged and battered no one will recognise him."

"That doesn't sound risk-free."

"It's the only option we have."

In truth, Talbot was right. There was no other way. That didn't mean that Thomas liked the idea of risking Philip's exposure.

Within the hour Talbot and Thomas had arranged all the equipment they needed in the auditorium. The other students had been invited back early, too, filing in one-by-one. A couple cast him a glances but didn't make any comments as Talbot closed the door behind them all. He wasted no time in detailing the plan for that evening, and cautioned the other students that they needed to wear as many thick, rubber layers as possible to prevent infection.

As he looked around the cluster of familiar faces, Thomas could see that they all wore the same mask of horror and apprehension. It was bound to be a long evening and Thomas was anxious that he hadn't been able to sleep. Somewhere in the labrynth of winding corridors and narrow hallways, Philip was waiting, panting, and scrabbling inside his cage.

With stiff muscles, they all changed into thick, rubber overalls, gloves, aprons and had metal collars slipped underneath their formal shirts just in case a wayward claw lashed out at them. As soon as they were all ready, the door to the office opened.

Talbot appeared in the doorway, a large iron ring of keys in his hands. "Follow me."

Filing out of the office, the group of students followed the tall dark-robed man down into the bowels of the hospital. The hallways were narrower, damper, and the air became stale and suffocating. The darkness was broken up only by the lantern Talbot held aloft. He picked a key from the ring and slipped it into one of five steel doors on the basement level. At least two of them had to be the boiler rooms. The room was dark and musty as they entered, Talbot taking his time to light the few torches and lanterns suspended from the ceiling.

In the centre of the room sat the beast in its cage.

'Philip. He's still Philip, underneath all of that.'

"Sir," Bennett's voice rang out in the low-ceilinged room.

"How exactly are you going to make that thing easy to strap down?"

"You leave that to me, Mr. Walpole."

The seven young men watched as the older man uncorked a large bottle of chloroform and soaked a rag before gingerly slinging it inside the top bars of the cage. The beast growled low in its throat and flinched as the sheet slumped down over its head, catching one of its pointed ears. It tried to shake the sheet of, but the wet fabric caught against its teeth, jaw and shoulder as it fought. Panting heavily, it wriggled around on all-fours, slobbering and pawing at its head to no avail. As it did this, Talbot sloshed more of the chloroform through the bars, dousing the marred skin of the creature within.

It took at least eight minutes before the werewolf was subdued.

Thomas watched with a heavy heart as Philip wavered on his unstable, mismatched legs, claws scraping against metal as he finally fell sideways and slumped to the floor. Once the beast was unconscious, it was easier to shackle the long, hairy legs and drag the drowsing creature out of the cage and onto a thick metal table on the other side of the room. It had been reinforced recently, no doubt for this very purpose. Thomas and Neville lit at least a hundred candles and positioned them in a large, intricate pattern on the floor.

Five of them needed to haul the wolf onto the table.

It landed heavily, its tongue rolling out of his gaping mouth. The body was steaming, the chest slowly rising up and down.

Each of its long limbs were shackled down and tightened over the furthest corners of the table. Talbot produced a large worn leather muzzle with a metal bit attached to keep the beasts' mouth open. It looked horribly uncomfortable as the straps bound the skin and fur tightly, but it needed to be done. Thomas drew in deep measured breaths, trying to calm his frantic nerves.

'*It'll be over soon*,' he assured himself. '*Just get through the next few hours.*'

At the side of the metal block table there was a crank. With Bennett's help, Thomas managed to lower the interior surface deeper into the steel borders. Philip's body sank along with the tabletop, his claws scraping against the sides as they rose around him.

"Remember what we are here to do," Talbot intoned. "Segdon, take charge."

Head snapping up, Thomas looked around the other expectant faces. Drawing in deep breaths, he addressed the others. "We need to douse him in the concocted mixture that's laced with silver, valerian roots and the formula I've been working on. Ordinarily, we'd need full exposure to direct moonlight but if he remains unconscious, we should be able to carry the body to the back courtyard where they make the deliveries."

"What if he wakes up?" Neville asked.

"We'll have to use more chloroform," Talbot stated.

"Won't that contaminate the formula?" Bennett asked.

"Perhaps," the professor agreed. "However, depending on how things transpire we may need to take that risk."

"What about after?" Clifford, a usually quiet young man, asked. "If it were so easy just to pour medicine over them surely someone else would have done it?"

"That's why we have these." Talbot unsheathed several long, engraved silver spikes. Thomas' eyed widened in fear. The spikes glimmered in the candlelight, the Latin words engraved into the silver made him shudder with revulsion.

"Sir, we don't need those," Thomas said.

"They're just a precaution, Segdon," Talbot stated coldly. "In case your way doesn't work, we'll do the rest my way."

Thomas opened his mouth to argue, but what else could

he say? Talbot always had the final ruling. Perhaps the spikes wouldn't be needed, and Talbot was right; they could just be a precaution. Still, his gut twisted.

Pressing his parched lips together he turned his gaze to Bennett. "I need you to turn the tap one; it should produce a solution mixed with hot, soapy water."

Bennett did as instructed. Pipes glugged and gurgled before chugging out gallons of the stuff. It sluiced over the furry body, rushing up over its limbs and pooling around the creature until it was soaked through and at least four inches deep. It wasn't enough to drown the beast, but it whetted most of his body. The fur seemed to writhe with bubbles under the skin.

It was unsettling to watch.

"Now I'm g-going to pour three vials over his body," Thomas spoke the words, but his mind was several miles away in the townhouse, where everything had been going so well. "T-This is so it soaks into any open wounds and is absorbed by the skin."

"What about the rest of it?" Bennett asked.

"They need to be ingested."

Everyone's mouths set into a grim line. No one wanted to be the one to tip a vial into a sleeping wolf's mouth. Thomas uncorked each of the first three vials and dribbled them over the beast's body. The creature let out a deep guttural growl but didn't wake up. The water sloshed. The flesh seemed to ripple and bubble a lot more and the men hummed in fascination.

"Sir, would you care to administer the first vial?" Thomas asked, holding a vial out over the table.

Talbot narrowed his eyes a fraction but took the vial. He popped the cork and held it down into the tub, hovering just over the glistening fangs and tipped. The smoking liquid trickled down into the creature's mouth. Once the wisp of smoke disappeared, they all waited with baited breath. A low groan started to drag itself out of the wolf's throat. The flesh-coloured skin bubbled and grew greasier as the creature rolled onto its back, the tweaked jaw turning up to the ceiling. Something gurgled at the back of its throat, growing louder and louder.

"Thomas ...?" Neville frowned, backing up a step.

"Is it waking up?" Bennett frowned panic ebbing into his voice.

"I ... I don't know."

"Hand me another vial, Segdon," Talbot ordered.

Thomas obliged, passing another vial over the tub, as the water started to bubble and froth. The candlelight flickered. Pulling the cork out, Talbot poured the liquid into the mouth. It smoked and seemed to hiss at the corners of the creature's jaw as it trickled through the fine layer of fur still clinging to its skull.

"Another!"

By the time the third vial was emptied, the wolf's eyes were rolling in their sockets. Its mouth was smoking, and its limbs were twitching, tugging at the shackles.

"Sir, are you sure those chains are strong enough?" Clifford asked.

"I had them forged specifically for this purpose. Yes, they're strong enough."

Thomas watched as the creature writhed in the water around its body; the chains clinked, its skin squirmed as though a thousand worms crawled underneath, and its matted hair started to slither away in greasy little clumps. They floated in the water like drowned hedgehogs. Suddenly the beast's eyes snapped open revealing milky grey orbs. Its jaw worked itself into a twisted mask and a long howl burst out, erupting through the silence that had befallen them.

Whilst everyone backed away, Talbot and Thomas stared down in horror as muscles and broken bones snapped back into place and untwisted themselves, a grotesque pantomime taking place under the marred flesh.

"Get back Segdon!" Talbot commanded, his arm knocking Thomas in the chest and snapping him out of his trance. He watched as the man raised one of the silver stakes high over the tub. In a low voice Talbot began to chant in Latin.

The sound rung in Thomas' ears, drowning out almost every other sound.

Flashing in the candlelight the stake was plunged down into the tub. It struck through bone and metal. Another, agonised howl ripped out of the wolf's throat.

The chanting continued.

"Professor, No!" Thomas cried.

He was dizzy from being thrown back against the wall. Had he hit his head? He couldn't be sure; the aroma of the potion was making him disorientated. None of the other men came to his aid nor intervened with Talbot. For all Thomas knew, they'd fled the basement. Another stake banged down into the creature, and then another and another.

"Professor ... please?"

All he could hear was the striking of those metal stakes, the sound matching rhythm with his fear. He wasn't even sure what he was begging for at that point.

On shaking legs, Thomas pushed himself up to his feet, his vision blurred and wavering as he advanced towards the professor. He needed to stop this madness before the man used all seven stakes. The beast was howling pitifully at this point, crying out for freedom and respite, tugging uselessly at the chains and shackles, water spilling out over the sides of the tub and onto the stone floor.

Thomas slipped in a puddle and caught Talbot's sleeve as he rose the next stake.

The sound of metal hitting stone was like a bolt of lightning.

"Segdon, what are you doing?" Talbot's distant voice sneered at him.

Thomas didn't –couldn't –answer. He clambered into the tub, terrified or both the beast and what would happen if he let this assault continue. He took the ring of keys of the side and fumbled with them. The creature's chest heaved underneath him, the blood oozing into the milky bathwater and turning it pink. Something tugged at the back of his collar, but he dragged himself away. His collar ripped against his throat.

'*Two more, two more, two more!*' was all he could think.

Finally the last shackle unlocked, sinking to the bottom of the tub.

A howl tore through the air.

Metal hit stone and water rushed over everything.

Thomas was flung to the floor. He clamped his mouth shut as the water washed over him in foul, frothy waves. Shadows danced through his eyelashes, but he was exhausted. His arm throbbed and bled into the bathwater. The cold was seeping into his bones and his mind was numbing everything, including the fiery pain at the back of his head.

Sounds echoed on the periphery of his consciousness.

"*Segdon, you've damned us all!*" were the last words he heard before he blacked out.

Saturday 3rd November 1888.

Thomas was out cold for three days.

That was the doctors told him on the afternoon that he woke up. His head was a cacophony of pain, weird humming sounds and a feeling like his scalp was on fire and being feasted upon by bugs. His hands were bandaged up too, which made scratching at himself even more difficult. One of the doctors had even joked that very rarely did they see the same patient return to them so quickly.

By early evening Thomas was able to sit up by himself in time for his dinner to be brought to him. It was then that it was announced that he had a visitor. Vague memories burst through his brain and he nearly threw-up at the idea of Stephen coming to see him.

To his surprise and relief, Xander came in.

He looked exhausted with dark bags under his eyes but he appeared in a much finer state than Thomas had last seen him; his dark hair hung in combed curls around his shoulders, his dark glasses gleamed as he took them off along with his top hat and placed them in his lap as he seated himself at Thomas' bedside.

"You've certainly proven your stupidity and bravery in equal measure," he commented blithely, a teasing smile playing on his lips.

Thomas relaxed a little more, despite the words. "I –I'm sorry?"

"Your little stunt the other night. During the ritual."

More memories ghosted through Thomas' head, barely skimming the surface of his conscious mind. The intruding thoughts made his skull ache. Xander took note of his pained expression and poured him a glass of water. Thomas drank from it gratefully, his bound hands lying uselessly on his lap.

"What happened to –the wolf?" Thomas hedged.

"I have been keeping tabs on the creature, don't worry," Xander stated, placing the pewter jug back on the nightstand. "For now, he is safe."

"Is he with you and Ri –er –the other one?"

"Perhaps," Xander nodded, his eyes flickering to the ward door. Thomas followed. The walls had ears wherever he seemed to be. The last thing he needed to do was expose names when any passing nurse could repeat the information.

Thomas rubbed at his forehead and grimaced at the gauze there. Turning to the man sat beside him, he asked, "Did they tell you what happened to me?"

"Not at first. However, as soon as I said I was your uncle and only living relative in London, they soon changed their tune."

"So what did happen?"

"It's hard to say, really," Xander confessed with a sigh. "They found you almost drowning in that room, covered in cuts and bruises and the foul-smelling formula you concocted. Old Talbot was half-conscious in the corner, mumbling something unintelligible. You were both brought here and tended to in separate wards."

Thomas swallowed thickly. "How –How is he?"

"He's alive."

"Was he ... bitten?"

"Not as far as I was able to tell."

"You examined him?" Thomas asked aghast, his jaw dropping open.

"As soon as everyone else left, yes." Xander smirked deviously. "As I said, I don't believe he has been bitten. Scraped a little but no, he shan't be turning into a were-beast anytime soon."

That was a small relief at least. Thomas drew in a deep breath and relaxed back against the pillows. He stared down at the dinner tray in front of him and then dumbly down at his hands. "Um ... would it be too strange if I ... um ... asked you ..." He held up his hands by way of explanation.

Xander smiled warmly. "Of course not, kid." He dragged his chair closer and, in a surprisingly fatherly manner, picked up the bowl of soup and the spoon and started to feed Thomas. "Try not to spill any."

Thomas flushed a little and tried to oblige. Some soup dribbled down his chin, but Xander swiped it back up with the edge of the spoon. Thomas couldn't remember anyone doing that with him since he'd been a child. It left him feeling low and longing to return home, to see his parents. Such familiarity would feel blissful at that moment considering the trauma he'd experienced. Xander was easily adapting into the role of a father-figure in that moment, but Thomas hadn't the heart to ask if the man had had any family prior to living in London. He didn't think his heart could handle anymore sadness at that point.

He ate the rest of his meal in silence.

Eyeing the room around him a = while later, Thomas found that something didn't quite add up.

"Xander –how is that I'm in another private ward? Philip paid for my last one, I don't understand how I'm here, now."

Xander didn't speak for a little while, his chin resting on his folded hands. He seemed to stare into space for a little while. The silence was somehow more irritating to Thomas' sensitive nerves than talking out loud.

"Philip didn't initially pay for the private ward. Once he found out about it, he switched the payments to coming from him instead. This hospital doesn't care where it gets its money from as long as they get it."

"So ... who did pay for my board last time?"

"Me."

Thomas' eyes went wide. "You? Why –why would you?"

"Thomas, haven't you ever wondered why you were granted the scholarship for your medical degree?"

Thomas shrugged helplessly. "I –I assumed I was some sort of charity case. That I needed to prove my worth against the others who had all sorts of resources."

"In a way, that's the measure of what everyone has to do," Xander stated.

"So –I wasn't a charity case?"

"Probably not in the way that you're thinking, no."

"Then ... why?"

"I paid for you, of course."

Thomas felt his insides churn. "I ... I don't understand."

"Thomas, I placed a large donation to this hospital on the understanding that they would not throw out your application simply because you were from outside of the city. It tends to happen, believe me. However, as soon as I heard the committee were intrigued by your grades and intelligence it made me feel terrible that they would just cast you aside, letting another, less intelligent person to take your stead."

Thomas listened mutely, his frown making his skull ache and buzz. Xander had taken it upon himself to pave Thomas' way to success –or at the very least to get him into the most prestigious medical school in the city. Why would he do such a thing though? Was there something for him to gain if Thomas was successful?

"W-Why did you make the donation?" he finally asked.

"Why wouldn't I?"

"You're a stranger to me! You cannot deny that! I have no prior connection to you until last week and now you seem to be dogging me around London!"

Xander's mouth twitched into a smile. Despite the truth in Thomas' words there was also a lot of information the young man didn't know. It hadn't been purely coincidence that he'd shown up at opportune moments.

"Thomas, did it ever occur to you that someone may have been watching you?"

The hairs on the back of his neck stood on end. "Y-yes, I had gotten used to the idea that it was Philip."

"For the most part, it was."

Thomas narrowed his eyes. The man didn't shrink away from him. He simply sat upright in the stiff wooden chair, his hands neatly folded in his lap and his expression open and neutral. "You? Why would you be following me?"

"I made an investment in regard to you, Thomas. You need to be alive and make well on the chances given to you."

"Bought for me, you mean."

"Does it really matter how you got the opportunity to study at the hospital? Or should it only matter that you are here, with these other men, excelling in your studies from what I overhear and are on the road towards a promising career after your exams, should you pass?"

Thomas couldn't describe what he was feeling. It was agitation and anger, but also a strange dabble of endearment that someone had cared enough about his future to take such a bold risk on his education. Not that he hadn't made every go of it he could, it was just incredulous to think that someone outside of his own flesh and blood would care.

His skull throbbed.

There was still one thing that didn't make sense to him.

"I'm sorry, sir, but there has to be another reason for your decision to invest your time and resources in me," he spoke with his head bowed to his chest.

"Oh, there is."

A pause. "May I know what it is?"

Xander closed his eyes. "Thomas, I don't wish to distress you whilst you're still recovering."

"I'm perfectly fine!"

"No you're not," Xander replied, calmly. "You've been through a terrible ordeal. You need time to recover properly. This information can wait for a few more days."

"I don't need another adult keeping secrets from me, Xander," Thomas stated tightly, wishing he could scrunch his useless hands into fists. "I'm sick of being kept in the dark! These last few months have been harrowing and I need to know as much as I can if I'm going to get through this *alive*."

Xander let out a weary sigh and stood up from the chair. For a brief, flickering moment he had been tempted to tell Thomas everything he wanted to know. However, he had not come to the hospital that night to enrage the teenager, but rather to make sure that he was still alive. The last thing he needed was for the kid to be scratched any more than he already had been.

Or bitten.

Patting Thomas lightly on the leg, Xander placed his top hat upon his curled hair and straightened the lapels of his jacket. "I'll be back soon, Thomas. Take advantage of the hospitals amenities while you can."

"Xander!" Thomas frowned. "You can't just leave!"

"I'm afraid I must, Thomas. You are working yourself up and may even burst some stitches. You need some solitude to decompress your mind, rest and recuperate. I sincerely hope it is a swift recovery."

"But -?"

"Rest, Thomas," Xander smiled in the doorway. "Just try and rest."

He didn't give the young man a chance to reply. He simply walked out of the private ward and let the sound of his shoes clicking on the marble floor follow in his wake. He couldn't deny that Thomas needed answers, but now was not the time. If he was going to divulge all to the boy, he needed all the information at hand to give an accurate depiction of what happened. There'd be time for all of that, but for now he needed to do what was best for him.

Xander had invested in his future.

Xander had spent a lot of his money in order for Thomas to get a good education.

Why would a perfect stranger to something like that?

The only time something of that nature would happen to other people, it would be a well-known wealthy benefactor, or a rich relative that had been abroad. Xander didn't seem to fit either profile in Thomas' life, so what were his true motives for financing Thomas' education? Was it so he could force Thomas to create an elixir in order to save his friends life? Was Richard's life more important than the way Thomas saw himself? More importantly, the way the rest of the world saw him? If he grew infamous for that sole discovery –he'd be no more than a joke.

A court jester.

Someone to laugh and jeer at as he walked down the street.

The subject of many conversations whispered behind gloved hands and handkerchiefs.

The feeling of despair pooled inside him like cold, black tar. Swallowing thickly, he brushed the hair out of his eyes and turned his gaze towards the window. Through the cobweb thin curtains, he could see the black sky stretching far and wide over the orange and black landscape of London Town. It had taken him a while to get used to the city skyline. He'd missed the rolling hills of home, the quiet and the crickets. It had all been so peaceful. However, peace and silence were rare in the bustling city; it was almost an alien concept unless one happened to be awake at such a late hour.

Now, however, the world was still.

The only thing Thomas could hear was the beating of his own, steady heartbeat. If he didn't know any better, he'd have guessed that he was the only person in that hospital.

His mind came back to Xander. He still didn't understand what that man was talking about and why it related to him. Scoffing at himself, he turned bodily onto his side and tried to make himself as comfortable as possible. He pulled the bedsheets higher over his shoulders and tucked them under his chin.

'*I wonder where Philip will be sleeping tonight*,' his mind hummed. '*Will he be warm and dry? Will he have food and water? Will he be human or ...?*'

He clamped his eyes shut, his breathing hot and heavy against the scratchy pillowcase. There was no need for such thoughts. He didn't need to sit there in bed and question all these ideas and problems. He was well enough –wasn't he? Pushing himself upright, he used his teeth to scrape and pick at the taut bandages. With a lot of tugging and snarling, Thomas was able to rip through one of the bandages and unwind it. Adrenaline helped him get the other hand free.

Numb and shaking, he stared down at his hands. They were both dark purple and his nails were marred, chipped and red. Yellow bruises marked his skin up just past his wrists.

Tears welled up in his eyes.

'*Don't cry. Panic later, but you don't have time to waste.*'

Sniffing loudly, he wiped his nose and eyes on the sheets before gingerly swinging his legs over the edge of the bed. The floor was cold underfoot as he pressed some weight onto the quaking limbs. It felt wrong –as though it weren't his body to control. It felt slow and limp as he shuffled a few feet to the window and back. Air caught in his lungs.

"I can do this!" he hissed to himself.

It took him a good half an hour or so to fully dress himself. With a tight chest, Thomas hobbled awkwardly across the room. Peering around the doorframe, he looked up and down the dimly lit corridor. He appeared to be alone. Getting to the back stairwell had him perspiring, lungs aching and his spine bending with pressure.

The cold, brick stairwells were refreshingly cold. However, by the time Thomas got down to the ground floor, he was drenched in a sticky sheen of cold sweat. Panting heavily, he dragged his body through the door. The main reception cast a sickly green glow at the furthest end of the wide hallway. Thomas wiped at his eyes and slowly, with his back pressed against the wall, made his way down towards the light.

Trembling, he peered around the corner. The main desk was empty.

Surely, they wouldn't leave the entire hospital unguarded all night? Perhaps there was an emergency that required all staff? Maybe the receptionist was out getting the police for statements. Perfect. The door to the outside world was within his sight. Drawing in sharp, shallow breaths, Thomas forced himself away from the wall and hobbled clumsily towards the double doors.

A tremor ran down his spine as he loped across the sparse, open area.

The rough wood bit through his shirt as he pushed all his weight against it. Grinding his teeth together, he did his best to force the doors open. They groaned weakly in protest but eventually gave. A sharp gust of wind ripped through the air. His entire body loped backwards with the pressure, but he continued to push through. He was sure he felt something 'pop' somewhere on his body and a trickle of warmth started to bloom on his left side. His mind was spinning as he almost fell down the stone steps leading up to the hospital.

The stars and moon welcomed him.

Emotions crashed over him like waves in a storm.

A desperate smile clawed at his mouth, tears burned in his eyes but there was no time to dwell on it. He had a lot of questions that needed to be answered and he was done being kept in the dark. Carefully using the iron railings for support, Thomas made his own, loping way down into the city of London, leaving a thin trail of bloody droplets in his wake.

Sunday 4th November 1888.

Philip's townhouse was the perfect place to take refuge and recuperate.

Thomas had managed to tend to his wounds with Joan's help. Thankfully she hadn't asked any questions. She'd simply run out and gathered all the necessary gauze and ointments that he requested. In the daylight he looked as though he were the lone survivor of a train crash. His mind was still trying to comprehend how he came to be in such a state. His hands were still a little swollen and mostly useless, which wasn't encouraging him to do much by way of practicality. He wanted to go outside and search for Philip, but how was he supposed to do that if his hands would barely turn a doorknob?

He used one of Philip's old canes to help him hobble downstairs. If nothing else, he could spend some time reading and drinking some tea.

Joan had lunch with him again. Thomas insisted afterwards that he was fine and could handle things for himself. She could take the afternoon off. She was troubled about leaving him in the mess he was in, however Thomas didn't plan on being at the townhouse for longer than a few more hours. He had something more pressing on his mind.

At late afternoon, the doorbell rang throughout the desolate house. Thomas could almost sense who it was before he even opened the door. The daylight fell, bleak and grey against the brocade of Xander's waistcoat as he swept into the hallway without invitation.

"You really didn't expect me to find you here?" he asked

tersely, rounding on the young man.

"Of course I did," Thomas replied, closing the door, and leaning heavily on the cane. "In fact, I expected you a lot earlier."

Xander sighed and removed his hat. "Why did you leave the hospital?"

Thomas didn't answer right away. Instead, he led the older man down the hallway and into the oak-panelled library where he'd been reading. Settling down into his armchair, he waited for Xander to sit down on the other side of the coffee table before speaking. "I needed more answers, and you weren't around to give them."

"So you thought you'd run amok and get them yourself?"

"Well, you're here, aren't you?"

Xander narrowed his eyes. "Thomas, you're not well. You need proper medical attention."

"You're a doctor, aren't you?"

"I didn't get my full license."

Thomas shrugged. "You're better than I am, especially in my current condition."

For emphasis, he held up his battered hands. Xander pursed his lips. He wasn't impressed by the severe bruising but chose to keep his thoughts to himself for the time being. They sat in silence for a while. Questions that had plagued Thomas all night, bubbled to the surface of his mind, each more important than the last. Swallowing against the lump in his bruised throat Thomas broke the silence.

"Have you managed to find Philip?" he asked, his voice barely a whisper.

The older man bowed his head. "Luckily, he was easy to track."

"W-Where did you find him?"

"I found him sauntering down along Spitalfields. How he managed to get all the way there without being seen I cannot fathom."

Thomas felt the blood drain from his face. Spitalfields wasn't exactly nearby. "Did he ... um ... was there any ...?"

Xander shook his head. "I did a preliminary search but as far as I could see, no, he hadn't hurt anyone. If he had, it was most likely by a drunk street-urchin."

"Where is he now?"

"He's in a safe place, as is Richard."

"I was going to ask. How are they coping? Are they still -?"

A sombre expression passed over Xander's face. "Yes, I'm afraid so. More human than werewolf at this point, but there is no denying that they are still caught in between."

"Is there anything we can do to help them?"

"I've noticed that the moonlight helps," the older man stated. Lacing his fingers together he drew in a deep breath and continued. "I leave them locked up with direct moonlight over them for most of the night. This seems to help heal their broken skin, bones what have you. It also seems to slowly cleanse them of their beastly attributes."

Thomas felt his mouth droop open slightly. "How slow are we talking?"

"Seven hours of moonlight seems enough to heal a single limb. Although it isn't directed at one place, Thomas. It's all over their bodies, which means the healing is stretched even thinner. Last night one of Philip's hind legs was able to snap itself into an almost human-like form. It's stopped about a foot longer than his other leg."

"And Richard?"

"He's looking less like a wolf and more like a fanged statuette at this point. Still has his tail, though."

For some reason the mental imagery was too much for Thomas. "Is Richard able to understand you at this point?"

"He can always understand me, Thomas. In answer to your next question, no, he cannot talk just yet. Not properly at least. He tries to, God Bless his soul, but his teeth cut his mouth up too much. It's ... rather distressing."

That meant Philip wouldn't be able to, either.

The notion weighed heavily in Thomas' chest. "Take me to him."

He didn't care if he had nightmares for months to come, he needed to see Philip –whatever form he was in –and know that he was okay. That he wasn't alone in this Hell anymore.

"Are you sure?" Xander frowned. "I still have reservations about it, and I've been aiding Richard in these matters for longer than you've been alive."

Thomas nodded with grim determination. "I need to be there with him, Xander. He has no one else. Not really."

There was the obvious argument of Talbot hanging between them, however he was still indisposed at the hospital. Thomas needed to remember to go and speak with his professor at some point. That wasn't a priority, however, going to see and help care for Philip was.

"If you're sure," the older man finally sighed. He stood up from the armchair, brushed lint of his cloak and turned for the door. "Be ready to leave in ten minutes and not a moment longer!"

Thomas took a few moments for himself before building up the strength to climb the stairs up to his bedchamber. There he packed his satchel with a fresh shirt, undergarments and his medicines and gauze before hobbling like an oaf down towards the front door.

'*I'm coming, Philip,*' he thought, grinding his teeth as pain shot through his body. '*Don't worry! I'm coming!*'

The carriage pulled up outside an old, grim house that

seemed to shrink away from the main road. The sky had darkened with the promise of rain. Thomas shivered and drew his cloak tighter around his stiff shoulders. Stepping out onto the pavement, he looked up at the tall, narrow house and instinctively wished to turn back to the carriage and run.

"This is where you live?" he asked, his stomach tying itself into knots.

"It was my mother's house before she died," Xander stated coolly. "I only use it now and again. It's useful for the basement; it's practically sound proof."

Thomas frowned but Xander had already moved past him and into the front garden. Instead of walking up the stone steps to the front door, the older man took a sharp right and began making his way around the side of the house down a narrow, brick path. There were tangles of dead nettles and ivy browning alongside the house's edge. Xander's thick boots trod over them easily enough. Thomas felt the odd prickly leaf nick at his skin but hurried on, not wanting to let the man out of his sight. As he rounded the last corner, it was just in time to see Xander pocket a heavy padlock and tug at a pair of ground-level slanted doors. They grunted open, the hinges in desperate need of oil. From somewhere below, Thomas could hear the scraping of claws and padding of feet against straw.

"You keep them down there?" he asked as Xander began to descend ahead of him.

"Where else was I supposed to keep them?" the taller man asked, arching an eyebrow. "I could hardly take them on the train up to the moors, could I?"

Thomas had to concede that he had a point. With anxiety spiralling inside his brain, he followed Xander down into the basement.

The basement itself was recently modified by the looks of the fresh, new wooden beams and the clean, scrubbed brick walls. There was a small stove off to one side giving off warmth and daylight coming in through the long, ground-level window above their heads. The grey light slanted down into the room. It gave off just enough light for Thomas to make out the long, gnarly half-forms that were Richard and Philip dozing in a strange nest. It looked to be made of straw, ripped sheets and there were two thick coverlets pushed to the side with fraying edges. Xander hung his cloak, hat and cane on some wooden pegs and then went over to the small stove.

"Tea?" he asked.

"Please."

The two creatures in the corner watched with their discoloured eyes, pointed ears pricked while the rest of their bodies remained motionless. It was disturbing seeing the half-formed Philip so poised and still in the beastly form.

Thomas took the seat opposite Xander, the warmth from the stove driving away the chill that clung to his skin and clothing. They drank an entire cup of tea in silence, only broken by Xander refilling their cups and letting out a soft sigh. Thomas eyed the two beasts who had laid back down in the nest, their breathing shallow and erratic.

"How long do you think they can live in that condition?" Thomas asked, keeping his voice low.

"I'm not too sure," Xander confessed. "It's only ever happened a few times before and never for this long."

Thomas felt his heart sink. Perhaps his potion had mixed with whatever Talbot had previously tried? Maybe Richard changing back to his human form had been a temporary fluke after all? Taking another sip, the hot tea rushing through his insides, he shivered and looked over at the creatures again. "Are they not healing at all?"

"As I said, Thomas, it's an arduous process and so slow it probably causes them more pain than good."

"I brought another couple of vials —to see if another recipe would work for them."

Xander frowned and then shrugged his shoulders. "I suppose there's no real harm in trying, not whilst they're in this state. Perhaps one of them could even speed up the process."

"What'll happen once they become human again?"

"At least a week or so confined to bed-rest to recuperate. Richard has been having a lot of problems in recent years, trying to maintain a job. For at least a week and a half each month, it got him branded as unreliable. That's why he stays with me."

"So that he can save some money?"

A pause. "For the most part."

They lapsed into silence again.

Thomas cradled the warm cup of tea against his bruised abdomen and drew in deep, calming breaths. It was the first time he had started to feel comfortable since the previous evening when he'd snuck out of the hospital. Stroking the fine china under his thumb, he took another sip and shivered. The sky grew darker outside the window. When the room became almost too dim to see, Xander went around lighting the lamps that hung across the ceiling at different intervals.

It cast a pleasant glow throughout the large room.

"Xander?"

"Yes, Thomas?"

"Would you mind if I stayed here tonight and monitor how you —how you interact with them?" He gestured at the half-formed beasts, only noticing in that moment how both creatures had shackles around their wrists and legs.

The older man smiled as he removed his waistcoat and tied his hair back out of his eyes and rolled his sleeves up. "It would certainly make my evening much easier."

"Is there anything I can do to help?"

"Yes, a fair bit actually. Try to get yourself rested in the next hour."

Thomas nodded, reclining back in the chair, and stretching his aching legs out in front of him. The tea did a lot to help him calm down –he mentally wondered if there was aconite in it but decided that he didn't care. It soothed his mind and kept him from focusing on the wounds that itched and scratched under the gauze.

He must have dozed off a little because the next thing he remembered was being shaken awake by Xander. *"Thomas? Thomas? Come on, kid, wake up. I need you to help me with this."*

Yawning, Thomas stretched and gingerly stood up from his chair, swaying a little on his feet. "Okay –what do you need me to do?" he asked, adjusting his glasses on his nose.

He took note of the long chains that clunked as Xander dragged them across the floor. Taking a hesitant step forward, he braced himself against the wall and watched as the two creatures clumsily climbed onto their haunches. They let out low, growling sounds but didn't aim to bite or lash out as Xander approached.

"What are you doing?" Thomas hissed, feeling hot panic surge through him.

Xander held out an arm and waved for him to be quiet. In his hands he had a long rope, looped at one end.

'*Like a noose,*' Thomas thought.

With one swift movement, Xander had the rope around Richard's neck and tugged. With a yelp, the creature's head lurched back as Xander tied the other end around his waist. "I know it hurts," he crooned, "I'm sorry but it'll be over soon."

Thomas watched with fear in his stomach as Xander advanced and splayed his fingers through the last tuft of fur on the animal's body. He stroked it softly. The smaller beast let out a warning growl, but Xander turned towards it and flicked some liquid at it. Still growling, the creature backed up a couple of steps. Thomas watched, scared, and intrigued as Xander returned his attention to Richard and continued stroking his free hand up and down the beast's body. In his other hand he held a muzzle with a thick, gleaming silver mouth-bit. As the Richard-beast whimpered and struggled weakly against the restraints, Xander managed to wrestle the muzzle on over his head. Once the buckles were secured, the curly-haired man untied the rope from around his waist and backed away.

Glaring, the creature let out a low rumbling whimper but didn't try and lunge. Turning to the younger boy, Xander held out the rope and a smaller muzzle. "Okay Thomas. It's your turn."

The blood drained from his face. "What? No! I —I can't do it!"

"Yes you can."

"No! No, I can't!"

"Yes you can Thomas. It doesn't hurt them as much as you think it does."

Thomas stared down at the offending muzzle. How could he do such a thing to Philip? His gut twisted inside him. He hesitated before reaching out towards the rope and muzzle and swallowing thickly. "What if —what if he attacks me?"

"That's why I'm here with you."

Thomas gave him a dubious look but didn't argue. Drawing in a deep breath, he took a step towards Philip. The animal cocked its head to the side, sniffing at the air and pulled its lips back in a grotesque snarl.

"*Talk to him, Thomas. Calm him. He can tell that you're scared,*" Xander murmured. Thomas nodded and advanced. The rope and leather bridle of the muzzle felt rough in his palms. "*Okay, I want you to toss the rope around his neck on the count of three. One ... Two ... Three!*"

Thomas tossed the noose and tugged Philip's head back, wincing as the creature yelped and pawed at the air. The guilt that ripped through his chest was immense. He almost let go of the rope completely, but Xander placed a hand on his shoulder.

"That's good Thomas. Now tie the rope around your waist and put the muzzle on over his head."

Thomas held his breath as he hurried forward and quickly fastened the bridle over the creature's head, fumbling awkwardly to secure the straps and make them tighter. Philip tossed his head from side-to-side, the metal bit scraping between his teeth. Thomas backed up, heart thumping in his chest. He could smell his own sweat and fear rolling off him in waves. He was sure he saw Philip's nostrils flare. Getting as far away as he could, he unfastened the rope and let the creature drop back down onto the floor with a whimper.

It took several moments before his heart calmed down. His eyes were damp and hot.

A hand landed on his shoulder making him jump. Xander gave him a comforting squeeze, "Come. Let's have some tea."

Thomas nodded mutely.

They drank in silence for a little while, the adrenaline ebbing away. Thomas downed the first cup in one gulp, hiccoughed, and then tried to calm himself down as he watched the two animals' paw awkwardly at their muzzles.

"Does it get any easier?" he found himself asking as Xander refilled his cup.

"Which part?"

"Literally chaining up and gagging someone you lo –care about?"

Xander ran a hand down his face. "I want to say '*yes, it does*' but there's no way you can get around it. It doesn't get easier, especially not when they're in this half-form state. Especially if they change in the middle of the night. Then you have to see your human companion in such a disparaging state with a bridle on their head."

Thomas watched as the two creatures shuffled about on their oddly shaped legs. Moonlight shone down through the clouds and fell over their mangled forms. Turning to Xander, Thomas pulled out two vials that he'd brought with him.

"Do you want to give them these vials? It's one of my other recipes. I don't know what it will do to them."

Xander held out his hand and took the glass vials. Popping both corks, he stood up and advanced towards the two animals. Their heads perked up, ears pricked, and a tension appeared in their posture as Xander grasped out for Richard's bridle and pushed the vial into the side of his mouth. He tipped the vial until it was empty, his muscles straining against the jostling creature, before letting him go and repeating the same struggle with Philip. Wiping sweat from his brow, Xander settled back down into the chair beside Thomas and took a long sip from his teacup. "Well, if this is what it's like having to take care of children, I'm glad I never bothered with them."

Thomas frowned. "You never wanted any?"

"I was tempted in my younger days," Xander admitted. "I just never found someone I wanted to tolerate for that long."

"You tolerate Richard."

"Richard is ... something else entirely."

"Didn't you have any friends who had kids?"

"Yes. I had two friends who got married and had a son. They moved out of the city because they wanted a better family-life for their child."

"Did you go and visit?"

"I used to try and get up there every month. However, when I reunited with Richard, my visits became irregular and then I just couldn't face letting my friends down all the time. I went up when I could, but it has been years."

"Were you very close?"

"We grew up together. I was even made godfather to the little boy. I feel bad I couldn't do more."

"I'm sure you did what you could."

"Well I'm trying to make up for it now."

"Oh? In what ways?" Thomas asked as he poured them both the last of the tea.

"I simply gave the young boy an offer he couldn't pass up."

"Like you did with me?" Thomas said offhandedly, before his hand stopped midway to his lips. His smile dropped. "Like you did ... with me ..."

"Thomas ..."

The teacup nearly shattered as Thomas let it slip from his hand. He turned to look up at the man. "You ... You're ... You're my godfather?"

Xander pressed his lips together and gave nodded.

Thomas sat still as he processed the information. The two beasts made low grumbling noises in the corner. Thomas just felt numb all over. He had a godfather? Why hadn't he been told? Why would his parents keep him in the dark? Were they worried that he'd have left them in search for this man? This wild, unruly man who kept werewolves as companions.

'*Actually,*' he reasoned. '*That's probably exactly why they didn't mention it. Papa must have known at least.*'

He let out a sigh and rubbed his temples.

"I understand if you're upset," Xander started, his voice trailing off.

Thomas ground his teeth together but closed his eyes. "You're here now, I suppose. At the times that I really need you, you showed up. In a way that's what a godfather should do."

Xander hummed. "I won't presume that this is okay or that you're happy about this. I understand it'll take time."

"Yes. It will."

"However, I'm more than willing to help you with Philip's problem. If you wish to speak to me after we help him, then that is entirely your choice."

"I suppose that's fair."

Xander looked up and felt his jaw slacken. Keeping his voice low, he tapped Thomas on the shoulder. "Look at them. Do you think your potion did that?"

Thomas followed his line of sight and sat up a little straighter. Both creatures' heads were lulling lower and lower, their eyelids heavy and their limbs slowly relaxing as the medicine took effect. Xander and Thomas watched in stunned silence until both Richard and Philip were asleep in their strange little nest of torn sheets and straw, Richard's elongated left arm sloping down over Philip's hunched shoulders.

"Wow..." he breathed out, not daring to believe his eyes. "This is incredible!"

"See? You were worth the investment."

For some reason that Thomas was unable to identify, he felt a ball of pride bloom within his chest. Revelling in the emotion for the moment, Thomas relaxed back in his chair. Together, he and Xander watched the moonbeams shift patterns through the windows. Only at dawn did Xander insist that he retire up to the house for some proper rest.

Thomas resisted at first but soon relented. As he drifted off to sleep, he couldn't deny that he still felt proud of what he'd accomplished that evening. He fell asleep before any other thoughts plagued him into misery.

Friday 9th November 1888.

The papers wasted no time in printing Mary-Jane Kelly's obituary.

Xander had returned that morning with the local paper tucked under his arm and a weary expression on his face. It had been a gruelling couple of days since Thomas had joined him at the house and had given his new formula to both creatures. Thomas had helped him as much he could and, just two days ago, when they went down into the basement they were both relieved to find a very naked, dirty and bruised pair of men, cradled in the torn blankets.

Baths had been run immediately and, once both men were escorted up into the main house and settled into the two large tubs by the stove in the kitchen, Thomas and Xander set about scrubbing them both and tending to their wounds. It was a long morning, but it had been worth the rewards once everyone was settled down, bandaged, drinking tea, and eating soup at their leisure in the parlour.

To have such an article in front of them only served to rack the tension that clung around their necks.

Philip read the newspaper and shivered violently. He drew the blanket tighter around his shoulders and bowed his head.

"Do you –Do you think I was responsible for that?" he asked hoarsely. His throat was still recovering from all the growling he'd done as a were-beast. "Do you think –I did that when I was ... when I was ...?" he trailed off, unable to finish that particular thought.

Richard reached out and tentatively squeezed the blonde man's forearm. "Accidents happen, Philip," he stated diplomatically. "Trust me, I've had my fair few newspaper clippings about my heinous behaviour."

Philip kept his eyes on the tabletop.

Thomas looked between all three of the older man, feeling completely at a loss for what to say. Instead, he reached for the newspaper and spread it out in front of himself to read. It was a short summary of events; Mary-Jane's body had been found mutilated –almost beyond recognition –and left to rot in her lodgings in Dorset Street, Spitalfields.

Spitalfields.

Where Xander had found Philip.

"Xander?" He turned to the man. "You said there were no casualties."

"As far as I was able to check, there didn't appear to be," Xander said defensively. "Need I remind you; I also had a seven-foot-tall werewolf to try and get control of without being bitten or wounded?"

Thomas bowed his head. He'd set Philip free from the hospital basement. In truth, this woman's death was on him. She'd only been twenty-five. She'd had her whole life ahead of her –not like the other victims that Thomas had helped dissect. A tremor ran down his spine. He hadn't felt any of those emotions for the other women.

"Do you think they will just bury this one?" Thomas asked quietly.

"It's hard to say," Xander stated. "I think they're going to leave this one open for a few days, get a thorough autopsy and most likely a second opinion from Talbot himself, then they'll bury her."

"Do you think someone should go and talk with Talbot?" he finally asked.

Three heads turned to look at him with unreadable expressions.

"Are you sure that's wise?" Philip croaked out, a bitter edge to his voice.

"Doesn't he deserve to know what's happened to you? That you're human again?" Thomas snapped.

"He was going to stab me through the heart," Philip sneered through gritted teeth. "I couldn't care if he were to never speak to me again!"

"He was only trying to help."

"Are you seriously defending him?" he spat.

Thomas flinched and averted his gaze. Philip appeared to remain animalistic in temperament after a full moon. Standing up quickly, Thomas flinched away as the chair crashed to the floor. Philip gripped the edge of the table, breathing heavily, before turning and storming from the room.

The door slammed shut.

A spattering of dust fell across the table.

Thomas felt horrid. He was ruining everything. He'd let Philip loose and been the indirect cause of the young woman's death and now he'd gotten Philip into a temper. Things were not going well.

'*Bad things always come in threes!*' his mama used to say. Thomas couldn't help but wonder what number he was actually on.

"I'll go and see if he's okay," Richard finally said, draining the last of his tea and making his way upstairs, trailing a hand discreetly along Xander's shoulders as he passed.

The silence was horrible.

"Do you … think I should go and see Talbot?" Thomas asked meekly as he toyed with his plate.

"I think you should do whatever you feel is right," Xander stated as he started to clear the table. The clattering of china being stacked filled the air, giving Thomas a chance to gather his thoughts. As Xander went to clean everything up, Thomas was left alone. He thought about it, he truly did, and in the end, there was no denying the truth of it all; Talbot needed to be told exactly what was going on with his nephew.

The roads around Dorset Street were still crammed with people. For the most part it was due to the police still sweeping the small back-building where Mary Kelly had apparently lived. They were trying to usher the people away from the crime-scene albeit unsuccessfully. Thomas let himself fall in with the crowd and slowly migrated to the other end of the street before making his way towards St. Barts.

He ducked his head as he briskly walked through the reception. The nurse behind it was too busy trying to deal with a couple of men who were bleeding through bottle cuts to pay attention. On the first floor, Thomas asked a nurse which room Stephen Talbot was staying in. A private ward on the third floor. Perfect.

Thomas followed the directions as quickly as he could, all too aware that the sterile lighting highlighted every bruise and cut on his skin. Tugging the collar of his cloak higher around his chin, he paused outside the door and listened. Considering the bustling noise in the hallway behind him, he struggled to determine whether the room was indeed devoid of medical staff.

Thankfully, there was only Talbot.

Thomas slipped into the room and closed the door quietly behind him. He needn't have worried as Talbot was awake, propped up against four or more pillows with a dismal hospital breakfast on a tray on his lap. His disdainful look only intensified when he caught sight of Thomas in his doorway.

"What in God's name are you doing here, Segdon?" he sneered.

Wringing his hands a little as he took a step into the room Thomas said, "I was hoping we could discuss last week. At the hospital."

"What of it?"

"I –I wanted to explain myself. For my actions."

"I don't want to listen to this!" Talbot seethed.

"I know I was just –"

"No, Segdon, listen to the words coming out of my mouth. I do NOT want to hear this. I know exactly why you did what you did. Regardless of your 'noble' reasons," he spat out, his voice dripping with sarcasm. "You endangered lives. From what I hear, there's another corpse awaiting my technical eye. So please; leave me to clean up the mess you've managed to create and get out!"

"Sir, I know what I did was reckless," Thomas hedged, trying to keep the distraught quaver out of his voice. "I know that young woman died. However, considering the alternative I don't believe you have any –"

"I am your professor. I have every right! I even have the right to permanently dismiss you from this program and send you packing back to your hovel in the moors!"

Thomas was struck by the words. Despite the bruises and lacerations covering the older man's pale skin, there was no denying that his bitterness seemed to thrive on discomfort. Swallowing past the lump in his throat, Thomas straightened his back, squared his shoulders, and tried to steel his mind. He'd left his family and everything he'd known to journey to a new, strange city in the hope of a better education. To have those doors shut to him was enough to break his heart.

"Sir, only one person died. Philip's –he's human now. I think I've found a new recipe that makes them docile –"

"Get out, Segdon."

"Sir, please, just listen –"

"*GET OUT!*"

It was the first and only time Thomas had seen the man lose his temper —and it scared him. There was an ugly pink flush to that sallow skin and the black hair hanging around his pinched features only accentuated the demonic side to the man before him. Fear spiked through his brain as he backed up against the door. Talbot continued glaring at him. Thomas fumbled for the doorhandle, twisted it, and fell back into the hallway.

He could smell the fear staining his body like invisible ink.

Turning his back on the room, his professor and —no doubt —his future career, Thomas left the hospital grounds and returned to Xander's townhouse.

"I don't think it's safe to stay in London right now," Xander stated over dinner.

He'd spent the early evening time cooking with Richard in relative silence. Philip still hadn't come out of his room despite the late hour. Richard had insisted, in his mild-mannered way, that Philip was fine, he was just keeping to himself out of pride, embarrassment and exhaustion.

Thomas set the table mentally preparing himself for the emotional upheaval of waking the blonde man up from his rest for dinner. Looking up at the two older men, he was suddenly overwhelmed by how young and inexperienced he was of the world.

"What could we do?" he asked. "Where would we go outside of London?"

"My family has an estate up in Scotland. It's been out of use for a while but it's large enough for all of us if we were inclined to move."

Thomas stared at Xander, his mouth agape. "How rich are

you? You have a townhouse, an old house out of town, and one in Scotland?"

'*Whilst my family lived meagrely,*' went unsaid.

Richard lit some candles and oil lamps around the room before getting some wine out for the table. "Don't pull at that thread, Thomas," he offered a wan smile. His lips were pockmarked with scabs.

Thomas shifted awkwardly. "I'll -go and see if Philip's awake."

"Don't bother," grumbled a voice from the door, "I'm here."

"Oh um ... Dinner is just about ready."

Philip stared down at him without really seeing him. He nodded his head and then took the seat closest to the door and slumped into it. He didn't seem to care how he acted around the other three men, any longer, considering they'd all seen him naked and covered in his own filth. The other three worked in silence in preparing the fish supper and boiled spuds. The smell of the food was enough to make everyone's guts growl with hunger and, thankfully, soon they folded their hands, said a silent prayer, and began eating. It wasn't a fancy or refined meal by any means, but food was food.

"So, has there been any more thought about our predicament?" Philip asked hoarsely some time later, as Xander poured everyone some tea to drink with the cakes, he'd gotten from the bakery that morning.

"Xander was suggesting we might move up to Scotland," Thomas replied.

"Oh? Where would we live?"

"I have a family estate up there. It's been vacant for years. I'm sure there wouldn't be any issue in transferring the deed directly to my name for us to live there."

Philip merely hummed.

"Would that ... bother you?" Thomas asked.

"I suppose not. Money will still serve me well up in

Scotland. The house was put into my name, so I can simply sell it." He looked up with sharp, clear eyes at Xander. "Would I be able to bring my own furniture and belongings?"

Xander grinned. "Yes, Philip, you could. You could have one wing of the estate if that pleases you."

Philip narrowed his eyes but remained silent, stabbing listlessly as his cake. They lapsed into silence, the weight of the situation descending upon them. Thomas glanced up at the clock and sucked in a breath. It was nearly nine o'clock. The night was getting on and he still hadn't gone back to the townhouse.

Standing up from the table he said, "Sorry, I need to head out. I was supposed to get Philip some more of his belongings from his house and I forgot on my way back from the hospital."

Xander wiped his mouth with his napkin before standing up. "I'll come with you. I don't like the idea of you wondering around this late, considering what's happened."

Thomas cast a look at Philip and Richard but didn't comment. It was safe to say that the two causes for the recent trauma's occurring in London were due to one or either of them. They had the decency to look ashamed of themselves. Thomas cast his godfather a stiff look before his shoulders sagged. He knew there was no way out of it.

"Okay. The sooner we go the sooner we can be back."

Richard and Philip didn't move or say anything as Xander grabbed his cloak and followed Thomas out of the house.

Philip's townhouse was tall, pale, and gleaming in the dim light as Thomas used the spare key for the front door. The locks drawing back echoed in the silence trapped inside. Xander was a solid, calculated presence behind him and Thomas hated to admit he felt much more secure with Xander there. He only needed to go to Philip's bedchamber and pack a few bags. That'd get him through his '*healing time*' before he was able to go back out on the streets again.

It had been a painful full moon.

The hairs on the back of his neck stood up on end as Xander lit a lantern on the end table and helped light the way up the stairs. Thomas followed close behind, tapping the man's shoulder when they drew near to the bedchamber. The lock snicked back as he pushed against the door. It creaked through the silence, echoing like a gunshot. Xander lit a couple of candles on the bureau to give some more light to the room. Thomas had his back to the room as he took some of Philip's freshly laundered garments and packed them into a satchel when it happened.

A lantern shattered on the floor, dulling the light.

Xander yelled out before being muffled.

Thomas couldn't see who it was, but he could see the vague shapes of two men grappling. They dragged one another onto the floor, landed blow after blow into ribs, muscles and limbs. Both men grunted, and Thomas panicked, trying to figure out what to do. Hurrying across the room, he grabbed the scruff of the assailants' neck and yanked him back away from Xander.

"Enough!" he yelled, as Xander stood up, cuffing blood from his chin. "Xander, the candles!"

Hissing and gobbing out mouthfuls of blood onto the wooden floor, Xander struck a few matches and lit the candles that had been knocked over in the scuffle. He had a few cuts across his cheek and chest from a scalpel. They beaded with blood in the dim light. In the glow of the candles, Talbot's face came into view as the hood was yanked back from his cloak. Xander growled loudly, grabbed the man by the throat and slammed him up against the wall.

"Why is it whenever there's a problem, I come face-to-face

with *you*?!" he barked, squeezing the doctor's neck.

Talbot sneered, blood leeching down his barred teeth. "I could say the very same about you!"

"What is going on?" Thomas snapped; his nerves frayed.

Talbot swivelled his eyes to look at the young man. "I came here to talk to my Godson. Now where is he?"

"He's with me!" Xander growled.

Thomas looked between the two men. They were on the verge of tearing one another apart. "Philip is safe," he spoke up. "He's –He's recovering. He'll be well enough before we leave."

"Leave?" Tablot snapped. "Why? Where are you going?"

"Scotland," Xander grunted. "NOT that it's any of your concern."

"He's my nephew! Everything he does is my concern!"

"*Xander*!" Thomas shouted over the din. "Go and wait outside. I need to speak with Talbot alone."

"You really think I'm going to leave you alone with this man after what he's just done to me?"

"Yes," Thomas said coldly. "Go and tend to your cuts. I need to speak with my professor *alone*."

Xander ground his teeth together but wrenched his hands from around Talbot's throat. He was rather brutal as he shoved the greasy-haired man aside and stalked out of the room in search of medical supplies, a feat not too difficult in that household.

As soon as the door slammed shut, Thomas turned his attention to the man he'd left in the hospital. "You have no right to demand anything of Philip after what you did."

"Perhaps not," Talbot croaked as he rubbed his throat. "However, being assaulted by your brute of a bodyguard is hardly necessary."

"You cut him!"

"Semantics."

Thomas resisted the urge to roll his eyes. "We're moving up to Scotland. It's not safe for Philip here anymore. Not with his current nature."

"You think he won't kill up there?" Talbot spat bitterly. "It'd just be easier to hide the bodies on the moors, that's all."

Thomas bristled at the accusation but didn't rise to the bait. Not this time. "Why did you come here? What do you want?"

"I had wanted to apologise to Philip for what I had been planning to do."

"An apology was going to fix that?" Thomas asked in disbelief. If he hadn't intervened when he did, Philip would probably be buried alongside Mary Jane Kelly.

"Of course not. However, I would have offered him a second chance at life. Much like you're trying to do."

Thomas, despite his anger and resentment towards the man collapsed in the chair before him, felt a ripple of understanding. There was no doubt that Talbot had enough of his own money from medical awards and investors across the board of directors at the hospital. Maybe the life he was going to offer Philip was better than the one Xander was.

Pressing his lips together, he crossed his arms over his chest and leaned against one of the posts of the bed for support. His own injuries were making him feel weak.

"Philip wants to move to Scotland," Thomas insisted, keeping his voice as firm as possible. "He's agreed to it, as long as he can bring his own possessions with him."

Talbot scoffed. "That's very much like him."

"We'll most likely be leaving London as soon as we can arrange it."

Talbot considered him through narrowed his eyes, his breathing shallow. "Very well. I'll let you take my nephew away from everything and everyone he knows –on one condition."

"What?" he asked slowly.

"Stay."

Blinking, Thomas shook his head trying to let the single word sink in. "I'm –I'm sorry?"

"Stay in London," Talbot rasped, clutching at his stomach where Xander had landed a punch. "Finish your degree. Get your license. Do as you please after that, but *do not* waste this opportunity."

"I –but –what about the murders? The women we cut up? Reports of the Ripper? Do you really think that's all just going to disappear?" he asked frantically.

"Of course not. However, if you can get Philip out of London now, then it'll be the end of it, won't it? It'll stop with one gang of prostitutes. People will simply brush it off as some Holier Than Thou Christian wanting to purge the city of the diseased evil that lurk in alleyways."

"I –don't know what to say," Thomas admitted.

His body felt clammy and sweaty as he stared down at the professor. A small cut on his forehead was starting to bleed. He tried to ignore the fact that the Ripper could very well be the only other man in the house with them, but he brushed that chilling thought aside.

"Can I –Can I think about it? At least?"

Talbot sighed heavily, clenched his fist to redirect the pain but nodded regardless. "Fine. You may *think on it.*" He grunted a little as he hunched over on the chair. "However, you may want to get all of this arranged before the next full moon. Who knows what may happen then."

Thomas swallowed thickly.

Within the hour Thomas managed to get Talbot into a carriage and paid the driver in advance to take his professor back to the hospital. Xander looked as though he was ready to grab a knife and dissect the man right there on the pavement, but Thomas reminded him that they had more pressing matters to attend to. Reluctantly, the man allowed his Godson to manhandle him into their own carriage and direct them across to Xander's townhouse.

As the carriage rocked along the narrow streets, Thomas fiddled with the frayed edges of his shirt cuffs. Talbot's words blurred through his mind, echoing in the silence as the wheels of the coach ground against the flagstones.

Sleep eluded him for the hundredth time that week.

Wednesday 14th November 1888.

I *t always ended the same.*

One minute he'd be taking a midnight stroll through damp London streets with Philip or Xander or just by himself. With the crack of lightning everything would change; Philip would be gone and down the other end of the street, standing in a pool of lamplight would be Mary Jane Kelly.

She'd reach a hand toward him and beckon him closer, a smile tugging at her lips.

Then her smile would pull too tight, the skin would split open and peel off the entirety of her lower jaw. The skin would hang and flap in the wet breeze, the stench of rotting flesh wafting from her. An eyelid would split open, her nose would drop from her face, leaving gaping, rotting holes in their place. Then, just as Thomas would step forward to help, her entire body would collapse into a heap on the cobblestones. By the time he'd reach her, only her mutilated body would remain; face completely unrecognisable, her chest cracked open and her organs running down into the gutter.

Another crack of lightning would wake him up.

"Another nightmare?" Philip asked just as Thomas swabbed at his face with a damp rag.

He closed the door behind him and edge into the room. Thomas shuddered and tried not to breathe in the water. He raked a hand through his hair and drew in several deep, soothing breaths.

"Want to tell me about it?"

"It was Mary Kelly again," he rasped.

Philip furrowed his brow, taking a moment to think. Then

realisation dawned on him, and the rosiness ebbed from his cheeks. Sparing the young man a sympathetic glance Philip reached out and squeezed his forearm. A draught made both men shiver a little. Winter pressed cold and brutal against the glass windowpanes. They sat in silence as Thomas drank half his jug of water before reclining back against the pillows, his muscles still tense.

"Have you given any more thought to what Stephen said?" Thomas finally asked.

Philip scoffed in derision. "Hardly. Have you?"

"I don't know what I want to do. Things are going to be hard for you in London right now and –"

"Thomas, even though it isn't my place to speak on your behalf, is it really wise to give up your place on this program? Even if you earn a place up in Scotland, you'll need to start from scratch –and none of this werewolf nonsense either."

"You can't fault it when you are part of it," Thomas hummed.

Philip gave a tight smile. "Perhaps. However, you cannot deny that you'd be setting your career back by not staying-on here."

"How can you say that after what the man nearly did to you?" Thomas croaked.

Philip's shoulders sagged. "As much as it pains me to say this –he was only trying to do what he thought was best."

"He was going to pierce your heart!"

"Considering you let me loose and the first thing I did was leave that whore's corpse lying in her bed, I think it's easy to see which scenario would have been easier!" Thomas scowled. "Don't look at me like that. He was trying to help. It's not his fault that those medieval books were –well –medieval."

"Regardless, it's basic biology that when you stab a creature in the heart, it dies!"

"So dramatic."

"I nearly watched you die, I'm allowed to be dramatic!"

Philip frowned. He'd only been teasing and decided to change tactics. "Thomas, what's done is done. Unfortunately, all Stephen can do is apologise. I'm not saying I forgive the man, or that I can forget what happened –as vague as that particular memory is for me –but I am still living, and he has suffered. There is no other way to move-on from this."

"As you said, it's a vague memory for you," Thomas stated, brushing the hand from his shoulder. "However, you forget that I was there, coherent, and conscious. I saw everything, and it still haunts me. Almost as much as Miss Kelly's body."

"Well I don't know why you insisted on seeing her corpse in the first place!"

"Morbid curiosity I suppose," Thomas sighed, cupping his hands over his face. He shuddered a little and pulled the covers higher up his chest. "I truly don't know, Philip. I can't get the image out of my head of Stephen raising that stake and –and –"

"Thomas," Philip drew the young man against his chest and rubbed soothing circles into the his back. The flush of his skin was clammy against Philip's chin as he rested it in the messed-up black hair. "I can't make the decision for you but look at what happened to that Kelly girl. It was either her or me. You spared my life, at the expense of hers. I cannot repay that debt to you."

"You don't have to –"

"Regardless, I owe you my life." He squeezed Thomas' body tighter. "Stephen may be eccentric and rash, but he isn't an imbecile. He wants to protect me. I think that night when he came to my old house, he had planned to do more than apologise."

"How can you know that?"

"He left the hospital despite a lot of heavy battering and internal bruising just to come and apologise? No, Thomas. He came to beg for my forgiveness."

Thomas blinked against the cotton of Philip's nightshirt. Beg? Stephen Talbot was going to beg? He'd kept Philip at arms-length ever since Thomas had known either of them. The imagery alone should have been too much for his mind to handle, however after the last couple of months, he could probably keep his composure upon seeing the Lord, God Himself.

"I can't imagine Talbot doing such a thing," Thomas managed to whisper, his eyelids drooping as Philip's warmth bloomed through him.

"Ah, then that just goes to show that you haven't known him as long as I have," Philip mused softly, threading his fingers through the soft, black hair. "Above all else, Thomas, he is human. He can't help the way he is. It's his nature."

A few days later they were all setting about their leisurely activities in the front parlour; Richard was mending one of the ripped coverlets from the basement, Philip was reading, and Thomas was sitting with his back pressed against the leg of the blonde's chair, making more notes in his journal. Even though he hadn't decided whether he was going to stay in London or not, he decided that he needed to complete his research to the best of his abilities. As he inked a detailed drawing of the half-formed shapes of Richard and Philip, he felt long, cool fingers thread into his hair and start caressing his scalp.

Philip had definitely relaxed in his affectionate behaviour around Thomas when Xander and Richard were around. At first, he was standoffish, almost hostile, but Richard tried to insist that it was because of a hard full moon for both of them. Thomas tried his best to just let the insults bounce off his skin —it was the least he could do considering that Kelly's death weighed on both their minds. Philip had brought it up one evening as they'd sipped spiced wine in front of the hearth.

In answer to his questioning, Xander and Richard had stumbled in, intoxicated from the local public house, and were pawing at each other like two dogs in heat. In that moment, any illusions that the two older men were nothing more than companions was instantly shattered.

Thomas drew in a sigh and tipped his head back against the cushion. "I cannot believe that within the next week, everyone I know and love it going to disappear to Scotland."

Richard chuckled quietly. "Don't worry too much, Thomas. You'll be coming up to see us at Christmas surely. As soon as you get your doctor's license, you can work wherever you please."

"I just feel at a loss again. I'll have to find new lodgings."

"Not necessarily," Philip hummed, his pointed nose still stuck in his book. His hand movements in Thomas' hair didn't stop either.

"Oh?" Thomas cocked an eyebrow. "What makes you say that?"

"You can just as easily stay in my townhouse. I'm only taking the furniture I actually use. The rest will be left there. It'd cost far too much to drag the entirety of that house up to Scotland."

Thomas smiled and shook his head. "No, it would feel too strange living there without you."

"You managed over the last few weeks."

Wrinkling his nose, Thomas straightened up. "As far as I was concerned, that was a temporary thing. I was right. It'd be completely different this time."

"A month is hardly something to whine about," Philip

chuckled. "Besides, I didn't intend for you to live there by yourself."

"What did you intend?"

"That you should speak with Stephen and live with him whilst you finish off your doctorate."

Thomas pursed his lips in response. Every muscle tensed, and he leaned out of the blonde's touch. His eyes and skin were burning with anger and resentment. In comparison, the tension between himself and Xander was a lot more manageable. Squaring his shoulders, Thomas gently closed the journal in his lap and turned to face his companion. Richard stealthily watched what was going on from under his fringe.

"I will not be staying in the company of that man!" Thomas seethed.

"Thomas, we've talked about this," Philip sighed, pinching the bridge of his nose. "Will you at least talk to the man? He's offering to let bygones-be-bygones. I'm not saying you need to speak with him outside of the lectures. The house is plenty big enough for you both to go about your daily business without interacting with each other."

"There's nothing you can say that will make me change my mind."

Philip opened his mouth to argue but, to both of their surprise, Richard held up a hand to silence them.

"I think I may have something that will change your mind, Thomas," he said with an easy smile. In that moment, that smile was unnerving. "As you know, Xander attended medical school around the same time as Stephen did. Unfortunately, due to complications, Xander was unable to complete his training. It hurt his pride and disjointed his mental faculties for a while."

Thomas nodded, narrowing his eyes.

"It has been a constant burden around his neck and – as you've seen –he's taken to putting his skills to use for my well-being and keeping my nose as clean as possible. Regardless of recent months."

Thomas looked between the two men. He was running out of arguments.

"Trust me, Thomas. Take the opportunities that life gives you. They will pave the way to a much better future. Besides, think how proud everyone will be that you're a fully licensed doctor. Who cares who you had to study with? It's a small portion of the rest of your life. You won't always get to like your job, or who you work with, or what you have to do, but at the end of the day those moments are temporary in the grand scheme of things."

Shoulder's sagging, Thomas glared at the triumphant look Philip pointed his way.

"Okay," he groused as he reluctantly settled down back at the base of the armchair. "I suppose I can at least speak with Talbot and see what he has to say."

"Keeping a calm mind goes a long way in this world," Richard stated with a sage nod. "Trust me. I've lived under the same roof as Xander for almost two decades. I may be the beast, but I have the tamest temper."

Philip let out a low chuckle.

Thomas managed a wistful smile.

Turning to the young, bespectacled man at the foot of his chair, Philip asked, "Would you like me to come with you when you go to see Stephen? I feel as though the two of you may need a mediator."

"I still don't understand how you can want to be in the same room as him," Thomas grumbled.

"He's family," Philip stated. "Unfortunately, that means something to me. Some breathing space between us would improve my outlook on him trying to kill me in cold blood."

"I despise your flippancy at your own morality!"

"Philip, stop antagonising him. Thomas, stop arguing. You're acting like children. If you want to act that way, I'll start sending you to your rooms without supper. Now, behave yourselves otherwise I'll set Xander on you."

"Oh please!" Philip scoffed. "What could that man possibly do to me that hasn't already been done?"

Richard gave a dark little smile. "You'd be surprised," he intoned, before turning his attention to his mending.

Philip and Thomas shared a look before clearing their throats and returning their attention back to their respective activities with renewed vigour. Within the hour Xander returned home and they started to prepare dinner for the night.

After looking in Philip's townhouse and then in the private rooms and the office at the hospital, Thomas was able to determine that Talbot was still at the hospital. The man was refusing to accept half his doctor's diagnoses and medicines they were giving him. It was causing a lot of difficulties in regard to his current residency as a patient.

Taking the stairs up to the third floor, they stopped outside Talbot's ward door. Thomas suddenly felt tense all over, his body warming up despite how cold the hospital hallways were. Philip reached down and squeezed his hand discreetly through the folds of their cloaks.

"Are you ready for this?" Philip murmured as he cast a glance down the hallway. There were a few nurses milling in and out of other private rooms, but none ventured down their way.

"What choice do I have?" Thomas murmured. "I have a week until you leave to head up North. Whatever my decision, I need to speak with this man. I need to understand why he tried to kill you and why I should risk my life living and studying with him if that's the way he behaves."

"Just remember what Richard said," Philip whispered. "Try to keep a calm mind. You'll do no one any good if you provoke the orderlies to come rushing in. The last thing you need is for the papers to report that you're attacking your former professor whilst he lies, defenceless, in a hospital bed."

"He may be in a hospital bed, but I highly doubt he's defenceless. Talbot doesn't strike me as being that careless two times in a row."

Philip smirked and pushed the door open.

Talbot scowled at the sight of them. "What do you want?"

"We came to talk with you," Philip stated bluntly. Thomas felt himself being nudged forward by a hand in the small of his back.

Talbot raised an eyebrow in disbelief.

"Thomas? Don't you have something to say to Stephen?"

Thomas glowered up at the blonde man but resigned himself to his fate. "I came to discuss the possibility of my staying in London to finish my medical degree."

Talbot blinked slowly. "Very well. What have you been thinking about it in regard to it?"

"That I don't know if I can study under you, considering what I've witnessed you do."

Talbot let a cruel, thin smile press his mouth into a line. "Do you really think being a doctor is going to require a lot of ethical decisions, above-board actions and complete honesty?" He scoffed. "Honestly, Segdon, you cannot be that naïve –not after all the things you've learned since you started."

Thomas bristled. "Technically no, I know there are some ethical issues involved. It just didn't really register in my head so much until I saw you about to stab your own nephew in his heart!"

"Philip, control your child," he sneered. "Are you going to continue acting like a brat, Segdon, or are you going to tell me what decision you've come to?"

"I haven't made my choice!" Thomas snapped. "I was hoping to speak with you and see if my mind could be made up. However, you're being as evasive and cold as you always are!"

"What do you expect? I've been working at this hospital for nearly two decades. Sensitivity and emotional attachments go out of the window within the first year."

"If I may?" Philip cut in. "I proposed the idea that the two of you could reside at the townhouse since I wouldn't be living there any longer. It's a large enough space for you to avoid one another outside of business hours and have enough space to work on your personal projects."

"It's ... an idea," Talbot grunted.

"I just don't know how comfortable I'd be with you as my mentor," Thomas said. "The only benefit at this point, would be that I'd be able to have more insight for my werewolf formula."

"It's a worthwhile ambition."

Thomas chewed on his lip before turning to look to his companion. "Philip, could you give us a few moments alone?"

Philip looked between the two men. Eventually, he bowed his head. "Very well. I'll be just outside. However, as soon as I hear any raised voices we'll reconvene to another time. Agreed?"

"Agreed."

With one last look at Thomas, Philip turned on his heel and left the room.

Focusing his attention on Talbot, Thomas felt his muscles tense up yet again. "I have some questions that I want to ask you. I want to try and be able to be in the same room with you without being consumed with hatred and anger."

Talbot didn't make any further comment.

"I'm worried that my emotional upheaval will impact the outcome of my work regarding the formula."

"That it will," Talbot agreed.

"I need to know that –that –you hadn't planned on killing Philip!" he finally hissed.

Talbot kept eye contact as he said; "I hadn't planned on killing my nephew. I had only planned on grazing his heart. The silver in the stake should have been enough to cause him to turn back into his human form. As soon as that had happened, I had planned on sewing up any cut arteries."

"It was an unnecessary risk!"

"More so than the death of that whore he mutilated?"

Thomas fell silent.

"That's what I thought."

"I still don't understand why you haven't turned any of us into the police?" Thomas queried, as he flexed his fingers over the cane. The wounds throughout his body were slow healing.

"That would hardly benefit either of us if I were to do that."

"How so?"

"If I were to land you into prison, I'd be destroying a young man's life in a way so mercilessly evil that even I have misgivings about it," Talbot licked his dry lips. "If I were to turn in my nephew and the beast that mauled him that first full moon, then I'd be throwing aside two prized specimens for this sort of supernatural study."

Thomas furrowed his brow. "What about Xander Holland? Would you not hesitate to throw him into prison?"

"Of course not," Talbot sneered, his thin lips curling over his barred teeth. "That mutt deserves everything that's coming to him and more."

"So ... then why are you letting him relocate everyone up to Scotland?"

"Whether I like it or not, he appears to be trained in the welfare and management of those in werewolf form. Until you go up there, they will need all the help they can get." There was truth to the professor's words as much as he seemed to say it begrudgingly. "Not to mention, I will insist on sending you up to Scotland for the week of the full moon, in order for you to try out variations of your formula until we can perfect it."

Thomas mulled over the information. As much as he wanted to loathe the bedridden man before him, there was a logic to his statements. It was almost too easy to plan, considering the predicaments they were in.

"I can't help but feel as though you're only agreeing to any sort of parlay because of the incredible chance that's dropped into your lap in the form of not one, but two werewolves."

"Does it truly matter?" Talbot asked. "If I were to turn you all in, you and Xander would probably serve life sentences and the other mutt and Philip would be put to death."

"You don't know that."

"Yes, Segdon," he said slowly with a pointed look. "I do."

'*He cares for Philip*,' he thought as he shifted his weight onto his other leg.

Despite outward appearances, and the general rockiness of their relationship, Talbot did care for his nephew that much was becoming clearer. Maybe there was hope for him to stay in London after all?

"Very well. I'll let you know my decision within the week."

Talbot didn't say anything more on the matter, so Thomas inclined his head and left.

"So, do you think it went well?" Philip asked as he tweaked a strand of Thomas' dark hair.

They were in the middle of having a hot bath in Philip's assigned bedchamber. The house creaked and groaned around them whenever the wind howled down the chimney. The brick walls were high and kept the heat inside. Despite the dust that had needed to be bashed out of the rugs, covers and canopy hangings, it was all very comfortable, even if the furnishings were a little dated. With the fire blazing, warming up their exposed skin, Thomas lathered himself over and shimmied lower into the water.

"I think it went as well as it could have gone," he said, "Considering that any yelling would have resulted in him being sedated. I think we both wanted to avoid that."

Philip gave a lazy smile as he scrubbed at his hands and nails. "Well, do you think it'll make your overall decision any easier?"

Thomas felt his smile drop. "I'm not sure. It's hard to say. A lot has happened that's impaired my judgement."

"How so?"

"I worry about you, Philip. You know that."

He chuckled as he raked two wet hands through his hair. "Thomas, you will have plenty of time to worry about me after you get your license!" He sat up straighter, so he could grasp the younger man's flushed cheeks between his hands. "Do something for yourself, then worry about the rest of the world, okay?"

Thomas looked up into the soft, clear eyes and felt his stomach flip. It was a surreal moment to be caught in, bathing in someone else's house in front of a roaring fire with a man who –quite literally –turned into a ravenous beast. His heart thumped in his chest as he was drawn in, closer and closer, until their lips met in a slow kiss.

Leaning back, eyes still closed, Thomas let out a soft sigh, "I adore the way you kiss me."

Philip smirked, teasing his fingertips around the shell of Thomas' earlobe. "Well, don't miss it too much. I can't have you hurrying up to Scotland without a medical degree."

"Does it really matter to you whether I have my degree or not?" Thomas murmured.

"Not in the way you think. I just don't want you to have any regrets."

"Do you regret me?"

Philip sat back; shock evident on his face. "Being bitten whilst coming to check on you, aside, no I couldn't regret you."

Thomas wasn't convinced. His eyes lowered to stare down at the soap suds fizzing around his bent knees. He raised them higher and pressed his chin against them. He felt a thousand emotions in the last couple of days and now all he needed to do was open his mouth and speak his mind.

With his mouth pressed to his knees he mumbled, "I worry that you'll grow tired of me and go off with some Scotsman whilst I'm studying."

Philip let out a bark of laughter. It sounded awfully uncanny to the way Xander laughed. "Oh, Thomas! Oh, you stupid little boy! Come here."

Before Thomas could protest, Philip had grabbed his arms, managed to spin him around in the narrow tub, and press his face against his pale chest. He looped his arms securely around Thomas' chest and tucked him under his chin.

"Whatever you're thinking you need to stop it," he said in an affectionate tone. "I don't want to be with anyone else, but you. I need you to trust that you're what I want in this world."

"How can you know what you'll feel a year or two from now?" Thomas asked, his heart sinking lower in his chest. There was a niggling feeling of impending fatalities in his mind and he just couldn't shake it.

"I can't know how I'll feel in a year," Philip admitted, "However I can make a comparison."

"Oh?"

"A year ago –two years even –I was alone."

"No you weren't, you had Stephen."

A pause. "As I said, I was completely alone," Philip

reiterated, making Thomas chuckle weakly. "I was depressed and filled my days milling around at high society luncheons, fencing, and going to banquets and lavish balls in the evenings. It was tiresome and there is only so much a rich young man can avoid, before getting ambushed by elderly women offering their young nieces or granddaughters for my bride."

"I can't imagine anyone wanting a sexless marriage."

"Precisely," Philip said. "Besides, I would have had to have sex with the girl for an heir and to stop rumours."

"How fun."

"That's high society."

Thomas wrinkled his nose. "Sounds terrible."

Philip chuckled, nuzzling his chin against the mass of damp raven hair. "Either way, I stopped going to those events and after about a year the invitations stopped coming through my door. I can't deny my relief. However, it just left a lot of long, lonely nights to escalate the demons in my mind."

Thomas ran his thumb down along Philip's forearm, watching as goose pimples prickled the skin, the fine blonde hairs standing on end. "Did you ever try to ...?" he trailed off, not truly wanting the question answered.

"Once. Stephen was not pleased. He gave me a hiding with his belt."

"You were grown man in your twenties, how did he manage that?" Thomas asked, tilting his head back with a perplexed expression.

"He may not seem like it, but he is a very agile man."

"Well it's a good thing he kept you alive," Thomas mused as he scooped handfuls of warm water over his chest. "Otherwise, we might never have met."

"What a terrible shame that would have been," Philip smirked teasingly before snatching Thomas' mouth in a deep, hungry kiss. The passion built up like gunpowder had been lit in their veins. Philip was on his knees and running his wet hands up and down Thomas' back before he finally broke the kiss and growled, "Perhaps we should move this to the bed?"

"Lead the way."

The sex that night was animalistic, passionate, and hungry as they devoured one another.

Thomas had to admit that now he knew what to expect, and that he readily wanted everything and anything Philip administered on him, having the older man buried deep inside him, rutting their hips together –it was enough to make every nerve inside him swell with heat and threaten to explode. He clung to the blonde's neck, legs pressed against his chest as Philip's hips thrust faster and faster, building to a climax that they both so desperately craved. Thomas tried his best to muffle his moans, but it grew harder as he succumbed to all Philip had to offer.

They barely rested for twenty minutes before Philip was ready to go again.

That second time, he somehow persuaded Thomas to sit astride him. He'd been hesitant as first, but as soon as he was completely sat in Philip's lap, his mind ran blank. All that mattered in that moment was feeling the older man.

By the glow of the firelight, Philip watched as Thomas gave into his baser instincts and ran himself ragged on him. It was the most beautiful scene he'd ever witnessed as Thomas spilled all over his stomach. Philip tried his best to stave his arousal, but all too soon, he reached climax.

Thomas fell asleep cradled tenderly in Philip's arm, listening to the beating of his heart and letting the sweat cool on his skin. He vaguely remembered the ghost of Philip's kiss on his temple and throat before their bodies were covered by a thick, cotton sheet and sleep enveloped him.

The following morning dawned bleak and frigid as the four men packed the remainder of their belongings into trunks and hauled them down the stairs to the two coaches waiting for them outside. The streets were almost empty, except for those few brave enough or desperate enough for the meagre shillings that they needed to keep alive. Thomas winced a little as the coach rocked along the road towards the train station. He couldn't help but notice that Richard had a similar expression. The idea brought a pink blush to his cheeks.

Once at the train station, Xander got their tickets sorted and helped Richard to stack the trunks onto the train. Thomas watched from a small distance away. It was strange to him, to think that someone who had been dubbed '*The Most Evil Man in Britain*' not only get away with manslaughter –or murder according to the tabloids –but also run off to a new life in Scotland.

The Ripper was fleeing London.

"Train leaves in fifteen minutes!" Xander called out from the platforms edge. "Try not to miss it!"

Richard gave Thomas a warm hug and murmured in his ear, "Come up to visit as soon as you have a chance. Don't waste this."

"I'll try my best," Thomas agreed. He watched as the greying man waved a final farewell and climb up into the first-class coach to take his seat.

Xander approached them then, a careful expression on his face. Things had still been a little tense since Thomas' visit with Talbot at the hospital. Though both men hated one another, there was no denial that Thomas' progression in the medical field was a top priority for both.

"Philip, would you mind if I have a moment with my godson?" he asked in a clipped tone. Philip inclined his head, spared Thomas a reassuring smile, and then moved away so that he was out of earshot. "Thomas, I know we've had some difficulties lately and I know this small token won't necessarily help in making things better between us but –*oof!*"

He stumbled as Thomas wrapped him in a hug. It had taken many restless nights to get to this point, mentally and emotionally, but he didn't care. After all the nightmares and all the trauma that he'd suffered with, it had all been made bearable by having someone looking out for him. There was no denying that Xander had been a low-key constant in his life. He hadn't aided Thomas in the same way as Philip had, but he had been there and that's what mattered.

"I'll try and do you proud, Xander. I –I really can't thank you enough!"

Xander let out a nervous laugh and returned the embrace. "You have no idea how much pandering and self-loathing it involved getting you onto the same course as –*that man.*"

Thomas smiled. "It's appreciated."

"Well, then I hope this will make things easier for you over the next few months." He handed Thomas a small paper packet. Inside was three hundred pounds. Thomas felt his jaw hang open, before Xander stuffed the packet into his pocket. "Don't go flashing it everywhere though. People get desperate in the Winter months."

They embraced one another one last time before Xander bade him a farewell and made his way into the first class cabin with Richard.

Finally, it was Philip's turn.

"I feel as though anything I say can't possibly match up to those words," Philip smiled softly as he came up beside him, discreetly brushing his hand against Thomas' as he turned to face him. "I almost wish we were getting a night train. Then at least I might have a chance to kiss you one last time."

Thomas felt desire stir inside him. "Don't say things you can't deliver on."

Philip smirked. "You'll write to me?"

"Every chance I get."

"I already can't wait to see you –again."

Thomas let the words wash over him. His heart was practically spinning in his chest. Opening his arms, Philip welcomed Thomas against his body and stroked the nape of his neck through his cloak. "Try not to stay outside too long. I don't want you getting ill. You have no excuse now that Richard and I will be in Scotland."

"I love you, Philip," Thomas whispered, almost hoping that the man couldn't hear him against the hubbub of the crowd. Yet, at the same time, praying that he would.

There was silence for a moment, before Philip lowered his lips to Thomas' ear and breathed, "I love you too. I'll see you soon."

The briefest of kisses was brushed against Thomas' cheek before he backed up quickly, raised a hand in a wave, and hurried towards the train just as the final whistle was blowing. Thomas remained on the platform until the train and its plume of grey smoke had vanished into the distance.

Taking a carriage towards the hospital to visit Talbot, Thomas asked to make a detour towards the old townhouse that he'd been staying at with the other three men –his strange little family –for the last few weeks. He barely even needed to slow down on the street as he caught sight of the 'FOR SALE' sign plastered up in the lower window of the front parlour.

That afternoon Talbot was officially released from the hospital and, together, they made their way to the townhouse. It was strange to see the empty spaces where Philip's furniture had once been. It felt a hole in Thomas' heart that needed to be filled with as much work as possible.

That is how Thomas became Talbot's lodger.

He remained in the bedchamber he'd occupied originally, whereas Talbot moved into the bedchamber that Philip had once used. Oddly enough, the large four-poster bed was one of the few things Philip had opted to leave most likely assuming that there were more ornate ones available to buy in Scotland.

After a small meal eaten in his room, Thomas settled back down with his medical journal in his lap by the fire. He hadn't seen Stephen for the remainder of the evening. The older man was probably resting in his room. He was still on a lot of medication.

As Thomas read by the fire, he couldn't help but have his mind wander to how Philip and the others were fairing. Had they reached Scotland yet? Were they settled in?

His stomach twisted in longing.

Rubbing at his temples, he closed his journal and reclined into the armchair. The loneliness crashed down on him like a rough, cold wave. His mind played tricks on him that night, to the point where he was almost certain –in the midst of the witching hour –that he'd heard a wolf howling somewhere in the far distance, crossing time and space just to reach his ears and let him know they were safe.

Friday 28th December 1888.

Upon returning from his Christmas visit to his parents in Yorkshire, Thomas received a letter in the post with the official results of his medical exam and the thesis he'd finally completed. It had been a long road, filled with a lot of late nights and heated discussions among his classmates –including Bennett who had had a few choice words the next time he'd encountered Stanhope at the hospital –but he could only hope that it had all been worth it.

He broke the wax seal on the back of the envelope and unfolded the thick sheet of parchment within. His heart was like a thick thudding lump in his chest, pressing down on his lungs and making it harder for him to breathe.

This was the moment he'd been toiling over for the last few months.

He opened his eyes and stared down at the neat calligraphy spelling his name. His eyes widened. He'd done it –He'd passed his exams! He had his official license and was invited to a dinner in his and the other graduates' honour to congratulate them, get them mingling with the inner circles of high society as well as getting their pictures taken for the newspaper. He staggered, almost completely floored by the revelation.

"Stephen?" he called out into the large house. "Stephen! Stephen! I got my letter! I passed!"

He found the older man residing in the study, his long nose in a book with a fire crackling merrily in the grate beside him. Looking over the rim of his newly acquired glasses, he smiled. "Congratulations Thomas. I knew you'd be able to do it. You put in more effort than half of your classmates."

Thomas beamed, a rush of softness and calm smoothing over him like thick treacle. He hadn't realised how on-edge he'd been over the last two weeks since his submission deadline had been met. Yet now, here he was, with his certificate neatly penned and held aloft in his hand. He only wished he could have celebrated with everyone who had made such an achievement possible for him. It had been a difficult six weeks living under the same roof as Talbot –however they had managed to set aside their differences for the most part and had managed to remain quite amicable towards one another.

It had all paid off in the end.

As soon as he'd eaten dinner, he went to his room, sat down at his desk, and penned a couple of almost identical letters to his parents and Philip. He had tried to write to everyone as frequently as he could, however as soon as his double lessons ramped up the studying for final exams, he found that there were only so many hours in the day. He had managed to keep both Philip and his parents updated on the daily goings-on of things down in London, but only just.

He had all of Philip's replies locked away in the top drawer of his writing desk. He kept the key on a ribbon around his neck. There was no way he could risk Stephen finding those letters, even by accident. He couldn't deny that he and Philip weren't as discreet as they could be in their outward approach to their affection for one another, however there was a difference between keeping it to themselves as opposed to shouting it from the rooftops.

Pressing his lips to the parchment, he inhaled wistfully before slipping it into an envelope and sealing it. Now that he was a qualified doctor, he needed to prepare himself for the dinner in his honour.

A plume of pale grey smoke rose into the air as a train on the opposite platform chugged off on its journey. Thomas watched it go for a moment before a hand on his shoulder brought him back to reality.

"You promise that you'll be back in time for the wedding?" Daphne asked, her smile bright and beaming as the wind caught her brown curls and tried to tug her hat off her head. She clamped it down quickly with one hand and tightened the ribbon under her chin.

"I'm only going away for two weeks," Thomas smiled reassuringly as he gave her shoulder an affectionate squeeze.

"I know. You do deserve a holiday and some fresh air," she conceded.

"Of course he does!" Rufus agreed enthusiastically. "He's been working himself to the bone just to get to where he is. He now gets to work on the same level as Stephen Talbot. That's something to be admired."

"Well he's not at the exact same level," Daphne corrected.

"Well perhaps not. However, he gets to work alongside the man and that speaks volumes to the medical community here."

"I'll take your word for it darling," she smiled, pressing a chaste kiss to his cheek. Turning her attention to Thomas, she took him by both of his shoulders and looked him square in the eye. "Now, are you sure you've packed everything for your journey?"

Thomas nodded. "Of course. I may just sleep. I was awake anticipating this all night."

Daphne frowned in dismay but didn't voice any of her concerns. Instead, she embraced Thomas tightly and squeezed. "Just make sure you come back soon. Rufus will be beside himself if he doesn't have his best friend to join him at all these high society functions."

Thomas chuckled. "I'm going to miss you both. I only wish I could have seen you more before the exams."

"Christmas is always busy for all of us," Daphne said sympathetically. "We'll see you soon."

She pressed a kiss to each of his cheeks. Rufus gave him a firm handshake and after hesitating a moment, gave Thomas a firm hug.

"Go on, off with you," he beamed down at Thomas. "Get on that train before it leaves without you."

Climbing up onto the train, Thomas spared his friends one last glance, raised his hand in a wave and then ducked into the carriage just as the final boarding whistle blew out. Settling down into the seats, Thomas watched the platform slowly roll away beneath him. He waved at Daphne and Rufus, and they waved back until he was out of sight. With his leather satchel between his feet, the soft tinkling of glass vials catching his ear every half hour or so, Thomas sat back in his seat and watched the city bleed away into the rolling hills of the countryside.

Soon, he'd left London behind entirely.

He dozed on and off for a few hours at a time. By the time he arrived in Scotland the sky had grown completely black outside, with no hint of stars to guide him. Through the bleak, black landscape that rushed by, small flickering beads of orange lamplight started flicking to life. The platform wasn't as busy as the one in London had been. He was surprised to find that Xander was awaiting his arrival. He was dressed in a fine brocade waistcoat, had his dark tinted glasses on his nose with his top hat and cane. He definitely stood out as one of the richest men in town, in that moment.

Once all of his belongings had been unloaded, Thomas found that he couldn't contain his excitement. He ran to Xander for a hug as readily as any toddler seeing their Papa for the first time in months.

"I am so excited to be here!" he gushed as Xander squeezed

tight.

"We're all excited to have you up here with us at last!" Xander grinned, releasing his godson and straightened up. "We've all been anticipating your arrival. Especially as it's a full moon tomorrow night. We want to have your first evening here being as calm and relaxing as possible."

"Will there be food?" Thomas asked.

"Of course. Richard and Philip are at the manor cooking right now."

"Oh," Thomas frowned. "They needn't go through the trouble."

"Nonsense, Thomas, we have been planning this all week. We want to make a fuss, especially as we didn't get to over Christmas. Just let us enjoy spoiling you? For one night? That's not too much to ask."

The young man had the decency to blush as the footman took his trunks and loaded them onto the carriage. "Very well then. I can't wait to see everyone again."

Xander agreed as they climbed up into the carriage and set off towards the estate.

The horses tugged the carriage along the rough, weathered roads. It was a lot bumpier than in London. Thomas had to hold on for support, but Xander had no trouble in keeping his balance. There was no way to see anything beyond the lace curtain.

Within the hour, they had pulled up to the large double doors and unloaded the trunks and satchels onto the gravel driveway. Grabbing a handle each, Thomas and Xander tugged the luggage up and into the entrance of the manor.

Inside it was even more extravagant than Thomas could have imagined. Even more so than Philip's townhouse –and that had been dripping in extravagance at the best of times.

His jaw dropped open as he took in the high, carved wooden ceilings, the pristine tiled floors, and the large mirrors in the gilt gold frames. Portraits of people long-dead hung on the walls and the doorways arched along the hallway, each one leading through into different rooms. Xander watched him with unmasked amusement as he spun in a slow circle, taking everything in.

"This place –this place is magnificent!" he gushed as he slowly unwound his cloak from his neck.

"I'm glad you think so," Xander mused. "Now, there's a lot to show you but I fear we've kept Richard and Philip waiting far too long. We can give you the tour later."

Thomas nodded in agreement and followed the older man down the hallway towards the kitchens.

The kitchen itself was made of bright, smooth sandstone and had a large set of ovens, all crackling with fires; strings of garlic, chilli and dried meats and cheese and other varying herbs hung from the ceiling in clusters, giving a dry spicy tinge to the air. Richard was just finishing setting the table when he caught sight of them walking through the archway.

"Thomas!" he beamed straightening up and dusting his hands off.

Thomas hurried forward and gave the mild-mannered man a tight hug. "It's so good to see you again!" he said, burying his face against the scarred man's shirt.

"Well, well, well if it isn't Thomas Segdon," drawled a low, silky voice from the far corner.

All heads turned to see Philip framed in the narrow archway with a bottle of wine cradled in his arms. Thomas felt himself flush upon seeing the blonde man for the first time in almost two months. He both had and hadn't changed; physically, he'd changed a little, he'd put on a little weight so that he didn't look as pinched and gaunt, and his hair had grown out a little, long enough to require it being tied back with a ribbon. It was strange but suited him beautifully.

This was the most casual Thomas had ever seen him; he was wearing pressed trousers covered in flour smears and his shirt was loose and open at the collar with the sleeves rolled up to his elbows.

"Don't I get a proper greeting?" he teased.

Coming to his senses, Thomas crossed the warm room and enveloped his lover in a tight embrace. He wasn't sure how long to hold for, or if he should even risk kissing the man in front of the other two, however all his doubts were erased when Philip lowered his head and pressed a firm, warm kiss to mouth, soaking up the rush of emotions that surfaced.

Thomas had to choke back a sob. He'd missed the intimacy so much.

Richard cleared his throat with a smirk, "If you'd please release the guest of honour, Philip, dinner is getting cold."

Philip raised his eyebrows with a matching smirk. "So sorry, my liege."

He gave a mock bow, before guiding Thomas over to the small wooden table. It was large enough for six people, however it just meant there was more elbow room at either end.

Dinner was a lively affair. They drank good wine, toasted any and every anecdote as well as recounting stories that had happened over the last six weeks since they had gone their separate ways. Under the table Philip constantly rubbed his palm over Thomas' thigh, teasing him and making him feel ashamed to wish for the end of the evening so they could retire for the night.

They laughed and drank and –before becoming too intoxicated –Xander raised his glass and bade everyone a happy and successful full moon and that they all hoped Thomas' next formula would bring them closer to such a day where a completely docile werewolf could be achieved. As soon as dessert was served with yet another bottle of wine, their third of the evening, they reminisced about Christmas and what they planned to do once all the celebrating had died down.

By midnight, Thomas felt his eyelids drooping.

"I think it's time this little one gets some proper sleep," Philip chuckled as he rested his almost empty wine glass on the table. Taking one of Thomas' arms into his own, he stood up and gave a gentle tug for the young man to follow him. "Come on, Thomas, let's get you to bed. You've had a very long, tiring day."

Thomas was barely about to stumble over saying goodnight to everyone as Philip gently escorted him from the room.

Arriving as Philip's bedchamber in the west wing of the manor, Thomas grunted as the blonde man laid him down as gently as possible on the beautifully carved four-poster bed. It had thick velvet curtains draping down from each corner. Everything was new, ordered within the first week of arriving in Scotland and Philip had paid extra to speed the processing time along. Now, he was grateful that he had when he had Thomas stripped down to his undergarments and sprawled before him like a gift from Heaven.

"Oh, Thomas!" he breathed as he hastily undressed himself. "You have no idea how desperate I've been for you. I've missed you so horribly!"

Thomas stirred so that he was more awake, tilting his head so that he could properly see Philip as he dragged his clothes off his body and climbed up onto the, bed straddling Thomas in the process.

"I've missed you too, Philip," he murmured, smoothing his hands up and over the blonde's body, committing every muscle to memory. "Mmmm you're so warm."

Philip lowered himself on his forearms over Thomas' head

and wasted no time in slipping his tongue between Thomas' soft pliable lips.

"Thomas, I've missed you. Let me show you, Thomas, let me show you just how much I've craved you?"

Through the haze in his mind, Thomas finally realised that Philip was begging him. He was asking for permission into Thomas' body. A smile tickled at his mouth.

"Please, Philip, I need you too."

He slipped his hands down the back of Philip's undergarments and gripped his buttocks. The blonde man moaned as he suckled on Thomas' throat, his tongue pressing and probing against the flushed skin with his hips rolling hot and heavy against Thomas' own.

"Make love to me Philip."

The blonde man needed no further invitation.

That night they did everything; they fucked hard and dirty over the end of the bed and the writing desk until they were both slick with sweat, claw marks and wet, raw bite marks over their necks and chest, they had energetic sex on the bed in as many positions as they could muster and then, finally, Philip stood up, naked and damp, and held out his hand for Thomas to take. Thomas was panting heavily as he stared up at the man before him and felt his heart lurch. Taking the hand, he was tugged off the bed and guided over to the thick, fur rug that was sprawled out on the hearth. There, he was laid down, the fur tickling his inner thighs, as Philip positioned himself between his legs, entered his body and made slow, aching love by the heat of the fire. It gave him a chance to breathe properly. It didn't matter at that point whether they finished or not –however Philip took his time and lovingly cared for him until they were both spent and collapsed into the rug.

Thomas must have dozed for a while because when he

came to, there was a blanket draped over him to ward off the chill. Philip was dressed in a robe and lounging on his side, his blonde hair still hanging down his back as he watched Thomas stir awake.

"Sorry," he mumbled. "I didn't mean to nod off."

"It's okay. It gave me some time to think and –I think I'm ready."

"To ... what?"

"I have a question I wanted to ask you," Philip admitted. "I wasn't sure if I should but I have to."

"You can ask me anything," Thomas stated as he forced himself to sit upright.

Facing one another, Philip gave a somewhat nervous smile before producing a blue velvet box from the pocket of his robes. "I wanted to give you this."

Thomas stared down at the box, his mind running blank. There was only one thing a box of that calibre could mean. His heart felt heavy in his chest as he took in with trembling hands. What would he say to Philip? He couldn't reject him at such a moment like this. It wasn't as though he wouldn't want to, if it were at all possible, but they'd both be hung if word got out. Whilst his mind raced and panicked, Philip was probably able to see that he was nervous at least. He pried the lid open for Thomas.

It wasn't a ring.

That was the first thought that went through Thomas' head. For some reason disappointment and relief washed through him in equal measure. He couldn't deny his confusion at what was in the box, however. Frowning up at Philip, he gingerly touched the silver metal bullet nestled within.

"What is this?" he asked, gently pulling the bullet free. It was attached to a silver chain with a heavy clasp. He laid it out in his palm and studied it in the firelight. "Is this real? How much did this cost you?"

"It is real silver yes, but the cost is not important."

Thomas smoothed his thumb over the silver and felt his stomach twist. "Philip, I really don't understand."

Adjusting his robe, he took both of Thomas' hands in his own and cupped them around the bullet. "Thomas, I need you to know that —I have never been so lucky to have met someone as remarkable as you."

Thomas felt his cheeks flush.

"You are kind, caring and intelligent. More so than I'd originally thought. You're inspiring and wonderful and are truly beautiful." He smiled as he watched Thomas blush even more. "I say all of this, not to flatter you —although that is a benefit —but also to draw attention to the fact that there are not many people like you in this world. It breaks my heart to think that flames as bright as yours get snuffed out by unnecessary means. No one, least of all you, deserves to be ripped from this earth ahead of their time, least of all by —by someone like me."

"Philip, I —I can't accept this."

Philip reanimated, pressing the bullet firmly between his palms. "No, Thomas, you *must*! You need to promise me that —should the need ever arise —that you will think of yourself first. I —I need to know that you are forever protected!"

Thomas felt his eyes brim with tears as he felt the hot metal roll between his palms. He swallowed thickly and tried to remember how to breathe. He let his mind process the words that Philip had just spoken. They hung in the air between them burning as fiercely as the flames in the grate. Without asking permission, Philip slipped the bullet from between Thomas' palms and undid the clasp.

"May I?"

Thomas hesitated for a moment, not wanting to promise anything as macabre as ending his lover's life in cold blood. That had been exactly what he'd tried to stop from happening nearly two months ago. He prayed he would ever need to use the bullet; if he did his research right and continued to find new ways to improve the formula, it wouldn't be an issue. The current batch rested in the kitchen, waiting to be used the following evening. If he was lucky, that would be the last time he'd need to make any alterations. He was hopeful.

Drawing in a deep breath, he nodded.

Turning his back to Philip, he shuddered as the bullet was draped over his chest, the heavy clasp fastened against the nape of his neck. He didn't have a moment to think before two arms wove around his chest and hugged him fiercely.

"This is how much I love you," Philip murmured in his ear. The words made his heart skip. "I love you enough, that I would give up my own life, if it means that you can live yours to the fullest."

"I want you in my life," Thomas insisted in a whisper.

"You probably will," Philip said. "Look at Xander and Richard. Two decades, Thomas. I hope to God you will never have to use that bullet, but promise me that if it's your only option –you'll use it?"

Thomas fingered the cooling metal, before he pressed back against Philip's chest. "Yes, I promise."

A finger hooked under his chin and turned his face around so that they could share a tender kiss. They remained that way for a while, wrapped in blankets and each other's arms. The fire dimmed a little, the wind howling in the outside world. Thomas nestled his head under Philip's chin and couldn't help but worry about the following night. Another full moon, another medicinal potion to test out on his lover. It was too much to take in, but at the same time it was a thrilling new step towards their future. Two decades?

Somewhere in the manor, a clock chimed 3 o'clock.

He continued to roll the cool, smooth bullet between his fingers as he laid down with Philip on the rug and turned so that his face was pressed to the older man's scarred chest. He traced a few of them sleepily, pressing a tender kiss to his skin as his brain slowly wound down for the night.

Soon, there would be another full moon.

Now, at least, he was prepared.

Acknowledgements

It's safe to say that at the end of every story, short or long, that there is more than just the one person behind a complete one. I have Melissa to thank, as usual, for putting up with me at the latest hours and Christian to thank for always reminding me of both sides of a wolf.

I would like to thank my tutor, Jack Johnson; without you, this renewed version of the story -including the new cover design -would never have come to be without your guidance and encouragement!

I'd also like to thank all my lovely friends who reviewed and gave feedback on the original draft and helped me to work out as many of the kinks as humanly possible. Above all else, I'd like to thank my partner, Tony, for always encouraging my writing and being proud of my accomplishments.

Thank you to everyone who reads this story. I hope you enjoy it! It was so much fun to research the Ripper's victims and to recreate the autopsies for this story. As grizzly as some of the details are, it definitely adds to the ambience.

Thank you all!

Printed in Great Britain
by Amazon